AN UNBREAKABLE BOND

AN UNBREAKABLE BOND

by

Mary Wood

Magna Large Print Books
Long Preston, North Yorkshire,
BD23 4ND, England.

British Library Cataloguing in Publication Data.

A catalogue record of this book is
available from the British Library

ISBN   978-0-7505-4406-1

First published in Great Britain 2013 by Books by Mary Wood

Published in Large Print 2017 by arrangement with
Macmillan Publishers International Ltd.

Magna Large Print is an imprint of Library Magna Books Ltd.

Printed and bound in Great Britain by
T.J. (International) Ltd., Cornwall, PL28 8RW

I dedicate this book to my darling husband, Roy, and our children, Christine Martin, Julie Bowling, Rachel Gradwell and James Wood. You made so many sacrifices to help me achieve my dream. Above all, you believed in me and held my hand through the journey. I wouldn't have made it without you. This, one of the first books I ever wrote, and the first I self-published and am now seeing traditionally published, is the product of the love, devotion, patience and encouragement you all showed me. I thank you all and love you all to the end of the world.

PART ONE
Innocence Lost
1913

1

One Door of Life Closes

Megan and Hattie's footsteps echoed as they walked down the draughty, stone-walled corridor towards the Reverend Mother's office. Within feet of it, Megan paused and motioned Hattie towards the internal window. Using this as a mirror, they checked their appearances, making sure their grey serge frocks were crease-free and their stiff white collars immaculate.

With shaking hands Megan tried to tuck the stray, unruly locks of her auburn hair under her mobcap. As soon as she tamed one curl, another escaped. Hattie giggled at her attempts. Megan made a face at her. 'It's all right for you.' Hattie's smooth dark hair always looked neat, for next to no effort. Giving up the battle, Megan knocked on the door.

'Enter!'

Reverend Mother's tone cracked Megan's already frayed nerves. Hattie squeezed her hand.

The moment she placed her foot on the carpet and smelt the wax polish, the small comfort of Hattie's gesture dissolved. The stark contrast to the cold flagstone floors, and the stench of carbolic soap and boiled cabbage of the quarters they shared with other born-of-sin and orphaned children, increased her sense of foreboding.

As they waited to be acknowledged, Megan's eyes fixed on the butterfly wings of stiff white linen cascading from each side of the Reverend Mother's bent head. The sudden lifting of the head made her jump. She tugged Hattie's frock, bringing her attention back from looking around the room in awe.

'Well, Megan Tattler and Hattie Frampton, you are now thirteen years of age and you are to leave us. And I don't have to ask to know how pleased you both are, do I?'

Neither of them answered, but Megan thought that if she were to, it wouldn't be to say she was pleased. Not altogether pleased, as both she and Hattie were deeply saddened at the thought of being separated.

'Hattie, you go later today, I understand – and, Megan, you are to leave tomorrow.' The Reverend Mother's eyes, shrouded by a brow that was squashed into a bulge by her veil, darted between them. A pinched smile crossed her face as she continued, 'Now, Hattie, I see you have a very fitting placement as a scullery maid in the household of Lord Marley's country residence. Very good! Are you prepared?'

'Yes, Reverend Mother, but...'

'No "buts", Hattie. Lord Marley is one of our benefactors and has given many of our girls a good start in life by providing them with jobs. It's up to you to make something of yourself.'

'Yes, Reverend Mother.'

'Good! So, Megan, it seems to me you think you can take up a placement far above your station. It is unheard of – someone of such low status becoming an apprenticed seamstress!'

The insult, and the look that went with it, froze Megan's hopes.

'However, Sister Bernadette has been very persistent on your behalf. And, although aware of the sinful circumstances of your birth, Madame Marie is still inclined to give you a chance. I have therefore had to give the proposal due consideration, and I am persuaded to approve it, after seeing what Madame has written in her letter to me. She states that she is taking you on merit, because you show exceptional talent in the drawings and the sample of stitches shown to her by Sister Bernadette. But she makes it clear that you will be expected to know your place, and to keep it at all times. You are not to try to engage with any of the young ladies who are training there and you will have a room in the attic away from the others. Do you understand?'

'Yes, Reverend Mother.'

'I hope you do.'

Megan struggled to hold down the joy surging through her. She stood still, head held high as was befitting and polite. She knew that Reverend Mother, aggrieved at having allowed her to take up the apprenticeship, would take it away from her if she gave her any excuse to do so.

The wings of the Reverend Mother's veil crackled as she inclined her head. 'You are dismissed. But remember, what you make of yourselves is up to you. If you work hard and stay true to the teaching you have received here, you will prosper.' The pinched smile had reached her eyes as she continued, 'If you don't, then the gutter is

15

where you will find yourselves, as many have before you.'

They turned to leave. The woman whose care they had been under since birth did not even say goodbye. Megan didn't want her to, and she knew Hattie would be feeling the same. She turned as she reached the door, but only the top of the stiff veil remained visible. Megan felt sure that she and Hattie had never really mattered to the Reverend Mother. She closed the door, glad to be free of the tense atmosphere. Now she could give release to her feelings. But before she had time to, Hattie's words dulled her joy. 'Will we ever see each other again, Meg?'

'Aye, we will. We'll make sure of it. We'll write regular. As soon as we get our first wage we can get paper and stamps...'

'I'm not for working in service, Meg. I'll be off from there just as soon as I can.'

'Eeh, Hattie, why?'

'Cos I'm scared of ending up like Daisy.'

'Daisy? I didn't know as she'd been in touch. Don't she like her placement?'

'I saw her the day I had to go into Leeds to have me tooth pulled. Sister Bernadette made me wait outside a shop. I wandered up the street and bumped into Daisy, and she told me she'd left her placement.'

'You didn't say...'

'I know. I couldn't think how, cos of what I found out, and you had worries enough over what would be happening to you. Anyroad, Daisy's working the streets. She hadn't eaten for two days, so I gave her the cab fare Sister'd pinned to me coat in case we got separated. I told Sister it must have come unfastened.'

'Oh, Hattie, is that the gutter as the Reverend Mother spoke of? This "working the streets"?'

'Aye, I reckon it is, by the looks of Daisy. But she said things'll get better for her. She's been accepted on the patch, and has a couple of customers of her own.'

'But what is it she has to do? Is it cleaning or sommat?'

'Oh, Meg! You daft ha'p'orth!' Hattie's giggling had Megan doubled over, as it always did, but she couldn't help feeling Hattie was privy to something she didn't know about.

'They sell themselves. Thou knows? To men. They let men do things to them. Things as men do to make you have babbies. Only they don't keep having babbies, cos they have ways to stop that happening.'

'How do you know of such things, Hattie?'

'Daisy told me everything as a sort of warning, cos she knew as I'd likely end up in service. She wanted me to watch out for meself. She told me her master forced her to do it with him, so she had to run away. She made her way to Leeds and looked for a job, but no one would take her on without a reference. She met this girl who tried to help her, but in the end all the girl could do was take her to the house where she lived. Daisy said she had no choice after that. There's this bloke who owns the house and he made her work the streets or she'd be for it.'

'Oh, Hattie!'

'I know. It's why I'm scared, Meg. The girl said

it happens a lot. She said as some top-drawer folk seem to think they have a right to do it, and him as did it to Daisy is known for it.'

'Eeh, no. What will you do?'

'Don't worry, I'll sort sommat. I'll work hard until Christmas and give them no reason not to give me a reference, and then I'll make up a story about having to leave. I don't know what yet.'

'But you might settle. It might be as your master is a good 'un. But if he isn't, you'll come to me, won't you? I'll help you, Hattie. I'll have me first wage an' all by then and I'll give it to you.'

'Ta, Megan. Eeh, I'm going to miss you.'

A silence fell. Hattie's hand felt warm and clammy inside her own and the fear Hattie felt had now entered Megan, but she had no idea what to do. A thought came to her, something that had bothered her for a while. 'Thou knows, Hattie? I don't even know how ... well, how babbies happen. I've been thinking about it since we started our bleeding and Sister Bernadette sent us to Mrs Hartley.'

'Aye, I know. I were the same. It were with Mrs Hartley saying we had to watch ourselves and not let boys have their way with us, or we'd end up pregnant. It set me thinking on it. But I know now. I could tell you, if you like?'

Megan said nothing, wanting to know, but not wanting to say so.

'Well, Daisy told me the man...'

A tickly sensation in her private part – as Sister Bernadette called the part of them she never allowed them to expose – shocked and embarrassed Megan as she listened to Hattie. And all she could think to say was, 'Does it hurt?'

'Daisy said it did the first time, but it isn't bad after that.'

'I suppose it can't be, cos women keep having babbies, don't they? Anyroad, happen as poor Daisy were unlucky in the placement they sent her to. Where was it?'

'I don't know. I were that shocked over what she told me, I forgot to ask her. Still, I shouldn't be going on. Your placement doesn't sound that good, either – not with that Madame woman thinking of you as she does.'

'Don't worry, I'll be reet. It'll be worth it. Just think: I'll be learning to make frocks and gowns! And maybe sommat'll come of me drawings. Wouldn't that be wonderful, eh? To see me drawings being made up, out of satins and such-like...'

'Ah, Megan and Hattie, here you are!'

Megan held her breath. Being caught in idle chit-chat was one of the deadliest sins. She hadn't heard the chinking of keys or the dull jangle of huge wooden rosary beads – the sounds that warned of an approaching nun. Peering into the dim corridor, she saw the outline of a plump figure, hazed by a flowing cream habit, coming towards them.

'Eeh, Sister Bernadette, it's you! You gave us a fright.'

'I expect I did, Hattie.' The twinkle in Sister Bernadette's eyes belied the strict retort. 'I have been looking for you both this good while. Tell me, my wee ones, is it your placements Reverend Mother has been confirming with you? And is it that you are happy now that you know for sure where it is you're going?'

Megan and Hattie nodded, but the sense of dread that had come over Megan on hearing of Daisy's plight and Hattie's fears deepened. Sister Bernadette was the only person they could share their worries with, but she couldn't talk to her about this. Not with her being a nun, she couldn't.

'And you, Megan? Is it pleased you are at knowing at last that you can go to Madame Marie's?'

'Oh yes, Sister. I can't believe it! Ta ever so much.'

''Tis the good Lord you have to be thanking for giving you such a talent, Megan. Not that He missed out on giving you something when He was at the making of you either, Hattie dear. You have many virtues: your kind ways and a willingness to help others, amongst many others. You will do well, too. I'm sure of it.'

Tears rolled down Hattie's cheeks as she nodded her head, and Megan felt her own eyes fill up at the sight.

Sister Bernadette patted Hattie on the shoulder as she continued, 'The house you are going to, Hattie, is beautiful, so it is. Lord Marley's country residence is on the outskirts of Leeds on the road to Sheffield. And Megan, Madame Marie's is in the centre of Leeds itself and her salons are wonderful.'

Even the new experience of riding the motor-bus to and from the station didn't lift Megan's spirits. The suffocating nearness of the strangers travelling with them, the rumbling and vibrating of the engine and the discomfort of the jolting over cobbled roads interrupted her reveries.

Sister Bernadette held her hand throughout the return journey, but didn't speak. Megan didn't want her to. Never had she felt so miserable. She'd known the parting with Hattie wasn't going to be easy, but she hadn't thought she'd feel such a sense of utter desolation, or that her heart would feel so sore.

The pebbles crunched under her feet as they walked across the courtyard of the convent, and a funny feeling overcame her when the huge wooden doors of the entrance came into view. It was like a fear mixed with excitement was churning in her belly as she thought of how tomorrow, she'd walk through those doors for the last time and leave everything she knew behind. As if sensing something in her, Sister Bernadette squeezed her hand. 'Megan, dear, 'tis as this day had to come, and I have a lot of pain in me because of it, but I have learned over the years to accept life as it is. Not all that it gives you is fair, and not all that is fair is good. You will come to know this and, when you do, I hope you understand. Now, wee one, I have things to tell you of, so I have, and 'tis as I have something to give you that belonged to your dear mammy.'

Sister Bernadette's words, spoken in her lovely Irish lilt, caused a sudden shock to jolt through Megan's body. Her mam had never been spoken of before. Questions had always been silenced. All she knew of her own birth was that it had taken place in St Michael's, a convent for sinful and unmarried pregnant girls.

Once they were inside the convent doors, Sister

21

Bernadette took Megan to her room. 'Sit yourself down, wee one, whilst I am getting for you what I know will be very special to you.'

No thick carpet hushed Sister Bernadette's footsteps or dulled the sound of her keys jangling against her hip as she crossed the room to her desk. Megan sat on the cane chair next to the brass bed; these two items and the desk were all the sparsely furnished room held. Square and with only one small window, it had a flagstone floor that resembled the one in the children's quarters, except that these flagstones shone as if painted with lacquer.

The tension that had been set up in her by knowing she was to hear about her mam made her fidgety. Her body felt hot and sticky with sweat. She watched Sister Bernadette sort through her keys and insert one into a drawer, before putting her hand inside. A panel to the side of the desk shot open, making Megan jump. Sister Bernadette pulled something from the opening and said, 'Megan, what I have here is a locket. Inside is a picture of your granny and granddaddy.' She paused and made the sign of the cross. 'To be sure, 'tis sorry I am to have to tell you, wee one, but,' she crossed herself again and looked heavenwards, ''tis as your poor mammy died just after giving you life. I helped at the birth of you, so I did.'

The pain Megan had held in her chest since saying goodbye to Hattie swelled up into her throat and threatened to strangle the life from her. 'She – she can't be dead. I have to find her. She...'

She had been about to say that her mam had been the daughter of rich parents who'd turned

22

her out of the family home and wouldn't allow her back, unless she gave her babby away. That had been the make-believe she'd lived her whole life by, along with Hattie, who'd always imagined that her mam had been a princess shipped away in disgrace, leaving her 'sin' behind.

'Now, now, my wee one...'

The urge to shout *I'm not your wee one! I'm nobody's wee one* fought against the part of Megan that could never hurt Sister Bernadette. But though she didn't utter the words, she knew them to be the truth. The innocent child she had once been had now gone.

The locket, cold against her skin, mocked her. Clamping her fingers tightly around it, she paid no heed as its clasp dug sharply into her flesh – better to feel this pain than look at the trinket, which linked her to her past and yet had also wiped out her hopes for the future.

'Look at it later, if that is what you have a mind to do, my wee Megan. But first I will tell you all I know.'

Lying still, her body stiff with anxiety and her mind in turmoil, the night-time hours seemed endless to Megan. A feeling of loneliness swept over her as she looked over at the bed next to hers. It no longer held the shape of Hattie, curled up in sleep. Always, when troubled, they would creep into each other's beds and snuggle up together, even though they feared being caught. But now Hattie had gone.

Sliding her hand under her pillow, Megan found the locket. She felt she would be able to look at it now. She sat up. Holding her breath, she waited, but no one questioned her movements. If any of the others were awake, they would whisper something to her. No sound came.

A chill shivered through her body as she tiptoed towards the door leading to the corridor. Once there, she opened her clasped fingers. As the light from the gas mantle that shone through the door's little window glinted off the locket, Megan's breath caught in anticipation. Opening the locket would let her see members of her family for the first time. Even the word seemed strange to her – 'family'. A nervous excitement rippled through her: *Eeh, I never thought to know of any family, and now I have pictures of me grandparents in a locket worn by me mam.* Did she look like them? Had her mam looked like them?

Sister Bernadette had said that her grandparents had died before she came into being. In a way she was glad of that, as it meant they hadn't abandoned her mam when she'd most needed them.

Turning the locket over, she read the words 'To Catch a Dream' inscribed in the tarnished, dented silver. Had her granddad had that engraved for her granny? She had so many questions that needed answering.

A tiny click and the locket opened. Two people looked up at her, but they didn't look like grandparents. The picture had been taken when they were young. Her granny's huge, smiling eyes held love, and her granddad, though not smiling, had a twinkle about his expression. Both were beautiful. Tears started to form in Megan's eyes, but then a warm feeling overtook the sadness as she saw that

24

she had some likeness to both of them. Granny had unruly, wavy hair just like her own, and the freckles on her nose were identical to Megan's. Granddad had the same high-cut cheekbones as she had, and his eyes, with their slight upward slant that gave them a near-Oriental look, mirrored her own.

The aged brown tint to the photo didn't hide the fact that her granddad's complexion was darker than her granny's. People often said that Megan had olive skin, so she was like him in that too.

Sister Bernadette had said she couldn't remember their names. She hadn't written them down, and she'd hesitated over her mam's name, as if she'd forgotten that too. 'I think her name was Br – Brenda. Brenda, that's right. Brenda Tattler,' she'd said. Then she'd told Megan that her mam hadn't been wicked, and that her conception had been the result of an attack by someone her mam'd trusted. She'd gone on to say, 'Everything isn't for being straightforward in life, Megan. 'Tis better you don't dwell on how you wish things to be, but get on with them how they are. Just be thankful your mammy left you something to hold on to.'

Getting back into her bed and laying her head on the pillow, Megan mulled over these words in her mind. Swallowing hard to stem the tears that threatened to flow, she told herself she'd do as Sister had said: she'd not dwell on the sadness of parting from Hattie, or of finding out her mam was dead; and she wouldn't agonize over being alone in an attic and not being good enough for the other girls on her placement to talk to. Instead, she'd think of her family and talk to them. She'd heard you could do that with those who had passed on. The locket had given her folk of her own – folk who would have loved her – and now she knew of them, they'd watch over her and help her. Lifting her head, she pulled the pillow down and wrapped her arms around it. A cold tear trickled down her nose. She held the pillow tighter and snuggled into it.

2

A Clash of Classes

The stagnant view of the symmetrical lawn, bordered by a tall, tailored hedge, epitomized what life had become for Laura Harvey as she gazed out at it from the window of Hensal Grange, the beautiful home in West Yorkshire that her husband Jeremy had inherited from his father, along with acres of land and the Hensal Grange mine.

Beyond the hedge lay the view she wanted to see: fields coloured with crops, and chimneys releasing gases from the bowels of the earth, where the men and boys sweated long hours to bring up the coal that was the mainstay of their income. And yes, the stables – once the centre of her life, but just a painful memory, now that her dream had ended.

How often she'd wanted to have the hedge chopped down, but Jeremy had laughed at her, thinking he knew better what privacy she needed in her own little 'sitting room', as he called it. He never referred to it as her study.

Yes, she'd had two Queen Anne carved sofas brought in, had smothered them with soft cushions and placed them either side of the ornate fireplace, making a comfortable sitting area. But the mahogany desk on the opposite side of the room – huge in its proportions, and flanked on either side with floor-to-ceiling shelves, stacked with all manner of books and files – told of the real purpose of the room. Her father-in-law's death, whilst Jeremy was still serving as an officer in the army, had necessitated her running the estate and had been the original reason for commissioning this room.

The hedge hadn't bothered her then, for the room had been a hive of activity. After all, the whole of Breckton breathed life from the Harvey estate.

Her mind went over how she'd had to learn the ins and outs of running the colliery, the farm and the stables, as well as continuing to manage this grand twenty-bedroom house that she and Jeremy now rattled around in. On top of all of that, over-seeing the maintenance of the tied cottages had been her responsibility, as had the shops, the leased farms and the buildings housing businesses such as the blacksmith's. The work involved in administering it all had been an immense task, especially for her, a woman who, up to that point, had never worked in her life.

Every day had presented her with a series of new decisions, and she'd risen to the challenge.

She'd revelled in it even, but now her life had become tedious. Household accounts she could do with her eyes shut, and listening to the continual whining of the senior household staff as they went about their duties was hardly riveting. Even her marriage no longer held anything for her, not since... No. She'd not dwell on that. Her loneliness would crowd her. Suffocate her.

Oh, how she hoped Emmeline Pankhurst would win through. Not that one altogether agreed with the woman's methods, but to be liberated enough to have the vote would help towards being seen in a different light.

Turning away from the window, she decided it would be best to sit at her desk for the task facing her. Observing a certain level of formality would be less of an intrusion on the woman's feelings. She allowed herself a moment of dread: meeting Tom Grantham's widow wasn't something she was looking forward to.

Laura's reflection on how much Tom's death had shocked and hurt her pulled her up short. She'd always thought of staff as dispensable commodities, but Tom had been different. He had been an expert horseman and the best damned groom in these parts. His death had made her realize that he'd become a kind of friend – a father-figure of sorts.

'God! What has one become, when one has to seek companionship from one's groom? And now I'm bloody talking to myself!'

She would have to do something. Write to Daphne. Yes, that would be the thing. It wasn't often that she envied her sister, because Daphne's life as the wife of a lord – the adorable Charles Crompton – meant she had a full social diary and had to embroil herself in charitable work.

Laura didn't think the charitable work would suit her nature at all, but she could do with socializing more. Jeremy just wasn't interested since... Anyway, she'd ask Daphne to come and stay for a few days.

Daphne would probably insist that Laura visited her in York instead. She wouldn't say so, but Laura knew her sister found the cold, polite atmosphere of Hensal Grange embarrassing, to say the least. Still, it didn't matter where. Just to be with Daphne and to talk silly talk, gossip about the latest goings-on and maybe go to a dinner party where young men would flirt with her and tell her she was beautiful, or just notice her even, would be enough.

A knock at the door interrupted her thoughts, and Hamilton announced Isabella Grantham. One glance at Isabella told her this was a homely woman, used to eating copious amounts of her own cooking. She had the appearance of someone who had scrubbed her face until it gleamed, but it didn't hide the sadness and apprehension in her eyes.

Laura knew the words of condolence she was going to utter would sound empty. Experience had taught her that they made no difference; they helped the speaker, rather than the bereaved. She supposed she should offer the poor woman a chair, but thought she'd probably refuse. 'I held Mr Grantham in high esteem, and as a very valued member of my staff, Mrs Grantham.

Consequently I want to do all I can to help you. The accident was most unfortunate, there being no warning that the horse would kick out in that manner. I am very sorry. It is sad, too, to think that this has come at a time when your daughter is to leave to take up the placement I found her at Tom's – Mr Grantham's – request. Are you still of a mind to let her go?'

'Yes, Ma'am. I can't see her waste a chance like this. I'm grateful to you for getting it sorted for her. She leaves this afternoon.'

'A good decision. Such placements are not easy to come by. I hope your daughter doesn't let me down, as Madame Marie took her solely on my recommendation. The type of employees she usually takes on are educated, and from middle-class families. Vicars' daughters and the like.'

'My Cissy is as good as the next one, I'll have you know. Oh, I – I beg yer pardon, Ma'am.'

Although the woman had apologized, the outburst shocked Laura. She was aware that she had alienated the woman, but she had no idea how. Better to ignore it.

'Now, about your own future. I understand you work at the local shop?'

'Aye, I do, Ma'am. I do three days, and some cleaning for Manny's wife.'

'Well, Mr Harvey and I have decided you may stay on in the cottage. There will be a rent of one shilling and three farthings per week, and you will be expected to help out in the house from time to time, to cover for staff sickness or any social events. We are not looking to employ a new groom in the foreseeable future, so your tenancy is safe for some time. The new enterprise Mr Grantham and I were working on – the building of a stud farm – is not to go ahead at present.'

The act of telling someone this news brought home the reality of it. Jeremy had been adamant, saying that he felt it an unwise investment and that she would never succeed in the face of strong opposition, especially from the Smythe stud farm just a few miles away. *How could he have such little faith in me? Or are his objections just another way for him to punish me?* She took a deep breath. If the woman noticed Laura's concerns, she didn't show it – she showed only relief for her own position.

'Ta. Oh, ta ever so much, Ma'am.'

'If we decide in the future to hire another groom, we will inform you in good time and will rehouse you. In the meantime, Henry Fairweather and Gary Ardbuckle are going to manage the stable. Henry hasn't lost his skills. He taught your husband, as you know.'

'Aye, Ma'am, he did. I can't yet grasp how someone like my Tom could be killed by a horse. Not with him being best in county with horses, and him being so strong.'

'Yes. It is unbelievable...'

'Me and my Tom thought as we had a lifetime together. We didn't count on that being until I were forty-live and him just on fifty. We–'

'Yes, of course. I am very sorry. Do let me know if there is anything more we can do for you.'

She didn't want or need to hear about how this woman's aspirations had been snatched away from her; she had enough of her own dashed hopes to contend with. Reaching behind her, Laura tugged the bell cord. Hamilton appeared immediately.

'Do wish your daughter good luck in her position, and remind her not to let me – us – down. Goodbye, Mrs Grantham. Hamilton, take Mrs Grantham through to the kitchen. Give her some supplies.'

'I don't need none, ta very much, Ma'am! I have plenty in me pantry, and me pot's still full. Full enough for me own care, anyroad, and I've no one else to care for now, have I?'

'Come along, Mrs Grantham.' Hamilton ushered her out.

Laura looked at the closed door in bewilderment. She shook her head. Whatever had she said to alienate the woman in that manner? Surely the woman didn't blame *her* for the accident?

Opening her silver cigarette case released the tang of fresh tobacco. Her hands shook as she placed a cigarette in her holder and lit it. The smoke stung the back of her throat, and coughing brought tears to her eyes. *Good God, I am going to cry! Damn and blast the woman! Damn and blast everything.*

3

Rules mean nothing to Cissy

'Which one of you is Megan Tattler?' Madame Marie looked from Megan to the girl standing by her side.

'I am, Madame.' Megan stood straight, with her shoulders pulled back, just as Sister Bernadette had told her to, though she didn't keep her eyes lowered to the floor. She didn't want to be seen as insolent, but neither did she want to be seen as someone who'd been dragged up from the gutter.

The imagined picture she'd had of Madame didn't match what she actually looked like. Her name, and what she had said in her letter, had conjured up a witch-like, beady-eyed person with teeth that stuck out. Not that she could describe the real-life Madame as pretty; she was more like ... *handsome*, yes, that was the word. A funny one to use for a woman, but that was the impression she gave, though her precise, almost sharp features were softened by the way she wore her hair: swept up into a roll that lay like a halo around her head, leaving curled tendrils falling onto her face. Her grey eyes didn't show any emotion. They, like her voice and her manner, remained businesslike at all times.

Madame turned her eyes to the girl standing next to Megan and asked, 'So, you must be

Cecelia Grantham?'

'Cissy...'

'Cecelia!'

'Yes, Madame.'

Megan heard the girl sniff as she answered and wanted to take her hand, to give her some comfort. They had met a few moments ago by the door of the office in which they now stood. They hadn't spoken. Cissy, as she now knew the girl was called, had given her a watery smile, and she'd sensed it was best not to question her. But she had thought that Cissy had the prettiest face she'd ever seen: her big, round eyes were of the palest blue, which even the puffiness of crying hadn't spoiled; and her hair – which reminded Megan of the colour of straw when the sun shines on it – had the look of a mound of bubbles, as it tumbled round her face in a mass of curls. It did occur to Megan to wonder why she looked so sad, but she hadn't wanted to intrude. And anyway, the sight of the rows of benches where young girls sat, bent over their sewing, had caught her attention. One of them had sniggered and nudged the girl next to her, but Megan hadn't let that bother her. Instead, she'd lost herself in the smell and the colours of the fabric, and the rows of shelves housing boxes she supposed held things like cotton reels and fastenings. All of it gave her a good feeling; one that no one could spoil.

Madame Marie let out the breath she'd been holding, as her glare left Cissy and shot between them both. 'Not that it matters what your Christian names are, as from now on you will be known as Miss Tattler and Miss Grantham. May I remind you that you are extremely lucky to be here – especially you, Miss Tattler. Though it is a concession on my part to have taken either of you on. You at least, Miss Grantham, come with a modicum of respectability and a reference from one of my best clients, whilst the only persuasion I have for taking you, Miss Tattler, is the talent you seem to display in design, and the exquisite stitching of the samplers I was shown.'

Megan lifted her body from her belly upwards and stretched her neck to lift her head high, keeping her eyes staring straight ahead. Although this outward sign of pride helped her, her inner shame made her face burn scarlet.

'Be aware: I will be watching your every move. Manners and attitude are just as important to me as hard work and ability. In all of these disciplines, you both have to prove yourselves worthy of being here.' Madame paused and stared directly at Megan, who dropped her head. *What does it matter? I know inside I am as good as the next one.*

'I'm glad that is clear to you, Miss Tattler. I hope the way you are to conduct yourself around the ladies working here is just as clear.'

Megan nodded.

'I was tempted to put you both together, but I don't want to risk offending Mrs Harvey. So you, Miss Grantham, will be allowed to sleep in the main dormitory. But remember, the other ladies there are above your station in life, and you must treat them as such at all times.'

'But, I – I don't– I'd like–'

'Never answer back, Miss Grantham! Never! Always remember: you may only speak to me

35

when I have spoken to you first, and then only if I require an answer. Do you understand?'

Cissy's body trembled and Megan again wanted to put her hand out and take Cissy's. She felt certain Cissy had wanted to say she would like to be with her. This gave her a nice feeling inside and made up for what she'd just had to listen to.

'Very well! Now, you will be working in the finishing room – that is the room just outside this office, where you will have observed the ladies at their benches. To begin with, you will practise on scrap material. You won't be allowed to touch the garments until I feel you are ready to do so. You will have every Sunday afternoon off. The morning, after you return from church at nine o'clock, will be spent cleaning the salon and window displays. Every month you will have the first Monday and Tuesday as your leave days. You will both be responsible for cleaning the workrooms, after the ladies have left to have their evening meal. You will take your own meal when this work is finished and the ladies have left the dining hall. You will be at your workbenches by eight every morning and will take your breakfast and lunch after the ladies have had theirs. Your salary, less deductions for your keep, will be paid to you on the Monday morning of your leave. You will keep yourselves and your rooms spotless at all times.' She rang the bell on her desk, an unexpected action that made them both jump. Cissy made a noise like a giggle being snatched back. For a moment, Megan thought that she would lose control and laugh out loud at this, but the years of practice at keeping a straight face stood her in good stead.

A girl not much older than Megan and Cissy answered the summons of the bell. Madame introduced her as Miss Stallton. Megan took an instant dislike to her when, at Madame's instruction to show them around, she gave them a look as if they were dirt on the bottom of her shoe.

As soon as they were outside the office, Cissy gave way to her giggles, and didn't stop even when subjected to another of Miss Stallton's disdainful looks. It was all Megan could do not to join in, but as they followed her through a door on the left of the finishing room and up the stairs, she realized that Cissy was just trying to cover her nerves and her earlier sadness. She took hold of her hand and squeezed it. This turned the giggles to tears, so she slipped an arm around Cissy's waist, whispering, 'It'll be reet, I promise.'

Miss Stallton turned round. 'I believe you have been told, Miss Tattler, that you are not to speak to anyone here unless you have been spoken to? Well, I am sure that includes Miss Grantham.'

Shock stung Megan and her breath caught in her lungs. She said nothing, but Cissy did. 'It don't include me. She can talk to me when she wants to.' This further surprised Megan. She'd had Cissy down as someone who would need looking out for, not someone who'd be looking out for her!

'Miss Grantham...'

'Me name's Cissy.'

'Miss Grantham! If you know what is good for you, and you want to retain this position, you will be wise to think carefully about your standing.

Which, I understand from Madame, is only just above that of Miss Tattler. And you, Miss Tattler, take your hands off Miss Grantham at once. I shall report this to Madame.'

Cissy, her eyes now dry and a look of defiance still on her face, didn't answer, and Megan was pleased that she didn't.

As they reached the top of the stairs, the smell of wax polish reminded Megan of when she'd stood in the Reverend Mother's office, and the same feeling she'd felt then entered her now. Unable to fit onto the narrow carpet-runner that silenced Cissy's and Miss Stallton's tread, her shoes squeaked on the shiny oilcloth covering the boards, resounding in the silence and causing Cissy to start her giggling again.

Fear stopped Megan joining in. She kept her eyes straight ahead, but the exasperated sigh of Miss Stallton undid her. Clamping her hand over her mouth didn't stop the nervous laughter that she could no longer hold in, but what Miss Stallton said next did. 'This is the dormitory you will sleep in, Miss Grantham. Your bed is the fourth one along. The washroom is through the door at the end, on the right. You are not to enter any of the others, at any time or for any reason,' she told Cissy. But it was when she turned to Megan and said, 'And you, Miss Tattler, are forbidden entrance to all of them, including this one,' that humiliation stung her, bringing a blush to her cheeks, and taking away her urge to giggle.

Looking through the door Miss Stallton had opened, Megan could see four beds. Each had a folded screen next to it, and a set of drawers displaying knick-knacks stood between the beds on the opposite side from the screens. Light flooded the room, and the matching pink curtains and candlewick bedspreads gave it a warm and welcoming feel.

'Now, Miss Tattler, you see those stairs at the end of this passage? They lead to your room in the attic. On the bottom step is a jug containing water. When you have washed and changed into your uniform, bring your bowl down and I will show you where you can empty it in the backyard. You will get fresh water from a pump out there and – well, there is a lavatory out there for your use. You are to empty your ... your chamber pot in the lavatory every morning. Please make sure you use one of the covers provided for it as you pass along here.' Miss Stallton's body shuddered with disgust. 'I will expect you at the bottom of the stairs in half an hour.'

Megan could no longer hold back the tears. Madame Marie had made her feel bad enough, but that girl – that spiteful girl with her 'Miss' this and 'Miss' that – had made her feel like she'd crawled out from the sewer. Her tears blurred her view of the room where she would spend her time when she wasn't working. She wiped them away with her sleeve and looked around. A well-worn rag rug served as the only floor covering. It lay between two narrow beds pushed up against the sloping wall on one side of the room. Someone had placed her bag on one of the beds and had spread her uniform out next to it. The wall facing the beds had a curtained alcove on either side of the huge chimney-breast.

Putting the jug down on the washstand that stood against the chimneybreast, Megan pulled one of the curtains aside. Behind it she found a rail with hooks on and some shelves at the bottom. She should put her things away and get herself ready, but she had no inclination to do so. Her relief that it wasn't the dungeon she'd imagined had done little to lift her spirits. Shame washed over her at the thought of how that girl had told her, in front of Cissy, about such private things as where she should go to the lavatory. And to think she'd even mentioned the pot under her bed!

Loneliness such as she'd never known before seemed to crush her, as the bed with no clutter on it took her weight in a comforting way. She buried her head in the pillow. What had she now? No mam to find, no Hattie and no Sister Bernadette. *Oh, Hattie, Hattie...*

A tapping on the door halted her sobs. She hesitated a moment before grabbing her hanky. Wiping her tears and blowing her nose, she called out, 'Who's that?'

'It's me, Cissy.'

The loud whisper warmed her mood, and Megan's body moved towards the door before she consciously told it to. *It seems all that has happened hasn't put Cissy off!*

'Aren't you ready yet? By, lass, you'll catch it!'

The way Cissy said this as she came casually through the door made it seem as if they'd known each other forever. 'Come on, Megan, it's time to get your frock and pinny on. I couldn't wait to get mine on!' She twirled around in her new uniform, and in an exaggeratedly posh voice said, 'Don't you think it is the height of fashion, Miss Tattler? The navy is the latest colour and the ankle length gives one ... modesty.' The twirl ended with Cissy falling onto the bed, giggling in such a way that it would take a saint not to join in.

The giggling felt good, but it didn't last long. Cissy stopped as suddenly as she'd started and sat up. 'I'm sorry about all me blubbing earlier. Only I haven't ever been away from me mam afore, and, well ... me dad – me dad passed on just a few weeks ago.'

Megan didn't know what to say. She took Cissy's hand and they sat for a moment, not speaking.

Cissy broke the silence. 'Anyroad, as me mam'd say, there's nowt to be gained from feeling sorry for yourself. There's always those worse off. Besides, we'll have each other, Meg.'

Only Hattie had ever called her Meg before. It sounded strange but somehow right that Cissy should call her that, too.

'Reet, come on, Meg. Slap that flannel round your face and get dressed. Miss What's-Her-Knickers will be at the bottom of the stairs any minute.'

'Miss What's-Her-Knickers?'

'Aye, that's what me mam'd call her, besides other things that would make your lugs go red! I'll tell you of them some other time, but I'd best go now. Me and you have to be secret friends, otherwise we'll catch it from Madame – stupid woman!'

As the door closed behind Cissy, Megan could have shouted out for joy, such was the glowing feeling that had replaced the loneliness inside her.

41

4

Hattie's Fears Come True

'By, you're up with the lark this morning, dear. You haven't wet the bed, have you?'

Hattie giggled. Cook had some funny sayings. 'No, Cook. I just thought as I'd give Betty a hand. She's lagging behind a bit, and I've plenty of time to do me own chores.'

'You're a good 'un, lass. You've settled well, and you only being here a few days. I've given a good report to the housekeeper, and she's reet pleased with you.'

Cook stood in front of the gleaming black range, stirring a large pan of porridge. The job of blacking the range was one of the chores Hattie had to do at least once a week, but she didn't mind. To her surprise, she found she liked the kitchen work. The smell of constant baking, the warmth, the hustle and bustle and the companionship of the staff when they gathered for meals around the large scrubbed table, or popped in and out as they went about their business, gave her a sense of belonging.

'Mind,' Cook continued, 'it don't do to be too kind, thou knows. You could be put upon. Though I'll admit as Betty needs a lift – her only having a few weeks to go till she drops her babby.'

Hattie didn't reply. She carried on gathering

the bucket, brush and shovel that she needed from the utility cupboard at the other end of the kitchen. She had to clean out the grates in the front room and the hall. She'd already done the breakfast room and the withdrawing room, and had set fires going in both, before she had helped Betty to get the sheets soaped.

'Are you happy then, lass?'

'Aye, I'm all right. It isn't what I want to do with me life, but it's working out better than I thought it would.'

'Good. It's a while since we had someone who knew how to go on, without being shown every five minutes. Daisy were the last, and she came from the same place you did. They teach you well, I must say.'

'Daisy? Daisy worked here?'

'Aye, she did, and she were a good lass. It were a pity – and unexpected, I might say – when she ran off. Just like that, without a by-your-leave! I hope you don't do the same, Hattie.'

Hattie couldn't speak. All in all she'd been happy, well fed and had a space of her own in a little room at the top of the house. She got on well with everyone. The hard work and long hours hadn't bothered her and she'd been willing to stick it out. But now her fear surpassed her happiness, and deepened it into dread at Cook's next words. 'Has Mrs Barker told you about the party next week? By, that's the start of it all, when the family arrive...'

'No. Is – is the family coming that soon?'

'Oh, aye, Lord and Lady Marley will be here come Saturday, and the rest of the family – ten of them altogether, with Lady Marley's sister and her brood – will be here come Wednesday. On the following Saturday there'll be a party to kick off the Christmas season. We'll have our work cut out that day, I can tell you. There'll likely be around fifty guests, with at least twenty staying over. But don't be worrying: you'll have your duties all mapped out, and as long as you carry them through and keep out of sight as much as you can, you'll be reet.'

Out of sight – she had a mind not to be found at all! She stood a moment, unsure of what to do. Should she tell Cook why Daisy had left? The sudden appearance of the housekeeper stopped her from doing so.

'What's this? Not slacking, are we? There's not enough time to stand gaping into space, Hattie. Not now, and certainly not when the family arrive, so don't be making a habit of it, girl.'

'No, Mrs Barker. I'm sorry, I–'

'It were my fault,' Cook said. 'I were telling her of the family coming. Mind, lass has been up a couple of hours and has been giving Betty a hand, so I thought it wouldn't hurt for her to slow down a bit.'

'Very well, Cook, we'll let it go this time. Now, Hattie, come to my room after breakfast. I need to talk to you about the extra duties you are to carry out whilst the family are here.'

Cook served up a breakfast of creamy porridge followed by scrambled egg on thick slices of toasted bread. It all looked delicious, but Hattie could hardly even pick at it. Thankfully no one seemed to notice, so she wasn't asked to account

44

for her lack of appetite. The banter that went on amongst the staff at mealtimes was something she usually enjoyed, but today she was relieved when Cook called the proceedings to a halt, sending everyone back to their chores and telling her to go along and collect the housekeeper's tray.

'Well, Hattie, you seem to be settling in well, I am pleased to see.' Mrs Barker had invited her to sit down as soon as she'd entered her office. 'Now, you know about the family coming home next week, so I will run through what is expected of you during the time all the guests are here with us.'

The list of extra chores seemed endless. She'd to step out of her usual role and assist the chamber-maids – women from the neighbourhood who all knew the routine well and would be in early the next day, and every day throughout the family's stay. She would be responsible for the fires, the turning down of the beds at the end of the even-ing and the bed-warming in five of the bedrooms, including that of Lady Marley. She must also be ready to run for trays whenever needed and gener-ally help everyone out. This meant she'd be on her feet for most of the day, from six in the morning till gone midnight on the day of the party, and till at least eleven at night on the other days, with only a two-hour break in the afternoon. The work didn't worry her, but with what had happened to Daisy still fresh in her mind, being around the bedrooms late at night did.

Lying awake in the early hours, Hattie thought about her situation and tried to dampen the fear building up inside her. She couldn't run away. She had no money and her wages weren't due until after Christmas, on her first leave days. Telling the truth about what she knew of Daisy and why she'd left, and divulging her own fears, wasn't an option. Everyone spoke highly of the family and the master, and because of this she had a feeling that she'd not be believed. She'd noticed, though, that Betty hadn't joined in when the others were gushing on. But then she wasn't one for saying much at any time. She walked around as if in her own world, and kept her head bent in the way someone would if they were looking for something. This worried Hattie. Betty had an aura of unhappiness about her and a look of fear in her eyes, and she always jumped when she was spoken to. No, she couldn't add to whatever it was that was troubling Betty by discussing her own worries with her.

Her thoughts went to Megan, and her eyes stung with tears. There was no one her own age here – no one she could make friends with. She liked them all, but it wasn't the same as the way she and Meg had been. She brushed away her tears. She would cope. She'd watch her back at all times, and make sure the corridors were clear of folk before she stepped into them. At least she would be safe in the bedrooms, as they were all to be occupied by ladies. They had connecting doors to the ones the gentlemen slept in, but she knew from the gossip around the table that the menfolk would never enter without the lady being present.

On the day of the party Hattie made her way to her room for her afternoon break. She'd been daft to be afraid. Poor Daisy must have been in the wrong place at the wrong time, because despite being around the house carrying out her chores from morning till night, she'd hardly clapped eyes on the master. On the two occasions she had seen him, he hadn't even glanced her way.

'Oh, there you are, Hattie. I wanted to catch you before you went for your break.'

She nearly jumped out of her skin as she rounded the corner and saw the housekeeper standing at the bottom of the stairs leading to her room.

'I'm sorry. I didn't mean to startle you. Now, I'm going to be very busy here, there and everywhere tonight, so I wanted to make sure you know to finish warming Lady Marley's bed and have her fire well banked up at precisely midnight, having first finished all the other rooms you are responsible for. This is very important, as Lady Marley has informed me that the carriages and motorcars are departing at eleven forty-five, and she and all the ladies in residence intend to leave the gentlemen just afterwards and retire. Do you understand, Hattie?'

'Yes, Mrs Barker. I'll have it all done on time.'

'That's a good girl. After you have finished all of that, I want you to make your way to the west-wing kitchen, using the back stairs. You are to see if you can be of any help. If not, you may retire to your bed.'

Hattie nodded.

'Good. Make sure you have a good rest now. It's going to be a long day – a very long day.'

For one moment she thought Mrs Barker was

going to take hold of her. A sweet sort of smile spread across her face as she bent her head to one side, just like Sister Bernadette used to, when pleased with Hattie. It was odd. But then, everything seemed odd today. Mrs Barker hovering around the bottom of the stairs waiting to give her instructions hadn't ever happened before; she always summoned the maids to her office. And then, only a few minutes ago, she'd seen Florrie Bateman, the chambermaid she'd helped, coming out of one of the gentlemen's bedrooms, even though they'd finished cleaning and preparing that room hours ago. She'd looked like she'd been in a fight. Her hair was sticking out of her mobcap at all sorts of angles and she'd been fastening her blouse. As Hattie watched her in her dishevelled state, she'd wondered where Florrie had got the coins that she'd seen her slip into her apron pocket.

With all this worrying her, and the excitement and noise of more guests arriving, Hattie didn't rest well during her break. Tiredness gnawed at her bones as she closed Lady Marley's bedroom door, having finished the last of her chores. The clock in the hall downstairs began to strike the midnight hour. The sound of the ladies coming up the main stairs as she turned towards the west wing hurried her step. Not being seen was another of the rules to be obeyed. Relief flooded through her as she managed to skip around the corner just in time. *Oh, how I hope with all my heart I won't be needed to help out when I reach the kitchen!*

Going down the first steep flight of stairs tired her even more, and her pace slowed as she

48

walked along the corridor towards the flight of stairs that would take her down to the kitchen. Doors leading to the bedrooms that housed the visiting staff led off one side. These were strange beings, with airs and graces, as if they thought themselves a station above the regular household staff. Most – though probably not the ladies' maids – would be tucked up and snoring by now.

The silence and the dimness unnerved Hattie. She walked faster. She could see the banister and the source of the only light: a single gas mantle placed just above the stairs. As she hurried towards it, the closed doors took on a sinister feel. She had only one more to pass. Just as she reached it, it flung open. Her heart plummeted into her stomach as a large man barred her way. 'Ah, so the little lady has arrived! Jolly good. This way, my dear.'

Shrinking back, she clutched the stair rail. 'I – I'm sorry, sir. I...'

'Come along now. Don't be shy. Your master is waiting.'

'But– but I'm on me way to the kitchens. I've to help out. I–'

'That's enough! You know very well why you are here. Mrs Barker will have told you. Now, come along and don't keep your master waiting, or you may find your pay is halved!'

The man grabbed her arm. She tried to pull away. 'You're mistaken, sir. Mrs Barker told me to go to the west-wing kitchen...'

He pulled her into the room. 'She's here, David, and my, she's a young piece and just ripe, I'd say. Pity it's your turn to go first, old chap.'

49

'Ha! Felix, you needn't try that one. I intend to take my rightful turn, and you'll not sway me.'

Hattie looked from one to the other. Her heart banged against her ribs. Lord Marley rose from where he had been sitting on a chair in the corner of the room and came towards her. His smile was a smirk that didn't reach his ugly, cloying eyes. 'Umm – very young, and petite with it.' His usually high-pitched voice now sounded deep, raspy and slurred. 'Come over here, little one, and take off your clothes. I've a mind to see you first. By the looks of you, you have tiny, firm breasts just emerging, and I'd wager a fluff's beginning to sprout between your legs. I'm in for a treat.'

A scream formed deep within her, racked her throat and assailed her ears as her body cowered away from him.

'Now, now. I like a fight, but there's no need to go so far as to scream. We don't want to wake the other servants, do we?'

He pulled her to him. The smell of cigars and wine tinged his breath, and his clothes reeked of musty perfume. Beads of sweat trickled down his fat jowls. He brushed her cheek with a clammy hand. Her stomach lurched. She swallowed hard, then kicked out with all her might. Her foot caught his shin, the pain of it causing him to wince. His hand shot out and slapped her face, bringing stinging tears to her eyes.

'Little bitch! Hold her, Felix.'

A burning pain ripped through her shoulders as Felix pulled her arms behind her in a grip so tight she feared they'd come out of their sockets. She couldn't move. Lord Marley's face stayed close to hers. He snapped in anger, 'I'll stop your antics, you little vixen. You bloody well know why you're here, so don't play the innocent. If you want the money, you do as you are bid. Am I making myself clear?'

'I don't know, sir. I should go to the–'

'That's enough!' Lord Marley looked over her head. 'What do you think, Felix?'

'Well, she's here now, and she's definitely the one pointed out to me. Her suddenly having cold feet isn't our problem, is it?'

'No, you're right, and I'm not planning on giving up now. As long as you're of the same mind?'

'I think the plaster and the cords will help our cause...'

'Good idea. Let's get on with it, then.'

Hattie fought until every bone of her body ached with exhaustion. Tears clogged her nose. The plaster stuck over her mouth was suffocating her, and yet it seemed that the more she struggled, the more they enjoyed themselves. They tore at her clothes, taking no heed of ruining her uniform. A deep shame overcame her as they gazed at her naked body, before dragging her towards the bed.

There was nothing she could do. They stretched her arms and legs as far as they would go and tied them to each corner bedpost. If she moved, the cords dug deeper into her wrists and ankles, and her struggles to breathe sapped all her energy. Lord Marley stood over her and undid the buttons on his fly.

Hattie found she couldn't look away from the sight of what he fetched out from his trousers and rubbed up and down in his cupped hand.

51

Was he really going to put that in her, like Daisy said men did? Her fear became a terror.

The bed sank as it took his weight. He knelt over her, his hand next to her head to steady him. His other hand still grasped himself.

She couldn't swallow. Useless prayers mocked her brain. Lord Marley crushed her as he bore down on her. His hand touched her private part, then a pain seared right through her as she endured a stretching, ripping sensation. Her mind couldn't take in the horror. Her thoughts swam away in the cold tears that ran down her cheeks. She was nothing, nothing, nothing…

The sound of splashing water woke her. Her head hurt, and her throat burned. Why was she lying on this soiled bedding in this strange room? Looking over to where the sound of the water was coming from, she saw the man that the master had called Felix filling the bowl from the jug on the washstand. The memory of what had happened slapped her. With it the pain and humiliation she'd endured revisited her.

With the gradual return of her senses came the realization that her mouth was no longer plastered shut and her arms and legs had been released, though her nose still stung from the stinking, cloying cloth that had been placed over her face after they had finished with her.

Looking around the room, she saw that the master had gone. Felix brought her attention back to him. 'When I leave, you are to wash yourself. There's a new uniform in the cupboard.' He moved over to the door then turned towards her. The coins he threw jingled as they landed on the bed next to her. His withering look made her recoil. 'Tell no one or you'll be out on your arse with nothing.'

As the door closed behind him, every part of her body trembled. Her teeth knocked together, as did her knees. But then the warm wetness dribbling down her legs and dampening the sheet beneath her spurred her to take action – an instinctive action born of the memory of standing for hours with wet sheets tied around her whenever she'd wet the bed back at the convent.

Easing herself onto the floor, she made as if to strip the bed, but the sight of the bloodstains and the smell of her own urine renewed her terror. She crumpled to the ground and wept.

5

A Misdemeanour is Rewarded

A forced cough brought Megan's head up from her work. She looked towards Cissy, then over in the direction Cissy had indicated with a nod of her head. She saw Miss Stallton walking towards Madame's office with a sketchbook in her hand. The words 'Miss Scot-Price, how nice of you to say you like my designs much better than Madame Marie's' flashed into her mind. Her body began to sweat with fear.

Just last week Miss Scot-Price had been in the

53

salon to choose the gowns for her debutante year. When Megan had fetched swatches of material for the girl and her mother to choose from, the colours and feel of the different fabrics had inspired her. She had sketched late into the night. Cissy had been enthralled with the designs and, as always, her fun-making had taken over. She'd picked up a crayon and drawn a figure with a bubble coming out of its mouth, with those words written inside it. Underneath she had penned 'Madame Megan'. The joke had grown, and they'd drawn another figure with huge tears coming from its eyes and had written underneath 'Madame Marie'.

The look of sheer delight on Miss Stallton's face as she wafted that same sketchbook towards her before entering Madame's office caused Megan to catch her breath in panic. *How does Miss Stallton come to have it?*

'Miss Tattler!' Madame's voice boomed out from her office. Megan's fear deepened. *Oh, no … she'll not stand for this. It'll mean the end of me time here!* A movement of the bench captured her attention. Cissy had stood up and was headed towards the office. 'No, Cissy! No...'

'It were my doing, Megan, and I'm not letting you take the blame.'

Megan jumped up and ran round the benches, but wasn't in time to stop Cissy. She'd already reached the office, knocked on the open door and walked in.

'Miss Grantham? Get out at once! I called for Miss Tattler.'

'But it weren't her doing – not the fun-making

weren't. It were me. All Megan did was to draw the designs and–'

'Are you daring to address me without permission? And to call Miss Tattler by her first name?'

'Aye, I am. Megan is me friend, and I'm not for letting her take the blame for sommat as I did.'

Megan's deep-seated fear made it hard for her to swallow the spittle forming in her mouth. She looked from one to the other: Cissy, red-faced and defiant, and Madame, just as red, but with a rage on her that made her eyes bulge from their sockets. Madame broke the stare and turned in Megan's direction. 'Miss Tattler, is this true? Have you gone against my instructions and formed an alliance with Miss Grantham?'

Megan nodded.

'You are two of a kind. I should have known. I should not have given you privileges you did not appreciate, Miss Grantham.' She paused, her eyes scanning the drawings. 'However, Miss Tattler, you have settled in well and apart from this – this...' – the pages of the sketchbook flapped with a snapping sound as she waved them in anger – 'I have to admit that I have been pleased with your work and your manner. The pleats you stitched into the bodice of Lady Gladwyn's frock were beautifully done. She commented on them.'

Megan kept her head bowed, not sure whether to say sorry for the drawings and the little figures in the corner, or to thank Madame for the praise she'd given. But the rasping of pages being torn from her pad made her lift her head.

'You have a talent, Miss Tattler, but if you think design is all about producing good drawings and having a lively imagination and flair, you are very much mistaken. The drawings are only the basis of design; they need to be broken down into pieces to form a pattern. Each piece must be precisely measured to fit – not only with the other pieces to build the garment, but to the figure of the client. All the details need to be enhanced in smaller drawings for the finishers, and only then can it all go to the pattern-makers who produce paper patterns for the cutters.' She stopped for a moment and gazed at one of the drawings that she had sifted through. 'Umm, yes, well, imagination and flair you certainly do have. This is very good, but without the technical know-how, you cannot call yourself a designer. It takes years – years.'

Without Madame seeming to make any movement, one of her desk drawers sprang open. She tucked the drawings into it. 'Now, Miss Grantham, what are we going to do about you? It appears from these early days that you are good at sewing on buttons, hooks and eyes and press studs, but not much else. Obviously there is a need in the finishing room for someone who is good at these tasks and willing to do them, but you are headstrong and, at times, very, *very* rude. This must change. Otherwise I will write to Laura – Mrs Harvey – and tell her you are not suitable. I know this won't please her and, as she is a valued client, I am reluctant to take that step. Therefore I want you to make an extreme effort.'

'Yes, Madame. I'm sorry, Madame.'

'Miss Tattler, I think you have earned the right to have a companion. Miss Grantham, you may move your things to the attic and occupy the other bed in that room. I have already spoken to Mrs Harvey about this, and she expressed surprise that I had allowed you to share with the ladies in the first place. You will carry out the task this evening, Miss Grantham.'

'Yes, Madame. Thank you, Madame.'

'I do not want a repetition of what happened today. And, Miss Tattler, if you do any drawings in the future, I want you to show them to me. If you continue to show promise, I may consider training you in the techniques of design.'

'Oh, ta, Madame. Ta very much.'

'You mean *thank you*. Oh, just get back to your work, and ask Miss Stallton to come to my office.'

They bumped into one another in their hurry to get out, and Cissy giggled. Megan's joy spilled out in her own giggles, but the smug look that Miss Stallton gave her when she came out of Madame's office deadened her happiness, and an uneasy stirring began in the pit of her stomach.

Two weeks later, engrossed in her work embroidering a rose on the collar of a silk blouse, Megan was thinking of Hattie. She listed the things she needed to tell her. She'd start the letter tonight, so that it would be ready to post by the time her leave days came and she had the money for a stamp. She could use some pages out of her sketchpad. She'd tell Hattie about Cissy's mam's letter inviting her to go home with Cissy for their leave days and – best of all – to spend Christmas there, too! She trembled with excitement at the thought of going to a real family home, but the feeling dulled to an ache as she remembered that it would be her first Christmas without Hattie. She hoped Hattie was as happy as she was.

A door banged at the other end of the room, bringing her out of her thoughts. The ladies were back from breakfast.

'Come on, Megan, I'm–'

Madame's voice commanded their attention, stopping Cissy from finishing what she was going to say. 'Gather round, ladies. This is the first of the garments for Miss Scot-Price. There is a good deal of smocking to be done.'

Megan glanced over at Cissy, willing her not to say anything. Cissy's mouth opened and then closed. Megan nodded at her, letting her know she was right not to speak out.

The emerald-green satin caught the light and enhanced the flounces of the skirt just as she knew it would, and the smocking would tighten the bodice in a soft way that was so suitable for a young lady. The frock was just how she imagined it would be.

'It is superb, Madame,' Miss Stallton said. Megan caught the sideways glance Miss Stallton gave her as she continued, 'The gowns you create are always exquisite, Madame. What did Miss Scot-Price think of this one?'

'Thank you, Miss Stallton. Miss Scot-Price is thrilled with *my* design, and when she came for the first fitting she had tears in her eyes. Now, Miss Tattler...' Madame's eyes narrowed. Megan read the warning; she dared not protest. 'I want you to do the smocking and, Miss Stallton, you

58

are to attach the lace edging around the bodice and sleeves.'

'Delighted to, Madame.'

Megan knew Miss Stallton's eyes were on her as she said this, and she didn't have to look to know that a smirk would be creeping across Miss Stallton's face. Madame must have sworn her to secrecy over the designs she'd seen in the sketchpad. Knowing that she could do nothing made an anger well up within her, and unsheddable tears formed in the back of her eyes. She took the garment from Madame Marie. The woman offered no further explanation. She didn't have to, as she knew Megan would know exactly where the smocking should start and end.

As she and Cissy left their benches and went towards the dining room, Megan acknowledged for the umpteenth time how glad she was of the rule that they took meals and breaks when the others had finished.

'Eeh, Megan...'

'It's all right, Cissy. Don't fret yourself. I'll get me own back one day. I'll show her.'

'How?'

'I'll tell you when we're sat down. I'm starving.'

'I'll make you some toast. The fire's glowing, so it won't smoke the bread. There's not much left to go with it, by the looks of things.' The lids of the breakfast trays clanged one after the other as Cissy made her fruitless search. 'Just a dried-up fried egg and some crispy rinds the ladies cut off their bacon slices – and that's your lot.'

'I'll stick with toast. I don't want any of their cast-offs.'

Whilst she worked, Cissy again asked Megan how she thought she could get her own back on Madame.

'Oh, it won't be for a while, but I've a dream in me and I mean to catch it.'

'Catch it? That's a saying as I haven't heard afore, Megan.'

'It isn't a saying as such.' Something stopped her from telling Cissy about the locket; it was as if she would lose something that was precious to her if she spoke of it. 'It just means ... well, thou knows: like a falling star carrying your dream, and you have to be ready to catch it.' She'd thought this explanation over when she'd been mulling over the engraving on the locket, and she hoped that was what it meant. It sounded nice.

'That's grand. What is your dream, Megan?'

'To own me own establishment just like this one, where the frocks and gowns I design are known as mine and...' The tears she had tried so hard not to shed spilled over and she brushed them away. 'But I've a lot to learn afore that can happen, and saying owt about Madame taking me drawings and using them as her own won't help me.' She knew what she said was meant for herself, as much as for Cissy. It helped, and her need to cry passed. 'I have to keep doing good work and giving Madame me ideas, and then hope as she'll keep her promise and one day teach me how to turn me drawings into garments.'

'But it isn't right. It's not fair as she–'

'Aye, I know it isn't right that she took me design as her own, and I've a mind she'll carry on doing so, but it's like Sister Bernadette always said to me and Hattie: "All that's fair isn't always right, and all that's right isn't always fair." Anyroad, it's not all bad, Ciss. Me drawings led to us being able to share a room and be open about our friendship. Hey, watch that toast, it's scorching! There's smoke coming from it.'

Cissy rescued the toast and set things back to normal, acting the fool as she juggled the hot bread. But although Megan laughed at her antics, part of her still felt low in spirits. Sister Bernadette's words were true; she knew that. But unfairness – right or wrong – still hurt.

6

A Misunderstanding Turns to Passion

Laura Harvey looked across the table at her husband. *Have I heard right?* 'You intend to rejoin your regiment? Jeremy, you can't mean that, surely?'

'I do, Laura. I have thought long and hard, and I think it's the only way I will have any peace of soul. I'm a military man through and through. My life here is a sham. I was forced to take over the estate after my father died, and I don't feel as though I'm following my true calling.'

'But if you go, what will happen about the colliery and – and the farm, and the estate?' She wanted to say *And what about me? Us? But then there is no 'me' or 'us' any more,* she thought.

'Laura, Laura, you know very well you can manage without me; you are the only woman I know who has a business head on her shoulders as good as any man's. Besides, you have done it before. And if, in the unlikely event you want to come with me and become a military wife, then I will appoint a manager.'

The scratching of his knife on the toast grated on her. It went on longer than necessary as he spread the butter to every corner, and gave him a reason not to look at her. He hardly ever looked at her. And of all the bare-faced cheek: to say that she had a good business head, just because he needed her to take over the running of the estate again! Taking a bite of his toast before placing it down and wiping his hands on his napkin, he picked up his paper and unfolded it. *Oh, why does his every movement affect me?* She was like a dog waiting for a titbit at his master's knee!

'I've spoken to Charles, and he said he will oversee the financial side,' his voice droned on. The pain evoked by his words stabbed deeper. Did Daphne know of Jeremy's plans? Surely Charles would have told her? But no, her sister wouldn't keep this from her. Daphne had been a tower of strength to her this past year, and Charles had offered to speak to Jeremy about his treatment of her, but she had refused to let him. Of course Jeremy would have had to speak to Charles: their financial matters were dealt with by his bank, and Charles himself oversaw their accounts... Jeremy's voice changed suddenly, bringing her attention back to him. 'So, what do you think?'

'This is my punishment, isn't it, Jeremy? My

God! Don't you think I've been punished enough?'

'Your ... punishment?'

'Yes. You've never said anything, but I've known. You blame me for the loss of our son. It's why you called a halt to my stud farm, and now this.'

'Good God! Is that what you think?'

'What else am I to think? You won't talk to me about what happened. You're distant. You no longer come to my bed, and now you want to go away and leave me.' Tears rained uncontrollably down her cheeks. Images flashed in her mind – images she'd denied herself access to for more than a year. The agonizing birth; the tiny, still body; the blond tufts of hair and the little fingers unable to reach out to her. Then the blackness – the clawing blackness – from which she'd emerged weeks later to face the truth: her child, her baby, was dead, and she would never again be able to conceive.

'Laura, darling, I – I thought you wouldn't want me. I thought – oh, my darling!' Jeremy rose and came round the table towards her. Taking her hands, he pulled her up from her chair and held her to him. 'I tried to comfort you. I tried.'

Her tears became draining sobs. 'It was too soon. I wasn't ready, but then...' She couldn't say it. She couldn't pile the pain of his distancing himself from her onto the agony of the loss she held in her heart. It was over, and she was in his arms. He was whispering his own anguish and love into her hair. After a moment Jeremy guided her to a chair, knelt down in front of her and buried his head in her lap. Her crying slowed. Seeing that he too was in pain helped to ease her own.

'He was so beautiful, our little son. He – Leonard – was so beautiful.'

His words shocked Laura. She hadn't known he'd been affected in this way, hadn't thought he could feel what she had. She'd been so selfish in her grief. My God! She had been just as guilty of shutting him out.

'Oh, Jeremy. Jeremy.' She stroked his hair.

His crying stopped. He lifted his head, and all that she loved about him was there before her, looking up into her eyes, loving her with his very being. 'Laura, I've missed you so much, darling.'

'Oh, Jeremy...'

They stood without bidding each other to do so. Joined in pain. Joined in love. They clung to each other. His kiss, when his lips found hers, brought together and helped to heal the torn seams of her world. Feelings she'd denied herself for so long crept over her and were answered in the deepening of his kiss. 'Shall we go upstairs, darling?'

She giggled at his question – a silly, girly giggle. 'The chambermaid...'

'Well, the guest wing then?'

'No, Jeremy, they will know. They'll have to redo the bed.'

'Stop putting hurdles in my way, wench! I mean to have you and will do so right here, if we can't agree on a suitable place.'

Her giggle became a belly-laugh of the kind she hadn't experienced for such a long time. She'd forgotten what a clown Jeremy could be. His laughter joined hers, but not for long. She was in his arms again, clasped so close that she could feel his need pushing against her. Her own desire became a hunger. Neither of them said anything. Their love, reignited, didn't need a voice or any clowning around. Their kisses expressed all of their inner feelings. It was Jeremy who broke away, took her hand and led her across the hall to her office, locking the door behind them. 'We won't be disturbed, darling. The servants know what's afoot. Didn't you hear the door open and then close again?'

She felt a moment's embarrassment, but it faded into oblivion when he took her in his arms and rained kisses over her face, her neck and her breasts as he manoeuvred her towards the couch.

Undressing wasn't a slow, dignified process. Garments were discarded in a frenzy of activity, and their eyes held all of their hunger and need. No time was given for fondling. None was needed; only a joining of their bodies would satisfy their craving. A joining that came the moment the soft cushions accepted Laura's naked flesh. The deep penetration was everything she wanted it to be, and the words of love Jeremy spoke were all that she wanted to hear. Her body accepted and responded to the desperate thrusting with an urgency that begged to be released – a release that came with an ecstatic pulsating that caused her body to stretch out beneath him. 'Oh, Jeremy! Jeremy. Stop. Stop, darling. *Please...*'

He held still. Her muscles clenched around him as spasms throbbed through her that were beyond endurance. His mouth covered hers and absorbed her moans. His hands searched and caressed her breasts, her buttocks and the deep crevice of her back, until finally she relaxed and allowed his deep thrusting to continue, until his body released his love into her.

They lay still, locked together for some time afterwards, cementing their love in the stillness. Their closeness, and what they had just shared, said all they needed to say. After a few moments Jeremy eased himself from her and looked down into her face, murmuring, 'My darling, I love you.'

'I love you, too, my sweetheart.'

A shadow of concern passed over his face. 'If only I'd known.'

'What is it, darling? What's wrong?'

He didn't answer her as he climbed off her, sat on the edge of the sofa and pulled on his trousers.

A sinking feeling banished any trace of ecstasy Laura had just felt as she anxiously enquired, 'Jeremy?'

He gathered up her clothes. 'Here, darling. Put these on and we'll talk.' Once they were dressed, he took her in his arms for a moment and then eased her down onto the sofa. 'If only I'd known before, I wouldn't have rejoined my regiment. But with everything how it was, it was unbearable. I wanted to get away. Oh God, it's too late – too late...'

'No. No! I don't want you to go! How could you have taken such a step without talking to me about it?'

'I felt so certain you couldn't bear me to be around. I'm sorry, my darling, I'm sorry. Forgive me.'

'Won't they release you, darling? Can't you change your mind?'

'I've signed! Oh, Laura...' He wiped a tear from her cheek. 'Don't cry, darling. I'll be home as often as I can be, and you can join me for functions. We can stay together in our London home.'

He pulled her into his arms again. She'd always thought of tears as a weakness, but she didn't try to battle against them now. It seemed her whole body wanted to weep. To weep for the feeling of loss, which she'd denied until now. To weep for the love that had been frozen for so long, and for the loss she now faced at not having Jeremy alongside her. Jeremy held her throughout. Slowly, she came to an acceptance.

Part of her knew she would relish taking the reins again and, as Britain wasn't involved in any conflicts, Jeremy would be safe. And it might work out that life would stay much the same as it was now, as they had always had their separate interests and often spent time apart. And yet somehow she knew it wouldn't be the same; it would be much more enriched, for she would be safe in Jeremy's love and she knew that when they were together there would be no more coldness. Instead there would be passion and good times, just as it was before ... before... No. She'd not let those thoughts in again. Instead she would delight in the second chance she had been given.

7

A Lonely Path is Taken

'You're looking under the weather these days, Hattie. Is owt wrong, lass?'

'No, Cook, I'm all right.'

'Is it your bleeding? Have you started with that yet?'

'Aye, I have, and happen it's that as is coming on.' Hattie hurried out of the kitchen, afraid to stand under Cook's scrutiny for long, and embarrassed at her blunt way of talking. It was her bleeding that she was worried about, but not its coming – quite the opposite, in fact. She'd been due over a week ago and nothing had happened.

There was no one amongst the staff she felt she could talk to about it. She wanted to, but it was a question of whether she'd be believed, and what would happen if she wasn't. She had a plan, though. As soon as she got her first leave days and her wages, she would be off. She'd go to Daisy and ask for her help.

She had thought of borrowing a stamp and some paper and writing to Megan to confide in her, but shame still burned in her and stopped her from doing so. Megan was a part of her life that was clean and trouble-free. She didn't want to taint that with the dirtiness she now felt was shrouding her.

Every time she thought of what had taken place, she became more convinced that Mrs Barker had had a hand in it. *Why would the master and that other one think I knew the reason for being there? In fact they had said, 'Mrs Barker will have told you...'*

Hattie had just sat down to have her breakfast with the rest of the staff when Cook questioned her again. 'Eat up, lass. You've hardly eaten owt for days now. Are you sure you feel all right?'

'Aye. I'm tired, that's all, Cook. I'll be reet when we get Christmas over and I get me leave days. I'm going to stay with a friend in Leeds. I'll be a different person when I get back.'

'You are coming back then?' This shocked Hattie, as did the way Cook was now looking at her. 'We've all been there. It's not easy to come back when you have your first time away from here, with your wages in your pocket an' all. But it's hard out there. You'll not find the same protection as you have in here, especially with you not having a family.'

As usual, everyone was surprised when Betty spoke, but what she said caused them all to take a sharp intake of breath. 'Has sommat happened, Hattie? We know the way of it and can be of help, thou knows.'

'Bet–'

Cook didn't have a chance to even finish saying Betty's name before the kitchen door flung open and there stood Mrs Barker, glaring at them. 'What is going on? I have my hatch open and ... well, it's obvious you all have more than enough to say.' She directed her gaze at Betty.

'Aye, well, you can't be at marrying this one off. She's only just on thirteen!' The scraping of Betty's chair on the stone floor before it crashed to the ground made them all jump, and shattered the death-like silence that had fallen. A sobbing Betty ran from the kitchen.

Cook stood up. 'It's not still happening, is it? By God, no! I thought after Aggie... But Betty and – and young 'un here?'

Beads of sweat trickled a shiny path down Mrs Barker's colourless face.

'God! You've sommat to answer for, Jean Barker!' Cook's voice shook with anger. 'Well, this time you can answer to Madam, because I'm going to do as I've told you I'd do if it happened again. I'm going to tell Madam everything from what part you play in it and how you profit from it, an' all!'

There was a moment when Hattie thought Mrs Barker would crumble. Her body shook and swayed from side to side, but she pulled herself together and walked out of the kitchen.

Cook took charge. 'Right, off with you! Go on, all of you. Get to your work. And you, too, Jimmy. And close your mouth before flies take root in there.' The stable boy did as she ordered, without his usual backchat. 'Florrie!' Cook's commanding tone stopped Florrie just as she was heading out the door. 'Find Betty and send her back in. Tell her I want her to help me with Hattie. I'm going to get to the bottom of this.'

The silence that followed the commotion took hold of Hattie. Cook came round the table to her, saying, 'Eeh, Hattie lass. Tell me what happened.'

The words wouldn't form. Her stomach lurched; her head swam. The heat of the kitchen was dragging at her tired limbs. She was sinking ... sinking...

'Come on, Hattie lass. Everything'll be all right. We'll help you.'

The soothing voice that met her as she emerged from the blackness caused her tears to spill over.

'There, there. Let it all out. Hold her a mo, Betty. There's a good lass. Come on now, tell us what happened.'

A feeling of safety surrounded Hattie. She could tell them the truth, and they would understand. She leaned heavily on Betty as she told them what she could, though the shame of her story only allowed her to tell some of it.

'Same thing happened to me,' Betty said. 'It were the start of the summer season. Mrs Barker made me pass this off as Cory's.' She jabbed at her stomach. 'She knew we were talking of being wed, but Cory hadn't touched me. He isn't the same with me now. He married me because he were told he'd lose his job if he didn't. He wanted to be first, as it should be, but now ... well, I don't know which one fathered me babby.'

'Oh, by God, Mrs Barker will not get away with this! I caught her out before. Years ago. It was a young lass by the name of Aggie. In fact she came from the convent you've come from, Hattie. Anyroad, you know how the tale goes. Well, young Aggie came screaming to me in the night. I spoke to Mrs Barker about it, but she played the innocent, though I always suspected she had a part in it, as Aggie had said. I noticed Mrs Barker were flush for a while after, going off and buying new clothes. She said it wouldn't be happening again, as she'd make sure it didn't. I didn't want to, but I left it at that and haven't had reason to suspect owt since. By, but she's been clever with it.'

'It happened to Daisy an' all,' Hattie told them. 'I didn't know it were here she'd worked, until you told me, Cook. But Daisy told me the master of the house where she worked had forced her to do it. That's why she ran off.'

'Right, that's it! Betty, get on with clearing this lot. You help her if you feel up to it, Hattie. I'm going to see Lady Marley.'

When Cook had left the room, Betty asked, 'Are you worried over owt else, Hattie? Have you started having your bleeding? And ... and did they hurt you badly?'

'Aye, me bleeding hasn't come, and it were bad.'

'Oh, dear. You could be caught. Aye, I know as you're only young, but once you have your bleeding, then you can get caught for a babby. Look, don't worry. Cook'll sort sommat out.'

'I'm not coming back. Don't tell Cook about me bleeding not coming, Betty. She'll not be able to help me and, if they know, I'll be shipped off to some convent, and I couldn't bear that. I have a plan: as soon as I have me wage, I'm off. I'm going to Daisy.'

'Aye, happen as that's best. I s'pose as I were lucky having Cory, even though everything's been spoilt by it all. But Hattie, you know you can come to me and Cory any time if you get stuck. We understand and we'll help you all we can.'

'Ta, Betty.' The words were barely discernible as Hattie's unshed tears took their course, and Betty cried with her. They held each other, finding some comfort in their mutual understanding.

Not even two hours had passed before Mrs Barker left, taking all her goods and chattels with her. Her parting shot at Cook was to flash her handsome pay-off money at her, as if in triumph. But Jimmy brought her back down to earth: he drove the trap round to the back of the house for her, but he didn't help load her boxes, and everyone laughed each time she dropped something.

Lord Marley left shortly afterwards, as did all the other guests, leaving only Lady Marley and her sister, Lady Carter, in residence.

In the hushed household the sound of Lady Marley's distress filled the corridors until later that evening, when the doctor arrived and she became quiet. Not long afterwards Lady Carter sent word for Cook to bring Hattie to her. She would see them in the housekeeper's office.

As they were about to knock on the door, Cook patted her on the shoulder and said, 'Speak up, Hattie. Don't be afraid. If there's owt as you want, I'm for thinking you will get it, in exchange for your silence. I'm going to see as Betty's looked after an' all.'

Desolation filled Hattie as she boarded the train early the next morning. The ten-pound silence money tucked into her blouse pocket, and what was left of her wages after deductions, did nothing to console her. She had been given the opportunity to stay or leave, but then neither Lady Carter nor Cook had guessed what was in her belly. And if she had stayed and they'd found out, she knew it would have been St Michael's for her.

Cook had done her best to persuade her to stay, but had been comforted by Hattie's telling her that she had a friend to go to. She hadn't said that friend was Daisy, or what Daisy did for a living.

She sat back on the hard wooden bench. The passing countryside and the sudden darkness while going through a tunnel had no impact on her, nor did she register when the scenery changed and the big houses on the outskirts of Leeds could be seen on the horizon. But when the rows and rows of poorer smoke-blackened dwellings and the tall city buildings and factories came into view, she knew Leeds Central was the next stop. This caused her to clasp her hands against the anguish and fear beating in her heart and to whisper a silent prayer: *Please, God, help me to find Daisy and let her know what to do to help me.* One thing she knew for sure: she wasn't going to St Michael's Convent, and though she wanted to with all her heart, she knew she couldn't go to Megan. Not yet anyway. Not until everything was sorted. *Oh, Megan. Megan...*

8

The Sorrow of the Divide

Megan turned into the road leading to Daisy's place with a sense of dread that made her body shake. What would she find? Once again, a thought that was never far from her mind since receiving Hattie's letter last week visited her: *Is Hattie having a babby?* Hattie had said her master had done that horrid thing to her, just like he did to Daisy, so it *must* be that!

Thoughts and images of what she'd heard about correction convents for pregnant girls caused her dread to deepen. No, she wouldn't let Hattie end up there – she'd find a way. She could get a job in one of the factories and find a room for them to share. But then, what of the babby? How would they cope?

The rundown building in front of her and the state of all the houses in the street further made her anxious. She checked Hattie's note again, but no, she hadn't made a mistake.

'Hello. You must be Hattie's mate. I've been told you were coming.' The door had opened without her knocking, and smiling down at her was a girl like none she'd ever seen before. Ribbons held her long blonde hair in two bunches, in the way a child's hair would be tied, and her face, painted with rouge, glowed red from her cheeks to her eyes. Her plump bosom bulged over the top of her blouse.

'Me name's Phyllis. I'm a mate of Daisy's, and I don't bite'

'Oh, I – I didn't mean to stare. I'm Megan. I...'

'I know. Come in. Hattie's in Daisy's room. She ain't well, and we're all worried for her. That woman Daisy took her to were no better than a butcher. Mind, she's not haemorrhaged, and that's a good sign.'

Megan didn't understand what Phyllis was talking about, but didn't ask questions. It was as if the answers would be too much for her to take. She followed Phyllis through narrow passages and up a steep flight of uncarpeted stairs. The brick walls had shed most of the distemper they'd once been painted with, and flakes of it littered the steps. Damp patches and mottled black areas showed, and the dank smell hanging in the air sickened her to her stomach. Her worry for Hattie increased.

Daisy met them outside a room on the left of the top landing. 'Eeh, Megan love, it's good to see you. Hattie's in here.'

Embarrassment seized Megan as she looked at Daisy and saw how the life she was now leading had changed her, both in the way she dressed and how she wore her face all painted with make-up. Her feelings were mixed with pity, but she hid this and managed a cheery greeting and a smile as she followed Daisy into the room. The smile soon dropped from her as Hattie's weak voice reached her. 'Megan. Oh, Megan.'

It only took two steps to reach the bed Hattie

lay on, for the room was that small. 'Oh, Hattie, love, what's happened to you?' The bed creaked as Megan sat down on it and leaned over to hold Hattie. Shock at how Hattie's small frame had become even tinier and how pain pinched her face, giving her the look of someone much older, made Megan feel helpless.

Hattie resisted her attempts to pull the grubby sheet back, as if she needed to hide as much of herself as she could. Her voice trembled with emotion. 'I – I told you in me note... It were bad, Megan.' A tear dropped onto her cheek.

'It'll be reet, I promise. I'll find us a place and get a job in the factory. And you, Daisy, you can come, and we'll all live together and look out for one another.'

'No, you've got to stay where you're at. It's what you want to do. Just as soon as I'm better I'll get meself right, don't be worrying.'

Megan wanted to ask if Hattie had had an operation or if there were a babby on the way, but she felt awkward, so all she said was, 'I brought some money with me for you. I've a mate at the salon and she lent it to you. She said not to worry over when you can pay it back.'

'Ta, Megan. It's needed, I can tell you. I wouldn't have sent a message to you, only we haven't eaten since yesterday morning. This mate of yours sounds reet nice. Tell her as I'll pay her back as soon as I can.'

'Here, I've brought some butties an' all. Me and me mate – Cissy she's called – made them up whilst we were having our break. We're the only ones to work on a Sunday, so nobody knew.'

'I'll go and put kettle on,' Phyllis said. 'Come on, Daisy, you can help me. A pot of tea'll go nice with them butties.'

Megan felt relief at this. She hadn't been able to talk properly to Hattie with the others in the room. 'Are you really all right, Hattie? I mean … did – well, thou knows, that thing they did to you – did it make it that you'll have a babby?'

'Aye, Megan. It did. It…' A sob like a hiccup jolted Hattie's body. She rolled over and turned away. Megan snuggled up behind her and held her close. She could think of nothing else to do at that moment and wished with all her heart she could call on Sister Bernadette and have her hug them both. 'Hattie, don't cry. We'll manage. You'll not go to St Michael's, and babby won't go in no orphanage. We'll care for it. I've thought on it, and it can be done. We can work shifts and–'

'It can't, Megan. Who's going to let a room to two young 'uns like us? Besides, there is no babby now. Daisy took me to a woman and she got it away from me.'

Sobs trembled through Hattie's body, and Megan held her even tighter. Tears wanting to be shed were denied their release by the cold feeling the shock had given her. She hadn't ever heard of a babby being taken from someone's inside before. Was the babby still alive when it'd been taken out? Her stomach turned over. 'Oh, Hattie.'

'I'll be reet. I'm going to stay with Daisy and do as she does.'

'No! Please don't, Hattie.'

'I've no choice, Megan. I've nowhere to live. If bloke as owns this place finds me here, Daisy and

Phyllis will be for it, unless they say I approached them to introduce me, so they brought me in. It's this or the workhouse, as I've no reference. I had the chance of staying in me placement, but I knew then I was in for a babby, so I left. They gave me money for me silence, but that's gone to that woman and to a doctor as came to see me. Well, he wasn't a proper doctor – Daisy said he was a quack, but he looks after the girls for a price, and I think he saved me life.'

'Oh, Hattie.' She couldn't bring herself to talk about what Hattie would have to do. 'What will happen if you are hungry again?'

'Daisy said they only get hungry at this time of the year. It'll be all right when Christmas has passed. They both have regulars – gents who work in the city – but with Christmas just around the corner, they can't get away so easily from their wives, as they have a lot of social events. Anyway, Daisy's regular is coming tonight. He sent word to her and she's going to ask him to give her a bit to tide her over. He thinks a lot of her and doesn't know she isn't fed right. She said she'll take a chance and not hand over all she should.'

Despair settled over Megan when she left Hattie. All her pleading had done no good: the Hattie of her childhood had disappeared. Life as she'd known it was over, and nothing was simple any more. But no matter what, she'd never, ever give up on Hattie. She'd always be her friend. She would visit her every Sunday and make sure she had enough food and money. Oh, if only they were older... But then, she did feel old. Old inside.

The next day it felt to Megan as if she'd visited hell and was now about to step into heaven.

The sign on the platform, with pots of greenery around it, stated that they had reached Breckton – the small town on the way to York where Cissy lived. Megan could hardly contain herself, but she knew she had to. For the thousandth time her mind asked what the house would be like, as never in her life had she been inside a real home. She had seen sketches and pictures in magazines, but to actually go inside one...!

'Come on in, love. By, I thought the day'd never come!' Cissy's mam held her daughter in her arms for an age, and tears streamed down her cheeks. At last she released her and addressed Megan. 'You'll be thinking I'm a rude old biddy. Come in. You're very welcome. I've cooked a pie and beat all me rugs in your honour.'

A giggle escaped Megan. It seemed a funny thing to say, but it warmed her and made her feel at home.

'Mam, you're daft, thou knows. Come on, Megan, I'll take you up to me room.'

'Don't be long, love. I'm not on with joking about pie – it's in oven and I've table all laid.'

Megan looked around her. It was as if she was in one of the books she'd read. Everything about the room made her feel happy, in a way she'd never felt in her whole life. She looked at the grate with the fire roaring up the chimney and the oven to its side, from which came a delicious smell. On top of the oven, pots bubbled on the gleaming black hob. On either side of the fire stood a chair and between them lay a rag rug made of bright colours and edged with black. The red-tiled floor was scrubbed until it shone. In the centre of the room a table was draped with a dazzling white cloth and was set for three. The far wall had a pot-sink in the corner with a chequered curtain prettily pleated round it, and a dresser – polished until you could see your face in it – stood against the opposite wall. It was ... it was – a home. Her throat tightened. If only...

An arm came round her and Megan felt herself being pulled into a soft, fleshy body. 'Think of yourself as being at home, love. Oh, aye, I know you've never had a home afore, but you have one now, lass. You have one now.'

She thought of Hattie and how, just a few short weeks ago, they'd been so young. Poor Hattie. Would she ever know anything like this?

The thought made her tears spill over, but Cissy's mam wiped them away with the corner of her pinny. It smelt of starch and cooking, and love.

PART TWO
The Letting Go
1918

9

A Shocking Discovery

Hattie stood with her back to the wall, trying to shield herself from the wind. The cold seeped through her thin coat and her limbs ached with fatigue. She'd been on her patch since two, and it was now going on four. She'd only had one customer, a regular. He'd alighted from a cab and asked his driver to wait around the corner. She'd found this strange, as he'd usually take her to a house about a mile away where he rented a room. She presumed he paid the landlord well, as there were never any questions asked, and as far as she knew he used it solely for taking his pleasure with her. 'I'm after a quick release, Hattie,' he'd said. 'I have a need on me, and there'll be nothing doing at home.'

They'd gone into the ginnel and she'd done a hand-job on him. She was good at that. She knew how to make it last, if that was what was needed, or she could make them come in seconds. But though he seemed more than satisfied, judging by his moaning, he'd halved what he knew were her charges, saying that was all it was worth. *A measly two bob!* She hadn't argued; she knew better than that. He was one of a few blokes who could cut up rough after it was done. It was guilt, or something, that got to them. The ones who came too quick or couldn't get it up were the worst, blaming the lass for their own shortcomings and using them as a punchbag on which to vent their frustration. She'd been lucky lately, but Phyllis, poor lass, had copped for a good beating a couple of weeks back.

A shiver trembled through her body. Oh God! She hated her life and everything about it – no, that wasn't true. She had Arthur. He was something good in her life. He loved her and she thanked God it was her he'd happened upon. She doubted if any of the others would've taken him on – not looking like Arthur did. And now, given how well she knew him, she couldn't think what being turned down by the likes of her, a common prostitute, would have done to him. He'd suffered a big enough blow when his own wife had rejected him.

No matter how much she told Arthur he'd no need to be, he was always so grateful to her. He was a lover, not a customer, although he made her take her due, and a good bit over. She was getting a good stash together because of Arthur, and she was still able to tip up plenty to Bobby Blackstaff, to keep him happy.

She thought of Megan. Five years had passed since they'd been together. *Oh, Megan, Megan. I miss you, lass…*

Their being apart wasn't down to Megan. She had never given up trying to find her – Hattie knew that. At first, after the bed-and-breakfast place had burned down and she and the other lassies had been moved, Megan had come every month and had traipsed the streets. Even now, after all this time had passed, she still came into the area every few months or so, looking for Hattie, but she didn't want to be found. She didn't want Megan mixed up in the life she led.

On the couple of occasions she had caught a glimpse of Megan, she had managed to dodge out of sight, and had asked one of the lassies to make her go away, by threatening her. How Megan must have felt about this played on Hattie's mind, but it wasn't safe for lassies like Megan to be in these quarters. Bobby Blackstaff looked out all the time for 'fresh meat', as he called it.

'You bastard! You're one of them! You thieving, murdering whore!'

The screaming voice shocked Hattie out of her thoughts. She turned to see a woman staring at her from eyes sunk deep into dark sockets. Desperation caused the woman's body to sag as she slumped against the hedge and wept.

Hattie took hold of her and guided her into the ginnel. 'You're right, Missus. I am a whore, but I'm no thief and I'm definitely not a murderer. What's this all about, eh?' The poor woman's tired sobs tore at Hattie's heart and she felt no resistance from her as she held the shaking body to her. 'Eeh, come on, love. Tell me what's wrong.'

'It were him as you work for. Everyone knows it were him – he's done it afore, and more than once. A few times. Young 'uns, not past their da's knee in height. Snatched! And – and, you lassies help him, you know you do. You make friends with the young 'uns, and then he moves in. And ... and the young 'uns are never seen again. Oh God! I can't bear it. I want my Janey! I WANT HER!'

Hattie took the blows. The woman pummelled her with her fists until her chest burned, but the shock of what she'd heard held her still. After a moment she caught the woman's hands. 'Don't ... don't. I know nowt of what you're saying. I promise you, I know nowt.'

The woman stopped fighting, and her body slumped against Hattie once more. Quiet, hollow sobs racked her.

'Look, love, let's go to Ma Parkin's for a cup of tea. She brews a good pot for a penny and I've enough on me for that. She's got a back room where she lets us go, if we want privacy with a customer. Well, I mean, not for well, thou knows. But some of them want to talk afore they– Well, anyroad, come on. It's warm in there and, like I say, it's private.'

The woman didn't say yes, but she didn't resist as Hattie led her away.

'Me name's Hattie. What's yours, love?' They were in Ma Parkin's back room and had a pot of tea in front of them. The woman had regained some control of herself and sat staring at Hattie.

As she poured the tea, the aches and the cold seeped out of Hattie, but worry for the woman and what she'd said took over her very soul.

'Susan, Susan Clough. I live over Chapel End. Me and me young 'uns. Me man were took in the war. He didn't have to go – him working down pit exempted him – but he wanted to do his bit.'

'Aye, him and a million others. I'm sorry to hear of that. If I could just get me hands on that Kaiser bloke! Anyroad, tell me of Janey and them others.'

88

Susan took a deep breath before she answered. 'It started a few years back, after war'd been on about a year. Then, as now, there were mostly only women looking after young 'uns, and a lot of them trying to do a job as well. I work at the cotton mill on the early shift meself. Anyroad, a young lass of only seven years went missing, and not long after that a ten-year-old, and there's been more heard of from over other end of the city. Nothing's ever been seen of them. It's said by other young 'uns that they were took by a woman. These young 'uns knew the woman to be a prostitute, though no one can find her – at least that's what the police say. Mind, some say the police are in on it, as they don't give it much attention. Then, three weeks back, my Janey. My Janey...'

She dropped her head.

After a moment she continued, her voice not much more than a whisper. 'She's only just on nine and ... and they say they take them for the gentry. They say good money is paid for ... for – oh God! Janey! Oh God!'

Hattie shuddered as her own memories made her insides turn over. The bile rose in her throat, threatening to choke her. She heard herself spit out the word 'No!' But as she said it, she knew it was possible, and she knew too that it was something she could put down to Bobby Blackstaff. There was evil in that man – an evil that seeped through his pores and lived in his blackened soul.

'You say it's been on three weeks since she's been gone?' Susan nodded

Hattie tried not to show it, but she felt that this was a hopeless quest. Three weeks was a long time to keep a child hidden, and if she'd served her purpose, she'd most likely be got rid of. It would be first pickings that would be of value. But she'd have to give hope to Susan, even if she thought that hope was in vain. 'Look, I've a friend in the police. He's a sergeant.' She didn't say he was more of a customer than a friend, but her thought was that she could use her knowledge of him to blackmail him into doing something. An up-standing figure in the community, he'd not want to risk anyone finding out about his association with her. 'He'll help, if I ask him. He probably knows of sommat.'

'Oh God! Do you think you can find my Janey?' Susan leaned over and took hold of Hattie's hands.

Hattie felt an overwhelming urge to take the woman in her arms and say she wouldn't rest until she had found Janey. But fear that it was too late stopped her, so she just patted the woman's hands.

A glimmer of hope shone through Susan's de-spair as she said, 'I trust you, lass, I trust you. I'm sorry I called you them names. I know you're one of them, but somehow I know as you're not. Not really, not where it matters: in your heart. You're not one of them in your heart.'

'No, I'm not, Susan, and a lot of the other lassies aren't, either. For most of us it were just circumstances that led us this way – but then, once someone like Bobby Blackstaff gets hold of you, you're trapped. Come on: let's get you home. I'll walk with you, so I'll know where to find you if I get to know owt.'

Susan didn't object, and Hattie held her arm

for support as she rose. There was no flesh on her bones.

'Here, lean on me, lass. I'll get you home.'

On the way Susan told her she had another child, Sally, just six years old, who was being looked after by a neighbour. 'I'm afraid for her, Hattie. What if they come back?'

'Don't think on it, love. Sommat'll be done to stop them, I promise.'

'But what if they know I have another lass, and are watching me comings and goings? They'd know I leave her every morning to go to me shift!'

'You mean she's left on her own?'

'Aye. I have a fear in me and I wish it were different, but if I don't work we'll starve.'

'Look, you said you're on early shift – that's six while ten, isn't it? I could come over and watch out for her. I don't go on me patch until two-ish, unless Bobby Blackstaff has someone lined up for me earlier. But it's never afore twelve.'

Susan was quiet for a long time.

Hattie sighed. 'It's all right. I know how you're thinking. After all, I really could be the one befriending young 'uns. You've no way of knowing for sure; you've only just met me. Don't take on about it. I'll get on with asking around and I'll talk to Sergeant Jackson. I'll come back as soon–'

'No, no, it isn't that. I do trust you and I don't think – well, to be honest I don't know what to think.'

'I know, love.'

They had reached a row of cottages and had stopped at the steps of one of them when Susan said, 'I've a picture of Janey. It's just the one.

Tallyman took it on her Communion day. I can show it to you if you have time? Only, if you know what she looks like, then you'll recognize her if you see her.'

The picture caught at Hattie's heart. The golden-haired little girl smiling out at her looked like an angel in her white veil and with her hands clasped as if in prayer. Hatred surged up in Hattie for Bobby Blackstaff and his cronies, and she vowed she would do all she could to try to stop their evil game.

The sound of Susan's sobs brought Hattie's attention back to her, and she put an arm around her and held her. She had no words that would help.

The click of the back gate opening brought Susan up sharply. She took herself from Hattie's arms, grabbed a piece of towelling from over the rail above the fire and used it to rub her eyes. No sooner had she done so than the door opened.

'I see you're back then, Sue. Any luck, lass?'

'No, Vera. Well, not luck as such, though I've met up with Hattie here and she's going to help me. Hattie, this is me mate Vera. She's been helping me search for Sally.'

Vera looked from one to the other.

'Aye, I know what I am; there's no need to look at me like that. Like I said to Susan here, a whore I am, and not of me choosing, but a child-snatcher and murderer I'm not. I knew nowt of young 'uns going missing, but now that I do, I'll not rest till those responsible are caught, and I have more chance of doing sommat about it than all of you have.'

'Well, I beg your pardon, but I were just shocked to see you in here, seeing as how it's one of your kind who had a hand in all this.'

'I can understand that. I don't blame you or Susan for not trusting me, but I'll try to prove to you, as best I can, as to me motives being the same as yours. I'll go now, Susan, but like I said, I'll be in touch as soon as I know owt. Just think on: Sally will be safer having someone looking out for her, and I would do that, I promise.'

'I've thought on and I'd be grateful, Hattie. Ta. I'm on shift every Monday to Friday morning, so if you could come tomorrow?'

She'd no time to answer before the door, which had been left ajar, was pushed open and a head of fair curls popped round it. The child's face mirrored the one in the picture, but this face wasn't angelic; it was very cross. 'Mam, you didn't come for me! I saw you come down the road and waited and waited, and then Aunty Vera left me behind... Who's this?'

'Me name's Hattie. What's yours?'

'Sally. Have you come about me sister?'

'No. Well, not altogether. Me business is with you. I'm being interviewed by your mam. She's thinking of taking me on to look out for you in the mornings.'

'I don't need no looking out for. I'm six and a half, thou knows! I can look out for meself!'

'Sally! Don't be so rude!'

'It's all right.' Hattie laughed out loud. 'She's got the same spirit as I had at her age. I can see me and you are going to be mates, Sally. I like someone who can look out for themselves. It

93

means they can look out for me an' all.'

'Do you need looking out for, then?'

'Aye, I do. And I can't think of anyone better to look out for me than you. How about I come for breakfast every morning when your mam goes to the mill?'

'I'd like that. We could toast butties on the fire. Me mam says I'm not allowed to do it when she's not here, but she'd let me if you were here. Won't you, Mam? We have a long fork and...'

'Aye, all right, Sally. That's enough. Hattie knows how to make toast. Now, get out back and get swilled down under the tap ready for your tea, there's a good lass.'

Sally went to do as she was bid, but as she got to the door she turned and said, 'Will you be here when I wake up in the morning? Only mornings are getting darker and me mam won't let me light me candle. She says I have to keep me eyes shut until it gets light, but it never seems to get light and I don't like the dark. Not when I'm on me own, I don't.'

Hattie laughed again, amused that the little one's spirit wasn't enough to stop her being afraid of the dark. 'That's sommat else me and you are alike in, because I wasn't for being on me own in the dark when I were a young 'un, either. I'll be here, I promise. And I'm not afraid of owt, now I'm a grown-up.'

Hattie thought over what had happened as she walked back to her patch. The sickening shock she'd felt still dwelled in the pit of her stomach. If she knew anything, the one who'd befriended the young 'uns was most likely to be Doreen.

Doreen was known as Bobby Blackstaff's woman, though he didn't have real feelings for her or any other woman. Doreen was more for show – a cover for the real type he was. Or at least that was the rumour. He wasn't above putting Doreen to work when it suited him, though. Being a beauty, she caught the eye of the fellas; and if the one who was asking could be of some service to Bobby, then she had to do his bidding.

You could feel sorry for the lass in some ways, as it was clear she adored Bobby. But Doreen was a sly one. She kept her eye out for anything she could report back to him and was the cause of many a lass being beaten or even disappearing.

Hattie's thoughts turned to her stash; she was always fearful where that was concerned. Doreen had been watching her lately, turning up on her patch and hanging around her room. She'd have to be careful that she didn't find out about Hattie looking out for Sally. Mind, Doreen was never about much before two-ish, on account of her 'duties', which is what she called the fact that she had to serve drinks and was at the beck and call of Bobby Blackstaff, and whoever he was playing cards with, until the early hours. It was rumoured that sometimes she was taken down by every bloke there, and in full view of the others! By, she'd been brought low at times, from what was said.

Hattie sighed. Happen Doreen was more to be pitied than blamed, even though she lived far better than the rest of them. But if she was mixed up in this rotten business, she'd not get any pity! God, it didn't bear thinking about.

10

Laura's Loss

The envelopes came on the same day, though not by the same method of delivery and not together. The regiment's buff one, with the crest embossed on the bottom corner, came first, causing Laura's heart to skip a beat. How often during these dark days of war had these letters from him lifted her gloominess and given her a sense of hope, whilst news filtered through of terrible losses in his regiment.

But now, there was so much talk of 'the last push', and if it was successful the bloody war would be over, that she felt certain Jeremy was writing to say he was coming home. She didn't take the letter to her room, as she was used to doing, but eagerly ripped it open as soon as she picked it out from the other post on the silver tray by her breakfast setting.

Her eyes scanned over the words – there was no mention of the war's progress or of when he would see her. But then, why had she expected there to be? She knew putting such things in letters was forbidden, in case they fell into enemy hands.

The pages spoke of his love and how he missed her. He told her how much her letters meant to him and how they kept him going in the darkest moments, as did thoughts of her and of them together. *'I hope it won't be long now, my darling. I count the seconds with the beat of my heart, which is easy when I am thinking of you, because then it thuds so loudly.'* As she read this, she pressed the letter to her own heart and murmured, 'Oh, Jeremy, Jeremy.' His name was a whisper on her lips, but an agonizing pain of longing in her heart.

Three and a half years had passed since she'd last seen him, and then they had had only two weeks together, as he had come home with the body of his commanding officer and had been promoted to command the regiment from that point on. She had begged him not to lead from the front, but had known that he would rise to the challenge, the thought of which had caused her to endure fear and agony every day, as well as the loneliness and longing of sleepless nights.

Please, God, let it end soon, and please send him home to me safe and sound. The prayer had hardly died on her lips when Hamilton came into the room. Her heart plunged like a stone as she saw his expression and noted how the silver salver shook in his hand.

'Wha ... what is it, Hamilton?'

'A – a telegram, Ma'am.'

He lowered his hand. The brown envelope screamed the news she'd dreaded every day. The moment froze. The clock on the mantelshelf took over the space, its ticking taking her towards a life she didn't want to face. *'Killed in action'...* *'Killed in action'...* *'Killed'...* *'Killed'...* The scream started low in her stomach and accompanied her into her blackness.

'Lord and Lady Crompton are here, Ma'am. Shall I–'

'Thank you, Hamilton. There is no need to stand on ceremony today.' Hamilton turned and looked surprised that the guests had followed him through to the sitting room. He bowed his head to acknowledge Lady Crompton's words, then turned sharply and left the room with an air of disapproval.

'Laura. Oh, my dear, I'm so sorry. I...'

'Yes, old thing, a bad business. Sorry we couldn't get here sooner. Poor Jeremy, and poor you. What happened? Have they told you?'

Laura looked helplessly from one to the other: her sister, distraught and lost, not knowing what to say or do; and Charles, her dear brother-in-law, uncomfortable, but trying to take some control. But how could he? How could anyone take control of this awful situation? 'I haven't heard anything. Just – just...'

'Leave it with me, old thing. I'll telephone George. He works in the War Office. He'll find out all the facts and if ... well, if they are bringing Jeremy home.'

Daphne's arms enveloped Laura. She sank into them, but the tight knot holding her together didn't release. Would she ever be able to let it? The bitterness she'd battled with since the news had come in two days ago resurfaced. 'Why Jeremy? Why? We had so much to look forward to. Why couldn't it have been young Gary Ardbuckle? What use is he to anyone? But no, he'll come back fit as a fiddle and–'

'Laura, don't talk like that! Don't even think it. Gary – whoever – has a right to live, and I'm sure he is loved by someone. His mother...'

'I know, but every young man who went from this village is safe, and for what? What do they have to give? Nothing! They only take, but Jeremy...'

'Come on, old girl. You're not thinking straight. It's to be expected. Has your doctor been in to see you?'

'I *am* thinking straight, Charles, and I don't need a doctor.' She lifted her head. Jeremy smiled down at her from the picture hanging on the wall between the long windows, and she drew strength from him. 'I've been making plans. I want to start up the stud farm again, just as soon as this lot is officially over.'

'But Laura!'

'No, Daphne. I know you mean well, and God knows I'd like nothing more than to curl up in your arms and just cry and cry and be comforted by you, but that won't help. I know from experience that it won't. I need something to focus on. The stud is just the thing – it was when I lost my son, and it will be again.'

Charles coughed. 'Yes, my dear, you are right. It is a good idea for you to have something to occupy you, but I would have thought you have enough on your plate at the moment, and you will have to concentrate on selling off Hensal Grange Colliery and–'

'No! Don't even think about it, Charles. No, no! Jeremy would want me, more than anything, to hang on to the mine and the estate. But it isn't enough. I have an excellent manager, as you

99

know – the day-to-day running of the mine goes ahead without me, unlike in the old days when I was needed everywhere. Jeremy, with your help of course, had everything running so well that my involvement is only to oversee and make final decisions. As for the estate, I find that work tedious and will be grateful for any suggestions you can make regarding the running of it.'

'All right, darling, but promise me you will give yourself some time. Come and stay a while with us until...'

'Yes, Laura, you need time and...' Charles pulled at his moustache. 'Look, I'd no intention of speaking to you about this yet, but as you are making plans I think I should. I've been thinking about your estate as a whole just lately and, I must admit, the possibility of what would be the best for you in this situation.' Again he paused. Laura had seen the disapproving look Daphne had given him.

'No, don't stop him, Daphne. This is just what I need to talk about. It is all worrying me. I know that I've coped reasonably well, but it was meant to come to an end. It won't now. I need to have a plan to enable me to face the future, because at least then I will be able to let go of the business worries and give myself the time you are right in saying I need. After all, the plans I have for the stud farm cannot take place just yet. Go on, Charles.'

'Well, my dear, I can appoint an estate manager to take care of the day-to-day running of the affairs of the estate – the letting of properties, and the hiring and firing, that sort of thing. I could also oversee all of the business and make sure you are not cajoled into making any decisions you don't really need to take. You know I have your best interests at heart.'

'I think that's an excellent idea.'

'That's settled, then. Leave it all to me. I have a young man in mind who will make a first-class estate manager, working as a mediator for the bank and the estate. He had great prospects before the war, but was badly injured. He needs a position that will be flexible, and an office in his own home. I was thinking maybe he could live in the gatehouse? I know it hasn't been occupied for some time, but it wouldn't take much fixing up. He has a young family, so that would be perfect. It means he will be near enough to you, if he needs to discuss anything with you.'

'Good gracious! You have been thinking about this, haven't you? Well, it all sounds fine to me, and I can't tell you how relieved I feel.'

'Well, that's good. I tell you what: I'll put into place what I can, and I'll try not to bother you too much with the details. But these other ideas you have – well, I suggest you give a lot of thought to them, make your plans, and then Daphne and I will stay over after ... well, after – you know, old girl – the funeral or memorial service, whichever it is to be.'

'Charles!'

Daphne's face was a picture. Laura couldn't help smiling at her. 'Don't worry, darling. Charles's matter-of-fact way of dealing with things is just what I need. You know you don't have to pussyfoot around me.'

Laura took a cigarette from the silver box on the occasional table in front of her and put it in her cigarette holder, before offering the box to Daphne and Charles. They each took one and Charles did the honours lighting them carefully. Laura relaxed back and inhaled deeply. It felt good to talk about the future and to make plans. None of them had done that for so long.

'Right! That's settled. Now, how about some refreshment? I don't know about you ladies, but I could do with a stiff drink. I'll go and telephone George while you organize that, Laura, and whilst I'm at it, I'll see if he has any indication of how we are doing over there and if the promised end is in sight.'

Hamilton had left the room after bringing in the drinks tray. Daphne had poured the drinks and they were settled back on the sofa. 'Laura, whilst Charles isn't here, I want to talk to you. I too have been thinking about what would happen if this was the outcome of Jeremy rejoining the army. Darling, you have been under so much stress these last few years, ever since you lost little Leonard. You need a break. You're living on your nerves. Look, in a few weeks when everything is settled, why don't we go away together? Caroline is always asking us to go and stay with her on her South Sea Island – whatever it's called – and I think this would be a good time to take her up on that offer. We could stay for three months or so. What do you think?'

Laura didn't answer for a while. She put her drink down and snuggled back into Daphne's arms to think. Could she take time out? Daphne's friend, Lady Caroline Harper, heir to her father's vast import–export business, owned a beautiful place where sun, white sand, blue sea and tranquillity could be found. But, Laura wondered, if she went there, would she be able to cope with lounging around with nothing to do but think? But then perhaps that's what she needed to do. Perhaps there was something in *giving yourself time*. 'Yes. Yes, Daphne, I will. I will come away with you.'

'Really? Oh, Laura, I'm so glad! Oh, darling, I can't believe it. I'll help you. I'll look after you.'

'Now, Daphne, I don't want you planning to mother me and fuss me – you know I don't like that – but I need to talk. Talk about everything, get this knot of pain undone, and sometimes I will need to be allowed to be weak and to cry and cry. Oh, Daphne...'

11

Hattie Pays the Price

Hattie closed the gate and removed her gloves. The house looked just the same as all the others in the street, where the buildings were tall, three-storeyed dwellings with small enclosed gardens to the front. Half-net curtains shielded its every window, and a sign on the gate pronounced it to be a hostel for young ladies.

The neighbours all knew the real business of the place, but Hattie had a mind that even if they were against it, they'd not cause trouble. Not with Bobby Blackstaff being a loan shark, amongst other even darker dealings that he was mixed up in, and them all being hocked up to their eyeballs in debt to him.

The girls living there each had their own room. Some rooms were more poky than others, as the larger ones had been divided into two. Furnishings were few, but each girl made what she could of her own space. Hattie was proud of hers. She had some good pieces – some of them she'd bought herself, and others were oddments from Arthur that he didn't need. This had been commented upon, but as the money coming from Arthur was more than that from any other client, Bobby let it go.

Hattie opened the door with confidence. Some of the stealth she'd used when she'd first started looking after Sally two weeks ago had left her. No one had seemed to notice her comings and goings, but she was troubled by the fact that nothing was happening in the quest to find Janey, despite the information she'd provided, and despite Arthur getting his solicitor involved.

Daisy's door opened as she went up the stairs. 'Hattie, quick! In here. Come on.'

'What is it, Daisy? What're you doing up at this time? You're not usually around until noon or after.'

'I'm not the only one up. Shush. Come in quick, lass.'

As soon as they were inside the room, Daisy

closed the door and motioned Hattie over to the window. Hattie's throat tightened at what she saw: Doreen stood out of sight, but for her head which stuck out around the corner, as if she was trying to see, without being seen. Seemingly satisfied that no one was around, and not noticing them peeping around the curtain, she suddenly dashed towards the house.

Daisy pulled Hattie away from the window. 'Quick, she might look up! We don't want her to see us.'

'Oh, Daisy, do you reckon she followed me?'

'Aye, I'm sure on it. She left just after you. I've been up most of the night with running out back to the closet, then, come five-ish, I heard someone on the stairs and the front door closing. I looked out me window and saw the back of you go round the corner. You'd only just got out of sight when Doreen appeared and hurried out the gate after you. What took you out so early? Have you been to see Arthur?'

'No, I look after me mate's little lass... Oh, Daisy, what am I to do?'

'Well, if that's all it is you've been up to, I don't see you have owt to worry over. I thought you were at deceiving Bobby, making a bit on the side that he didn't know of. Anyroad, who is this mate? I didn't know you had one outside of this house. Well, not since you dropped off seeing Megan.'

Hattie hesitated. She couldn't tell Daisy – it'd be too dangerous. 'I've got to go, Daisy, but I'll tell of it some other time. I can't let Doreen think you know where I've been.'

'But why? I can't see as Bobby could object to you helping a mate.'

'Just leave it, Daisy love. I've to go. Doreen mustn't be at thinking you're involved.'

'But...'

Hattie gave her no time to say anything further. She was through the door and skipping along to her own room just as she heard the door at the bottom of the stairs closing.

Once in her room, she found that her body wouldn't settle itself. Her stomach churned with fear as she paced up and down. What could she do? What could she do? They'd not believe her if she said that all she was doing was looking out for a mate's young 'un. Not if they knew her mate was Janey's mam! Oh God! What if they found out she'd been asking questions of Sergeant Jackson? Or that he'd had meetings with Arthur and Arthur's solicitor?

One thing gave her hope: the cowardice of Sergeant Jackson. He was likely to be mindful of his own skin, and that's what would keep her scheming from being found out by any of Bobby's lot. Thinking about it, it was probably Sergeant Jackson's cowardice that was holding things up. He'd be afraid to move until he was sure of trapping the whole gang, as he knew he'd be dead if even one of them was left free. Bastard that he was, he deserved to be dead an' all. Her skin crawled at the thought of lying with him, of how he sweated as he pounded her, and of the things he wanted her to do to him. And for no payment! At least, not for her – it was his payback for favours owed to him by Bobby. But that aside, what sickened her most

106

was how he worked things so as to get a night with her. He'd have her and a few lassies who were getting past it, and who Bobby wanted rid of, arrested. They would be thrown into the cells, but she would be taken to his office to pleasure him. In the morning the lassies would be up before the magistrates and would end up being sent to a workhouse or, worse, to some prison to rot, and she'd be let free with no charge. There was nothing she could do about it. It just happened to be her that Sergeant Jackson wanted.

The lassies knew how it was for her, and knew how much it hurt her to be the bait that helped Bobby to get rid of the others. They didn't hold Hattie to blame. In fact, if she knew anything, it was more than a good bet that the sergeant had alerted Bobby to her goings-on, but he'd not say he knew what she was up to. He'd not dare. With Arthur's solicitor knowing everything, he'd be caught out. No, he'd just hint as to her being seen out and about in the early hours. One day she'd get even with that bloody sod, and in the meantime she'd have to think of something. She'd have to.

A knock on her door made her body stiffen. Opening it and seeing Doreen leaning against the wall, arms folded across her middle and a look of triumph on her face, made the small hope that Hattie had harboured sink.

'Bobby wants to see you.'

Just that – 'Bobby wants to see you' – but it was enough. Enough to strike such fear into her that she broke out in a sweat, but she'd not let Doreen see it. 'All right, I'll be up in a minute. I'm just taking off me outdoor things.'

'I wouldn't be long, if I were you. He isn't in a good mood.' A sickly smile spread across her face and her eyes gleamed maliciously.

Anger replaced some of Hattie's fear – an anger that urged her to hit out at this vile woman. If she did, she'd not stop beating her until one of them was broken, and that wouldn't solve anything. But she'd not spare Doreen the lashing of her tongue. 'Why's that? Haven't you been at licking his arse all night then? Because you might as well, as everyone knows you'd do his bidding, no matter what that bidding be. By, Doreen, you've been brought low. So low you're not fit to clean the shit off the closet the rest of us use, and that's saying sommat!'

Doreen faltered. Her shock at the attack registered on her face, but she recovered quickly. 'We'll see about that, shall we, when you're begging for mercy and I'm watching. We'll see who's been brought low then, eh?'

'So it's a beating I'm in for, is it? Well, well, and it'd have nowt to do with you snooping in what doesn't concern you, would it? You're a bastard, Doreen, a vile bloody bastard!' As she said this last, Hattie slammed the door in Doreen's face. The action helped, but as soon as it was shut, she slumped against it.

She knew she hadn't long; knew it would be worse for her if she kept Bobby waiting. Her mind tried every avenue she could think of that might convince him she didn't know anything, but in her frantic state she had no answers. She knew in her heart that it was hopeless.

'Ah, Hattie!'

Bobby's greeting surprised her. He didn't seem in a bad mood; he was lounging in an armchair, the like of which she was more used to seeing in Arthur's house, though it didn't look out of place with the rest of the furnishings in this light and airy room. She looked at Bobby. His attention seemed to be taken up with cleaning his nails with a long, thin paper-knife. Smoke curled from an ashtray on a polished table next to him. He picked the cigarette up and drew heavily on it. The smoke came out of his mouth and down his nostrils as he spoke, causing his eyes to squint. 'I hear you are taking a little walk every weekday, Hattie.'

'I look after me mate's young 'un whilst she's at her shift. She lost her man in the war.' In an instant Hattie decided she couldn't avoid mentioning the missing child. She knew it would be better if she did, as it would make Bobby think she didn't know he was involved. 'Her other young 'un's gone missing, so she's in a state.'

'Gone missing? Well, well.' He swung his legs to the floor, stood up and moved towards her. She couldn't think what he was up to. This increased her fear even more. His voice was still smooth and held no malice as he continued, 'And where do you think she's gone, this other one?' His body brushed hers. She thought he intended to walk on towards the window, but without warning he turned, grabbed her hair and yanked her head backwards. The suddenness of his action shocked rather than hurt her, as it wasn't in keeping with his friendly tone. She could feel his breath fanning her ear as he said, 'I think you know only too well where she's gone, Hattie, don't you, eh?'

She tried to lessen the pain by bending with him as, with her hair coiled around his hand, he started to circle her, tightening his grip and tearing at the roots. Her voice whimpered from her, 'No, I...'

'Oh, I think *yes*. I can't have the likes of you lying to me now, can I?' With his other hand he grabbed her left arm and twisted it up her back. His face was near hers – so near she could smell him. Smell his perfume, which brought to mind the preference she knew he had for getting his sexual pleasure with men, more than he did with women. It shocked her to think at this moment that she pitied Doreen when Doreen had been instrumental in all of this happening to her.

Just as quickly as he'd grabbed her, Bobby let her go. He walked away from her and picked up his cigarette again. His movements were graceful, yet menacing, like a cat ready to pounce. 'Well, let me tell you something, Hattie. The first chicken I took from your mate's nest served me well in making me some good money, and now I'm going to pluck the next one from the same nest, and you're going to help me to do it.'

'No!'

'Oh, yes. I think you will bring the pretty little thing to me. I'm so confident of this that I have already put out the word of her coming, and have a customer waiting. I can't believe how easy it is all going to be.'

'No! I'll not. I'll not do it!'

'You have no choice. Bring her here and you

live; don't and you die. It's as simple as that! Oh, actually,' he blew his inhaled smoke in her direction, 'it isn't that simple, because your death wouldn't be pleasant or quick.'

He'd moved closer to her again, his expression mocking her. As if on impulse, his hand whipped out and caught hold of hers. Her skin seared with pain as he ground the stub of his cigarette into her arm.

Using all her strength, she pulled away from him. 'I don't care what you do to me, you bastard! You'll not get me to bring Sally here – not ever!'

'Sally, is it? Pretty name. And I'm a bastard, am I? Well now, whilst we're on names, let's see. What was the other one called?'

Again his body reminded her of a cat, as he stretched forward and picked up a bell from the table next to his ashtray. Its tinny peal hung in the air as he said, 'Hmm, Janey. Yes. "Janey's me name, sir." Ha! A treasure. A little treasure! What pleasure she gave. So much that I could charge double for the younger version.'

He was talking as if Janey was dead. She swallowed hard. The implications of his words had taken Hattie's fear away and cleared her head. She had to think; she had to do something. Something that would save Sally and make Bobby Blackstaff pay!

The door across the room opened. Doreen entered, her satisfied smirk unmasking her inner evil. Bobby spoke to her in a different voice – softer, kinder – confirming the conspiracy between them. 'Fetch Wally and Doug, please, Doreen my love.'

'Yes, Bobby.' Her look in Hattie's direction came with a raising of her eyebrows as if to say: *I told you so.*

The gesture didn't have any impact on Hattie. Her mind soared far above what Doreen felt or did. As plans formed, she knew what she must do. She'd take as much of the beating coming to her as she could bear, and appear broken and ready to do as Bobby bade. Bobby knew her, knew that she had spirit. He'd not believe her if she gave in at the threat of being hurt – he'd suspect that she had a scheme of sorts up her sleeve. Once she was trusted, she'd set something up that would trap them all. Arthur would help her. He'd find a way to keep Sally safe and get this lot their just deserts.

When the door opened again to admit Wally and Doug, her newfound courage all but deserted her. They were brutish, and had no concerns for the pain of others. She'd heard the screams coming up from the basement when they were at their work, and she'd helped in the nursing of the bloodied and beaten lassies who'd displeased Bobby in some way. Even worse, there'd been times when the screams had stopped suddenly, and the lass being beaten hadn't come back up the stairs or ever been seen again. Oh God! Could she hold out long enough to convince them?

Bobby gestured towards her with his head. 'Just until she agrees. I don't want her dead – not yet. Make it last a few days, if you have to. Only call me if she's near to death and hasn't given in. I make the decision on whether she dies or not – is that understood?'

'Yes, boss.'

Bobby's tone changed. 'Now then, Hattie, you are about to find out for yourself just what a bastard I am!'

As the men moved across the room, the fear she'd almost let go of as she'd plotted a way out gripped her in a tight knot once more. Without warning, Wally, the small, fat one, punched her in the stomach, causing her to double over and gasp for breath.

'Make her holler loud enough for me to hear, boys. I like the sound of pain. And I like my other whores to hear as well. It gives them a lesson.' Prowling round the room like the animal he was, Bobby had come up close to her once more.

'Look at the boss when he speaks!' Doug grabbed her, twisted her arm and yanked her head so that she was looking into Bobby's evil eyes. She could do nothing. Her stomach cramped with pain and her arm burned. 'Don't! Please, don't.' No one answered her or even acknowledged that she'd spoken.

'Try not to mark her face. It hasn't got a beauty to it, but some of my more useful customers seem to like it. And leave her intact where it matters. She's good to have a go at, so I'm told. Sample it and let me know what you think – yes, that would be fun. I've heard she'll do anything rather than let her arse take it, so give her some of that – get her ready. You do it, Wally. The size of you will definitely loosen it up. Sergeant Jackson often complains that he can't get her to let him up there. I think he'd be pleased enough to tell me more of what he knows of her, if he thinks it's been made ready for him.'

113

Spittle gathered in her mouth and she spat her hatred at him. 'Fuck you!'

'You fucking whore!' Bobby's hand whipped out and stung her cheek, but it was worth the pain, to see her spittle run down his face. Wiping it with his handkerchief, he ground out the words, 'You'll pay for that, you filthy bitch!' Then he told his thugs, 'Use the chair after you've raped her. Take it to its limit.'

As she was dragged by her hair like a dog on a lead along the corridors and down flights of stairs, the doors of the bedrooms they passed remained closed. No one dared to intervene, she knew that. When they approached Daisy's room, she forced herself to clamp her lips together and endure the pain, because if Daisy heard her, she'd be out like a shot. Hattie didn't want that to happen. By the time they reached the kitchen, the terror inside her had reached fever pitch. She fought for all she was worth, but her resistance was futile.

A cold shaft of air brushed her face as the door to the cellar clunked open. They shoved her into the dimness. Her foot missed the step and she crashed down onto the stone floor. Wally stepped over her, swiped a match on the brick wall and lit the gas mantle. The light took time to reach each part of the cellar. Fear caused her mouth to dry. The implements of torture, now visible, seemed to snarl at her. Straps, whips, knives, chains and unidentifiable objects lay on a huge table. In the far corner, a chair that wasn't a chair in the proper sense mocked her. Made of wood and iron, it spoke of pain and death. Leather clamps positioned on the arms, feet and at chest-height hung ready to hold a victim like a vice, but what etched dread into her heart even more was the cage-like contraption fixed to the top. *Please God, don't let them put my head into that!*

Fighting achieved nothing, serving only to amuse the men as they ripped the clothing from her body. With her arms screwed up behind her back and held as if in a clamp by Doug, she watched Wally send the implements clanging across the room with one swipe of his hand. The dreadful noise they made echoed around her, as Doug forced her backwards over the edge of the table.

She wouldn't beg. She wouldn't kick out or utter a sound, because to do so would only heighten their pleasure. She closed off her mind. Doug took his turn first. And though the skin on her back seared with the soreness of his thrusting her against the rough wood, she felt nothing of what was happening. Wally's voice, thick and guttural, goaded him on. 'Go on, Doug. Give it to her.'

Thankfully it didn't last long.

'Eeh, Doug lad, you enjoyed that, I can tell. I've never known you come that quick. It must be right, what's said about her.'

Doug laughed, a breathless sound that repulsed her. Wally shoved him. 'Right, move over and let the big boy in!'

Doug's laugh this time was pitched to a high, stupid-sounding note. He took her hands from Wally and together they turned her over.

Clenching her fists, she willed herself not to think about what was going to happen. Her only hope was to stay relaxed. The pain of him entering her tore through her and she screwed up her eyes. Her breath hissed through her gritted teeth. Spittle ran down her chin. Every thrust ripped her, causing a soreness that made her flesh feel like it was being rubbed with sandpaper, as he forced himself deeper and deeper. At last it was done. Wally groaned like an animal, then pulled himself from her and threw her onto the floor. She could see him leaning on the table above her, panting. Doug hovered around him. 'You all right, Wally?'

'Aye. Christ, that were sommat else. Get me baccy. I need time to recover.'

Their smoke filtered down to her, clogging her throat, and their talk was like that of schoolboys congratulating each other. Hattie screwed herself up tightly into a ball. Shivering, a tear trickled down her cheek. If she had a mam, she would have called out to her, but instead she thought of Susan and little Sally. And remembered why she'd had to endure them using her as they had.

In order to help her cope, she tried to bring Megan to her mind – sweet, untouched Megan. Thank God – thank God Megan's fate had been so different. At least one of them had escaped, and how glad she was that it had been Megan.

'Right.' Wally dropped his fag-end on the floor and scrunched it out with his foot. 'Back to work. Let's make this whore pay for spitting at the boss. Get her in the chair, Doug.'

'No – no. Don't. I'll do it. Tell Bobby I'll do it. Tell him I'm sorry...'

'Ah, but it's not about that now, bitch. No one gets away with what you did.'

Her screams resounded off the wall, bouncing back at her. The nutcrackers clicked in her face, glinting in the flicker of the gas mantle, before crushing the bones of her fingers to the chant of *'This little piggy went to market...'*

Her soul hollered out cries for mercy, but they showed her none. Her mind sank into the vilest of places, where she felt the despair of a despising God as well as her very own being. But then the agony eased, as a blackness swept her into a deep, dark, closed part of her mind. There, the laughing, mocking faces of the hated Reverend Mother, the vile, filthy Lord Marley, his friend Felix and the rotten-to-the-core Mrs Barker yo-yoed at her, and she knew she was descending into madness.

The shock of ice-cold water hitting her body dragged her back to the present, and an acrid taste of smoke clogged her throat. Heat burned inside her nostrils. Terror gripped her as she came to the confusing realization that the room was on fire, and that the fire was licking at her, searing her skin. But, as her head cleared, she saw Doug wafting a lighted torch backwards and forwards before her eyes. The flames lit up the evil in his eyes as he smiled down at her, before dragging it along her arm. She opened her mouth to scream, but only a hoarse moan came from her.

12

Megan Enters Hattie's World

Megan clutched the crumpled note in her pocket:

Megan, I need to see you. Forgive me for losing touch. Please come. I'll meet you at six, down at the end of Fell Lane next Sunday. You know where it is. It's the one as you turned off to go to the guesthouse when you visited me that time. Please, please come. All my love, your friend, Hattie x

Going over the words Hattie had written gave Megan the courage she needed to turn the corner into the dark ginnel that would take her into the streets where Hattie and the lassies who plied the same trade did their business. Hattie's having made contact at last spurred her on. To think she'd been considering giving up trying to find Hattie, and resigning herself to having lost her for good!

As she turned into Fell Lane, she made out the shadowy figure of a woman pacing up and down just a few feet away. Could it be? The woman turned towards her. 'Hattie? Hattie, is that you?'

'Aye, it is, Megan. Eeh, Megan... Megan...'

'Oh, Hattie!' The years of separation rolled away as their laughter and tears mingled in a hug, but a wince of pain from Hattie made Megan jump back. Before she could ask what was wrong, Hattie's urgent whisper beckoned her: 'Quick, step into the ginnel. Don't let anyone see you.'

'Who? Are you all right? Are you hurt, Hattie? Is someone–' She went to take Hattie's hand. Hattie jerked it away from her, but not before she'd seen the bulky bandages. 'Hattie love...'

'Don't worry, I'll be reet. Come on, let's get off the street. Oh, Megan, it's good to see you!'

'I tried to find you, Hattie. I looked.'

'I know you did, love, but I weren't for being found. I'll tell you of it all, I promise. But first we have to get ourselves to a safe place.'

They walked in silence, keeping as close together as they could through the narrow pathways. Neither wanted to let go of the other, even though they sometimes had to walk sideways so as not to unlink their arms. Hattie had asked Megan to hold on to her left arm, as she'd said it wasn't as badly hurt as the other one. But even so, the feel of the bandages wrapped around it deepened Megan's worry. It wasn't just the injuries that were causing her concern, though: Hattie's sudden gestures telling her to get into a doorway and to keep quiet added to the fear already stirring in her stomach.

The winding paths went on and on. The stench of poverty worsened with every step, as they passed rows of neglected houses, their back yards strewn with rotting masses of dumped waste. More than once pity at what had become of Hattie dragged at Megan's heart, and she thanked God and Sister Bernadette for her own fortunes.

When they came to a wider but just as muddy

119

road, the air became fresher and was tinged only by the smell of the horse dollop they had to weave around. There were gas lamps here, and though they only gave off a dim light, Megan could see the gates to a park on the other side of the track. Hattie's whole body relaxed when they came up to these. 'Nearly there, love. Just got to cross the grass. We'll be fine now. I have a friend... Well, he's a sort of friend. He started as one of me customers and got fond of me. He's a gentleman. He got hurt bad in France, lost a leg and part of his face, and his wife won't have owt to do with him. Anyroad, he came looking to satisfy his needs and that's how we met. He's took this house just round the corner from the other side of the park, and he's helping me to get away from the fella who controls the patch I work on.'

Megan didn't know how to react to all this information. Everything Hattie had said was far from what she already knew of her friend's situation. She wanted to say she was pleased for Hattie, but on the other hand she didn't want Hattie to be used by any man, gentleman or not. It was easier just to squeeze the unbandaged bit of her arm gently and smile at her.

'Me man's name is Arthur. He isn't good to look on, with his injuries, but I know you'll be like me and take that in your stride. He's after me moving in with him, but I've other plans. I want to look out for all the lassies on the patch, and I have an idea for a business that would help them and could see me right an' all.' The damp undergrowth at last gave way to a cobbled road leading to a street so bright that it looked like night had turned into day. A dozen lamps lit the whole area and light shone from the windows of the type of houses that folk far above Megan and Hattie's station lived in. Hattie grinned at her. She could only smile back. It was as if someone had tied her tongue in knots, making it hard to form words. But if it were possible for such a thing to happen, speaking became even harder when they stopped in front of huge ornate gates and Hattie said, 'This is it': before her stood what looked to Megan like a palace.

'Come on, love. Stop trying to catch flies.' This from Hattie, who strode not towards the servants' entrance but right up to the front door, prompted a giggle from the pair such as they used to share. The sudden opening of the door, however, stopped the flow of their laughter, and a tall, up-right young man smiled a welcome. 'Hello, Hattie. Is this your friend, then?' His voice didn't go with his accent, which had a posh tinge to it.

'Aye, this is Megan, Harry.'

'Pleased to meet you, Megan. I'll take your coat. Captain Naraday is still at his rest, Hattie, but I've a fire lit in the front room. If you and Megan go through, I'll fetch some tea in for you.'

Megan handed him her coat and smiled at him, then watched as he helped Hattie off with hers, asking as he did so, 'Are you feeling any better, lass?'

'Aye, I'll be reet. It'll all be worth it in the end.'

The obvious friendship between them warmed Megan. Hattie *did* have folk who cared for her, and that was good to know, no matter what the circumstances.

The friendly welcome made her forget her awe at where she found herself. The hall they'd stepped into held beauty, in a manly kind of way, the dark mahogany of the doors and banister standing out against the background of the cream walls. Framed photographs of men in uniform hung in straight military lines, and the stairs, winding up from the centre, were carpeted in a plain, rich brown carpet.

The room they were shown into had a different feel, and its grandness made her catch her breath. There was a plush red carpet, and gold-and-red curtains formed a backdrop to pink-and-gold cushioned chairs and sofas with elaborately carved legs. The tables, some small and placed next to sofas and chairs, and one larger and round-topped standing in the window, were of a rich mahogany, and they too had beautifully carved, bowed legs.

'It's grand, isn't it, Megan? And it could all be mine, if I wanted.' Hattie's smile didn't reach her eyes, and a touch of bitterness had crept into her words, but Megan's shock as she turned to answer stopped her from querying this. Without her coat and in the full glare of the many burning lamps, the full extent of Hattie's injuries hit her. Looking gaunt and frail, her eyes were sunk into their sockets. Bruises – red, purple and angry-looking – covered every part of her exposed skin. The sight brought Megan down to earth with a painful jolt. 'Oh, Hattie, what happened?'

'Don't worry, love, I had it coming to me. Fella I told you of as owns patch I work wanted me to do sommat, and I wasn't for it. But I thought on how I could do it and get him caught for what I'd found out. Taking me beating and not giving in until he'd near killed me made him think I'd agreed, and hopefully kept me scheme from him.'

Megan clutched at her sleeve awkwardly. She didn't understand Hattie's world, peopled as it was with folk who would beat her and with others who would use her, but also with kind people like Harry. But what of Harry's master, this Captain bloke? What would he do to her?

'Tell me what's been happening with your life, Megan. You look well. You've not changed. Only I didn't think you'd make such a beauty!' The laugh that accompanied this remark lightened the moment.

'Go on with you! I'm no beauty. You should see Ciss – by, she's sommat. I've never seen anyone prettier. Mind, you've not turned out so bad yourself, though you're a mite thinner than you should be. Oh, Hattie, I've missed you. Why haven't you been in touch until now?'

'I wanted to – I did – but me life wasn't what I wanted you mixed up in. Lassies as threatened you when you came looking were doing so at my bidding. It's a dangerous place where I live, Megan; lassies like you – innocent lassies – are snatched regular and raped and such, then put on the game. And not only lassies of an age. Oh, Megan, I know things. Things I shouldn't know of, and I'm–'

Harry came in at that moment. If he noticed the sudden silence, he didn't say. Crossing the room, he put the tray laden with tea, sandwiches and cakes down onto the table next to the sofa. Hattie spoke to him as if she was used to dealing with servants: 'Thank you, Harry. Is Captain Naraday up yet?'

'His bell rang a few minutes ago. He asked for a tray and said he has a headache. He sends his apologies, but he won't be joining you. Though he hopes you can go up, after your business with your friend is done. Now, if I pour for you both, will you give Hattie a hand, Megan? She's not a good patient, so be careful when you feed her, so as you don't lose a finger or two!'

They both laughed at this and, as he left the room, Hattie said, 'That means Arthur isn't up to seeing you after all. Poor Arthur, it's hard for him looking like he does, and he's afraid of meeting folk for the first time. Mind, he's lucky to have Harry – he's a good man, is Harry. He's been with Arthur for all of his army career. He was his batman, and he'll not leave him now. Especially how he is.'

Again there was the hint of a suggestion that there was something Hattie wasn't telling, which she covered up by saying, 'Well, tell me how things have worked out at that Madame Marie's place, and then I've a lot to tell you an' all.'

'It's worked out better than I thought it would, Hattie, and I know as it sounds funny, but the war has made me life better, which isn't a good thing to say, seeing how so many are suffering. But business took a bad turn with the war. It wasn't as if folk hadn't got the money, more that it'd not be right to have parties and things. Even weddings are quiet affairs now.' The expression of bewilderment on Hattie's face made her giggle. 'I'm not at making much sense, am I? I can see as you're wondering how all this doom and gloom have been of benefit to me.'

'Aye, I were at wondering.'

Megan helped Hattie take a sip of her tea, and lodged a sandwich between the only two fingers showing through the bandages, rather than feed it to her. Then, taking a sip of her own tea, she began to relax. It was easier to talk about her own life than to listen to Hattie's tales about hers. 'Well, it's like this: me and Ciss'd thought at first we'd be down the road when Madame started cutting back, but it were the others – the posh lot – that she let go. She had us in her office and said as she'd keep us on if we took a dock in our wages and learned other skills, so as we could help out where needed. I were that glad to think I were going to get a chance to learn things like the cutting of patterns and making up that I were ready to agree straight off. But Ciss! Eeh, Hattie, you'd like Ciss; you wouldn't think it to look at her, but she's got some clout. She only ups and says me and her'll only agree to stay if the rules are relaxed some. Madame looked right put out, but it were like Ciss said later: she'd not have been able to ask the posh lot to take a dock and do all the other work an' all. So we were her only hope. Anyroad, Madame took on what Ciss'd said and now, once our work hours are done, we can come and go as we like and we get to go home every three to four weeks or so.'

'Home?'

'Aye. I've a proper home, Hattie. Like me and you always dreamed of. Issy – that's Cissy's mam – treats me like a daughter, and Ciss has become...

125

Well, I mean–'

'It's all right, love. I'm happy for you. I know as you've never forgot me, so don't go feeling guilty. It were my fault we've not kept in touch, and you're still like a sister to me an' all. You thinking on Ciss in that way won't bother me. I'm just glad your life's going so well, and I've never forgot Cissy's kindness in lending me that half a crown that time. Tell her I have it for her, and with some interest on it an' all.'

Hattie had reached out and taken Megan's hand as best she could. Megan let it lay in hers, wanting to ask and yet not wanting to know how she'd been so hurt, and how badly injured her hands really were.

'Now, I've sommat to tell you,' Hattie said. 'I'm for giving up this game – well, that is, in part. I mean, I'm not going to sell meself to all and sundry, but I will still be Arthur's ... mistress, sort of.'

'Oh, Hattie, that's good news. I can't stand to think of you doing what you've been doing. But are you sure you want – well, thou knows...'

'Aye, Arthur's a good man, but I'll not come to him on his terms, and he knows that. Anyroad, he's helping me. Not just with money, though I need that, as me own stash isn't enough for what I'm planning. No, he's helping me with all the legal stuff and with the police–'

'The police! Are you in trouble, Hattie?'

'No. Well, not as such. Not with the police, that is, but what I am involved in could go either way. I mean, it's very dangerous and I could be killed.'

'Hattie! No! Oh, Hattie. Oh God!'

'I'm sorry, love. I wasn't for wanting to shock or

126

hurt you, but I had to see you before I do what it is I have to do.'

'Whatever it is, don't do it. Please don't do it. Look, I've got some money saved and it sounds like you have an' all. Let's find a place, a little house. You, me, Ciss and Daisy.'

'It wouldn't work, love. Me and the lassies would be hounded down till we were found, then punished – or even murdered – as an example to others not to try to get out. I have to do this thing. I have to. It's me only way. Now listen: I need to tell you what I want you to do if owt happens to me. Me stash is with me solicitor. Eeh, that sounds grand! Me solicitor!' She giggled and, though it sounded good, the fear and pain inside Megan wouldn't allow her to join in.

'He's Arthur's solicitor, really,' Hattie continued, 'but he's acting for me in the business I mean to set up. I've been at saving for a long time – holding back what I could whenever I could, and stashing it away. Then, when I met Arthur ... well, he always paid me over the odds. He's always wanted to get me off the game. He thinks a lot of me, Megan, and he's willing to put in a lot more money an' all.'

'What business are you talking of, Hattie?'

'I mean to buy a house – a good-sized one – in an area where it's pretty decent, but won't have neighbours as such. I don't want any young 'uns living around it, or folk who might poke their nose into me business. I've seen just the place. It's at the end of a cul-de-sac. Houses line one side of the road leading down to it and there's the canal on the other. The houses used to be homes, but they're used as offices for solicitors and

127

suchlike now. It's ideal for me purpose, because it's still in the city, but it's not a thoroughfare or place as police go on their beat.'

Still mystified, Megan waited, listening with rising confusion. She had so many questions and fears, but they were all tangled in her brain. She wasn't sure if she wanted to know of this business venture of Hattie's, her part in it all, or the thing Hattie had to do that could get her killed.

'I can see as I've put you in a stew, with me going from one thing to another, Megan. Look, me business is going to be a home for the lassies: a safe place, a clean place, a place where gentlemen come to them and they don't have to walk the streets. They'll have regular meals and medical treatment. That quack I told you of who helped me, do you remember? Back when I first left being in service? Well, it turned out he were a trained doctor, but had been struck off. Sommat to do with a married female patient. Well, he's good, so I'll be taking him on to look after the lassies. Lassies will pay me a percentage to have all this provided for them, plus a bit on top, as'll be me profit. Mind, I won't have any visitors meself – only Arthur, and sometimes I'll be staying here with him. And it isn't like I'm going to be a pimp or owt, as I won't be selling the girls or enticing others to be prostitutes. I'll just be providing proper conditions for them as are already doing it. Them as have no other choices.'

With this explanation, it all became clearer to Megan. 'It sounds good, love. Well, that is, if it's what you want. I'd be more glad if you said you were opening a tea shop, though. But is...? I

128

mean, is there sommat stopping you taking up Arthur's offer? Wouldn't that be better for you?'

'No. Why do you ask that, Megan? I'd have thought you'd have known.'

This surprised her. Hattie sounded upset and Megan couldn't think what she'd said to cause her to be. 'I didn't mean...'

'I know. But, well, I never planned it like it's happened. I'm no different to you, Megan.'

There it was again: the bitterness.

'I've just not had the chances. I don't want the life I lead, but ... well, an arrangement like that wouldn't sit right with me. I always thought that when I went to a man, it'd be as his wife, and that's still what I want. Thou knows – someone like Harry. Someone of me own class. I'd come here gladly and live in servants' quarters as Harry's wife.'

'You mean, you love Harry?'

'No, that's just it. I love Arthur. I do, despite everything. He's good; he's kind. The man inside the broken body is everything I've ever wanted, but when I found him, he was everything I couldn't have. Not proper, like. Not someone who could take me to be his wife and let me live a decent life, like we were brought up to do.'

'I don't know what to say, Hattie. I carry a guilt at how things have turned out. You'd never take me up on ways I thought we could have got by.'

'Don't, Megan. You're the best thing in me life, and'll always be. I know you'd have given up everything for me, but I couldn't have bettered meself at your expense. I would have dragged you down. I'm sorry. Me moaning about how me life's

129

turned out isn't fair on you. I could have had chances. You tried to give me some. I could've set up in a cottage or sommat with you.'

They dropped into a silence that wasn't comfortable. It was as if they were at odds with each other – something Megan had never known to happen before. She tried to think of a way to break it. Thinking some encouragement might help, even if it wasn't what she'd choose for Hattie, she said, 'This house you're getting will change things for you, love. I know it isn't life as you'd really want it, but it sounds like the next best thing, and I'll be able to visit you regular.'

'Aye, you will. I'll have me own private rooms an' all. You should see it, Megan! It's grand. I'll have a good life there, I know I will, and don't worry over other things I've said. I'll be happy. I've long since learned to be happy with me lot. I don't know what prompted me to bring all that stuff out. It must be being with you. We were always able to say what were in our hearts. I've missed that, Megan.' She smiled her lovely kind smile, and Megan gently took Hattie in her arms and held her. It felt good as she told her, 'We'll never be separated again, Hattie. Never! I'll come to see you as often as I can, I promise.'

'I can't wait, Megan.' As Hattie said this, her body trembled.

Megan drew back. 'Are you all right now, love?'

'Aye, it's this other business. I've to get that out of the way first. Every time I think on it, me body shudders.'

Megan had been dreading this moment, hearing about the *other business* Hattie had mentioned, and

130

this didn't lessen as she listened to what Hattie said. 'I need to tell you what I want you to do. If anything happens to me, Megan, I want you to go to me solicitor. Me money as I've left with him is to be yours. You're to use it how you want, though I'd like you to see as Daisy and Phyllis are all right. Arthur'll help you sort it all out.'

'No, Hattie! I couldn't. I don't want your money. I want everything to be right for you.'

'I know, love, and I hope it will be. But if the worst happens, I'd be happy knowing you and Daisy and Phyllis are looked after.'

'Oh, Hattie, I can't bear it. I can't think on you being in so much danger. Do you have to do this thing as you're talking of? Isn't there any other way?'

'No, there's no other way, and when I tell you of it you'll understand, like Arthur does. He knows that I couldn't live with meself if I did nothing...'

13

The Devil's Work is Done

The fear and agony in Susan's face planted a seed of uncertainty in Hattie. Was Susan thinking of stopping the plan from going ahead? She tried to reassure her by saying, 'It'll be all right, love, I promise. I'll not let owt happen to Sally. Sergeant Jackson'll have a dozen police in plain clothes around and about. None of them local, so they'll not be known to Bobby Blackstaff and his cronies.'

'But what if they get away with her? I'd not bear it, Hattie, and what if they don't find Janey?'

Susan's thin, drawn face was tinged with yellow, the colour of failing health, and her eyes held desolation. Hattie's worry over her deepened. Susan was always being sick and constantly complained of pain in her stomach. The little flesh she had on her bones sagged as if the life had already left it, and the simplest of chores took it out of her. She'd stopped going to the factory weeks ago, living on the parish relief and whatever she would take from Hattie. Thank God that had been more lately, as Hattie had convinced her the money was for Sally. No matter what, she knew Susan wouldn't allow Sally to go without.

But now she needed to see that Susan got some attention, so she told her, 'I'm getting me doctor friend to come and have a look at you, when this is done, Sue. Now don't protest. I know you're a proud woman, but you need help, and who else can you take it from, if not from your mates, eh?'

A weak smile creased Susan's cheeks. 'Aye, and you've been a good mate to me, Hattie. I'd have not got through it without you. I can't believe what they did to you, and you standing it all so as to help get that lot caught and get me Janey back. But I'm feared over Sally. I keep thinking on what it'll do to her. She's bound to get a big fright when they come to take her. It don't seem right to put her through it, no matter what it might mean.'

'They won't frighten her – not if I know owt, they won't. It won't serve their purpose to. They wouldn't want to deal with a screaming young 'un and the attention that would attract. No, I think they'll get her to go willingly. Doreen can put on a kind and gentle side when she wants to, and she has a knack of making people like her. I've seen her with new girls as Bobby's brought into the game. They're all taken in by her, until they get to know what she's really like. Anyroad, the police will follow her, so Sally will be protected all the time, and if all goes to plan they'll catch the lot of them.'

'And Janey? They'll make them tell where Janey is, won't they?'

'Aye, of course they will. It's hoped they'll be able to uncover the whole bloody show Bobby Blackstaff and his lot run: selling young 'uns to gentry, taking money for protection, prostitution and God knows what else. And while we're on mentioning His name, pray to Him they all get their just deserts and swing from the end of a rope for what they've done.'

Hattie hoped her words about Janey would bring some comfort to Susan, but internally she admitted to herself that she didn't think the youngster would be found. Not alive anyroad, although she hoped with all her heart that she would; it didn't bear thinking about what might happen if Bobby Blackstaff didn't get caught or if he didn't get the death penalty, as he'd know she was the one who had planned it all.

Ten minutes passed before Hattie spotted Doreen walking towards her and Sally. A sick feeling entered her as she took a deep breath to speak, but there was no going back on her words now. 'Look, Sally, love, I'm going to leave you for

133

a mo. I've to pick sommat up from me mate's house. She just lives around the corner. She's got some medicine that might help me with me hands.'

'But me mam says you're never to leave me alone, Aunty Hattie. She'll not have it, thou knows. Why can't I come with you?'

'It's not a place for young 'uns. Me mate's man don't like anyone round.'

She willed Sally to accept her lie, but another protest came: 'No, no, don't leave me. I don't like it on me own.'

Oh God, now what? There was nothing else for it but to involve Doreen. Fear of what this would mean trembled through Hattie. She'd wanted Doreen to come across Sally on her own and to persuade her to go with her, not to have to hand her over. Now, Sally might never forgive her, but there was no choice. 'Look, lass, I need sommat for the pain I'm in. Oh, look, there's Doreen, another of me mates. I'll ask her to watch you for me. How would that be, eh?'

'I don't want her to watch me. I want to go with you!'

'My, what's this? A cross little girl? Are you cold, love?'

'Hello, Doreen. This is Sally, the little girl I told you of. I look after her when her ma needs a rest. She's a good 'un really, but she don't want me to leave her and I need to go and get some stuff for me hands. I'll not be a mo. Can you watch out for her?'

'Aye. I tell you what: how about me and you go over to Ma Parkin's, Sally? She'll have done her

134

trays of tuffies by now, and they'll be cooling on the wires in the window. We can buy a farthing's worth and be back here munching it afore Hattie gets back.'

'Can I, Aunty Hattie?'

Though it worried her to agree, she nodded her assent. 'Aye, go on with you. I'll see you in about ten minutes.'

Sally tucked her hand in Doreen's and looked trustingly up at her. 'We'll have to hurry some, Dorween, if we're to be back. Ta-ra, Aunty Hattie!'

'It's Dor-reen!' Doreen laughed out loud as she shook the little hand in hers, causing Sally's body to shake, and making her giggle. 'You're a cute little thing, aren't you?'

Sally smiled up at her.

Doreen smiled back – a smile that would make the devil love her. But when she looked back at Hattie, the smile had a mocking twist to it. 'Bobby's going to be reet pleased. You've done well, Hattie.'

Hattie thought she was going to retch. Instinct told her to snatch Sally and run, but there was so much at stake: so many pretty young 'uns who might be in danger in the future; and then there was always the hope of finding Janey.

She turned and walked away as fast as she could, not daring to look either way to see if anyone was following Sally and Doreen, but praying to God they were.

Hattie looked in disbelief at Sergeant Jackson. 'But you said Sally'd be away in no more than a few hours! Oh God! I can't believe she's not

135

home yet. Why? Why?' She heard her own voice screeching in her ears and felt a sick fear in her belly. She clutched the back of the nearest chair.

'Try to keep calm, my dear. Everything will be all right, I am sure. Let the sergeant explain.' Arthur leaned on his crutch and put his arm around her waist. A flicker of what looked like disgust passed over the sergeant's face, turning Hattie's desolation into anger. She glared at him. He shuffled from foot to foot, coughed and twiddled his helmet in his hands. A disgust of her own came over her – disgust at how he'd used her. His vileness sickened her. He should be protecting people and stopping the filth that happened, not contributing to it. And he dared to stand in judgement of her!

A sweaty anxiousness stood out on his forehead as he spoke. He'd sensed her thoughts, she could see that, and his discomfort gladdened her. His voice held a plea as he said, 'Bobby Blackstaff didn't show up, so we couldn't make a move. He was followed to London a couple of days ago and seen outside a gentlemen's club talking to Lord Marley – him as has a country residence not far from here.'

Hattie's sharp intake of breath provoked an immediate question from Arthur, his concern obvious in his voice. 'What is it, dear? Oh, my dear, you're shaking!'

'That's him! You remember? I told you of him. He and his friend...'

'Lord Marley! You didn't say it was him! You only told me–'

Sergeant Jackson interrupted. 'Does that

gentleman have some significance in all of this?'

'Yes, he does. I know of him. I know from me past experience that he likes young lassies. He used to take young 'uns into his service from the convent I were brought up in. Then he'd rape them. He were stopped at his games when Cook found out and told Lady Marley of his antics. Oh God! Do you think this could mean he's getting young 'uns through Bobby Blackstaff?' Her head reeled. Memories made her stomach turn over so forcibly that she felt she'd be sick.

'Sit down, my dear. This is all too much for you.'

'No! I must go to ... to Sally, to Susan. Oh God! I don't know which one to go to. Poor Susan. She'll be out of her mind. And Sally! Sally'll be scared and–'

'You can't go anywhere. It isn't safe. They'll know you didn't return to the house. They'll smell a rat. Our worry is that they don't go through with it and get rid of the young 'un.'

'No!'

'We've got to see that as possible, though unlikely, before Bobby Blackstaff returns. He'll be the one as says what goes. But it's a risk we had to take. Getting half the gang wasn't going to do no good. It's got to be all of them.'

'You bastard!'

'Hattie!'

'I'm sorry, Arthur, but he is. He stands there saying he'd sacrifice a young 'un to get them all, and yet I know, as he does, the real reason for that. I'll not stand for it. I'll not! Tell me where she is and I'll go there. I'll–'

137

'You'll be doing no such thing. They'd kill you as soon as they saw you.'

'My dear, the sergeant is right. You will be in too much danger, and you going there won't save Sally. It will only serve to have you both killed!'

'I can't bear it. What have I done? Oh God, what have I done? Please, please let me go to Susan. She'll be distraught and she's already poorly.'

'Look, Sergeant, what if you brought Susan here? I think Hattie is right. They need to be together. The poor woman must be going out of her mind.'

'Well, sir, if that's what you want, but it is very dangerous. She isn't implicated at this moment, but if police are seen to go to her house and she is seen leaving, well...'

'It won't be like that, Jackson, and you know it. What game are you at playing? Susan isn't meant to know anything, so the natural thing to do when her young 'un doesn't come home is to call you lot in. Police being round her place wouldn't look suspicious at all. If you're trying to get at me through all this, you're a bigger bastard than I thought you were.'

'Get at you, my dear? Why should he?'

'It isn't like that, sir. Hattie, I...'

'Then get Susan over here, and get Sally out of wherever she is. I don't care about me being safe. Just make it so as they are!'

'I'll get Susan, but Sally stays put. She's all right. She was spotted yesterday evening, playing with that Doreen in the yard of the house they took her to.'

'But that were hours ago. They could have told

her I were delayed – but a whole night! She'll be scared.'

'Well, according to my man, there's been no sound of a young 'un in distress.'

'Oh no! That means they've used sommat on her – sommat to quieten her. They've used it afore on lassies they've brought in. They sleep for hours. Oh, Sally! Sally, what have I done?'

'You've done the best thing you could've. If they've used something on her – well, that isn't a bad thing. As long as they know what they're up to, it'll be like you say and she'll sleep for hours, so she won't know anything is going on. This'll turn out, you'll see. If we give up now, we'll lose. It'll all have been for nothing. We have to get the whole gang, and get them good and proper. If, in doing so, we get that Lord Marley as well, then scandal or not, a good job will have been done.'

'But at what sacrifice? At what sacrifice?' Hattie could no longer stop her tears. Her body folded and she sank down onto the sofa nearest to her. Despair, fear and shame – yes, most of all shame – brought her low. Because wasn't the outcome of all this going to be her own freedom? Freedom from Bobby Blackstaff? Freedom from her life on the streets, and most of all freedom from the likes of Sergeant Jackson taking her down! Oh God! What had she done?

Arthur sat down beside her. Relaxed in a seated position, he had the strength of a man with no handicap. This strength, and his gentleness as he took hold of her, gave her comfort. Her head sank onto his chest and she begged of him, 'Help me. Oh, Arthur, help me!'

'Come on, my dear.' He rang the bell on the table next to him and Harry came into the room. 'Take Hattie upstairs, Harry. Run her a bath and get her bed ready. She's all in. Go on, dear, leave all this to me. Go on, trust me. I will sort it all out. Susan will be here before you know it. We'll look after her. Leave it all to me.'

14

The Nightmare Returns

The room was veiled in darkness when Hattie woke. Disorientated, she searched her thoughts, knowing that something bad lay in them. As the shocking truth came back to her, she curled up into a ball, but wallowing in her own pity would do no good. She mentally shook herself. She had to take some action: take matters into her own hands. Reaching out, she felt for the matches on the bedside table. Finding them, she lit the gas mantle, and in its flicker she could see the clock. Half-past nine! It didn't take her long to dress.

How was it that every stair creaked, when it never had done so before?

'Is Susan settled down, Harry?' Arthur's voice drifted up from the drawing room. *So Susan is here! She's safe! Thank God.*

'Yes, sir. She is tucked up and asleep. She took some persuading to take the medicine the doctor left for her, and she'd not eat anything. I let her peep in on Hattie, and that settled her mind. Hattie's still out for the count.'

Hattie turned and tiptoed back up the stairs. She hadn't thought things through! Arthur was bound to look in on her, so she had to make it look as if she was snuggled up and fast asleep.

When she next peeped over the banister, Harry was crossing the hall. She hoped the mound arranged in her bed would fool Arthur. This time she was ready to attempt to get out unnoticed.

Relief settled in her when, taking a tray towards the kitchen, Harry didn't stop to bolt the front door as he passed it. She felt a longing to confide in him, but would he help her? Or would he stop her and tell Arthur what she intended to do? If he did that then all would be lost. Arthur would never agree to her plan and so she just couldn't take the chance. Her heart beat like a drum, and beads of sweat trickled off her forehead. But fear or no fear, she had to move quickly; it wouldn't be long before Arthur came out of the drawing room to retire. He was likely to be drinking his nightcap at this very moment, so she had just seconds to get out of the door without being seen.

Once outside, she took a moment to catch her breath. Which way should she go? If Jackson's lot were prowling around, they'd stop her if they spotted her. She had to get to Daisy. Daisy might know where Sally had been taken, but where was Daisy likely to be?

Making her mind up to go to Ma Parkin's, where she might get information on the lassie's whereabouts, Hattie sped across the park, keeping her route to the darkest ginnels. But as she came out of one ginnel to sprint across an opening to the next one, a hand grabbed her arm. Terror overrode the physical pain of the firm grip, but a familiar voice settled some of her fear. 'Hello, Hattie. You've not been on your patch lately. I've missed you. What were you doing up the posh end, then? Had some good pickings, have yer?'

'Kenny! God, you gave me a fright.'

'Aye, and that's not all I want to give you. I can't believe me luck, coming across you like this. Come on, there's no one over at my place – the missus has took the young 'uns to a show and won't be back till late.'

'I can't, Kenny. I've to be somewhere.'

'Don't give me that. You know what I gave you last time you were hasty with me. Well, it'll be a darn sight worse if you think as you're not giving me owt at all. And I'll tell you sommat else for nowt: I'd drag you to that pimp of yours afterwards and put a complaint in. Here, what's happened to your hands?'

Kenny could cut up rough if he didn't get what he wanted, so she knew he meant what he was saying. A man of means, he owned a pawnshop, and his business was in lending money to the poor and letting them have goods on tick. The tallyman, they called him. He put fear into everyone – in particular those who couldn't pay their dues. She had to think of something to say to satisfy him, as she dared not take the time out to see to him. She decided on the truth. 'Me fingers were broke by Bobby Blackstaff's lot, and they burned me arms an' all. Look, Kenny, I'll tell the truth of it, then I'll ask you to be helping me in what I have to do. But if your need is too much for you, I can send Daisy along to you.'

'Hold on a mo. I don't want to be mixed up in anything as Bobby Blackstaff's got a hand in. I don't mind paying for what he sells, but I want nothing to do with owt else. I'd rather make do with me missus and put up with her opening up under sufferance. But I'll say this, Hattie: I'd not be letting you go, if it weren't for the fact that I can tell as there's sommat not right with all of this.'

'Thanks, Kenny. I owe you one. We'll do it for free next time you come looking, and it'll be good, I promise you.'

'Go on, get going, or you'll have me thinking on it so as I'd have you anyroad, and right now in the ginnel!'

Glad to hear amusement in his voice, Hattie turned and ran for all she was worth across the clearing and into the next ginnel. She hesitated at Ma Parkin's, peeping through the window just to make sure there were no police in there. It was empty. Lifting the latch with difficulty, she nipped in as quick as she could and faced a startled Ma Parkin. 'Eeh, Hattie, you gave me a fright! Where'd you come from? I didn't see you pass me window.'

'Sorry, Ma. Is there anyone in your back room?'

'Aye, Daisy's in there, but she isn't with a client. Though she might be waiting for one. She didn't say.'

Daisy! She couldn't believe her luck. 'I'll have a brew, Ma, and I'll take it through and have it with Daisy, ta.'

'Naw, I'll bring it in to you. It's quiet the night. Don't know where everyone is. Mind, there's been a few strangers milling around of late. Some reckon as they're police in plain clothes, so everyone's keeping a bit low.'

This news was unwelcome. If folk were talking about the strangers being police, then Bobby Blackstaff's lot would know of them as well. But Daisy's welcome put this worry out of her mind for a moment. 'Hattie! Where've you been? Oh, Hattie, are you all right? Your poor hands...'

'I'm reet, love. The pain isn't nowt as I can't bear. Arthur got his doctor to look at me and he's put some splints on me fingers and some soothing stuff on me arms. Mind, you're going to have to help me with me tea.'

'Oh, love.'

'Don't be at giving me sympathy. It'll get me started, and I've a lot more on me plate than what's happened to me hands. Have you seen owt of Doreen?'

'Aye, but not as much as usual, and not back at the house. I saw her go into the corner shop a while back. When she came out she had a big brown bag full to the top. I were curious, so I followed her, and she went into an end terrace house up Gollan Street. I waited a bit and she came out again and went into the one next door. What d'yer reckon she's up to?'

'Daisy, love, I know what she's up to, and I need your help. Are you on with waiting for a client?'

'Aye, but he hasn't showed. He were a new chap as has been hanging around a bit. Talk is as they're police, but...'

'They *are* police, Daisy. Look...' After she'd finished telling Daisy everything, Daisy's face

144

reflected all that Hattie felt. She sought to give her comfort. 'Aye, I know, love. Brings back pain we suffered, don't it? I'm on with having it stopped, only I don't trust Jackson. The thing is, though, I do have on me side the fact as he's scared of Arthur's standing, and what could happen to him if he is caught at being in league with Blackstaff, which we all know he is. So that gives me some clout. If I can get into the house, he'll have to shift himself and do sommat. He'll know he has no choice. I just hope I'm in time.'

'But, Hattie—'

'No "buts". I have to do this. Will you help me, Daisy?'

'What would I need to do?'

Hattie could see Daisy was scared out of her wits, but the question hadn't been asked as if she would make up her mind after hearing the answer. Daisy was with her, no matter what.

'That's them – the two on the corner. But how do we know which house young 'un's in?'

They were in the ginnel just across the road from the houses Daisy had seen Doreen going into earlier. Hattie weighed up the possibilities. 'I'm going to make a guess at it being the end one that Sally's kept in. It'd be the best bet, I'd say, as any noise wouldn't matter. There's no neighbours the other side to hear owt, and it looks like Blackstaff owns the house on this side an' all, if Doreen went into it.'

'I'm scared, Hattie.'

'Aye, I am an' all. But let's do it afore thinking about consequences puts us off, eh? Now, as soon

145

as the door opens, you run like blazes. Get to Arthur's as fast as you can. You're sure, now, that you know how to get there and which house it is?'

'Aye, I does. Oh, Hattie...'

'No more now, love. I'm sorry to put this on you, but we best get on with it.'

They hugged each other as best they could with Hattie's arms in the state they were. Daisy kissed her cheek. 'Be careful, love.'

Hattie crossed the road. No one challenged her. But then another thought occurred to her: was this the right house? What if these houses were just some that Blackstaff owned but didn't use for the purpose of sex with young 'uns? Well, she was here now. With a determined attitude, she kicked the door hard several times. The noise she created increased her fear, but there was no going back... Doreen opened the door. 'Who is it? And what d'yer want?'

Outrage overtook Hattie's dread, making her want to claw Doreen to pieces. 'Where's Sally, you bitch?'

'Hattie! Ha, it's Hattie. Bloody hell, you've got some clout, lass, I'll say that for you... Hey!'

Doreen reeled back. Hattie felt no pain in her hand from the blow she'd landed on Doreen's face. It was as if the rage burning in her had taken her out of her own body. 'Tell me where Sally is, you bastard!' She stepped into the house. She lingered for just a second to take in the sumptuousness of it, before she lifted her arm again. Doreen cowered. 'You idiot, Hattie! For God's sake, what're you thinking? Wally and Doug are next door!'

'I don't care. Just tell me where Sally is. Come on, Doreen, if there's a shred of decency left in you, you'd tell me. Where is she?'

'Don't come near me – I'll scream! Let me get out. Let me get out of it, please, Hattie. I promise you, I couldn't help owt as I've done...'

'Then do the decent thing now, and help me. I can't do much with these hands, but there's nothing wrong with me feet, and by God, Doreen, I'd think nothing of kicking the life out of you.'

'She's next door. That Lord Marley's with her.'

'WHAT!'

'No – Hattie, I told you. Wally and Doug are there. They're downstairs keeping guard...'

'Oh God! How could you?' Hattie pulled her arm free from Doreen's grasp and hit out with all her might, ignoring the pain searing through her arm. Doreen landed on the floor. Looking down at her, Hattie hesitated, wanting to grind her foot into the hateful face. 'You vile scum!' Her foot lifted, but the urgent need to get to Sally took over. Tearing out of the house, she reached the one next to it in seconds. The force of her kick at the door trembled through her. It opened and Wally stood there, a look of astonishment on his face. Recovering from his shock, he shoved her backwards. 'What's your game? What yer doing here?'

The railing separating the pavement from the road broke her fall. Rebounding off it and using the leverage it afforded her, she lifted her foot and kicked him in the crotch. Wally doubled over, his strangled cries telling of the pain she'd inflicted.

Inside the hall, the stairs loomed ahead of her. Her body seemed to fly, not run, up the steep

147

flight. At the top, three closed doors gave her a moment's dilemma. The agonizing sound of a distressed child calling for her mam came from one of them. It was as though the sound created a power in Hattie: she barged into the door, and it gave way as if it were no more than a curtain. Time suspended, then rolled back into the past as the scene playing out before her unleashed years of pent-up hatred for the man who stood there, stopped in the act of putting himself away. Her body grew as if it wasn't her own. She threw herself at him. He crashed backwards over the bedstead. As she stared down at the source of her wasted, rotten life, a rage boiled up inside her giving her a strength she never knew she possessed.

Hattie's vicious kick found its mark. 'You bastard! You bastard!' Each time the words spat from her she kicked out at him. Unable to right himself or shield his manhood from her, Lord Marley hollered for mercy. Tears ran down his bloated face. Spittle foamed at his mouth, but she didn't stop; not until Sally's screams crushed her fury and replaced it with heart-rending anguish. 'Sally, Sally... Oh, Sally love, I'm here. No one'll ever hurt you again. Sally, come on, my love.'

Sally's staring eyes held unspeakable horror. *Oh God, how can I help her? How can I put this right?* They rocked back and forth together, the child's hurt and sadness torturing Hattie.

Over the sounds of their weeping, the door clicked open. Doug's huge body filled the frame, but Hattie had no fear where he was concerned. He couldn't inflict anything on her that would give her more pain than she was already in. 'It's over,

Doug. Get out while you can. You know about Arthur, don't you? Well, he knows where I am. Sergeant Jackson can't save you, so I'd take me chance, if I were you, and scarper. You might get lucky.'

Doug opened his mouth, then shut it again. His moment of uncertainty lasted a moment too long: Bobby Blackstaff stood behind him with a look that Hattie recognized, his face curled into an ugly mask. His voice held the menace she dreaded. 'He's going nowhere. And the police will do nowt. I've the lot of them in my hands, as you well know, having been part of the payment, you fucking whore!'

He shoved Wally out of the way, stepped round the still-moaning Lord Marley, and was beside the bed in a flash. His eyes held cold evil. As he lifted both hands in the air, the knife he held glinted as the gas light flickered over it. Hattie pulled Sally closer, trying to shield her. The moment froze. No scream came from her, no begging for mercy.

Only a fear for Sally... As if in a nightmare, she saw his outline as a gigantic shadow on the wall, depicting his movements. The knife came down towards her. She cowered forwards. A thud resounded through her body, but no pain came with it. *Has the knife missed me?*

A vicious shout assailed her ears, bringing into focus a searing, ripping pain in her shoulder. She looked up. The bloodied knife soared above her once more. She couldn't move. She saw it coming towards her, but her mind couldn't decipher what happened, as Bobby fell forward and the knife flew through the air. He lay silent and still across

149

the bottom of the bed. Looking to her left, she saw that Lord Marley had hold of his legs. He had saved her. Lord Marley had saved her life!

A moment passed in which Lord Marley's bloodshot eyes held her gaze. In them she saw a flicker of recognition. He opened his mouth as if to speak, but the sound of clanging bells blotted everything out, and she watched the colour drain from him. He slumped to the floor, a defeated man. It was over...

The room filled with men. Handcuffs clicked. Sergeant Jackson came into view. His face drew near to hers, his voice holding concern. 'Are you all right, Hattie? Is the young 'un all right?'

Her mouth, which had dried with terror, became wet again. She gathered up the saliva and spat it forcefully into his hated face. He didn't react. His hand wiped away her spittle as he turned away.

15

Broken Lives and Uncertain Futures

'Megan, you've been quiet since you came back from seeing Hattie. Are you sure as there's nowt wrong?'

'I can't tell you of it, Ciss. It isn't sommat as you'd understand. There's stuff as goes on you've no idea of.'

'Tell me, then. I'm not a young 'un any more, thou knows.'

Not a young 'un? Oh, if only Cissy knew how young and innocent she was! Megan wished to God she could be like her and not know all that she did.

'Look, Megan, you've to talk to someone, love, because whatever is bothering you is making you ill. You're not eating nor sleeping proper.'

'Must you girls talk so much? That gown has to be finished for collection tomorrow and I need you, Miss Tattler, to work on some designs this afternoon. Here, Miss Grantham, a letter arrived for you, but I don't want you reading it until your break-time.'

'Yes, Madame Marie.'

Cissy sounded as though she was going to do as she was told and picked up her work again, but the minute Madame's office door closed she got up, grabbed her letter and went towards the back door, laughing. 'She can't stop me going for a pee, and she'll not lower herself to come out to the closet to see if I'm reading.'

Megan laughed back at her, but once she'd left the room her thoughts returned to Hattie, rekindling the worry she felt for her and the little girl she'd told her about. It had all been set to happen yesterday. She hoped, with everything that was in her, that it had gone well.

'Megan...' Cissy's whisper drew her from her thoughts. She looked up. Cissy was red in the face and all of a fluster. 'It's me mam. Eeh, Megan, you should see what she's wrote. I'll not be able to go home ever again!'

'What? Is she for taking you on again? You're easy pickings for her fun-making, Ciss, as you

151

always take her bait.'

'Not this time. She's got a lodger and she's trying to line him up for one of us. Oh, Megan!'

Megan wouldn't have put anything past Issy, but her amusement at this was tinged with a worry that it might just be true. But, no, it couldn't be. 'Come on, it's snap-time. Let's go and get a cuppa and I'll have a read. A lodger! Honest, Ciss, do you really think she'd do that without asking you? If I know owt, she's been at thinking of ways to make a bit of fun afore we go home. You know what a one she is.'

'Here.' Cissy handed her the letter. 'I'll make a brew and some toast for us whilst you read it. I tell you, Megan, she's gone too far this time.'

Megan smiled. She didn't think Issy knew what 'too far' meant. In Issy's book, if there was a laugh to be had, then that was all right and she could say and do as she liked, though there was never any malice in her and she wouldn't intentionally upset anyone. She opened the crumpled sheet of paper:

Dear Cissy,
You and Megan must come home as soon as you can. I've a young bloke lodging with me. He's come to take over your dad's old position as head groom at big house. His name's Jack Fellam.

I told you of young Mr Harvey copping it, God rest his soul. I knew him from being a babby. Me mam – your granna – brought him into the world. He loved your dad, and used to help him in the stables. His mother, a lovely lass as I used to work for, encouraged him to be normal, like, and let him do the things he

152

enjoyed. He took after her, and his dad as well, in many ways, though I knew stuff about his dad as would make your hair curl – more than it does already, and that's saying sommat, with how yours and Megan's does!

Anyroad, to get back to young Mr Harvey getting himself killed. Henry Fairweather's been saying that, since it happened, Mrs Harvey's talking of rebuilding the stud, but with Mr Harvey not yet cold as they say, and them not able to lay him to rest proper, no one thought as it would be just yet. But it seems them considerations are not for Madam Posh-Knickers. Anyroad, she's gone away for a while, sunning herself, but before she went she took on this new man. He and his family live in the gatehouse and he's running the estate. He's a nice bloke, been badly injured in the war. He lost half of his right leg, but he gets about right well with some crutches and manages to ride his horse around the estate. It was him as found Jack.

Jack's been to war an' all. Him and his dad and brother. But his dad and brother both got killed, so they brought Jack home, but then, with all the heartbreak, his mam didn't last long and though he had a position he could've gone back to, he needed a change. He's not down about it all – says he's seen too much for that. That seems a pity, don't it, Ciss? Young men who can't feel grief any more?

Don't worry, though, about me cottage, because I've been told as they'll not be giving Jack tenancy till he marries, so until then, as long as I agree to give him bed and board, I'm safe. Mind, I'm pretty sure as he'll be snatched up, and soon an' all. I tell you, our Ciss, if I was just a few years younger, I'd snatch him up meself! He's a right handsome bloke, and a cheeky bugger to boot. I've told him all about pair of you, and he can't wait to meet you. I've told him, though, if he takes a fancy to either of you, he's not to muck you about, but to make his choice and stick to it. Write back and let me know when you can come.

Love to you both, Mam.

Laughter bubbled up in Megan. Just reading the letter brought Issy's presence into the room; she wrote just as she spoke, and her fun-making got to you. 'Eeh, Cissy, it's right then. She *has* got a lodger. I wonder where he sleeps, because she doesn't say he's got our room.'

'Mam'll have put him on the shake-me-down in the parlour, I should think, but how're we to face him, with what she's said to him?'

'I know, and I bet she has said it an' all. She'd not think on how she might embarrass us. Let's hope, by the time we go home, he's forgotten it or he's so used to Issy by then that he takes it as a joke, eh?'

'I hope so. Oh, me mam! You're right when you say she's a one. Though it sounds interesting, don't it? I wonder what he's like and if he will be at taking to one of us.'

Megan couldn't stand it any longer. It was Sunday, her half-day, and she was going to find Hattie today, even if she had to walk the streets begging for information.

Cissy came over to her. 'Megan, please tell me what's to do – please! Whatever it is, I can take it. I know you say as there are things as goes on – things I know nothing of – but how can I know if you don't tell me? Besides, I reads, thou knows.

154

I've a lot of knowledge of how things are in London from Mr Dickens's books, and I'm for thinking as them sort of things go on in every big city, so Leeds probably isn't much different. This mate of yours – Hattie – the way you keep her secret, anyone would think she's a prostitute or sommat!'

Megan felt relief enter her with Cissy's words. Not at what she'd said, but the matter-of-fact way in which she'd said it. It meant she wouldn't be shocked if she knew. Nor would she be disgusted, by the sound of her, though she felt a shock of her own. She wasn't a reader herself, not unless it was the magazines on the latest fashions that Madame bought and let them have when she'd finished with them. Megan couldn't get enough of them. But Cissy always had her nose in a book. She hadn't thought, though, that they dealt with such subjects as prostitution. And they'd been written by a man, too! Still, she'd not comment on it; she was just glad to have a chance to talk about everything, now she knew she could. 'Aye, she is, but it wasn't what she wanted to be, nor wants to be. It was circumstances, but she has a chance to get out of it.' She sat down and, with relief at the unburdening, told Cissy everything. At times during her telling she hesitated, as Cissy paled and shock made her eyes widen and her jaw drop, but always she urged Megan on, insisting that she needed to know it all.

There was a silence when she'd finished, then a stunned whisper. 'Young 'uns? And ... and Hattie? Raped? And when she were just thirteen years old? Oh, Megan.'

Her arms opened, and as Megan went into

155

them she thought of how lucky she was to have Ciss and Issy and her job. Poor Hattie. Why had their lives turned out so differently? Cissy drew away from her and held her by the shoulders. 'What're you going to do? Are you thinking of trying to find Hattie?'

'Aye, I have to. I have to know she is all right. That she's safe.'

'I'll come.'

'No!'

'Please, Megan, I'd be going out of me mind here. We'll be safer together. You on your own – well, owt could happen.'

It hadn't been any use arguing with her. Ten minutes later, Cissy – her face pale, but her lips set with a determination Megan knew well – stood beside her in the hall, pulling on her gloves.

'Look, I've been thinking, Ciss, and I've decided I'll start me search at Hattie's fella's place. He might know sommat. After all, he knew what she were about to do. He'd backed her in it, and his solicitor had sorted things with the police.' She finished buttoning her coat and reached for her own gloves. 'And I've a mind to take a cab to his place, as I only know his address. I've been there, but I don't know as I could find it again. When Hattie took me, we went down ginnels and along back lanes for more than a mile.'

'A cab! By, that'd be sommat. Do you remember that Sunday we tried to take a ride in one, to the park?' Cissy went into one of her fits of giggles, but Megan didn't join in. She knew it wasn't a proper giggle. It was more of a nervous one, so she thought it better to ignore it and carry on the conversation.

'Aye, I does. The driver looked down his nose at us and geed his horse up and left us standing on the pavement! Well, that won't be happening today. We look like two young ladies in our outfits.'

'That's thanks to you, Megan. And to Madame, of course, for letting us have them offcuts at a cheap price. I love me coat as you cut for me, and its reet warm an' all.'

'And you look lovely in it. Come on, let's go.' Her stomach felt ticklish deep down with the nerves, and she felt that if they didn't get on their way soon, she'd not go through with it.

'Look, Ciss.' They were standing at the side of the road, where they were most likely to see a cab pass by. 'Hattie's man ... well, he's a gentleman, by all accounts. He's rich, anyroad. He lives in a big house and has a servant.'

'Eeh, Megan, you didn't say owt about that!'

'I know, but that isn't all. Well, I haven't seen him, but Hattie said he's been injured and isn't good to look on.'

'Poor fella. What's going to happen when they all come home – well, them as are coming home. How's it going to be? Who's going to look after them all? This fella at me mam's, he isn't hurt in his body, but from what me mam says, he must be hurt inside. Things as he must have seen...'

'I know, and they say lassies like us are going to be lucky to get a man, there are so few of them left. It doesn't bear thinking on. We've been fortunate, thou knows. War hasn't affected us much, and what bit it did were for the better.'

'Well, I'm glad it's over. Well, in the main it is. Will it bother you if you don't get a man, Megan?'

'Aye. I've me heart set on getting married and having young 'uns of me own. I'm not for thinking I'd like to be left on the shelf.'

'Well, there's always Bert Armitage. I'm sure he's took a shine to you.' Cissy pushed her gently on the shoulder and laughed as she said this. Megan shrugged. Cissy often teased her about Bert, and she did feel an attraction to him. He weren't bad-looking and he was of strong build, but his surly nature put her off. Still, he'd probably change, and he did seem to like her. He often stood on the corner when they came out of the station at Breckton, where Cissy's mam lived. But now wasn't the time for thinking about suitors and, even if it was, she wasn't sure she would really consider Bert Armitage. It was to do with her dream, really. She didn't know why, but she felt that Bert wouldn't want his wife following the path she intended to follow. He seemed a proud man, one who would want to be seen to provide for his family. She allowed herself a moment to wonder about him. Where had he come from, for instance? He'd not been in Breckton long; his arrival came just as the war was starting. Not that that was unusual. Miners were badly needed, and anyone with flat feet or some other condition that rendered them a hindrance were sent to work in the pit or in the factories.

'Are you on with dreaming about him?' Cissy giggled again and nudged her.

'Go on with you!' She feigned a laugh in response, and then changed the subject. 'Anyroad,

Ciss, you'll be all right, won't you? With Hattie's fella, I mean? You won't cringe or owt? Hattie says he's sensitive about it.'

'Why're you asking me that? I'll not like seeing him hurt, but I have more about me than to show it and embarrass him!'

Megan had to smile. Cissy was put out of sorts by her question, but was funny in her indignation, huffing and pulling a face.

Despite the reason for their journey, the girls got into the cab giggling, and held hands as their bodies jolted from side to side as it trundled along. More than once Cissy said, 'Eeh, Megan...'

Megan had no need to ask, 'What?' She knew what was causing Cissy an excitement that she couldn't speak of, because she could feel it herself, though her nerves revisited her when she stood at the huge front door and pulled the bell cord. Harry opened it as if he'd been standing behind it, waiting for her. 'Miss Megan! By, you're a good sight. You're just what Hattie needs. And who's this, then?'

'She's here? Oh, Harry, thank God!'

'Aye, she is, but she's not well. She's been through a lot. She'll tell you of it. Come in and warm yourself. Let me take your coat.'

After taking her coat, he looked towards Cissy. 'Miss...?'

'Cissy. I'm a friend of Megan's.'

'Well then, as such you're very welcome. But not if you stay on the doorstep and let the cold into the house.'

'Eeh, I'm sorry. I'm just in awe of all this. I haven't ever been to such a grand place, and now

159

I'm here. I didn't expect to have someone to take me coat and suchlike.' Cissy was giggling again, and Megan could see that Harry was captivated. Cissy was playing to his attention. Megan shook her head at her, but had to smile.

'Right, Megan, you and your friend come along in here and I'll fetch Hattie.'

Megan didn't even notice her surroundings this time, but Cissy did, gasping as they entered the room. 'Oh, it's beautiful. Look at those chairs! Oh, I daren't sit down, Megan.'

'I know. It's grand, isn't it?' Just as she said this, Hattie entered the room. A pain clutched at her heart as she took in the gaunt appearance of her beloved friend. 'Hattie, what happened? Your shoulder! You've been injured again. Oh, but thank God you're safe!'

'Aye, safe, but not sound. Oh, Megan.'

'What is it, Hattie? Is the little 'un all right? Is she safe?'

'She's safe, poor thing, but what she's been through...'

Megan helped Hattie to a chair. They listened as she told them what had happened, though it was plain to Megan that Hattie wasn't telling all. Even so, her anguish at what she did speak of filled the room. 'I shouldn't have done it, Megan. And Sue, Sally's mam, she's so ill. She's not going to live. She's upstairs. Her other one – Janey. They found ... they found her body.'

The silent tears falling down Hattie's face spoke of her distress. Megan sat on the arm of the chair and took her in her arms and held her, trying not to hurt her. She didn't know what to say. She had so many questions, but her throat had dried out on her, rendering her speechless, and her heart felt so heavy to see Hattie in this state. It was not what she ever thought she'd see. It was as if Hattie was broken, her spirit gone. 'Hattie, you can get through this, you can. Me and Ciss'll help you.'

'Hattie, I'm Cissy. I'm Megan's mate, and I'm for being yours if you'll have me and, like Megan says, we'll help you.'

As she heard this, Megan felt a love for Cissy that was more than she'd ever felt before. Ciss was able to see past the horror of the tale, and her only thought was for Hattie's welfare.

'I'm pleased to meet you, Cissy. I've known of you a good while, and I've not forgot how kind you were in lending me that half-crown when I most needed it. I've got it for you. It's been kept separate from everything, and I've added some to it for you.'

Cissy tutted. 'You daft thing! I've been at worrying over that, thou knows!'

They all giggled at this, and it felt good. Megan took her hanky and wiped Hattie's face. 'See, I told you she were a one. Mind, she's nothing to what her mam's like.'

Hattie's laughter hadn't reached her eyes. She leaned her head on Megan's shoulder. 'It's been a bad time, Megan. I've felt heavy with grief and guilt. After all, some of me motive in doing it all were to get meself out of the way me life were. And for that I put little Sally in danger, and dragged Susan down so far in her spirits that she can't rise up again. Oh, Megan, I'm so ashamed.'

'Hattie, you getting free wasn't your main motive. It wasn't! Aye, it were going to be one of the outcomes, but you were at trying to find the other little girl and stopping the terrible things as were happening to young 'uns off the poor streets. Oh, I know your life stood to get better if it went well, but don't forget: if it hadn't, you were certain to be killed.'

When Hattie looked up, Megan saw there was a light in her eyes that hadn't been there before, so she pressed on. 'Hattie, you thought losing your life were worth it, if you saved young 'uns from the terrible things that man and his gang were doing. That's a good thing to have done, not a bad thing. And Susan – well, poor Susan. You knew she wasn't well afore; you knew she wasn't going to make it, even if you found the other one alive. And little Sally... She'll forget, she will, Hattie.'

'I hope so. She's young. I mean, she's a lot younger than I were.' Hattie hung her head, and the tears were silent no more: huge sobs shook her body.

Megan waited, letting Hattie reach a calm place, a place where she could cope. Her own mind had filled with horror. *Poor, poor Sally! Oh God!*

'I were too late...'

Megan patted Hattie affectionately on the arm and looked over at Cissy. Her friend looked as though she were being held in a vice. Only her bottom lip trembled. Poor Ciss – she'd taken in information she'd had no idea of, and in such a short time. Megan had an urge to go to her, but she couldn't move. Hattie needed her more. There was a silence, then in a stronger voice Hattie said,

162

'Mind, Megan, it's like you say. If there's owt good to have come out of this, it's that other young 'uns are now safe. And I'm for thinking Bobby Blackstaff'll hang for Janey's murder, and that'll be the fate of Wally and Doug an' all. But as for the rest, I hope they rot in jail – Doreen and Lord Marley included. In fact, Doreen more than most, because for a woman to help to get young 'uns, knowing what were going to happen to them, is vile beyond owt I can think on.'

The door opened and a quiet, refined voice asked, 'Are you all right, Hattie, dear?'

Megan looked up. She swallowed hard. This was the moment she'd been dreading, and she hadn't wanted it to come at a time when she wasn't ready. Her heart went out to the man who stood in the doorway, leaning heavily on his crutches. Both of his eye sockets were pulled down, showing the blood-red of the insides. His nose was twisted to one side, and his skin was puckered with burn scars. On one side he had no ear, but when her eyes rested on his mouth and chin, these were untouched and perfectly formed, as were his teeth. These features told her he'd been a handsome man at one time.

The effect his presence had on Hattie was as if he'd taken away all her troubles. She straightened and dried her eyes. 'Aye, I'm all right, Arthur. In fact, I'm a lot better now, as Megan's helped me to look at things in a different way. This is Megan, me mate as I'm always telling you of, and this is Cissy. Cissy is Megan's mate from where she works. Me and her have just become acquainted, but we're liking each other already.'

163

Arthur smiled. 'I'm so glad, my dear, and I am pleased, too, to meet your friends. In particular you, Megan, as I have heard a lot about you. You and Hattie were brought up together, I understand?'

Was he judging her? Was he thinking that she'd done all right for herself? Her mouth still felt dry. She could do no more than smile at him, and hoped he wouldn't take her nerves for rudeness. Or, worse, think she was struck dumb at the sight of him.

'I think it is wonderful how you never gave up on Hattie. Many would have done, given the circumstances. I think you are a true friend, Megan. One doesn't come across friends of your kind very often.'

There was a sad note in his voice as he said this, and it was this that helped her find her own voice, more than what he'd said. 'I'm pleased to be meeting you, too, Arth– Sir.'

'Arthur. Call me Arthur.'

He'd moved further into the room and came over to her. She stood up and took his outstretched hand. That too was maimed – two of the fingers had gone and the skin was wrinkled, but all she could think of was that it was a funny world, her shaking hands with gentry as if she was an equal.

Arthur extended his hand to Cissy next. As she took it she said, 'I can't believe as I'm meeting someone who's done such a lot to make sure as we are safe from that Kaiser bloke and been through such a lot an' all. I mean–'

Hattie's sharp intake of breath had stopped

164

Cissy in her tracks. Megan bit her lip. She knew what Cissy had meant by what she'd said, but wondered if Hattie and Arthur did.

'Thank you, Cissy. It is nice to know that what I have been through is appreciated.'

Hattie breathed a sigh of relief, but the moment was still tense and Megan wished Cissy hadn't brought up the subject of Arthur's injuries. She knew he was sensitive about how he looked, but there was no stopping her now. 'It is, Arthur, very much so. And while I'm talking, I might as well say that there isn't no one that's been more of a friend to Hattie than you. Me mam'd say as you're top-drawer, but without the tight knickers pulling your nose high.'

Arthur looked surprised for a moment, then put his head back and laughed out loud. They all joined in and the moment relaxed.

'I'd like to meet this mother of yours, Cissy. She sounds a card! Well, Hattie, I will leave you and your friends to carry on your conversation. No, it's all right, dear. I will see you later. Everything upstairs is fine – Elsie is seeing to that. Anyway, Susan was asleep when I looked in, so she's not having to listen to Elsie preaching, which is a blessing.'

The sense of relief that was beginning to settle in Megan didn't stop her from feeling surprised at someone of Arthur's standing giving a small bow to her and Cissy, and at how he spoke. 'Bye for now, ladies. It was very nice meeting you. In fact, it was a pleasure.'

The smile he gave them was sincere, and what he'd said sounded genuine. Suddenly she was

165

able to see past his injuries, and the fact that he was a member of the gentry. She just saw a man – a handsome, young, kind man. And because of this, a peace settled in her. Hattie would be all right, Arthur and Harry would see to that.

After seeing Megan and Cissy off, Hattie climbed the stairs and opened the door to the bedroom where Susan lay. Elsie, Susan's sister, rose from the chair next to the bed and put her finger to her mouth in a gesture that told Hattie to be quiet. The action, like everything Elsie did, had a stern edge to it.

It had been a surprise when Susan had said she had a sister living over on the other side of Leeds – just as it was to learn that this sister and her man had a corner grocery shop. But she'd gladly asked Arthur to contact them, even though it had set a fear stirring inside her as to Sally's future. She'd been hoping that that future would be with herself, what with the love she held inside her for the child. When she'd seen how different Elsie was from Susan, her worry was compounded. Susan was gentle, fragile and loving, while this one walked like she had a plank stuck up her backside reaching up to her collarbone. Her hair was scraped back into a bun so tight that it pulled her face into a permanent expression of disapproval. But then that was exactly how she was: disapproving. Disapproving of everything she saw. That is, if she bothered to look, which she didn't at Arthur. How she could be a guest in his house, taking everything as if it was her right, and yet openly and rudely reject him, beggared belief!

166

Part of her bristled as Elsie showed her the door. It was as much as she could do to keep her hands by her side and not knock the woman off her feet. In fact, even thinking of doing this made her feel better.

Once outside the bedroom, Elsie said, 'It is clear to me, Hattie, that me sister isn't long for this world.' She sniffed and used her hanky to wipe her eyes. 'And I am not surprised after what she's been through!' Her eyes held none of the emotion displayed by her actions as she sniffed again, more loudly. Then, holding her head high, she appeared to look down her nose as she continued. 'I don't know how you are going to live with yourself after this, Hattie. I really don't.'

'Live with meself! I were willing to give me life to find Janey...'

'*And* Sally's! My God, I'm going to have sommat to say about all of this, if it's the last thing as I do.'

'Aye, and it might be the last thing you do, if you carry on. You know nothing – nothing! Do you hear me?'

'Don't you dare talk to me of knowing nothing! I know as me sister is lying in there dying, and me niece is hurting so badly on the inside that she's scared even to talk. And me other niece lays cold on a slab. God alone knows what she went through afore she died, poor little mite. And as for you! You live here as ... as *his* mistress!' Her whole body shook with her disgust, but she'd hardly drawn breath before her rant gained pace. 'My God! I know all I want to know, or ever thought I would know, about life as you lot live it.

167

And for decent folk like me, who make an honest living, knowing *that* much is a mile too far.'

Hattie hung her head. The momentary comfort Megan had provided her with left her, allowing the guilt she'd borne throughout it all a chance to weigh down her shoulders once more.

'Elsie, you may think you know everything. But all you know is what you want to know, which is just enough to salve the guilt you bear for how little you have cared for your sister and her children's welfare since her husband was killed. And all you see is what you want to see, and how you want to see it.'

Both Hattie and Elsie turned in surprise at this outburst from Arthur. To Hattie, it seemed that a different person stood before her: not a being who was apologetic for even existing, but a man – forceful and, well ... manly.

'I don't know what you mean.'

'I mean, Elsie, that Hattie is not responsible for what happened. She didn't have to listen to your sister when she approached her about Janey. She didn't have to try to find Janey, or put herself in extreme danger to help the police catch the per-petrators of these heinous crimes. And she isn't responsible for what happened to Sally.'

Hattie stood in awe of Arthur. He stood squarely in front of Elsie, his body hardly supported by his crutches, forcing Elsie to look at him. His voice, though quiet, was commanding, and his stature grew as he went on to talk about how Hattie had had nothing to do with the way things turned out. That she had been betrayed by the police, who were the ones who had sacrificed Sally for the ultimate prize of nabbing the gang they'd been after for so long.

But Elsie wasn't daunted. 'Well, say what you might, but she's one of them – and, well, things here are not what they should be!'

'That, may I remind you, is none of your business. And while it's necessary for you to remain under my roof, you will kindly refrain from giving your opinions on anything that is my business, and my business alone.'

'Don't worry, I'll not be under your roof a moment longer than I have to be, and nor will Sally, because when I leave after my poor sister departs this world, Sally will come with me and live as one of me own. She'll be brought up with decent folk who behave in a Christian manner, and she'll not be having to look on you every day. Injured through no fault of their own or not, folk like you should be locked away some place where they can't be seen and can't carry on like you do, because not only do you look like the devil, you behave like him!'

Hattie saw that these last words had cut deep into Arthur. His skin paled and his stature shrank, and he leaned heavily on his crutches, as he was used to doing. But her own agony was such that she couldn't help him or fight Elsie for him. She just stood next to him and watched as the triumphant Elsie turned and went back into the bedroom. As the door closed, a desolate sigh escaped her, bringing Arthur's immediate concern back to her.

'Don't worry, my dear, we'll be all right. We don't have to face such people very often. Do you know, Hattie? What she fails to realize is that I am locked away. Wherever I am, I am locked away.'

'Oh, Arthur.'

But then her mind and heart were agonized by a different thought: Sally. How was she to say good-bye to her? And to think she was to be brought up by that woman! She could do nothing about it; Elsie was kin, so she had a right and a duty to take Sally. If only she would be taking her as a right and not a duty, because all too often duty can become a burden.

16

Love Strikes

'He's there!' Cissy cried.

'Who?'

'Bert Armitage. I just caught sight of him. He's standing on the corner of The Row, and it pouring down, an' all. He must've asked me mam what train we were coming on.'

'Don't be daft! He's most likely just having a smoke. Old Stan, as he lives with, has a bad time with his breathing. Bert says as the poor man's lungs are near gone, so he has to smoke outside for fear of choking him. Anyroad, how come you sound so pleased? I thought you didn't want me to take up with him, because of his surly nature!'

'I know, but you said yourself he isn't unattract-ive, and you thought he'd get less surly if he had a good wife to look after him.'

'It is possible. It can't be much fun being a bloke on your own with no family. I always think it's worse for men, somehow.'

'You could be right. Anyroad, with situation how it is, if someone takes a shine, then we've to grab them with both hands and take our chances. And I reckon as Bert's definitely took a shine to you!'

'Aye, he does seem to have. Oh, I don't know. Anyroad, get your bag down and pass me mine. Train's pulling into station.'

Megan looked out of the window. She couldn't see much through the rain-spattered pane and the cloud of smoke that the slowing train belched out. She just made out the sign 'Breckton', and felt the usual flip of her belly as the excitement at being home gripped her.

As they turned into one of the streets known as the miners' rows – a maze of back-to-back, two-up, two-downs that housed the miners and their families – Bert stepped forward and came alongside her. 'Hello. You got here, then?'

'Why, were you expecting me?'

'No. Well, I've been after asking Issy when you were coming. I've sommat to ask you.'

The rain was running off his flat cap, and Bert's voice and expression were those of a man unhappy with his situation. Megan asking whether he'd been expecting her seemed to have put him out some, but she wasn't for letting him off the hook.

'I think as you should get on with asking then, because I'm getting soaked and so are you.'

'It don't matter none. I'll see thee later.'

And with that he threw his nub-end onto the

ground, turned, and walked away from her. Out of the corner of her eye she saw Bert cross the road and hurry into the pub that stood just before the turn into the lane where Cissy lived. 'Well! What d'yer make of that, Ciss?'

'It's you as beggars belief, Megan! You know what he's like, then you taunt him, then you find as he can't take it, which is what you knew in the first place! Anyroad, never mind him. He'll stew or he won't, but isn't this grand, Megan? Just sniff the air. I love the rain. It dampens smell of the pit and freshens everything. Come on.' She skipped ahead, not stopping to adjust her scarf as it fell from her head, allowing the rain to plaster her hair to her face in tight curls. Her laughter and joy rang out.

Megan shrugged and decided to put Bert out of her mind. She'd not join in with the skipping, though, at least not until she'd passed the pub. She couldn't help noticing as she did so that Bert was at the window watching her. She pulled up her collar and quickened her step. As she turned into the lane, Cissy called out, 'Come on, slow-coach. Does you remember song as were sung to us when we were young 'uns? Well, it were to me, but I bet as you've heard it.' With this Cissy put her arms in the air and twirled round and round, singing at the top of her voice:

'It's raining, it's pouring,
The old man is snoring,
He bumped his head...
On the bottom of the bed
And couldn't get up in the morning!'

Even though the rain and her encounter with Bert had dampened her spirits and excitement some, Megan couldn't help but feel lifted by Cissy's joy, and laughed at her antics. Cissy didn't see the tall, handsome young man turn into the lane from the ginnel, but Megan did, and as she looked at him it was if a bolt of lightning had struck her. She couldn't call out to Ciss to tell her that she had an audience, as she couldn't find enough spittle to wet her mouth to help her form the words. It was as if her heart had been ripped from the inside of her and given to him. She stared at him, taking in every detail, and as she did so, feelings she'd never known before assailed her.

His hair lay in flat, wet strands over his forehead, and rain droplets dripped from his nose, but he had the most perfect face she'd ever seen. Even though his body was huddled against the rain, she knew that it, too, would be perfect. His smile was broad, and his teeth white and even.

When his eyes shifted briefly from Cissy to glance in Megan's direction, she saw that they were a deep blue. They didn't linger on her, but then she thought, compared to Cissy, the attractive bits she was blessed with wouldn't catch a man's eye at first glance, even if she wasn't looking like a dog coming out of the beck! A pang of jealousy entered her and she wished with all her heart she'd one ounce of Cissy's beauty.

Cissy became aware that she was being watched and stopped dancing. She stared at the young man, and then embarrassment took her. She bent double in a fit of giggles, before taking hold of

Megan's hand and running with her the last few yards to the cottage. The run didn't break the spell for Megan, or stop the feelings burning inside of her.

'That must've been *him!* Oh, Megan, he's so handsome.' They were shaking their wet over-clothes in the back porch. Cissy hadn't noticed any change in her and chatted on. 'D'yer think as he'll like me? Oh, what'll he think of me dancing around like that?' The sound of the latch clicking told them he'd come in. Cissy looked at Megan, her eyes wide and more beautiful than she'd ever seen them. Her damp curls framed her lovely face like a halo. 'He'll think I'm an idiot, Megan. I'm reet embarrassed. You go in first and get him talking. Give me time to get meself together...'

Megan did as she was bid, still unable to speak. As she entered the scullery the warmth that hit her only added to her already reddened, glowing cheeks, as she looked into those wonderful blue eyes again. He stood just inside the doorway, drying himself on a piece of towelling. Now that he wasn't huddled against the rain, she could see his size and the strength of his body. She noted the flicker of disappointment that crossed his face.

Cissy's mam had her back to them, stirring something on the stove. 'Right, lad, these are girls as I told you about. This is–' She turned around. 'Where's our Cissy? What's she playing at?'

Cissy came sheepishly through the door. Jack looked at her and smiled. Cissy coloured and lowered her lids as he said, 'You've a lovely voice, lass.'

'Lovely voice! Where've you heard her sing,

174

Jack? Don't tell me – she's daft as a brush, that one. I bet she were singing whilst rain soaked her?' Issy looked over at Cissy. 'You've got nothing up top, lass. I wondered how it were as you were twice as wet as Megan. You'll catch your death.' She nodded in Jack's direction. 'This is Jack, as I told you about in me letter.' Her head then bobbed in their direction. 'And this here is Cissy, me daughter, and her friend, Megan, as I expect you've gathered by now, lad.'

Jack looked over at Megan and she held his eyes for a moment, wondering at the sound of her name on his lips. 'Hello, Megan. I'm pleased to meet you.'

She could only nod her head at him. She noticed that his eyes lingered for a little longer on Cissy, and she heard Cissy say something to him about folk who stare, and Jack's head went back in laughter. The sound made her heart dance further.

It was a relief when Issy said, 'Well, that's a good start. I think as you'll all get on fine. Now, get yourselves sat down before me stew is spoiled. By, it's good to have you home, me lassies. Tell us all your news.'

The relief Megan felt at the activity of sitting down and the serving of the meal, and the general banter going on between Cissy, Issy and Jack, was short-lived. It was replaced by a feeling of something akin to heartbreak, because in the time it took to eat their meal it became painfully obvious to her that, even though they had only just met, Cissy and Jack were meant for each other.

'You've been quiet all day, Megan. Are you all right?'

They were getting ready for bed when Cissy asked her this, after going on and on about how wonderful Jack was, and did she think he was taken with her?

'Aye, I'm just tired and worried about Hattie,' she lied. It sounded like a good excuse, and Cissy accepted it.

It was in the dark and the silence of the night that the tears flowed. She didn't stop them; she needed to empty her pain. She asked herself over and over how she was going to bear it if Cissy and Jack took up together – or married! She knew without doubt that moving away wouldn't be something she could think of doing. How could she live without ever looking on Jack? Without being near to him? And what of Cissy and Issy? She couldn't imagine her life without them in it. Her last thought before falling asleep was: *There's always Bert...*

PART THREE
Choices Lost
1920

17

A Proposal of Sorts

The wind brushed Megan's hair away from her face. It would look like a mop when they pulled into the station, but she didn't care. After all these years, her stomach still knotted with joy as the Breckton sign came into view. She leant a little further out of the window, trying to see over Cissy's head. She caught sight of Bert. He was on the platform as usual, leaning against the wall at the bottom of the steps. Cissy turned and winked at her as she spotted him, and then turned back and strained her neck even further to see if Jack was coming.

As the train came to a halt, Bert stepped forward, and at that moment Jack came through the gate. Megan looked from Bert to Jack. An 'If only' came into her head, but she'd have none of it and banished it away. She'd found a place deep within her where she kept her feelings for Jack buried, and only in the dead of night did she allow herself to visit them.

'Oh, Megan, it's good to be home! Mind, I'll tell you sommat: by the looks of Bert, you've to make up your mind. You can't keep him hanging on forever.'

She didn't answer. She just smiled and hoped that the smile had reached her eyes.

'I mean it, Megan. I think as you've kept him waiting long enough. Mam says as Lillian Cole's been at sniffing around of late. And Pauline Sedgefield. Thou knows – her from the back row as–'

'You've not been at saying owt of this afore!'

'No, I know. Me mam told me not to. She's not for you taking on Bert. She has a feeling in her about him, only she didn't want to be seen as if she were trying to make trouble between you. She says as you'll do as your heart tells you, and that'll be that. Anyroad, it's bound to happen that lassies who have no man will go after Bert, him being the only unattached male in the town.'

'Aye, I s'pose so, and I'll think on. Now, let's get off the train, eh?'

Jack overtook Bert and ran towards them. Taking Cissy's bag from her and putting it on the ground, he lifted her up and twirled her round. 'Eeh, me lass, I've missed you!' He hugged her to him. Their happiness nudged at the dull pain Megan felt in her heart. 'Hello, Megan lass.' Jack had put Cissy down, but still held her close to him.

Megan drew on her inner strength and answered him as if she hadn't been affected by his and Cissy's love for each other. 'Hello, Jack, you look well. The sun's been at scorching you as brown as a berry.'

'Aye, it's been grand. You lassies need to get out in it whilst you're home.' He bent down and picked up Cissy's bag and then, looking at her, he motioned with his eyes in Bert's direction. 'We'll take your bag, Megan, and we'll see you later, eh? Oh, by the way, Issy said to tell you as it's cold ham and tatties for supper, and it'll be on around six-ish.'

Megan watched them greet Bert as they passed by him, but he only nodded. He'd stepped back to his original stance and was leaning against the wall as if he'd no care as to her being there. His dark expression didn't change when she walked over to him.

'Hello, Bert. Are you all right?'

'Aye, but not as good as the big fellow by all accounts, but then it isn't often as the sun gets down in the bowels of the earth.'

'Don't be daft! You look fine.'

'It's daft that I am, is it? Well, I must be, hanging around for the likes of you!'

He turned and walked away from her. For a moment she thought she would let him go, but fear gripped her. Did she really want to lose him? Oh, she didn't know what she wanted.

'Are you coming, then?'

'Where to?' She stood her ground. 'And why should I go anywhere with you in that mood? Some welcome!'

Even though he was a few yards in front of her, she could sense his anger. Bert had a funny way about him. It was as if she was to do his bidding at all times, or she'd know about it. But then he had another side that was sort of ... well, vulnerable – like he didn't think anyone could like him. It was this side she was attracted to. Not that it was the only thing about him that drew her to him. No, there was something else, something she couldn't fathom. She knew it wasn't love. Well, not love like she felt for Jack.

After a moment, when it seemed they'd stare each other out, he shrugged his shoulders and grinned. 'I thought, seeing as it's a nice afternoon, we'd take a walk across to the beck, and if you're up to it we could take in Mire Hill.'

Her relief came from her in a sigh, which she covered up with a smile. 'Aye, I'd like that. I need to go home and change me skirt and shoes, but I'll not be long. I'll bring some of Issy's ginger beer and meet you at the ginnel in about fifteen minutes, eh?'

His grin widened, and he motioned to her to catch him up. She did as he bid, but left him at the corner and hurried down the lane to Issy's.

It felt good to be held in Issy's arms. To feel the comfort and safety of her love. To smell the familiar fresh, clean-linen and home-baking smell of her. It was so good that the tightness Megan could feel coiled up inside her nearly broke.

'Eeh, lass, it's grand to see you.' Issy held Megan away from her. A knowing look came over her face. 'Bert?'

'Aye, some. I feel I'm not being fair to him hanging him on, but I want...'

'I know. You want what is the right of us all, and what so many are missing out on. It's up to you, lass. Think on your choices, and when you decide which is the best for you, then that's the path to take. Only don't leave yourself regretting. Put your heart into what you choose and make the best of it.'

She hugged Issy to her again. She knew this wasn't the advice Issy wanted to give her. She knew she'd sooner have told her not to take Bert on.

Bert still had a grin on his face when she met up with him a little later on. It settled her some, but she'd no knowledge of what she'd say to him if he did ask her to marry him, which is what she suspected he had in mind, with this walk he wanted to take her on.

They were standing at the side of the stream known as the beck, watching the cool water bubbling over the stones, when he reached out for her hand. She felt herself stiffen, but fought the feeling and let him take her hand in his. This hadn't happened before. He'd never touched her. His hand felt hard and rough, and a tremble went through her. She looked up at him. His face was different; there was a longing there. A hunger. The feeling she'd had when she'd seen his vulnerable side earlier gripped her again.

'I want to ask ... well – thou knows...'

She couldn't help him. Her mouth dried and words wouldn't come to her. They stood awkwardly for a moment. Megan knew such moments shouldn't be like this. Was it because it wasn't right?

'Look, let's climb hill, eh?'

She just nodded.

It was a hot climb, and she felt grateful that it didn't give leave for talking. Her thoughts battled on. Should she...?

'Here it is! This is the place I wanted to bring you to. It's grand, isn't it? Me half-sister were brought up round here and she were always on about it. Telling me tales on how it were good to come up these hills with her dad and our mam. She said as Mam lost a babby at birth, and as it hadn't been baptized, priest wouldn't bury it in the consecrated ground, so they brought it up here and buried it. She said as they held their own little service for it. I've often looked, but never found owt as could be a grave.'

'You've not said anything of your family afore, Bert. Where does your sister and mam live?'

'We lived down in Sheffield. Mam'd come from there – well, not originally. She were Irish by birth. Anyways, she moved back after she were widowed and then she married me dad. She'd known him afore she'd left. Me mam and me dad are dead now. Me sister lives somewhere in the Midlands, but I don't bloody care about her. She's nowt to me. She may as well be dead, for all I care. She left me with me dad not many weeks after me mam'd died, after her promising me mam as she'd take care of me and find a way of getting us out of it. I were just on six; she were ten years older than me. Anyroad, I got up one morning and she were gone. Never even said goodbye.'

He was quiet for a long time, but feeling that he needed to be with his own thoughts, Megan didn't break into them with questions. After a while she poured him a mug of ginger beer and handed it to him.

He took a swig and then started his tale again. 'I'd not heard of her for years, thou knows. Then suddenly I had a letter, a bit afore I came here. Said as she'd married some doctor and wanted to get together with me. She said as she'd known as

184

me dad were dead and that's why she felt she could now get in touch. She had things to explain. Ha! That were a laugh! How do you explain leaving a young 'un in that hellhole and saving your own skin! She were everything to... Anyroad, I wrote back and told her as she were no sister of mine and I'd sooner she kept out me life, and that me dad'd long since made me understand as she'd had what were coming to her when he beat her.'

Megan wondered about the bits of his story referring to 'getting us out of it' and about his sister being beaten, but thought better of asking. He'd said a lot more than he'd ever said to her before and she didn't want to upset him by probing further. He'd most likely tell her in his own good time.

It was funny him choosing Breckton to come to, and him looking for the babby's grave. It was as if* he was trying to be near his mam again. A feeling of kinship grew in her – they were not unlike, in what they'd been through. 'I'm sorry to hear of all that, Bert. You having no family as such is sommat as I can relate to. I've no family meself.' She'd not mention her granny and granddad, not yet. 'Me mam died giving birth to me, and that was in a convent for them as had no man.'

'Well, we're in same boat then, so that's a good start. But what I've told you is just for you. I don't want anyone else knowing. No one! D'yer hear? Especially not the likes of Issy Grantham. Because I know as me sister had sommat to do with her, when she was a young 'un. I don't want any interference from that quarter. Me business is me own.'

This shocked her. To think that Issy knew of his

mam and sister, yet knew nothing of them being related to Bert. She'd not to speak about them, either, but it wasn't going to sit easy, keeping stuff from Issy. She was bound to ask. She'd always been curious about Bert.

'You've gone quiet, Megan.'

'I were thinking on me and you not having family as such. Have you pictures of your family?' She hesitated. She thought of her locket, but no, she'd not tell of it. She'd kept her granny and granddad to herself for so long that sharing them would be like spoiling something special.

'No, I did have. I had them in a tin, but when I come here I vowed I'd put it all behind me, so I chucked them out. I didn't have a good child-hood and it's shaped me. Hardened me. I've no time for owt that has gone. You should do same, Megan. Don't think on what's in the past. Think on what future can be like.' He'd moved closer to her. 'I reckon as you must know what it is I want to say to you, Megan. Are you ready for it?'

'I want to talk some...'

'Talk? What's there to talk of? We've an idea of each other now. Either you're for being me wife or you're not.'

So, that was it then? No going down on one knee. Oh, well, what had she expected of Bert Armitage? He wasn't exactly known for being romantic, was he? Hadn't it been on two and a bit years that he'd been showing his leaning towards her, and today was the first time he'd even held her hand?

A laugh bubbled up inside her, but she swallowed it back. It wasn't right to laugh. Besides, it

186

wasn't a good laugh. More a feeling of – of anger. Yes, that was it. She was angry. Angry at her mam and Bert's sister and Cissy and Jack; and, yes, she was angry with Bert. Bert more than any of them.

'Well?'

She turned and walked away from him. It was all she could think of doing. She'd climb higher. There was still a way to go to the top.

'Where're you off to? Megan. Megan!'

He caught up with her and grabbed her arm and held it in a painful grip. 'What're you up to? You bloody knew how I felt! You bloody had me on, you bitch!'

'Let go, you're hurting me! I just want to think.'

'Think?'

They'd reached a small thicket, and Bert pulled her in front of him and pushed her back against a tree. His hand was above her, leaning on the tree trunk. He was so near that she could feel his breath on her and smell his body. It smelled of coal dust and his brand of smokes, but mostly of freshly washed clothes tinged with sweat. This last was like Jack smelled when he came in from the stables. Her imagination always stirred up images of Jack. Something fluttered in her belly, and a tickly feeling between her legs sent a gripping spasm through her. The feeling surprised her. She dared not look up at Bert, in case he knew.

'Megan.' He lifted her chin. He was gentle, loving. The feeling inside her increased; she couldn't breathe. His lips touched hers. She didn't stop him. She wanted the kiss – wanted more. Wanted... 'No! Not that! Not afore...'

The touch of his hand on her breast brought

187

her back to reality. The shock it sent through her wasn't unwelcome, but woke her to what might happen.

'I'm sorry, Megan. I didn't mean – you said "afore"! Afore what? Are you thinking on marrying me, Megan?'

'I don't know, Bert. Don't get mad at me again. I just want to think on some. I know it isn't being fair on you, but I've things I've to give up, and I'm not sure as I'm of the mind to give them up. Not altogether.'

'What things are you talking of?'

'Well, I've talked of them before. Thou knows. Me dream to have a place of me own, so as I can design clothes for folk and make them up. A place like where I work, only smaller. I'm good at it, Bert, and I could make a good living for–'

'It isn't a woman's job to make a living! Not a married woman's job. Besides, it'd make me a laughing stock. If you marry me, you can forget all that. I'll be the only breadwinner. Look, Megan, I want a woman as'll be a proper wife to me.'

'I know, and it's that as worries me. Would I be the one as could make you happy? Because I don't know if I could be happy, giving up what I love doing. I've had me dream for so long and I've been at saving this good while.'

'Aye, well, that'll not go to waste. With what I've got an' all, we could do the cottage up some. You'll not like it how it is. It needs a good coat of distemper all through. And we'll need some bits of furniture and stuff. Mind, it'll take you a while to get it cleaned up – it's in a bit of a mess.'

'Bert Armitage, you can go and fish! I'll not

wed you so as I can be your skivvy. If I do say as I'll wed you, then you can clean up the cottage before I step foot in it.'

'Oh! So it's a possibility, then?'

'I told you. I'm thinking on.'

'You liked it when I kissed you, though, so that says sommat.'

'Aye, I've feeling towards you.'

'Do you love me, Megan?'

The question shocked her. He'd never spoken of loving. She had only one way of dealing with it. 'Do you love me, Bert?'

He was quiet for a moment, then looked into her eyes and said, 'Aye, I do, Megan. I have done for a while.'

'I – I'm thinking me feeling for you is love. I think of you a lot and I – yes, I think I do love you, Bert.' And she knew she did. Not the searing, painful kind of love she had for Jack, but what she felt was a love of sorts. She wasn't cheating him by saying it, and she'd liked the feeling when he'd kissed her. Maybe they'd go along all right together. If only she could keep her feeling for Jack where it was – deep inside of her – and if she could live without her dream.

'Well, I'm glad to hear it. But, thou knows, I've no give in me, on how I want it to be. If I take you on, you're to be a proper wife and no less.'

'I told you, that's what I've to think on. And I need time. I'll give you me answer when I come home next, I promise.'

'Aye, well, I might have taken up with someone else by then.'

'You can if you like. It won't hurt me none!'

189

His move was quick. He took hold of her arm and pulled her to him, his fingers bruising her flesh. His eyes were dark, deeply dark, and his body shook. A fear trembled through her, then he loosened his grip and smiled down at her.

Confusion clouded her; she couldn't figure out what had happened as his mouth came crushing down on hers. He sucked her lips into his mouth and held her so close she could feel every part of him, even – oh God! Sensations she couldn't control rushed through her body. She knew if he tried to go further again, she'd not want to stop him. Was this love? Was this enough? Could she give up her dream for it?

18

Unwelcome Feelings

Jack finished brushing the hindquarters of the grey mare he'd been grooming. 'There you go, Karinda-lass. You're more than ready for your sire.'

'She is looking rather well, Fellam. I think Charing-lad will be a good match for her. You know he sired Finny-boy, the best runner on the flats there has ever been, don't you? I'm hoping he and Karinda can produce something just as special.'

Jack hadn't noticed Mrs Harvey coming into the stable. He felt unnerved, and wondered how long she'd been watching him. He nodded and touched his cap. She came closer and took the horse's rein from him. Stroking its mane, she spoke softly to the horse, 'Good girl. You know I'm relying on you, don't you?'

Karinda shook her mane and whinnied. 'Ha! She understands everything I say to her.' Handing him back the rein, she surprised him by abruptly changing the subject. 'How are your wedding plans going, Fellam? Has Henry cleared out the barn for you yet?'

'He was working on it this morning, Ma'am. I think he'll have it ready in time. He tells me it's a job he's done on many occasions, and as Cook dresses it up reet nice.'

'She does. I've always been amazed at how it looks when she and the others have decorated it. They have different garlands and drapes and cushions for each occasion, all hand-made. They work magic on what is, after all, just a barn with bales of hay around it. And besides that, they bake for days, making delicious pies and cakes. I hope you have a really good time and everything goes well for you.'

'Thank you, Ma'am. I'm sure as it will. And I'm grateful for all as you've done for me and Ciss.'

'Not at all! It's a tradition. Mr Harvey's father started it. All the wedding receptions of the farm and household workers are held in the barn, and the spring and autumn barn dances and summer fete. Though we haven't had any of those since... Anyway, your wedding will get us going once more. It's about time there was music and celebrations on the estate again.'

To hide the embarrassment of the nearness of

her, Jack fiddled with the horse's rein. Laura Harvey had made him feel uncomfortable a few times of late, standing too close and even touching his arm on occasions.

Her jacket brushed him. There was nowhere he could move to.

'And did you know, Fellam, there is also a tradition around these parts that the mistress of the house has the first dance with the bridegroom?'

She was laughing at him. She knew he felt uncomfortable. The opening of the stable door saved the moment, as her attention was drawn elsewhere. 'Ah, Ardbuckle. Keep Charing-lad out there. It is too confined in here. If he has a problem mounting her, he could end up hurting both himself and Karinda. Take Karinda outside, Fellam.'

With this she'd moved away, and he could breathe again. He caught Gary's eye, and saw the usual teasing grin and knowing raise of the eyebrow. Gary hadn't missed Laura Harvey's obvious fancy for him, and used the fact to have a laugh at his expense. He thought about what had been said and hoped to God he was right in thinking she was only teasing about the dance. He knew it was tradition for the gentry of the manor to come to the wedding do, but only for half an hour or so and not to join in – she wouldn't change that, would she?

Concentrating on helping Charing-lad mount Karinda eased Jack's mind as he gave his attention to what could be a tricky task. As a rule, the job didn't take long once the stallion was inside the mare, but the eagerness and anticipation of

192

the horse to achieve this could overexcite him and waste the sperm. Guiding and helping him was a business that allowed no time for chatter or to think of anything else until the job was done. The first experience he'd had in this stables had been a source of embarrassment to him. He'd found it unusual to have a female boss as it was, but to have her around and helping with this particular task had unnerved him. It had been her matter-of-fact way of tackling it that had helped him to get used to it.

'Well, let's hope she takes. Ardbuckle, get Charing-lad into the box and take him back to Smythe's. We don't want him trying again. Smythe's may have another filly lined up for him later today. Well done, both of you.'

As she walked away, Gary winked at Jack and said in a low voice, 'She were forgetting who were to mount who, I reckon, Jack. I'd say you're in with a chance there.'

'Don't talk like that, Gary! I'll have none of it. Get about your business!'

It wasn't how he usually took Gary's teasing, and the lad looked taken aback, but the anger inside of him – not at the lad, as he had meant nothing more than to have a bit of banter, but at Laura Harvey – had sharpened his tongue. She'd no right putting him in such a position. She was his boss and was taking advantage of the fact. It wasn't unknown, he knew that. Such things went on, but even though she was a beauty, he wanted none of it. Besides, she knew he was to be wed soon.

He thought about Cissy. He had a need in him, and he knew this was letting Laura Harvey get under his skin. And with the wedding only days away, his anticipation made his need more intense. He couldn't wait to make Cissy his wife. He'd cope better with how Laura Harvey acted around him then, and when she saw she wasn't having an effect on him, she'd be more likely to back off. Well, he hoped so...

'Eeh, Megan. I can't believe it! Ten days. Only ten days!'

'Aye, I know, and if you say it once more, I'll not finish your gown for you.'

'What's wrong, Megan? Every time I mention me wedding you sound like you don't want to hear of it.'

'I'm sorry, love. I'm just worrying. Everything is going to be different.'

'Aye, that part does spoil me happiness some, but...'

'No, I'm being selfish. Of course things change. They have to. I'll be reet. I'll see you every few weeks and I'll get used to it. I will.'

'You haven't thought on saying yes to Bert, then?'

'No, I haven't me mind straight on Bert as yet. I've a feeling in me for him, but anyroad, as I said, I'll be reet. I'll stay on here a while and keep on with me saving and see how things go.'

'Bert's not for waiting for you, thou knows. I told you afore about that Lillian Cole. Well, it seems me mam's seen them together a couple of times and they weren't just talking, neither! Mind, Lilly would have done all the running.'

'Well, if he finds someone else, he does. I won't

cry over it.'

'Look, I'm sorry, but I don't want you missing out. That's the only reason I tell you. That Lilly's a pest where men are concerned. She's had a go at getting Gary Ardbuckle from Jenny afore now. Mam says Jenny moved that quick when she realized, and now she and Gary are to get engaged. She says as Gert's over the moon, now it's all settled. And Gert's for living with them an' all. Not like me mam. I wish me mam'd think on. I don't want her living so far away.'

'It's only York. It's no different to you being here and her in Breckton!' The sharpness of her tone made Megan feel ashamed, so she changed it to jokiness. 'It's a good position she has with them priests, thou knows, Ciss. It'll suit her, looking after three men. By, she'll knock them into shape, if I know Issy.'

'Aye, you're reet there. But why doesn't she want to stop with me and Jack?'

'She's told you. She thinks as you'll have a better start without her, and I think she's right. If she stays on, she's afraid as any advice she gives could come to be looked on as her interfering. And that could lead to a bad feeling. Anyroad, she's looking forward to the change, and she'll have every third weekend off and come and stay with you. And I reckon as that'll be plenty!'

'Oh, Megan! What a thing to say, even if you are right.'

'Aye, I know. She'd skin me if she heard!'

They giggled at this and Megan felt better. She'd covered up her surliness and hadn't given away the reason for it. She gave her attention

195

back to her work, but her thoughts didn't rest and she didn't feel better in them.

Her mind went to the wedding gown. Madame had allowed her to work on the making of it in the evenings after they had finished here. She'd also let her use the workrooms and the machines. She'd only to finish the bow at the back, and then every painful stitch would be done. Though she'd still to get on with her own frock! She couldn't bear to think about it, nor how it would be to be in the position of bridesmaid and have to watch Jack promise to love and honour Cissy for the rest of his life! Oh, Jack. Would she ever get rid of this feeling she had for him? This longing, this...

'Oh, damn!'

'Megan Tattler! Was that you swearing? Oh, what...? You're crying! Megan, what is it?'

'No, no, I'm not. I – it were the giggling, Ciss, honest. It made me eyes water, then because I couldn't see proper, I stuck meself with me needle.'

'Was it me going on about Bert?'

'Well, aye, it were a bit of that,' she lied. 'I were shocked to hear as he'd taken up with someone. He said as he'd give me some time to think about it. Oh, I don't know. I'm in a reet tizzy inside. I just don't know what to do. Everything is settled for you, Ciss, and I'm glad, I am, but I just don't know how things will work out for me. If I go for Bert – that's if he still wants me – he's made it clear as I'm to go on his terms. He's a proud man. He talks of me stopping at home and having young 'uns and him providing for us.'

'That's been worrying me an' all, Megan. Thou

knows – well, having young 'uns – I don't know exactly what happens...'

A dread settled in Megan. She knew, of course, what Cissy was referring to, but the last thing she wanted to talk about was her and Jack coming together. Not in that way, she didn't. 'Is that what's behind you not wanting your mam to go?'

'Aye, some.'

'Hasn't Jack tried owt on?' *Oh God! I don't want to know!*

'Aye, he's – thou knows – touched me, but...'

'It'll be reet, love, don't worry. Jack'll take care of you. I knows of what happens, but it isn't easy to tell of and it sounds bad. Mind, Hattie tells me it isn't. She says if the man loves you, and you love him, then it's – well, she says it's wonderful. Though it might hurt a bit first time.'

'But what is it? Tell me, Megan.'

'I can't, love. I haven't words as'd sound right, but just to say as Jack – well, Jack will put sommat in you. His...'

'Oh! Is that why it – it sort of grows? Only I've felt it against me when we kiss and that.'

The agony in Megan increased, and her heart thumped in her throat. What did it feel like to be held by Jack? To feel him wanting more than kisses; to feel him kissing... No! She must stop this. She must change the subject before the tears came again. 'Aye, that's it, love. Now, talk of sommat else, eh? You're embarrassing me. I don't want to know what you get up to. And don't be telling me after, either. It's for you and Jack to know, and that's that!'

Cissy looked red in the face and put her head

down, seeming to concentrate on her work. She had a look of rejection about her that caused Megan to feel ashamed again. Cissy needed her, and all she could do was snap at her. It was as if she'd to punish her because Jack had chosen her. And it wasn't Cissy's fault. She reached out and took her hand. 'I'm sorry, love. I didn't mean it. Of course I'll always be here for you. If it – well, when it happens, if it don't go right or owt, you can talk to me. I don't know much, but I can ask Hattie for advice and she'll help. Now, what you're best doing is to think on about Jack. That'll help you to be less worried. Do you think as he's not going to be careful with you? He will be. And men seem to know how to go on, so he'll be at teaching you an' all. Come on now. It's your wedding you should be looking forward to, not your funeral!'

A sudden clapping of hands made them jump. Madame Marie had come into the workroom and stood looking around at them. She had an air of sadness about her, and the usual stiff way she held herself was gone. Megan felt uneasy and she saw that Cissy did, too.

'Girls, I have something to say. I'm afraid the garments you are working on are the last. I have to close the business. I–'

'Close! But...'

'Yes, Miss Tatt– Megan. I'm sorry. I cannot avoid it. I'll be honest with you all. I just about managed to keep going through the war, largely thanks to how hard you all worked. I thank you for that. But the lean times that followed, and the continuing worry over the predicted recession, is making it impossible for me to continue. I know you are not altogether knowledgeable about current affairs, but things are not good for businesses at the moment, and I am not capable of fighting through a recession. The cutters and pattern-makers have already been given notice earlier today and will be gone by the end of the week. You girls in here will be kept on for a further week. Miss... Megan, when you have done the trimming on that frock, you can work on finishing Miss Gr– Cecelia's wedding gown, and your own gown. I want you to be able to finish them in time. The cutters will help. That's all I have to say. I'm very sorry.'

She turned and almost ran back into her office.

During the silence that followed, Megan wasn't sure what part had shocked her more: being told they were all out of work or hearing Madame using her own and Cissy's first names!

Gradually the chatter started up again. Some in the room seemed happy to be escaping, but Megan wasn't. With a realization that put a sick feeling in her belly, she knew her choices were gone. She'd only one path that she could follow. Her life had suddenly been mapped out for her and the feeling that this evoked wasn't welcome.

19

Megan's Choice

A disappointment settled in Megan as they left the station, even though she knew she shouldn't have expected Bert to be there. He'd be in the pub with that Lillian Cole, if he wasn't on his shift.

'Are you all right with that box, Ciss?'

'Aye, Jack should be along. Oh, Megan, I can't wait for him to see me in me gown! And you look lovely in yours an' all. How you got them both finished I'll never know. I'll not ever be able to thank you enough.'

'Just make sure as Jack don't see it before the day! It's unlucky, that, thou knows.'

'I'll not let him. Or more to the point, me mam won't.'

'Aye, you're reet there. She's got him lodgings at the pub from Thursday, hasn't she? There's not a chance you'll see him after that until you walk up the aisle.'

'Well, it'll not be so bad. We'll be back at work till Friday. Oh, I wish we hadn't to go back. There doesn't seem much point now, does there?'

'No, but it'll make the time pass and we do have a duty to Madame, so it's only right that we go back and help her to pack everything up.'

'What're you going to do after, Megan? Have you thought about it?'

'Aye. I'm going to see if Bert's still for me, and if he isn't, I'm going to go round the mills and see if I can get set on and get some board and lodgings for meself.'

'So it's you as is after *me* now, is it?' A gruff male voice interrupted their discussion. 'Well, I've not been for waiting round for thee, thou knows.'

'Oh, Bert! You made me jump. Sneaking up on me like that!'

He'd no time to retort before Cissy jumped in. 'Hello, Bert. Have you seen Jack?'

'Aye, he were just coming down the road. D'you need a hand? I'll help you.'

'No, ta. I'll wait for Jack. Put that box down here with mine, Megan, and leave them to Jack to carry. You go with Bert. I'll be reet.'

'I haven't heard meself invite her anywhere as yet.'

'You needn't be like that, Bert Armitage. I know as you haven't been waiting for me, even though I did ask you to give me some time.'

'Well, what did you expect? You weren't at encouraging me, were you?'

'Will you walk with me to the beck then? I'd like to talk to you.'

'I don't see as I can refuse, not when I'm being asked by such a pretty lass.'

Despite the grin that spread across his face as he said this, Megan felt hot with embarrassment, and Cissy's giggling didn't help matters.

'Well, here we are again. Though it seems as boot's on other foot, and you've to do the asking this time, Megan.'

'Aye, I know.' She'd waste no time. She'd no

choice, she knew that. She deserved the humiliation she felt. 'I – I were wondering if your offer to take me on were still open? I have to be truthful and tell you as sommat happened as I didn't expect and it's helped me to make me mind up to come to you.'

'What's that, then? Are you saying as you don't come willing, like?'

'No, I'm not saying that, Bert. It's that I were helped in me decision. Me livelihood's gone and...'

His silence after she'd finished telling him had her holding her breath.

'But you were leaning towards coming anyroad, you say? And it isn't as I'm your last hope, is it?'

'No, you're not. I've a plan of what I'm to do, if you'll not take me on, and I know as you've other choices in the offing. It's up to you.'

'Come here.'

He reached out to her and pulled her close to him. 'Course I'm for taking you on. Lillian's nowt to me. I were just not for having no one and chancing losing me cottage.'

He held her close. It felt good. Megan tried to take something from his strength in order to banish the feeling of dread inside her. She was to make the best of this, because despite her words about going into the mill, it wasn't really an option. She would find it difficult to pay lodgings out of the meagre wages she knew the mill workers were paid.

When Bert's lips pressed against her own, she didn't let it be just him who was doing the kissing. And as feelings woke inside her, she allowed them to flourish and didn't stop him from gently caressing her breast. She wanted to know what longing felt like – wanted to be sure he could rouse in her the sensations she had experienced with him before, as she was sure that would help her in her mission to be a good wife. And he did. She was near to begging him to take her down, before she eventually gathered all that was in her and pulled away.

'Christ, you're being a tease! Well, you bloody well needn't think as I'll take them games when we're wed.'

'I'm not playing games! I ... wanted to. It's just – I want to be wed first.'

'Well, I'm not bloody going to say as I'm sorry for me actions. You were to blame just as much as me.'

Though his reaction wasn't what she'd anticipated, and his quick temper was frightening, she understood. She knew she hadn't been fair to him.

'And I'll tell thee sommat else while I'm at it. I'm not for waiting no time to be wed.'

'I know, Bert, and I want to be wed as soon as it's possible. I'm sorry. I've no experience of it all. I were letting me feelings carry me, but then I suddenly realized what I were doing.'

He shuffled the dirt around with his feet. It seemed an age before he spoke. 'Aye, well, I s'pose as it goes good for us. At least I know as you have feelings for me, and you weren't just for taking me on because you've no other choices. Let's talk about the arrangements, eh?'

They sat down on the grass. Relief filled Megan. It seemed Bert could emerge from his temper as quickly as he could slip into it. Her body hadn't

203

truly let go of how she'd felt. She still had an urge to take Bert to her. She had a need in her, not just to do it, but to know if what Hattie had said about it would happen for her and Bert. Though she had to admit to herself that, above all of this, she needed to know if it would be enough to stop the longing and the pain inside of her, at the thought of Ciss and Jack together.

'We can arrange it all in three weeks, thou knows. I were asking Father O'Malley about it afore I brought you up here last time.'

For a moment she was unsure what Bert meant. His words didn't seem to match her thoughts or what she was feeling.

'The wedding, Megan.'

'Oh! Sorry. I were daydreaming.'

'Aye, well. I know, lass. But we've to sort things out. I have to put in for me cottage proper, to make sure on it.'

'Three weeks – is that all it takes? Well then, let's do what we have to. There won't be a problem with you getting the cottage, will there?'

'No, it's mine for the asking. Only thing is, I have to have a wife or be getting married. I've been on with getting it all cleaned out. Well, best as I can. And I've the two bedrooms whitewashed...'

'You took on what I said, then?'

'Aye, I did, even though I weren't sure of you. Mind, I'm not for doing women's work. I've only shifted stuff out as were of no use. As I see it, I'll do the distempering, but any cleaning is down to you.'

His mood had changed again, and she felt a dread. But she'd to get on with it – if she was to take him on, she had to take this side of him, too. 'How about I stay in the cottage until we're wed? I've nowhere to go after next Friday. I mean, if you could move out for a couple of weeks and stay at a mate's or suchlike.'

'That's a good idea, love. I'll soon find a place to kip, or I could take a room at the pub. And as you'll be at home all day, you can really get things sorted.'

'We've to post banns an' all. What about we do that on Sunday? We'd have to attend mass, and it's likely Father O'Malley'll need us to go for some lessons.'

'Lessons! What's he going to be on with teaching us? I reckon as we could teach him a thing or two, even afore we're wed! Ha, that's a turn-up. Lessons, from a Catholic priest!'

Megan had to laugh with him. It did sound funny. 'I think it's on the religious side of stuff. Cissy said as he talks about the sanctity of marriage and bringing young 'uns up in the Church. It's got to be done or he'll not marry us.'

'Aye, all right. I'll go along with owt as long as it gets us settled. Come on. Let's get ourselves away, afore I start in on you again.'

He stood and offered her his hand. She took it and he helped her up. For a moment Bert looked like he would be for starting in on her, as he put it, but she didn't dare visit the feelings again, so she made a joke in an attempt to deter him. 'You needn't look like that, Bert Armitage! You've three weeks to wait, so from now on until we're wed, no more meetings without Father O'Malley being present to bless us.'

Bert put his head back and laughed out loud. It sounded good, and she couldn't help but join him. She felt a happiness swell up inside her, where before there had been a dread. Things would work out. She was sure of it.

20

A Change in Fortunes

Hattie sat up in bed.

'What is it, my dear? You often look so sad. Is it me?'

'No, Arthur, no. You couldn't make me un-happy. It's ... well, I'm worried about me lassies. It isn't working out as yet, and they're not getting enough to line their pockets. Some of them are getting grumpy about tipping up me due, and others are not making enough to tip up anything. I'm at digging into me standby money to keep them in food and pay me bills.'

'Well, it will take time to get known. It's not as if you can advertise. I hadn't thought you were struggling. You haven't said anything before.'

'I know, but I didn't want you to worry. And besides, you weren't for me taking on this busi-ness, even though you helped me to get it.'

'That wouldn't stop me helping you again.' He hauled himself up to a sitting position, and his sigh told her he'd other things on his mind besides talking. 'Yes. I do hate the thought of you having to be involved in a business such as you have. I worry. I am concerned, as it isn't legal to do what you are doing. Oh, I know the girls would do it anyway, and you are providing a safe place and caring for them, and I strongly believe it can be a necessary service. No one knows that better than I do – did – but I'm surprised that after being up and running for eighteen months, you're still not breaking even.'

'It's like you say. I can't advertise. Some of the lassies have kept in contact with old customers, and they're visiting, and I'd hoped as word would spread that way. And it is, but not enough. Mind, I've been at vetting all the customers first. I'll not have some of the bast– I mean blokes in the house, as used to use the services of the girls.'

'Look. I'll go round to my club tonight and drop the word in an ear or two. It might help. There are a few members saying they are missing out. Most upper-class wives are of the "lie back and think of England" type, which must be less than satisfying after a while. Only the other day I heard a remark on how the street girls were missed, since the Lord Marley busi– Oh! I'm sorry, my dear. I shouldn't have mentioned it.'

'It's all right. I know as it's still talked of. Besides, if they're at talking because there's nothing available on the streets, then it shows as there are customers looking. Though I don't want the Lord Marley type. Anyroad, would you try that for me, eh? I mean, don't embarrass yourself, but...'

'Oh, don't worry. I'd only have to mention it to one chap I know and word will get round to the right ears in no time. But I shouldn't have mentioned – well, you know.'

'It's all right, honestly. It's funny, but it don't bother me so much now. In fact I've hardly thought on it since the executions. The day Blackstaff, Wally and Doug hanged seemed to bring an end to it. And with Doreen serving a long sentence and Lord Marley rotting in his grave, I feel free of it all. I never stop thinking of Sally, of course, and it all comes back when me hands are paining me, but...'

'I know, my darling, though sometimes it doesn't feel as though justice was done on account of David – Lord Marley. Him keeling over like he did seemed to let him off the hook. And you, my poor darling, left with the legacy of your painful hands.' Arthur took the hand nearest to him and gently kissed it, letting his lips travel up her arm. It felt good. He was the only person she'd let see her scars laid bare. He understood how she felt about the ugliness of the gnarled fingers and the red-raw, stretched skin on her arms. When his lips reached her shoulder, he kissed her scar there as he turned his body and pulled her into his arms. 'Hattie ... Hattie...'

His lips – his perfect, firm lips – were on hers, and she tasted the sweetness of him as his tongue explored her mouth and she sucked gently on it. She had a need in her to talk, to tell him her worries, her fears for Megan and her longing to know if Sally was being cared for. It wasn't with an easy will that she lay down beside him. Arthur set about changing that, as if he'd a notion that he'd to fight for her attention. His touch was light and caring, and helped her to come to a quiet place, where her love for him was all that mattered for the moment. Her body and mind relaxed and then filled with an intense desire. She let her kisses tell him he could come into her.

Helping him to do so was something she'd perfected, to make it a pleasure for him rather than a struggle, and to enhance her own enjoyment. Once achieved, he found the strength he needed to thrust into her body with a deep, pleasurable intensity that brought them both to a release.

Lying in his arms afterwards, she felt safe and would have chosen to lie there forever if she could, but Arthur wasn't for lazing about. After kissing and thanking her, he moved his arm from around her. 'Well, my dear. I'd better make a move. You know how long it takes me to get ready.'

'I'll help you. I don't want you to be calling Harry in – it spoils it for me. Brings it to an end and puts me back in your world. I want us to be staying in our world.'

'You are funny sometimes, Hattie. All right, you go and run my bath whilst I get myself out of this bed. And, Hattie, you won't go home, will you? Not tonight. I'll give Harry an early night and we can have some supper when I get back. What do you think?'

'Aye, I'll stay, love, and be glad to. I've things as I need to talk of. Nowt as you can do anything about. Just me concerns. And I'll cook supper. I've never cooked for you afore, have I? Will Cook be gone an' all?'

'Yes. I'll send them all to their rooms with strict instructions not to come out until further notice.'

'Oh, poor things. They'll be on with starving

afore I've finished with you!' This set them giggling, and even more so when Arthur swung himself over the edge and made as if to chase her, forgetting his crutches and falling straight back on the bed.

Making her way home two days later, Hattie felt better and more settled in herself. They had made love so many times they were both exhausted, and when they weren't making love they'd talked through her worries. He'd said the club had been buzzing with the news of her facilities, and he'd every confidence she'd see a difference and her business would pick up soon. This hadn't stood well with the way Arthur had tried to persuade her to give the business up, or at least let one of the girls run it. He'd told her he wanted to set her up in a place of her own, where he could look after her and visit her freely. He no longer pressed her to move in with him – he'd accepted that that arrangement wouldn't suit her.

She'd told him she'd think about it, but if she did accept, it wouldn't be for a long time in the future. She had to be sure of making her money first. She never wanted to be in the position of not having any choices, not ever again. *And if I had owt to do with it, I'd be a woman of means as could take care of myself afore I went to Arthur proper. Or to any man for that matter...*

When they'd discussed Megan, Arthur had said he was sure Megan was capable of making a sensible decision. He reckoned she had a good head on her shoulders. He was right in that, but he had no notion of what it meant to a lass to think of herself as being left on the shelf and how it frightened lassies like Megan, sometimes influencing them into making the wrong choice. Hattie didn't know why, but something told her that marrying this Bert Armitage wasn't going to be good for Megan, even though she'd never met him herself.

As for her worries over Sally, he'd said it was better that she didn't interfere, and should let her settle with her new family. He thought it possible Sally had already forgotten them all and what had happened to her, but that wasn't what Hattie had wanted him to say. She'd been hoping he'd make enquiries as to how Sally was. Her love for the little lass was so strong that it felt as though a pain was gnawing away at her heart, but although she'd thought to go and see her on many occasions, she'd never got further than within a half-mile of the shop. Fear had always stopped her – fear of upsetting Sally or awakening bad memories. And, yes, fear of fully opening up wounds hidden in places within herself that she didn't want to visit.

Silence greeted her when she opened the door of her house. 'Daisy! Phyllis! Where are you?' *Lazy bitches! I'm at making things too easy round here.* 'Dais–'

'What's all the shouting? Eeh, Hattie lass, you're in a mood. What's up?'

'Up? It's gone twelve and this place looks like it hasn't seen a duster in days. You know as you're all to muck in. I especially rely on you, Daisy, when I take a couple of days away. And yet I come back to find this mess and you still in your

211

robe. It isn't right. It isn't what we agreed.'

'Sorry, love, we were busy till late. It seems as word has got round we're here. Last night we had a crowd from that gentlemen's club, that one around the corner. I tell you, lass, they were all top-drawer. And they all went away pleased. I reckon as some of them'll become regulars.'

'Aye, well, that's good.' She didn't tell her it was down to Arthur's help. 'But thou knows how I've been worried of late as to whether I'd done the right thing? It's been a while taking off, and one good night don't make a good business! Besides, if we let standards slip we'll not keep good customers. Now, get the windows open. It smells like a brothel!'

A howl of laughter broke the moment's silence that had fallen at her words. Bemused, Hattie looked at Daisy, but then it dawned on her what she'd said and she joined in the laughter. As they quietened down again, Hattie slumped into the nearest chair. 'Oh, Daisy love.'

'Is owt wrong, lass?'

'No. Well, nowt as we can have any bearing on.' She stood up again. 'Get Phyllis up and tell her to get the rest of them roused and start cleaning up. Tell her I want every room in the house shining and clean afore I walk round on opening time. You leave them to it and come to me room, once you've got them organized. I'll make us a brew. I need to talk to you about Megan. I'm reet worried over her.'

The whistling of the kettle on the hot plate filled the room as Megan entered with Daisy. Hattie had her back to them, and Daisy winked at Megan. 'I've someone here with me, Hattie. She were knocking at front door as I came across the passage.'

Hattie turned. Her surprised look turned to a grin, and Megan felt the warmth of her welcome. 'Megan! Eeh, it's good to see you. I've been on with worrying over you. And me and Daisy had fixed up a mo to chat over me worries, and now you're here. It's as if I've conjured you up. What's to do? I thought as you'd be gone back to Breckton by now for Cissy's wedding. Are you all right, love?'

Hattie had released Megan from her hug and stood back, looking at her. 'I've lost me job, Hattie, and with it me choices. Me and Ciss are catching train to Breckton later today. I'm going to marry Bert.'

'Lost your job! Sit down, love. Daisy, pour tea out, there's a good 'un. Tell us what's been happening, Megan.'

Megan didn't take long to tell them about Madame Marie having to close the gown shop, and how she'd been and asked Bert if he'd still take her on.

'Oh, Megan, are you sure as that's what you want?'

'No. Oh, I don't know. One minute I am, and the next I'm not. I've just no other road open to me. Besides, me mind's made up and I've to get on with it. Me wedding day is in three weeks.'

'Oh, love. Did you tell Bert as your mind had been made up for you?'

'Aye, I did. And he were all right about it, as I said I had other plans if he'd not have me, so he didn't feel as though he were me last hope.'

'Well, if your mind's made up – and as you say, you haven't got much choice – I hope as it goes well for you, love. But if he ever cuts up rough, don't be for taking it. Walk out and come here. We'll sort sommat out for you.'

'That's a funny thing to say, Hattie. I know I said Bert is surly, but I don't think he'd hit me or owt. He's been through a lot. Anyroad, I'm going to do me utmost to make him happy.'

'Well, you know best, love. So, wedding'll be in three weeks then? You've not much time to get sorted.'

'It'll not take much organizing. When Madame heard about it, she gave me a gown she'd had on display. Mind, that'll take me some time in sorting. It's a gown as a young miss would go to a ball in, but it'll be reet when I take all the flounces and bows off it. And it'll be a quiet do, not like Cissy's, on account of me and Bert not having a lot of friends in Breckton and us having no family. Well, Bert has, but...'

She took a moment to tell Hattie of Bert's sister, and wasn't surprised to hear them speculate as to what had caused her to run off.

'Anyroad, the only ones attending so far are Ciss and Jack, and Issy – Cissy's mam. Bert has a couple of mates as he works with as he wants to ask. Would you come, Hattie? And you, Daisy?'

As she asked, she wondered if Breckton, or Issy or Jack, or even Bert, was ready for the sight of Hattie and Daisy, and she nearly giggled at the thought.

'We can't, love. I think thou knows why.

214

Besides, there's not a chance we can be away for a Saturday. That's a busy night. I'm sorry.'

'But I never thought as we'd not be at each other's wedding day, Hattie!'

'Well, you'll not be at mine and that's for sure, lass, as I'm not destined to have one. Now come on. Be sensible. How would your Bert deal with the likes of me turning up at his wedding, eh?'

Megan rocked with laughter at Hattie's antics as she thrust out her ample bosom and wriggled across the room.

'Aye, and me an' all!' Daisy joined in, flashing open her robe to reveal underwear the like of which Megan had never seen before. That's if you could call it underwear, because it didn't cover anything that undergarments were meant to cover. There was … well, what she could only think of as 'peep-holes' everywhere that was meant to be private.

As she collapsed in a heap of giggles with the pair of them, Megan felt more akin to Hattie and Daisy than she'd felt to anyone for a long time, as now she found herself in the same position they had once been in: with her choices all gone. And, with this realization, the guilt she'd shouldered for many a year – especially where Hattie was concerned – lifted from her.

21

No going back

The bells clanged in Megan's head. The sound that was meant to be joyous caused her pain to increase with every peal. How was she to get through today?

'Come on, Megan. Turn round so I can fasten you. Oh, Megan, you look beautiful.'

'Go away with you, Ciss. I'm not beautiful!'

'You are, Megan. You look grand. The gold colour of that frock does sommat for you, lass. And your hair scraped back like that ... well, it gives you an Oriental look, even though we can't get all of the frizzy bits tamed.' Issy held her shoulders and looked into her eyes as she spoke. 'Thou knows, you have a look of someone as I once knew. And funny thing is, he had a name similar to yours. He were called Hadler. Will Hadler – that sounds a bit like Tattler, doesn't it? And another thing: his wife Bridie had hair the colour of yours, and she told me her mam were called Megan. In fact, they put it in their little girl's name. Bridget, her name was. She had four names...'

'Mam! Don't be going on with that. Take no notice of her, Megan. She'll have you on with thinking as she's found your family next!'

'Eeh, I'm sorry. It wasn't right of me to say such a thing. Anyroad, Megan, I think as Bert's

216

going to be surprised when he sees you. You look a picture. He's going to be feeling his need and wishing as it were his wedding day today.'

'Mam!'

Megan laughed, although inside she felt like a piece of lead had fallen into the pit of her stomach. *Issy was referring to Bert's half-sister! Her name was Bridget and she and her mam and dad lived around here. Bert told me of them all and now Issy is talking of them.*

It hurt Megan that she couldn't acknowledge that she knew of them, or tell Issy what had become of Bridget. She couldn't break Bert's confidence; she'd promised. But it didn't sit well in her not to do so either, as she had always been open with Issy and Cissy. Funny, though, that Issy should think that she looked like them. With this thought, Megan pulled herself up quickly before she weakened, and covered up her guilty feeling at knowing something they didn't know of by chastising the pair of them. 'Stop taking her bait, Ciss. And Issy, you behave!'

'Why? You've got to have a laugh, thou knows!'

Issy went over to the window. 'It's a lovely day an' all, lass. June's a nice month to get married in. Me and Tom were married in June. Happy the bride that the sun shines on, eh, love?'

'Aye, Mam, me and Jack are going to be happy an' all. I–'

Megan cut her short. 'Come on, Ciss, let's be at getting you ready. I've a mind to gather your hair up and let the curls tumble down at the back, what d'yer think, eh?'

Wearing the long cream gown Megan had made for her, and with a beautiful lace veil – the same one Issy had worn at her wedding – draped over her face and hair, Cissy looked a vision of loveliness.

As they walked down the lane to the church, which stood in the grounds of 'the big house', as the locals always called Hensal Grange, children ran in front of them strewing petals. Every step caused a pain to enter Megan's heart, but she kept a smile on her face and teased Cissy, as was traditional.

Issy walked beside her. The tears filling Issy's eyes, which she constantly mopped away with a pretty embroidered hanky, Megan knew were mostly for joy at what the day held, but she suspected that some were for Issy's Tom. She must be feeling the loss of him today. Besides which, her life was set for another huge change. Megan made a mental note to take special care of her, once her duties to Cissy were done.

The route they took passed by Tom's grave. Cissy stopped when she reached it, took a flower from her posy and laid it near to her da's headstone. Henry Fairweather stepped forward at that moment and offered her his arm. As Cissy's mam and dad's lifelong friend, the honour of giving her away had fallen to him. 'Are thee ready, lass? Jack's waiting for you.'

'Aye, I am, Mr Fairweather. Ta.'

When they entered the church and Jack turned round, Megan felt like she'd never catch her breath again. To her, he was beautiful. The sunlight beaming through the stained-glass windows lit the whole of his body, creating a picture that she wanted to keep in her heart forever. She let the tears run down her cheeks. They gave her some release from her pain and wouldn't be noticed, as she wasn't the only one crying – even Jack had tears glistening in his eyes as he looked at Cissy. No one would know hers were due to her heart breaking in two.

Falling into step behind Cissy, they walked slowly towards Jack. Megan couldn't take her eyes off him. Suddenly, Jack's gaze left Cissy and he glanced at her. She saw the smile he would normally give her die on his lips as a look of shock flashed over his face. It was as if he was seeing her for the first time. She hadn't imagined it. The way he turned his attention quickly back to Cissy told her that. Her spirits lifted. It wasn't much, but it was enough. At least he'd noticed she existed, and she was more than just good old Megan.

What am I thinking? Shame washed over her. He'd more than likely just been surprised at the look she'd given him. Oh God! Suddenly she wanted to be anywhere but here. How could she have let her feelings for him show like that? And on his wedding day, too – on Cissy's wedding day!

The nuptial mass went over her head. Not even when they exchanged their vows did she register what was happening, so deep was the shame inside her. What would Jack think? What would everyone be thinking? They must have seen how shocked he'd looked.

The bells started again. It was over, then? She'd to face the world without the man she loved by her side, and in two weeks she'd stand here again and make her own vows. To love, honour and obey a man she didn't love – well, not *didn't love*, exactly, but wasn't *in love with*. The thought at this moment was unbearable.

They were on the porch of the church, with everyone talking at once and congratulations and kisses and laughter all around her, when Jack spoke to her. 'By, you look bonny, lass. I reckon as you're the most beautiful bridesmaid there's ever been. And we're lucky at having her as ours, aren't we, Mrs Fellam?'

He said I was beautiful!

'Aye, Jack, you're right there. Megan's done us proud. She'd not believe me when I said as she were beautiful. Eeh, Jack – Megan, *Mrs Fellam!* I can't take it in, as that's me name at last. I'm so happy!'

'Aye, lass, you're me own Mrs Fellam.'

The pain that ripped through Megan's heart was short-lived, as someone grasped her arm. She turned to see Bert, his face red with anger. Her shame increased. Had he seen? Had he heard Jack? He pulled her away from the crowd. 'What's your game? What're you playing at, eh?'

'What? What d'yer mean, Bert? I'm not playing at owt. I'm just doing me bridesmaid's duty.'

'So, it's your duty to ogle the bridegroom, is it? And to have him tell you as you're beautiful, eh?'

'Well, he's probably the only man as is going to tell me owt like that, because you're not for noticing!'

'I weren't given a chance, were I? You never even looked round the church to find me. So now I know how the land lies. Well, thou knows, you can forget being wed to me. You can go on with your other plan, and you can get out of me cottage an' all.'

Shock kept her from going after him. *Oh God! What have I done? How could I have let my feelings show, after keeping them locked up inside me for so long?*

'Are you all right, Megan lass? What bee's got into his bonnet? Eeh, he's a funny cuss. Come on. Don't let Ciss and Jack see as you're upset.'

'Oh, Issy. He says as he isn't going to be marrying me, and I can get out of the cottage! He thinks ... he...'

'Aye, lass. I know what he thinks, and he isn't wrong at that, now, is he?'

Megan's head dropped with the weight of her guilt.

'Look, you aren't the first lass to fall in love with another's man, thou knows. It happens all the time. And in particular when that man is as handsome as Jack is.'

'You knew?'

'Aye, I knew, lass. But I also know as you're not one to do owt about it and hurt our Cissy, so I had no worries on that score. Me worry were for you and your feelings not being returned, and that making you settle for such as Bert Armitage.'

'He isn't so bad, Issy. He loves me and I have a feeling for him. There's another side to him that I can love, but now I don't know what to do. Should I go after him? Will I be missed?'

'If you're on with being sure as you can make a go of it, then go after him. I'll cover for you. They'll be dancing afore we sit down for the meal, so just make sure you're back for that, eh? And, Megan, if it's what you want, then do your best. Tell him as you were daydreaming that it were him as were standing at the altar waiting for you, and as you got a shock when reality hit. And say the words: say you love him, because he strikes me as one as hasn't had much love in his life. Go on, lass. And good luck.'

Bert was where she thought he'd be: in the pub. She couldn't go in after him, as it wasn't the done thing for a woman to enter the pub on her own, so she stood tapping on the window. He turned round, as did all the men who had escaped the wedding party to get a quick jug of ale in before the formalities. Bert's face turned red, and she guessed by the laughing men around him that he was taking some leg-pulling. She hoped it wouldn't make him angrier, but as he came out of the door he was on the attack. She'd expected that, as he had to save face. 'What d'yer want? I've said me piece.'

'Aye, you have, but I haven't been at saying mine, so I came to say it.'

She could see that he was put out by her retort. He didn't like her chatting back at him, but he'd to get used to it, because he wasn't going to have it all his own way.

'Well?'

'Bert Armitage, you've got it all wrong. I walked into that church in a dream. I was on with imagining as it were my day and it were *you* waiting at the altar for me.'

The words Issy had given her were having an effect. His expression softened.

'I haven't ever been to a wedding afore, and I haven't ever dressed up like this, either, or had folk tell me as I'm beautiful. It all went to me head. I felt like I were somebody. I started thinking of me own day, as is to come. My look at Jack was one of shock, as I came to me senses and seen as it wasn't you! I felt daft and confused. I – I love you, Bert Armitage, and if you were to say as I were beautiful, then that would mean everything to me.'

A cheer went up, then calls of 'Go on, Armitage!' and 'By, you've caught a fiery one there, Bert!' and 'She loves you... Ahh.'

Bert's expression changed. He looked like he was about to explode; his eyes bulged with anger and sweat stood out on his face. He grabbed her arm so fiercely it made her cry out with fear. The men quietened down and one by one went back into the pub.

As he dragged her by the arm, she stumbled and caught her heel on the cobbles, but he took no heed. When they reached the cottage, he opened the door and flung her inside. 'You bitch!'

'But, Bert, I–'

His hand shot out. Her face stung. Shock held her breathless.

'I'm sorry... I'm sorry. Megan, Megan me love, forgive me. Oh God! I can't believe as I did that! Megan, I do love you, lass, and you *are* beautiful. You're the most beautiful thing as has happened in all me rotten life. I'll never be at hurting you again. I don't know what come over me.' Tears streamed down his face.

The shock of the slap made her body shake, but

the shame she felt at having brought him to this crushed her. 'It were my fault, Bert. I've kept you unsure of me. And – and then today ... saying all that stuff in front of your mates. It's me as is to be sorry, Bert.'

They held each other close. Bert slowly stopped crying and telling her how sorry he was, and a love deeper than she'd felt for him before kindled in her. His kiss took her to a place her body wanted to be. Yes, Jack was there, and yes, it was him caressing her, but the feeling was so good she responded with all that was in her.

It took a moment to remove her frock, as she had to make sure it didn't get crumpled. Once it and her shift and underbodice were off, she surprised herself with how little embarrassment she felt as Bert looked at her. 'Megan, Megan lass, you're beautiful. You're me beautiful lass.'

His words further enhanced the feelings in her, but the pain when he tried to enter her brought her back to reality, and she stiffened as she tried to hold him back.

'No, Megan, no. You're not stopping me now. Stop fighting and lay still.'

'It's hurting, Bert. You're hurting me.'

'I'm not for stopping. Oh, Megan – don't stop me...'

'Slow down. Stop! Bert, please stop!'

'Christ! Megan, you're a bitch. A cock-tease! Well, I'm having none of it. You're having it now and that's the end of it.' He pushed her back down and forced her legs open. 'Come on, Megan, I'm telling thee–'

'No. No!' Pain shot through her with greater

intensity as he forced his way into her. *Oh God, help me!*

Bert stopped pushing and lifted his body so that he looked down on her. 'It'll be reet now, lass. It's just the first time. You're mine now. I'll not take long – just be a good lass and let it happen, eh? Next time you'll be at liking it.' His kiss soothed her, and her body relaxed. It was going to be all right. She had a shame in her because she'd not been wed before she'd allowed it, but it'd be all right.

As Bert moved above her, the pain lessened. There was a soreness, but that was how it would be. Hattie'd told her, and she was daft not to have remembered and to have fought and made Bert angry. He was all right now, though. He was enjoying it; his moans told her that. When it was over, he lay on the floor next to her. His face, hot and sweaty-looking, held the happiest expression she'd ever seen on him as he said, 'That were grand, lass. I reckon as I'm going to like being married to you, Megan. Aye, but look at you! You've to get some work done to cover up what you've been up to, thou knows.'

A feeling of emptiness overcame her as Bert rose. His praise had been something, but she had a need to be held – soothed and loved. The hollowness of this aftermath pushed the disgrace of what she'd done away and left her feeling as if she was nothing of worth. She hadn't wanted to feel like that. It wasn't how she should feel. *But then,* she told herself, *I only have meself to blame.*

22

Reality Sets a Path

From her window, Megan could see Cissy hurrying up the lane with a lightness to her step as if she would have liked to have broken into a skip.

Megan's cottage stood on the road running along the top of the lane where the farm cottages and Issy's cottage were. *I must stop thinking of it as Issy's; it is Jack and Cissy's now.*

There were no houses opposite, as Megan was on what was termed the *front row*, and the pub was the only building on the side of the road where the lane emerged. With the hedges cut back as they were at the moment, she had a full view over it and behind the pub, so she could see the comings and goings in the lane. The lane was a nicer place to live than where she was, though she knew she was luckier than those who lived behind her.

The layout gave the impression that the farm labourers were up above the miners. The farm labourers' cottages were bigger, too, with a parlour and a scullery as well as a back porch covering the coalhouse, and they each had their own closet. They were only joined to one other cottage, whereas the miners' cottages were in back-to-back rows, with some twenty or so in a row. And, to Megan's disgust, they had only one closet between two cottages, and that backed

226

onto the one belonging to the row behind. It was a regular thing to be sitting out there and have your neighbour from the back row doing his business in the lav that backed onto yours. Worst of all, they always wanted to carry on a conversation whilst they did it! She knew she'd never get used to it, and always tried to time her visit when there would be no one around to join her.

Keeping the closet clean, she found, was a task that only she took on. Mrs Braithwaite, who lived next door, laughed at her for this, and only yesterday had said, 'Eeh, lass, it'll only get dirty again, thou knows. Specially when me man comes home and does his business. You'll never keep it clean. I should give up, like the rest of us!' But Megan knew she wouldn't, as much as it sickened her stomach to scrub and swill it out every day. She'd never give up trying to keep it clean, between the times the cart came and it was emptied.

When she opened the door, there was a look of joy on Cissy's face. It brightened her out of her thoughts, though of late she wasn't at her best in the mornings. Not since she'd taken to emptying her belly into the bucket as soon as her feet touched the floor.

'You look happy, Ciss. Come in, love. I needn't ask if everything's all right with you. I can see as it is.'

'Aye, it is. I've missed me bleeding. I think as I'm going to have a babby, Megan! Oh, I'm so happy.'

'Ha! You won't be in a week or so, not when you're reaching for the bucket like me every few minutes!'

'You mean...? Megan!'

Cissy was round the table and holding her in a hug that felt good – so good that she nearly let the tears come. They'd been needing a release for weeks, but she swallowed them back and tried to hook onto some of Cissy's happiness.

'You never said! When ... I mean, when did you miss yours?'

'I haven't seen owt since I were wed and ... and it were some weeks afore that when I last seen it.'

'You'll have tongues wagging if your babby comes early, Megan lass!' Cissy giggled. 'You must have caught first off. By, Jack'll be jealous of Bert. He thinks as he's the best stud in the town for getting me took so quick.'

'Ciss! You sound just like your mam. We'll not be at missing her with you around. If you were in the convent as I were brought up in, you'd have your mouth washed out with soap.'

They both started giggling then, and somehow Megan didn't feel quite so alone. She and Ciss would go through their pregnancies together.

It wasn't that Bert didn't try; he just had no understanding of such things. He'd not ever been around women before and ... well, it was his way. His temper! He did try to keep it under control, and he was always sorry. Anyroad, it was mostly her fault when he snapped.

'Is sommat up, Megan?'

'No. I were in me thoughts, that's all. We'll be reet, won't we, Ciss? We'll get through it, eh?'

'What is it, Megan? Is there sommat you're not telling of? We said as we'd tell each other, and we said as we'd see Hattie if we needed help. Does you need...? God! What's that on your arm? Megan, I've never seen the like of such a big bruise. How did that happen?'

'It's nowt. I – I banged meself. I'm always at banging meself. Thou knows how clumsy I am. I were like a pin-cushion at work.' She swallowed hard. The tears were going to come. Damn! She couldn't stop them.

'Eeh, Megan love.'

She sat down on the fireside chair. Cissy sat on the arm and leaned over her and held her close. Megan could no longer control her sobs as they racked her body.

'He didn't mean to. It were me. Thou knows how I get 'is 'eckles up. I've always done it. I rub him up the wrong way. I should learn. You told me of it afore, you remember?'

'Aye, I did, but it doesn't give him leave to hurt you. It isn't right, Megan. He can't have things his own way all the time. You've to have your say an' all.'

'It's not just that. I – I'm not much good at ... well, thou knows.'

'It probably isn't your fault, love. He's the man. He should be patient and be on with teaching you. Jack–'

'It's all right. I'll be reet. Don't – don't let's talk on it. It were only the once. Let's put kettle on, eh? We should be at celebrating!'

'Aye. It'll turn out. How about we do go and see Hattie, though? She'll have some tips for us. Because though I'm at being happy, I don't feel as I have it right as yet. I'm still at trying.'

Megan doubted Cissy was telling the truth, but

229

loved her for what she knew she was trying to do. 'I think a trip to see Hattie is just what we need, and she must be dying to hear all our news.'

'Let's go tomorrow then. Only ... well, Jack doesn't know owt of Hattie, as I've not been at telling him of her. That sounds bad, doesn't it?'

'No, I understand. I haven't told Bert of her either, so we're in same boat. Let's just say as we've some shopping to do, on account of our conditions. That should satisfy them and stop them being curious. Mind, I can't be going until after eleven. I can't leave me bucket until then.'

They were giggling again, and Megan was glad for it. She'd had a fear in her of Cissy and Jack finding out about how Bert was when he lost his temper. They'd want to try and help her, which mustn't happen. It would only make things worse. She hoped Cissy would just take it as something that had only happened the once; and besides, Bert had said as he'd never do it again. Oh, she knew he'd said that the first time, but she believed he meant it this time. He was in such a state afterwards, and so loving towards her.

Doing as Hattie had suggested on their trip to visit her – relaxing and letting it happen, then gradually taking more of an active part – made Bert much happier when they coupled. Over the next few months it made a difference to his mood and to how he viewed Megan's feelings for him. It'd pleased her, too. It wasn't what she would call 'wonderful', but it wasn't without some pleasure for her. The trouble was, it was getting more difficult and uncomfortable to take him.

230

Her pregnancy had caused her to swell so much that she was now like a barrel.

As she dipped doorsteps of bread into hot fat for his breakfast, she could still feel the pain he'd put her through during the night. He'd wanted her to turn her back towards him. They'd done it a few times in that position since she'd got bigger, and she'd liked it, but with the babby so low it had hurt. Hattie had told her how to use her hand, and she'd suggested doing that instead from now on. Bert had liked it as part of their love-making, but he wasn't for it being all he had. She'd ended up in tears after taking a clout as well as the pain of him forcing himself into her.

He hadn't spoken to her while she'd been cooking his breakfast, and neither did he speak while he ate it. She decided to leave things, and got on with putting up his snap tin. She wasn't for saying anything if he didn't. But then, as he pulled on his boots, he said, 'Are thee all right, Megan?'

'Aye. We've to talk, though, Bert. I'm not for going through what happened last night again. I'm not saying as I'll leave you wanting, but there's other ways.'

'I know. We'll talk on it, but it seems as it isn't reet having a wife as you can't use. I can do the other meself if I want to, and you've two months to go as yet.'

'So you "use" me, then? It's for your pleasure only, is it? Not to show me your love or owt.'

'Don't go twisting me words, Megan. You're good at that. I just can't see me getting by for two months having nothing. And besides, you'll not be

231

ready for a few weeks after babby's born, either.'

'Well, you'll just have to go calling on Lillian then, won't you? I'm sure as she'll be willing to let you use her. Because I'm telling you, Bert Armitage, I'm not for it. Not until babby's born.'

'Aye, I might just do that. Like you say, she'll be willing. She's always hanging around me. She showed willing afore you decided you wanted me, and it were good an' all. And it weren't given under sufferance, either!'

The door slammed behind him. Megan sat down. What had she done? If anybody should be accused of 'using' anyone, it was her. Hadn't she used Bert because she'd nowhere else to go? He might have been happy with Lillian. It seems they had been at it, and he'd liked it, but what if he went off with Lillian now? What then? The cottage was in his name. Could he chuck her out? No, he'd not do that. He'd be an outcast amongst his own. It wasn't done. Oh, having a bit on the side would be accepted – some would even put him on a pedestal for it – but would she be able to stand the shame? No. She knew she wouldn't. She'd just have to let Bert have his way. She would have to bear the pain and pretend it was good. It was the only way.

Megan looked anxiously at the clock as she waited for Bert to come home from his shift. He was late. He was never late. He'd often go out again for a walk or, if it was later, to the pub, but never until after he'd been home and eaten his meal and had a swill. Thoughts of what had gone on between them that morning had made her mind up to say she was sorry and to tell him she'd try harder. But now it was four o'clock, and he'd been due back before three. Was he with Lillian? Had he taken what she'd said as leave to do it? Oh God!

She looked out of the window again. Lillian walked by with a smile. Was it a satisfied smile? One that said, 'I've got your man'?

Bert came in just after, looking sheepish. Her temper flared, and she shot at him, 'Did you do as you said then?'

'What was that?'

'I saw Lillian go by just now, looking like she'd been made happy.'

'What yer talking of? I haven't been near her. But I tell you sommat, Megan: I will if you keep on.'

'Well, that's up to you, isn't it? So where have you been then?'

'Oh, I'm not to be trusted now, am I not? Some marriage this is turning out to be. No having what's me right to have, no trust. And I'd like to bet as me dinner isn't on, either! By, I took sommat on when I took up with you, Megan Armitage!'

He came towards her, his anger rising with every step. 'So, you want to know where I've been, eh?'

'No, Bert. It ... it's all right. I was just on with worrying about you.'

'You bloody wasn't! You thought as I was with Lillian Cole, didn't you?'

He pushed her in the chest with each word, until she had her back to the table edge. 'Don't, Bert. Don't get all worked up. I'm sorry.'

'Sorry, is it? Thou knows, if anybody's bloody sorry it's me for taking you on. You bitch!'

His fist dug into her stomach with such force that she crumpled to the floor.

'And that's where you bloody belong an' all. You're nowt but a cock-teasing bitch! I'm off. I'm going to see if I can find Lillian and see what she's got for me.'

Megan thought the pain would never stop. It caused every part of her body to cramp and a wetness to seep between her legs. *Oh God! The babby! No. It's too soon! No. No...* She tried to sit up, but couldn't move. Waves of pain took all her strength. Panic rose in her. It couldn't happen. Not here on a stone floor, and her all on her own. Her babby would die! 'Help. Help me. Oh God! Someone help me!'

The door opened. 'Oh, Megan lass, what's to do? Is babby coming?'

'I – I think so, Mrs Braithwaite. Oh! Help me, please help me...'

'Can you get up if I give you a hand? You need to be on your bed, love.'

'No – no, don't move me. Oh – oh, it's coming... IT'S COMING!'

'I'll fetch Gertie. Hang on. I'll not be a mo.'

'Don't leave.'

A deep despair engulfed Megan as the door shut behind Mrs Braithwaite, but it didn't last long, as an urge she couldn't stop took her and a pain more intense than any she'd suffered before made her push down with all her strength. The babby slid from her onto the cold floor.

Gertie Ardbuckle and Mrs Braithwaite came in

just at that moment. 'Eeh, Megan love!' Gertie moved swiftly, grabbing a towel off the fire surround and wrapping it around the little form. 'Get water from kettle into that bowl, Bertha. Come on, move yourself! We've to act quickly.'

Bertha Braithwaite did as she was bid, as she did for all the instructions Gertie called out. Megan dared not ask any questions as they worked. It was as if time had frozen. Suddenly there was a mighty yell from the babby and Gertie said, 'It's a boy, lass. And he's reet bonny. You must've been at getting your dates wrong. He's a good size for an early one. I'd say he's on five to six pounds.'

With the relief that came with the cry of her babby, her body started to shake and, through chattering teeth, she asked, 'Is he all right, Gertie? There's nowt wrong with him, is there?'

'No. He's perfect. He's a mite sleepy, but then little ones are.' She cut off there and shouted at Bertha, 'Put him down on the settle, Bertha, and run upstairs and get the bedding. We've to get Megan warmed. She's on with the ague. Don't worry, Megan lass. It's a thing as happens, especially when babby comes quickly like that. We're to get you warm and get sommat hot into you. You'll be fine.'

Megan didn't think she'd ever be fine again. She couldn't keep a limb still, and drinking the hot tea Bertha had made for her wasn't easy. Gradually she felt her body steadying.

'Right, that's good, lass. Now, we need to get you cleaned up and get you to your bed. You need a good rest.'

Megan found she couldn't speak as they washed

her down and helped her into her nightgown, securing a clean rag between her legs. Weariness flooded over her and it took all her strength to get up the stairs. Gertie walked behind her, steadying her with her hand. Once in her bed, Bertha passed her son to her. As she took him and held him close, Gertie said, 'He'll take some raising at first, on account that he'll not be able to take much food all at once. He'll be at your breast near on every hour of the day and night. You've your work cut out, lass.'

She just nodded her reply. It was a strange feeling – a strange but wonderful feeling – to be holding her child. She couldn't believe it, and neither could she take her eyes from him. A love she'd never felt for anyone in the whole of her life took her over.

'There! It was worth all the pain, I'd say, wouldn't you, lass?'

'Aye, I would, Gertie. And thanks. And you, Bertha. I'd not have known what to do without you.'

'Go on with you. Anyroad, I'm to go now. I've to call at the corner shop, which is where I were going when Bertha stopped me. I've nowt for Gary's tea on the go yet, but before I go, tell us what you're going to call him. Then I can have the full story for anybody as I see on me travels.'

'I don't know. I'd not thought about it, as I thought I'd ages to go. I'll see what Bert thinks.'

'Is he on shift?' Gertie asked.

'No. He ... he went for a walk.'

'Don't be on with worrying, love. I told Mr Braithwaite to be going after him as soon as I'd got

Gertie to come. He said as he would when he'd finished his dinner. Bloody men!' tutted Bertha.

Gertie chuckled, but Megan didn't smile. All she could think was, *Please, God, don't let Bert be found with Lillian. The shame of it would be too much to bear.*

'Megan! Megan...' The sound of Cissy calling from downstairs stopped any further thoughts or worries. The bedroom door burst open. 'Oh, Megan, I've just heard. I were in the village and I saw Mr Braithwaite. Oh, love! Babby's here then? What is it? Are you all right? Oh, let me see!'

'I'll leave you to it. She's fine, Ciss, and so is the babby, so don't be fussing. Happen she could do with another brew – one as she can enjoy this time. I'll see you later, lassies.'

'Aye, and I'll be off an' all. I've to do me pots. I'll look in tomorrow after Mr Braithwaite's off on his shift.'

'Thanks, Gert. Thanks. Thanks, Mrs Braithwaite. Thanks for all as you've done. I'll see you both right.'

Bert was back within the hour. She didn't ask him where he'd been. He sat down on the end of the bed, holding his head in his hands. Cissy had left when he'd come in. Megan tried to soothe him. 'Don't take on, Bert. I shouldn't have said what I did. Things'll be better for us now babby's born. You'll see.'

'Oh, lass. I never wanted to be one as knocked you about. You've to stop getting at me, thou knows. You make me that mad at times.'

'Aye, I know. I were for saying sorry when you

237

got home, but you coming in late set me off with imagining things, and me mouth ran off with me.'

'Well, I knew as you were spirited when I took you on. I haven't been with Lillian, thou knows. I missed cage as come up, and got on a later one. First time as that's happened to me. And just now I went for a walk up Mire Hill. I were on me own. Anyroad, I'd better be at getting me swill and then I can have a look at the babby.'

'Have you a name as you'd like to call him, Bert?'

'Aye. Me half-sister Bridget told me of her da once. He died young, but were a good bloke. He were foreman at pit, and though folk don't know as I know of him, he's still talked of. And what they say is good. He were called William. Folk called him Will, but I like Billy, the other short form of his name. So how about that then?'

She didn't tell him she knew of Will, that Issy had spoken of him on Cissy's wedding day. That would form a connection that she didn't want to make, as it could upset him again. 'Aye, that's grand. Billy it is, with his christened name as William.'

'Good. I'll bring you a brew up, lass.'

As she lay back she wondered how Bert could act as if nothing had been his fault. He hadn't been sorry or asked how it'd been for her. Their babby could so easily have been born with problems. He hadn't thought about that, and the last thing she'd expected was for him to want the babby called after his sister's father. He'd a funny side, had Bert – look at how he'd tried to find the grave of his mam's lost child. It was as if he wanted some link with family. Mind, she could understand that. He was like her in that and, even though he'd not got any photographs of his family, he'd kept his sister's letter – hidden away, just like she did with her locket. She'd found the letter when she had been clearing things out. She hadn't told him, but she'd read it. She'd noted how crumpled it was and thought that Bert must have read it more than a few times himself. It was as if each time he'd thought to throw it away, he'd changed his mind and flattened it out again.

It had been strange reading about her sister-in-law's life, and it was funny to think that this woman knew nothing about Megan's marriage to her brother. She wondered about Bridget, and what she was really like. She didn't sound as bad as Bert had painted her. Her letter read as if she'd been forced to leave him for some reason – happen it was to do with the beatings Bert had mentioned.

At that moment she made up her mind to write to Bridget – to tell her that she and Bert were wed and that he was all right. She'd tell her about Billy. She wouldn't be able to give their address, or post the letter in Breckton – she'd have to post it in Leeds when she went to see Hattie. And another thing: it wasn't going to be long before she went to see Hattie, either. She'd go just as soon as she was allowed up. She needed her help on what she had to do so as not to get her belly up again, because she was never going to bring another babby into this world. She had feared for Billy before he was born, and something in her feared for his future. She wished she never again had to do that as had made him ... at least, not

239

with Bert. But then she let in some of her despair as she told herself, *Eeh, lass, you're to think on, as that isn't sommat as you have a choice in.*

PART FOUR
The Parting
1927

23

A Moment of Joy –
a Future of Apprehension

'By, you're beautiful, me little lass! I couldn't believe me eyes when I turned the corner and you were stood there waiting for me.' Jack pulled Cissy to him. His heart swelled inside his chest and the intensity of his love for her burned through his body. 'I love you so much, Ciss.'

'I know you do, Jack, and I love you an' all. I thought as we could walk over the field by the thicket and back through the ginnel. Have some time on our own next to the beck.'

'Will Sarah be all right?'

'Aye, I've left her with Megan. Bert's on late shift, so Megan's on with her sewing, and Sarah and Billy are playing on the green. Megan's keeping an eye on them from the window.'

'Bert's never found out about her sewing, has he?'

'No, and I hope as he don't Megan's making a nice bit of money, thou knows. Oh, I hope as she gets enough soon to get out of it.'

'Aye. She's no life with Bert Armitage. There's been many a time I'd have liked to sort him out, but interfering will only make things worse for her. Still, at least we're doing sommat to help, by letting her use our parlour and Ma's old sewing machine. And she seems to get a good bit of work from Manny, the owner of the corner shop. What's she on with now?'

'It's Manny's second grandson's bar mitzvah, and Megan's making the frocks for the women-folk. It's a big order for her. I've been helping her out, though, with hems and stuff. And Manny's good. He lets the women come to the rooms above his shop for fitting and he tells no one. I took the last batch over. Jenny Ardbuckle from next door leaned over her fence, just as I was taking it down the garden. She asked a few questions, but I just said I were taking in some washing and ironing for Manny, as his wife misses me mam doing it for her. She took that as a truth. No one else has said owt. There's not a soul as knows, I'm sure.'

'Well, that's good. I don't like to think that folk believe you have to work, but if it helps Megan I'll put up with that, because if anyone does find out and drops the word into Bert's ear, she'd suffer.'

Talking about Megan, he knew, was only delaying things. He had to face what was troubling him. 'Right then, lass. Shall we make a move? It's a lovely evening, but nights are starting to draw in and it's on six now.'

'Aye, we best had, as I've brought a picnic for us. And I've brought a towel so you can swill yourself under the waterfall.'

'That sounds grand. It's been a hard day, and this heat doesn't help. Besides that, I've things on me mind to talk over with you.'

'I know. I mean ... I know as sommat's been at worrying you, love. That's why I thought up this idea.'

Jack didn't answer her, but took the basket from her and held Cissy's tiny hand in his.

As they made their way to the beck, he hoped with all his heart there was no one else with the same idea of picnicking. It was a favourite spot for the folk of Breckton, but then if there were others about, he and Cissy could make their way up Mire Hill after he'd freshened himself under the waterfall. There was always somewhere up there to be on your own.

'Jack, whatever it is that's bothering you, you can tell me of it. I might be able to help some.'

He smiled down at her and wished he could tell her all, but she'd be hurt if he did and he couldn't bear that. He had to tell her, though, of his main worry, and that would help relieve his troubled mind. But of how Mrs Harvey was with him ... well, that would have to be kept from her.

They settled on a flat, grassy area some way up the hill. There'd been one or two people out for a walk, so they'd had to climb up the hill a bit to find some privacy. Jack felt relaxed. They wouldn't be overlooked, as they'd had to climb around some rocks and walk through a clump of trees before coming to this clearing.

Cissy handed him a cheese doorstep, and then surprised him as she said, 'So, come on then – out with it. Are you on with planning to leave me for another?'

'No! I mean, don't be daft. I'd never leave you, Ciss. You're me life.'

'Jack, you scared me. I were at fun-making.'

'Aw, me little lass. Come here.' He took her in his arms. The guilt he felt crept over his whole body. Damn Laura Harvey! Damn her! 'I were on with being shocked at you saying such a thing, that's all.'

She moved in his arms and lifted her head, and her beautiful eyes misted over. He felt his heart wrench with pain. He'd never hurt her. Never!

Without either of them seeming to move, his lips were on hers. At first the kiss gave him reassurance, but then it deepened and filled him with a longing. Only Cissy could make him feel like this ... only Ciss. But then, how was it that Laura–?

Cissy's soft moan banished all doubts from his mind. The silky feel of her hair and the hardening of her nipple as he cupped her breast in his hand set up feelings within him that he couldn't deny. As he gently eased her down to lie in his arms, the feeling became an urgent need.

Cissy moved, looked up at him and giggled. 'Here?'

He couldn't answer her, but eased himself over and undid his trousers. Tracing his hand up her thigh, he felt that her legs were bare. She didn't resist as he rolled onto her and pulled her knickers aside. Her cry of joy as he filled her told him how much she wanted him, and the writhing of her body to meet him and her calling of his name told him she was reaching her special feeling.

He moved himself forward to help her, knowing that the place he needed to thrust would be better reached like that. His own feeling was akin to agony. He needed to burst into her. Her legs, wrapped around him like a vice, pulled him ever deeper into her, and his agony increased when her body stiffened and he felt her pulsate. Her cry filled his ears. 'Jack – ooh, Jack!'

An intense pleasure took over his whole being as he came into her. He couldn't speak the love that encased him. A moan shuddered forth from the very depths of him.

They lay still a while, unable to part and unable to descend from the ecstasy. When a few moments had passed and they could cope, he gently eased himself out of her.

Cissy curled up into him, her breath wafting onto his face. Her sweat mingled with his. He tasted the salt of it as he kissed every part of her face. They spoke of their love and how it had deepened, not lessened, as the time went by. But then Cissy brought them back to reality. 'I haven't me protection in place, Jack.'

She didn't seem concerned, but he felt a fear set up in him. 'But what if you get caught? Oh God! Why didn't you tell me?'

Memories of the pain they'd been through, with two lost babbies since Sarah was born, cut into him. They had vowed never to put themselves through that again, and Cissy had sought Megan's help to stop it happening. He'd no idea how Megan had known about the contraption or where she got it from, and he hadn't asked. He'd just been pleased there was a way they could make love without him having to pull himself from Cissy at the very moment he needed to thrust deeper.

'It'll be reet. It's been on three years now since I were caught last. And Megan says as it happened once as Bert took her, afore she'd had time to put her protection in, on account of him not knowing as she uses owt. And she didn't get caught. We were on with thinking that after a time it makes you so you can't have babbies.'

'Oh, lass. I hope so. I'd never be able to forgive meself. I can't bear to think of you going through all that again. I thought as I were going to lose you the last time. How soon will it be afore we'll know?'

'Look, Jack. As I see it, you've enough on your mind. Just forget it. Besides, you'll be spoiling the feelings as are still in me. Tell me what's at worrying you instead, eh?'

Ignoring the fear that lay in the pit of his stomach, he put his mind to telling her part of his worries. 'It's me job, lass. It's likely as it's going to be changing some.'

'Is that all? Why didn't you tell me afore?'

It wasn't all, although he wished to God it was. 'Well, it weren't sommat as I could say much on. I'd heard rumours, but there's been them afore, and I didn't want to worry you on account of rumours. But Mrs Harvey's had a word with me. She's no choice but to sell the stud horses. She says it's the recession, and the miners being out for so long last year, that's brought it about.'

'But what will your job be then? You will have a job, Jack?'

'Oh, aye.' He'd have a job all right, but not one that he wanted. In fact, the way Laura Harvey had said it would work out worried him deeply. 'Mrs Harvey's on with thinking of buying a motor-car, and I'm to learn to drive it and take care of it. I'm to be a chauffeur!'

'But that's grand. I can't understand why you're on with worrying. It's like a promotion. Oh, I know as you love the horses, but – a chauffeur!'

'That's not all there is to it, though, love. It'll mean me going away a lot, taking her places as she now takes the train to, and staying away nights to be on hand when she needs me to be.'

'Oh, no! Oh, Jack, I couldn't bear it. Is there no other job in the offing? There'll still be horses to be seen to. The farm horses and–'

'No, love. It's the only option she has for me. Gary's to take care of the horses as are left – thou knows, the farm horses and Mrs Harvey's own horse – and I think she's keeping another two for when her sister visits.'

Cissy was quiet for a long time, and he didn't break the silence. He held her close, trying to put out of his mind what might happen if he spent days away from her, and Laura Harvey got up to her tricks. To his shame, she was getting at him. Oh God! He held Cissy even tighter.

'No wonder you were on with worrying. Let's think on it some, eh? How long will it be afore it happens?'

'Oh, it'll be a good few months. It'll take a while to sell the stables, and then the motor-car has to be made. Them as top-drawer have are made to order.'

'Well, we've time to think on. I'll write to Mam and arrange a visit to hers. She might know of sommat going on the estate as she works for. We've not been since the beginning of the summer, and it'll be good to see her. It's been tough since she changed her job. We hardly ever see her now and it'll make a nice day out for us.'

'Eeh, me little lass. Nowt gets you down for

long. You're always at seeing another road. I feel better already. Come on, we'd best get back, as the sooner you write to Ma, the better.'

He hoped with all that was in him that his ma-in-law would know of something going. A part of him was unsettled by Laura Harvey. He didn't know how it could be so, but Mrs Harvey wouldn't let up on him, and he wasn't in a position to do anything about it.

24

The Loss of the Past Comes Home

'Megan! Oh, Megan love. Come on in. It's good to see you. It's been a while.'

Hattie's heart lurched. Megan's eyes, pitted with pain, sank into her hollow face. She thought better of asking how Megan was, at least until they were in her rooms. She had a feeling that broaching the subject would undo her friend. She'd give Megan time to compose herself. Talk about other things for a while.

'Cissy hasn't come with you this time then. Is she all right?'

'No. She's having a babby, and I'm worried over her. Like the other times, she's not carrying good. She's not expected until June, some eight weeks or more away, but she's had a couple of shows already.'

'Oh, no! I'm sorry. Please God she'll be all right

this time!' The thought crossed Hattie's mind as to how it was that the cap had let Cissy down, but her worry for Megan took over.

As soon as she opened the door to her room, she took Megan in her arms. 'Oh, Megan lass, come here.'

Safely inside Hattie's comforting embrace, Megan let out her fears. 'Oh, Hattie, Hattie...'

'It's still going on then, love?'

'Aye. It's got worse as time's gone on. There seems no pleasing him. I try, Hattie. I do try.'

'I know, love. Don't cry. Come on, sit down by the fire and warm yourself.'

She helped Megan off with her coat, and as she did so, the pain showed again in Megan's slow movements. She felt a deep anger towards Bert Armitage. 'If I could get me hands on the bastard, he'd not hit you again. I could get sommat done, Megan. I know folk...'

'No, Hattie, don't.'

'I won't, though I don't mind saying as nowt would give me more pleasure. Oh, Megan, I wish as you'd leave him.'

'I am on with a plan to, Hattie.'

'Really?'

'Aye. It were Cissy's doing. It were back end of '26, just after strike finished. Me and Ciss were on with remembering how it were when we worked at Madame Marie's, and I told Ciss as I still did me drawings. When she saw them, she said I should be doing sommat with them.'

'And you have? Oh, Megan lass, I'm so pleased! I can't believe it's more than a year since I saw you. I've been on with worrying meself sick.

Couldn't you at least write to me, love? Just to let me know how things are, with you and the lad?'

'I'm sorry, but with Ciss as she is and me sewing and everything, it's not been easy to get away. I thought meself about taking your address down this time, so as I could write. It's funny as I've never taken it down afore. I just knew where it were, and that were that. Mind, you'll not be able to write back, unless... I'll tell you what. I'll ask Ciss if I can have letters at hers, because if Bert found out about you, I'd never get to see you again, Hattie. He'd not like me having a friend. He hates me seeing Cissy, and I've never told him of you.'

'I know, but me mind would be at rest if I heard from you. Now, I'll make us a brew whilst you tell me what you've been up to.'

At the end of her telling of how Cissy had shown her drawings to Manny and he'd taken them home to his wife, and how she now sewed for Manny's family and friends, Megan said, 'Eeh, Hattie. It's like me dreams've come alive again.'

'Good for Ciss. It sounds just the thing. I'm reet glad for you, love. So what're you aiming for?'

'I keep thinking on getting a place. A shop, p'raps with some rooms above, as me and Billy could live in.'

'That'd take some money, wouldn't it, love?'

'Aye, I know, but I don't care how long as it takes. I'm not going to give up.'

'What have you got so far?'

'Six pounds... I know it isn't much, but I only have the one lot of customers. I know as I'd have a customer in Mrs Harvey at the big house, as she was a regular at Madame Marie's. She liked me designs, though she didn't know they were mine – or know me for that matter. But trouble is, with half the daily staff at the house coming from The Row, it'd be too risky and Bert'd be bound to find out. And I can't sell me stuff to the lassies around me. They can't afford to have clothes made. They get their stuff from jumbles and the tallyman.'

'Ah, but my lassies can afford to have clothes made for them. And they'd pay good money an' all. They have to get what they want from a catalogue, as they can't get it round here. Stuff comes up from London, but it's at a price. You'd have no trouble making what they like.'

'But how? I mean, how could I do it? I couldn't come here...'

'Why not? It's perfect! You could have my rooms. I'm not here often now. I've to tell you of it, but as it happens you're lucky to catch me. There's plenty of room for you and Billy, and Bert'd never find you here. You could be at making a good bit of money and have your own place in no time.'

'Oh, Hattie. I'll never be able to thank you for making me the offer, but I can't. I couldn't be bringing Billy here. He'd not settle, and though you say as it's separate, he'd see things.'

'Well, I'll help you find a place nearby then.'

'No, Hattie. It's not just Billy – it's Cissy as well. I can't leave her.'

'What about Issy? Won't she come back and look after Ciss?'

'I'm sure she would and be glad to, but there's not much room at the cottage, and Issy has a job.

They don't let her have much time off; I've not seen her for nearly two years... Mostly Ciss goes to visit her. Besides, even if she did, I'd still not leave Cissy and ... I mean – well, not until babby's born and she and babby are all right.'

'Were you going to say Jack? Oh, Megan love, you got a raw deal in the end. But listen, I know as it'll turn out for you, though I wish as you'd think on. You can't go on like this, thou knows.'

'I will think on, Hattie. You've given me some hope and, aye, I was on with thinking it'd be hard to leave Jack an' all. Though in the end it'd be for the best and it will come, as I have to leave them both. It isn't easy seeing Jack all the while. Anyroad, ta, love, but I've always known I could come to you. It goes without saying.'

'It does, Megan. I wish–'

'Let's leave it there, love. I haven't got much time. I'm to be back afore Billy and Sarah come from their lessons, and Bert'll be in on six. So tell me of your news and where it is as you are most of your time.'

'Arthur's set me up in a house. Oh, I know I said as I'd never go to him on these terms, but it's different now. I've me own place here and money enough to take care of meself if owt goes wrong, and the house is going to be mine, not Arthur's. He'll still own it, but it's to be my home. I'm on with getting it just how I want it. It's not far from Breckton, out in the country on the way into Leeds. In fact, you'd see it from the train. It stands in its own grounds. It's grand, Megan! Arthur comes to stay as often as he can. He's happier, as he never liked staying here with me, and he knows as I didn't like staying at his. I always felt as though I were his visiting prostitute. Well, I know I am in some ways, but in most ways I'm not. And now I feel I have more of a position in his life.'

'It sounds wonderful, Hattie. I'm so pleased for you.'

'Only thing is: Arthur does some sort of secret work for the Foreign Office, and that takes him away a lot. He says he could be away for months at a time in the future.'

'How does he manage? It's years since I've seen him. Can he get round, and that?'

'He's doing grand. He went off to America and was gone just on six months. They're on with pioneering some work as can remould people's faces. You'd not know him. He looks so much better; they've managed to make his eyes so as the red bit don't show, and that's made all the difference to his appearance. And his hair's grown back so that it covers where his ear was. Not that it ever bothered me how he looked, but it's given Arthur all his confidence back. I don't know owt of what he does at the Foreign Office – as I said, it's secret work – but it must be important or he'd not leave me so often. It were hard for us both when he was in America.'

'I'm glad for him. I only met him a few times, but I liked him. So, what happens here when you're away?'

'Daisy takes care of things, though she's had enough. And Phyllis has, too. I'm thinking on taking them to me house, to take care of it for me so that it's not shut down and empty when I'm not there. They've ... well, I don't know if you can

255

understand this or not, Megan, but they've become a couple.'

'A couple! How? I mean – well, that don't sound right. A couple, like...'

'I know. But it goes on. There are men as only likes other men, and women as–'

'No! It ... it sounds...'

'Look. Don't take on. It's a fact, and there's nowt as can be done about it. You just have to keep quiet about it. It's up to you whether you accept it or not. It's asking a lot, I know, but they're still the same lassies as they've always been – better in fact. They're reet happy now, and I'm not going to be looking at them any differently. They're family to me, no matter what.'

Hattie could see Megan was struggling to understand. She might have gone through hell in her marriage, but in many ways she had led a very sheltered life. Hearing about Daisy and Phyllis was bound to shock her.

'I have to be going now, Hattie. Will ... will you give Daisy me love? Tell her I'll happen see her next time, eh?'

'All right. Now don't let it go bothering you, and think on about me offer. And, love, there'll be plenty of room at me house for you as well. In fact, whilst I'm thinking on it, there's some outbuildings. I could...'

'Oh, Hattie. Thank you. Look, I'll come and see you again after Cissy's babby's born and she's coping. It'll most likely be around July time. I'll see how the land lies then, and I'll write to you in the meantime.'

After hugging and kissing each other and exchanging addresses, Megan hurried out. Hattie stood on the doorstep to watch her go. Megan looked like she was scurrying to get away as far as she could. She was most likely afraid she would bump into Daisy, and Hattie couldn't blame her. It wasn't an easy thing to come to terms with.

The concern she had for Megan was eased by knowing that she was on with a plan, and she hoped there would be a way that Megan could work for the lassies. The way they spent money on clothes, it would take her no time to reach her dream.

Megan waved as she reached the corner and then disappeared out of sight. Poor Megan. She'd to take a lot on board, from the differences in the way their lives had turned out. She knew of things other lassies of her own standing knew nothing of, and each new thing was always a shock to her.

Once back in her room, Hattie warmed herself for a few minutes in front of the fire. She had to get back to doing the accounts that she had been compiling when Megan had arrived.

It had been Arthur who had advised her to keep books on all the money that came in and went out. That way she knew what was needed to keep the place going and what she could take as her own, especially when she wasn't here as much.

Hattie had hardly given her attention back to the task when she was startled to hear someone knock on her door. She sighed. The lassies knew what she was doing and had been told not to disturb her.

Daisy opened the door and put her head round. 'Was that Megan going up the road?'

'Aye, it was. Look, Daisy love, I'm busy. And Megan'd no time to wait for you returning.'

'Oh, I'm sorry as I missed her and I know as you're busy, but I have sommat to tell you that can't wait.'

'It'd better be important, lass. I've to get on.'

'It is. Mavis has heard as Doreen's died in prison and...'

'Doreen! Well, that isn't owt as'll make me sorry. In fact, I'm glad to hear of it, as that means we're not faced with her release coming up. What happened? And how does Mavis know of it?'

'It seems as it were a bit back. Mavis's mam has a mate who's just been released from the same prison, and she told of it. She said Doreen just took ill, and that were that. But there's sommat else as well.'

'Are you sure it can't wait, Daisy love?'

'Aye, I think as you're going to want to know this, and would skin me if I kept it from you a moment longer. Mavis reckons as she saw Sally.'

'Sally? Good God! Where?'

'She ... she were on the old patch.'

'The patch! But ... well, how did Mavis know her? And what were Sally doing there? And come to think on it, what were Mavis doing there?'

'She has to go that way to visit her mam, and she said she were just crossing over by Ma Parkin's when she saw this lass sort of peeping round the corner. Like as if she didn't want to be seen and...'

'Get Mavis in here. Let her tell me of it all. Oh God! Sally, Sally!'

Her anguish was such that as soon as Mavis entered the room, Hattie blurted out, 'Tell me of this young 'un as you saw. How do you know as it were my Sally? I mean...'

Mavis's eyebrows arched in surprise.

'I'm sorry, I didn't mean to shout at you. And aye, I do look on the little lass as mine. Tell me everything as you know, lass.'

'Well, when I first saw her, I thought I were at imagining it to be Sally, because her mam Susan were in me mind. You know, with me mam just on with telling me as Doreen were dead, it'd brought back into me mind all that'd happened.'

'Did you know Susan then?'

'Aye, I did. She lived on the next estate to ours, and when her young 'un went missing, I saw her trawling the streets. Folk pointed her out, and she often had Sally with her. She had a go at me mam an' all, on account as she'd heard as I were making a living on the streets.'

'So, knowing what you knew of Susan and Sally, you're for thinking this lass might have been Sally, even though it were some nine years or so ago now?'

'Aye, she has the look of her mam. She ran off when she saw me looking at her, but I followed and called out her name. She stopped when she heard it and turned and looked at me. Then she ran off again.'

'What do you think she were doing?'

'Well, at first I thought as she were after learning the game, but I'm not so sure. She seemed as though she didn't want anyone to see her.'

An unease settled over Hattie. If it was Sally, what was she doing? Was she starting on the game? Or was she looking for... *God! She might have been*

259

looking for me! Oh, poor Sally.

'What are you thinking on, Hattie? Are you all right?'

'No, this news has upset me. I … well, I came to love that little lass, and I've missed her every day since it happened. She mustn't be allowed to go on the game. I won't let it happen. Did she look cared for?'

'No. She looked like a street urchin. I'd say as she were living rough somewhere.'

'Why didn't you bring her in? Oh God! I can't bear it!'

'To tell truth, I didn't know how things were between you and her. That's why I told Daisy first. I mean, we all knew what happened, but with how it turned out – well, it isn't spoken of much.'

'It's not your fault, Mavis. I should've been on with finding Sally this good while, but I were always counselled to leave well alone. I'll get me coat. Come on. Take me to where you saw her. I just hope as we find her afore it's too late.'

They'd been searching for over an hour when Dolly Makin – or Dolly the bag lady, as she was more widely known – came round the corner.

'Eeh, Dolly, you always come as if from no-where. How are you, love?'

'I'm at being alreet at the moment, Hattie. I've got meself a companion. I lost me Posy as thou knows, and I've been at being lonely ever since.'

Hattie had to smile. Posy was the name of Dolly's cat, but the way she spoke you would think a man had taken her down. Dolly was what was termed 'a penny short of the full shilling'. She had been part of street life for as long as Hattie could remember, and the many nooks and crannies she called her homes were in derelict buildings and under railway bridges. Each one was decked out with an oil stove and an armchair.

Dolly would call at Hattie's a couple of times in the winter for a hot meal, but she would never stay the night. She preferred her own cubbyholes and her bottle of meths. She dressed in a confusion of colours and a variety of garments all worn at the same time, and the smell of her was enough to knock you off your pins at times. For all that, she was loved, and many folk took care of her in the best way they could without her knowing it.

'So you've got yourself another cat, then?'

'No. It's a young 'un. She were on streets, so I took her in.'

'A – a young 'un?' Sally– *Oh God! Sally with Dolly!* 'Dolly, you can't look after a young 'un. Where is she?'

'I didn't say as it were a girl!'

'It's just that I'm looking for a girl, Dolly. Her name's Sally. I've got to find her, to take care of her.'

'She's mine! She don't want to be found. I'm taking care of her reet enough.'

'How will you feed her, Dolly? And keep her warm? It's only April and it gets cold and wet at night. You're used to it, but she's not. Please let me see her. Let me see as she's all right, eh?'

'I'm not giving her to you to turn her into the likes of your lassies, so go away!' This shocked

261

Hattie. For all that she was, it seemed Dolly had morals. Not that they stopped her from visiting Hattie when she was hungry.

'I'd have thought as you'd rather have another cat. After all, they can fend for themselves, get their own food and then curl up on your lap for stroking. Not a grown lass as'll take some feeding and'll be on the want all the time.'

'Aye, well, I haven't got another cat, have I?'

'I'll get you one, Dolly. I'll trade you for the lass, eh?'

'When?'

'Tomorrow. But only if you let me see the lass tonight and, if she'll come with me, you'll let me take her.'

'Aye, all right. I can trust you, Hattie, for all what you are.'

Hattie wasn't sure how to take this. She never thought to be looked down on by the likes of Dolly.

They followed Dolly for what seemed an age. She would be going along one way and then would suddenly turn and retrace her steps. Hattie tried to keep her patience, but in the end felt she had to say something.

'Dolly! Stop playing your games. We all know where your homes are. You've took most of us in them when times were hard and given us a brew. It's getting late and it's cold an' all. Just take us to Sally, there's a good lass.'

Dolly let out a bad-tempered groan and then turned down into the next ginnel that led to some tumbledown sheds. As soon as they were within a few yards of them, Hattie called out,

'Sally, Sally. It's Hattie, love. Do you remember me? Hattie as used to take care of you?'

An animal-like scream filled the air. Sally, hardly recognizable, crawled out of one of the sheds. Her scream held pain and tears as she lunged forward at Hattie. 'I hate you! I hate you...' Her fists flailed at Hattie's body.

'Sally love, no. No, I...'

Daisy moved forward and grabbed Sally. 'Hey, stop that, lass. Come on now. Hattie's come to help you.'

Sally collapsed in a heap, wretched sobs shaking her tiny body. Hattie knelt down beside her.

'Sally. It weren't my doing, love. I'll tell you of it. Oh aye, I were one as thought up the plan, but it didn't go as it should've.'

'How? How could you do that to ... to me? I thought ... I thought as you loved me.'

'I do, Sally. And I've never stopped loving you. I were let down. How much of it are you on with remembering?'

'Everything. Me Aunt Elsie would never let me forget. She told me how dirty I were, every day of me life, and how what you did to me made me dirty and – and how me actions killed me mam.'

Her sobs tore at Hattie's heart. 'How did you get here, love? Did you run away?'

'No. He kicked me out. Me so-called uncle. Me Aunt Elsie died. She had a sickness and I nursed her. She spat at me every day and told me vile things about you and me mam, and when she died me uncle showed me the door. Said he were not for keeping me no longer and I'd to make me own way. He put it in me head to come to you,

263

He … he said as I were as rotten as you are. And you are. I know that, from what you did to me.'

Sally's hands clawed at Hattie's face once more.

'Please don't, Sally.' Hattie caught hold of her hands. 'Give me a chance to put it right, love. Let me take care of you.'

'I want me mam. I want me mam. Maaaaam!'

'Oh, Sally. Sally, I'm so sorry. Please come with me, love. Please, just give me a chance.'

Sally rolled herself into a ball, a small defeated ball.

Hattie put her hands gently on either side of Sally's head and lifted her face till they were looking at each other. Her own tears streamed down her face, and her heart felt like it was breaking. To see Sally in such a state! She prayed like she'd never prayed before. *Oh God! Forgive me and be at helping me. Please help me.*

'Oh, Hattie. Make it all right. Make it as it was.'

'I will, Sally, me little love. I'll do everything I can. And I mean it when I say as I love you. I've been where you are, Sally, and I know that someone loving you is the best thing anyone can give you, and you have me, love. You have me heart for your taking. Come home with me. Please, please come home with me.'

25

Seeking a Release

Laura Harvey sat back, releasing a sigh of pleasure at the progress she'd made as she stretched out her limbs and then relaxed.

'And what is making you so pleased with yourself? Did you enjoy your ride?'

'Umm, very much, thank you, Daphne. It's a lovely morning, but it's what transpired before my ride that is pleasing me so much.'

'Oh? What have you been up to? Darling, you haven't...'

'No, but I'm making progress.'

'I wish you wouldn't, Laura. He's your groom, for heaven's sake!'

'I'm not going to marry him, you goose! I just want some fun. And it happens to be Jack Fellam that I want to have that fun with.'

'But have you thought about how unfair your actions are on him and his wife? Didn't you tell me a while back that she is pregnant?'

'Yes, she is, and he is missing out, I'd say, as she hasn't long to go. What's unfair about it? I'll make sure he enjoys it as much as me!'

'Laura, you're incorrigible!' Daphne's mock-indignation set them both laughing.

Laura stood up and walked over to the window. She was impatient to bring all this to a conclusion.

She'd played around at first, amused at Jack's embarrassment and enjoying the little gains she made. But now she was serious – really serious.

She held her stomach as a sensation of desire caused her muscles to clench at the thought of the chances she'd have, when Jack became her chauffeur. The prospect almost made up for the loss of the stud farm.

As if she'd read her thoughts, her sister said, 'How are things progressing with the sale? Charles tells me there's a serious buyer in the offing.'

'Yes, but I can't say I'm happy about it. It happens to be my rival, Smythe. It took a long time to build things up to take his place as the best stud farm in this county. Bloody miners! If they had just gone back to work when the rest of the country did, I might not have had to sell! They want too bloody much these days. Why can't they be satisfied with their lot?'

'I know, dear. They nearly brought the country to its knees, but it isn't just commodities and manufacturing that are suffering, you know. Charles is very upset about having to consider selling shares in his bank. He feels he is letting his father and grandfather down. They wouldn't allow anyone to muscle in on the family business, but the general strike has changed things and he may have no choice.'

'I'm sorry. I can be selfish in what I say sometimes. It's just that things were going so well. Anyway, darling, I have to go back to the stables. I...' Laura floundered, desperately trying to think of a plausible excuse. The feeling inside her hadn't gone away, and she wanted to try once more. Jack was weakening. She might be lucky. They could ride out together. 'I forgot to tell Fellam that Diamond stumbled. He may have hurt himself. I'd just like to make sure he is all right.'

'But I thought you said you were going to get changed and we would go shopping?'

'Yes, and I haven't changed my mind, darling. I just wouldn't be able to relax and enjoy myself unless I sort out Diamond first. I won't be long. That is, unless we have to call the vet in. I'll send a message back to you if I'm going to be delayed.'

Jack felt his stomach turn over. He looked at Gertie Ardbuckle, unable to take in what she'd come to tell him. Cissy in labour – God! The babby coming early! Cissy had at least three weeks to go, by their reckoning, and she had been all right when he'd left her this morning.

'You say as Megan's with her, Gert? Are you sure Ciss is alreet?'

'Yes, she's doing well by all accounts. Megan just asked me to let you know. She said as Ciss'd said she hoped you could get home for a while sometime today. I reckon as she's a few hours to go yet, so don't be on with worrying just now.'

'Thanks, Gertie. I'll go up to the house and see how the land lies, and ask if I can get an hour off. Tell Cissy I'll try me best.'

As Gertie left, Jack turned back to the task of grooming Diamond. His nerves had settled with Gertie telling him everything was going well, but still, he'd do his best to get home soon. He voiced his relief and happiness, talking to the horse as he brushed him down. 'Well, what d'yer think to that, lad, eh? Me Ciss is having the babby today. By, that's good news, is that. She'd not have been able to go on much longer, thou knows.' He patted Diamond's rump. 'There you go. Her Ladyship must've ridden you hard this morning; you've a reet good sweat on.'

The happiness inside him at the news smothered the guilt he'd been feeling. Nothing had happened. He'd let his guard slip, but he'd given Laura Harvey short shrift in the end. He'd get through. It was nearly over. Cissy would soon be back to normal and she'd be feeling more like helping him get his release before long. He couldn't wait. It'd been a long time since Cissy'd even felt like getting close, let alone anything more.

'Ah, there you are, Fellam.'

Jack had started to clean Diamond's saddle. He stopped and turned in surprise to see Laura Harvey back in the stable again so soon.

'I forgot to say that Diamond stumbled whilst we were out. Is he all right? Did you notice a limp or anything?'

'No, Ma'am. He seemed in fine fettle, though glad of his rest.'

Laura Harvey had moved closer to him. He felt a familiar internal twinge, alongside the rekindled guilt that caused him to burn up. He turned his attention back to the saddle.

'I'm not surprised. We really had a good time and set a good pace. Diamond was anxious to please me.'

He looked down at her. She was so close. His mouth dried. She smiled up at him.

'Is Prince ready? I thought I would accompany you on the exercising of the horses today. Lady Crompton is planning a shopping trip and I'd like to delay it for a while. I feel very restless.'

The way she said this last got at Jack even more. He needed to do something to change things. But then a part of him didn't want to...

There was a look in her eyes – a longing. She was different. She wasn't playing games. She... *Oh God! What am I thinking? Ciss ... Ciss, I'm sorry, lass.*

'You seem very distracted, Fellam. Is there something troubling you?'

Relief flooded him. She'd given him a way out.

'Aye, me lass is having her pains. It seems as babby is likely to come today, Ma'am, and I were wondering on whether I could...'

'Oh, I see.'

The expression on her face changed – he didn't think she would agree to him going! She turned from him, and there was anger in her movement.

'Very well, Fellam. Bring Prince out. I will exercise him, and then get Ardbuckle to see to the exercising of the other horses.'

By the time he brought Prince out, her mood had changed.

'I'm glad for you, Fellam. It must be a relief to think it's soon to be over, especially after what has happened in the past. Of course you can go, and I do hope it all goes well for you both.'

'Thank you, Ma'am.' The happiness in him at her decision seemed to relay itself to Prince; he became frisky and shook and nodded his head, then pulled on the rein in an eager manner. They both laughed at his antics.

'Hold him steady, Jack. I'll never mount him whilst he's like that.'

He was shocked at the use of his first name and how it sounded, in the posh tones of her voice.

'I'll tether him to the post a while and give you a lift up, Ma'am. By, the fella's lively! Steady, boy.' He took a sugar lump from his pocket and fed it to Prince. 'There you go, me lad. Quieten down now and you'll get your rein.'

With the horse tethered and Laura Harvey ready to mount, he bent down and cupped his hands. His confidence in handling the nearness of her boosted him, but then she slipped and he was forced to catch her. She was in his arms, the velvet of her jacket brushing against his cheek. It was like no other cloth he'd ever felt and it affected him in ways he didn't want to be affected. He swallowed hard. Her feet touched the ground, but she wasn't intending to move away from him any time soon and he wasn't for letting her go. After a moment she turned and released herself, but stayed close. Her eyes – her beautiful violet eyes – were looking deeply into his. He couldn't breathe. Of all the tricks she'd played, he'd never been put in the position of holding her before, and the feeling it gave him blocked out any guilt. He couldn't move his eyes from hers. He looked at her parted lips. If only he dared to kiss them...

'So, the coat of armour you wear does have holes in it then, Jack?'

She was mocking him. She'd known the effect she'd have on him and it was enough for her. Her bloody games were undoing him, turning him from his Cissy! God, he hated her.

'There aren't any holes in owt as I wear, Ma'am. I'll fetch the mounting stool.'

It was a relief to get away from the nearness of her. He felt sick in his stomach. Why was he so weak? How could he have let her have even a part of him? Because, he knew, he had given something of himself to Laura when he'd held her.

When he returned, she was already mounted.

'Call at the kitchen on your way, Fellam, and give a message to Hamilton. Tell him to tell Lady Crompton I am delayed. I will see her in about an hour. I'll expect you to be back in the stables to bed the horses down later.'

Jack watched her ride away. He heard her soft laughter, and saw the pace she set once through the gates. He allowed the anger in him to have its way as he threw the stool against the stable wall. He'd finish a few chores before he sought Gary out. He needed to calm himself and get himself ready for ... for being good enough to stand in the same room as his Cissy.

Laura Harvey rode to the southernmost part of her estate, a secluded haven surrounded by old trees, a place where no one other than the family was allowed to go. A place where she could indulge in the only activity that gave her body sexual release.

As she unsaddled Prince, she thought over what had happened and recalled the look on Jack's face. His humiliation and shame had reddened his cheeks, and his expression had changed to one of contempt and dislike. Why had she mocked him? 'You're a bloody fool!' she told herself out loud. She should have realized that he hadn't the sophistication to cope with the subtlety of her double meanings.

But then she remembered the feelings and sensations she had experienced when he'd held her, and a pulse of desire throbbed inside her with the memory.

Prince pulled on his rein and shook his head. Laura laughed at the pleasure the horse was showing at being free, and yearned to feel that freedom herself. Her desire intensified with each restricting riding garment that she removed. She looked around, although there was no need to. The place was very private, but she wanted to take everything off and ride Prince with just her loose, silk French-cut knickers on, so she needed to be sure.

The sun caressed her naked skin and enhanced her desire, dispelling any niggling voices inside her telling her this was wrong.

She led Prince over to the tree stump that she used to help her to mount and, pushing herself off it, seated herself, straddling her legs across his bare back. Slowly she trotted him round the clearing. A heat permeated her as the friction gradually stirred her senses. Her thoughts drifted to Jack. In her imagination it was him that was caressing her deeply.

Pressing her knees hard into the horse, she urged him to go faster. Her hair came loose and the cascading locks stroked her shoulders and licked the dark tips of her breasts. Sensation built on sensation, and soft moans escaped her lips. Beads of sweat trickled down her face and neck and found the deep valley of her cleavage.

'Yes ... yes!' Her breathless plea urged her body to accept the almost painful crescendo of feelings that burned her loins and gripped her whole body in a spasm of thrills that she could hardly endure.

Desperately hauling in the reins, she brought Prince to a halt. Holding herself still and taut, she allowed the thrills to pulsate through her. The agonized cry that came from her held Jack's name. As the feeling subsided, her body slumped forward and shame washed over her. Damn this loneliness! And damn this longing that she couldn't deny! A tear ran down her cheek.

She closed her eyes, then let out a deep sigh and brushed away the tears. What was the point? Thank God Daphne was here. She'd go home now. She'd tell her sister what had happened at the stable between her and Jack. Make a joke of it. She needed some light-hearted banter, something to lift her, then they would go shopping and everything would be all right again.

26

An Anguished Goodbye

When he reached home, Gertie was coming down the steps of his cottage. 'Oh, Jack. I'm reet glad to see you. Things are not going well. I'm to fetch the doctor. Megan said as you've enough to pay for him.'

Shock held him from speaking.

'Go on up, lad. You'll be a comfort to her.'

He took the stairs two at a time. 'Megan, what's to do, lass? What's happening?'

'I don't know. She's been at pushing some good while, but there's nothing to show for it and just now a lot of blood came from her. Oh, Jack.'

'Ciss, Ciss lass. Ciss...' There was no response. 'I'm sorry, lass, I'm sorry. Oh, Ciss, what have I done?'

'Don't take on so, Jack. Doctor'll not be long. He knows she's labouring; he passed this way earlier and Gertie told him. Things were going as they should've been then, but he said he'd be on with being ready to come and assist if we needed him, and we weren't to hesitate to call him.'

Cissy stirred, her body bent double in pain. Her face reddened with the effort to push, but a weakness took her and she slumped back.

'I'm here, me little lass. Everything'll be reet. I'm sorry, lass.'

'It's not ... not your fault. I love–'

Cissy's eyes closed, and her hand went limp in his.

'Oh God! No! No, Ciss.'

The door opened. 'All right, Jack. Let me get to her. Anything else happened, Megan?'

'She just had another pain. She tried to push, but...'

'Aye, I can see. She's haemorrhaged. It'll have weakened her.'

Jack had moved to the other side of the bed. He felt despair enter his heart. Cissy had lost the colour from her face. Her eyes were sinking into their sockets and her lips were blue. He heard the clinking of the doctor's bag and saw the shiny instrument he held, but couldn't register what was happening.

Megan's every nerve felt tense to the point of snapping. The babby was here and was wrapped in her arms, sleeping as if nothing was going on. It hadn't taken her long to get the babby cleaned, as she'd had everything ready for the task. Throughout the birth she'd kept her attention and her heart on what was going on across the room. Her whole being willed Cissy to respond.

'I'm trying to release the afterbirth.'

Dr Cragshaw didn't seem to be speaking to her or to Jack, and neither of them answered him. When Megan looked towards Jack, her heart jolted painfully in her chest. The ever-present guilt she felt at her feelings for him increased, causing her to bow her head and close her mind to him.

'I'll have to get it away, or I'll not be able to stop her bleeding.'

She was so worried for Cissy that she barely registered the doctor's anxious words; it seemed as though they were bouncing off her closed mind. After a few minutes he stopped massaging Cissy's stomach and took hold of her wrist. The wait seemed eternal. A tangle of fear knotted deeply inside of her. When he looked up, his face told her before he spoke that her fear was going to become a truth.

'I'm sorry...'

There was a pause, when it seemed as if nothing in the whole world moved or made a sound.

275

Dr Cragshaw broke the silence and said something, but the feeling deep inside her welled up now, and drowned out his words. A hollow moan filled her. Had she made the noise, or had it come from Jack?

She forced herself to look over at him, watching his face stretch and twist in a contortion of agony. His body slumped, and he sank to his knees and buried his head into Cissy's still breast.

His pain entered Megan, and intensified her own anguish. The doctor spoke again. 'Megan. Megan, come on now, lass.'

Her mouth opened and closed, but nothing came out. She could only shake her head.

'I know, lass, I know. Have you seen to babby? Good. Put her in the cot for a moment while I clean myself up, and then I'll take her downstairs so I can have a look at her.' He turned towards the dresser where the bucket of hot water stood. There was still some left in it, and he plunged his hands in, then looked back at her as if a thought had struck him. 'Do you feel up to fetching Father O'Malley? If we get him here quickly, he can give Cissy a blessing and baptize babby.'

She nodded. She understood his urgency, as it was said the body didn't give up its soul for some hours, and its anointing would send that soul straight to heaven. She wanted that for Cissy.

The brightness of the outside world shocked her. What time was it? She hadn't counted the hours. The light in Cissy's bedroom was such that she'd had to light the mantles, but then the small window in that room never allowed much light to enter.

She looked over at the gathering of women in the lane. They were all there: the women from The Row and those from the tied cottages. Gertie would have put the word round that things weren't going right.

The group moved towards her as she went down the steps. 'Will one of you go for Father O'Malley? Tell him to come as quick as he can.'

'Oh, no! Is it Cissy or babby?'

'It's Cissy, Jenny. She's...'

'Don't stand there asking questions, lass.' Gertie stepped forward and took hold of Jenny's arm. 'Get yourself away. You're youngest and'll be quickest. Go on now.' She turned to Megan. 'Is there no hope, lass?'

'She ... she's gone.'

Their gasp cut through her.

'Gone? Eeh, no! No! Oh, dear God, why? Poor Jack. Is babby all right, Megan?'

'I don't know, Gertie. She seems all right, but...'

'Come on, lass. I'll come in with you. You'll need a hand.'

It was quiet in the cottage, quiet and unreal. Even the babby, lying on the kitchen table being examined, was quiet. Neither Megan nor Gertie spoke, though questions of all kinds were popping in and out of Megan's head. It was a relief when the doctor finally stood up straight and put his stethoscope back in his pocket.

'Is she all right, Doctor?'

He didn't answer, but stood pulling at his lips with a forefinger and thumb on either side of his mouth. After a moment he shook his head.

'Not totally, I'm afraid, Megan. She's not in any

277

danger, but things are not right with her.'

She knew that already. Inside her, she'd known. It was the babby's face – it'd seemed sort of flat. And the shape of her eyes had reminded her of the pictures of the Chinese boys and girls in Billy's school book. He'd brought it home once. It was all about other countries and the people who lived there.

'What's to do? Is she faring badly, Doctor?' Gertie asked.

'No. Not ill as such. Anyway, we'll not worry ourselves over it now. We'll talk about it later. Let's take her up to Jack, shall we?'

They followed him up the stairs and stood just inside the door. The gentle pressure of Gertie's hand on her arm steadied Megan, but it didn't stop the strange feeling that flooded her body. She felt such a sense of disbelief; it was as if none of the things that were happening seemed connected to her.

'You've another little girl, Jack,' Dr Cragshaw said.

Gertie went over to Jack and patted his shoulder. 'Jack lad, I'm sorry. Poor Ciss. What can I say?'

Jack looked up at Gertie, his face wet with tears. He made no sound, but nodded his head.

Megan closed her eyes. It was all too much to bear. A knock at the door made her jump, and Father O'Malley entered the room. The strange feeling that had taken her increased. She couldn't have said in detail what happened after that. The anointing, the baptism – it all seemed to go on without her, though she knew she'd acted as god-mother. Her mind had left her body doing things and travelled its own road back in time. Pictures of Cissy as a young 'un of just thirteen came to her mind, her sweet and infectious giggle drifting into the space around her.

Cissy couldn't be gone – she couldn't! *Ciss … oh, Ciss*. Tears streamed down Megan's face, wetting her neck and breast, and yet she wasn't crying. Not crying the kind of tears that would help. Instead her body was emptying itself, leaving her stranded and alone – more alone than she had ever felt in her life.

The terrible sound of Jack's sobs penetrated her thoughts. The rituals were over. She looked over to him. He was standing, but it seemed his large frame had shrunk with the weight of his grief. Gertie and Dr Cragshaw were supporting him.

The ache of the love that her soul held for Jack almost moved her body, but she stayed still. She knew her soul would betray her if she went to him. Knew, too, a moment of intense guilt. She looked over at Cissy. Cissy's beauty and goodness were locked in her still and waxen face. She silently begged her beloved friend for her forgiveness.

'Megan.' Dr Cragshaw held her gently by the shoulder and spoke to her in whispered tones. 'Take babby downstairs. Father O'Malley will help me to bring the cot down. She'll be better in the kitchen.'

Before he left, the priest promised to call in on the undertakers and to make sure Jenny knew to keep Billy and Sarah away until Megan could see to them later. When he'd gone, Megan allowed herself some time to address her own worries. Her fingers found the corner of her pinny and she twisted it in her hands. 'Doctor, what's to do about babby? She'll need feeding and ... and caring for.' She willed him to understand. As Cissy's best friend, it would be natural for her to take the babby and care for it, but Bert wouldn't stand for it.

'Don't worry yourself on that score. I know what's in your heart, and I know it isn't possible for you to do what you'd like to.' He snapped his case shut. 'If she's fretful in the next hour or so, give her some boiled water with a little sugar in it. I'll call in on Franny Bradshaw and arrange for a supply of breast-milk for the first few weeks.'

The relief that washed over Megan was eclipsed by his next words. 'You've seen how things look for the babby, haven't you?'

'You mean her eyes and that?' Suddenly it dawned on her – the slanted eyes and the flat features. 'Oh, no! Oh, poor little soul! She's ... she's a Mongol!'

'Aye, I'm almost certain she is. The signs are all there.' He heaved a huge sigh. 'Anyway, like I said, Franny'll help, though I don't think she will take the babby in. Wet nurses can be funny about putting these children to their breasts. That wouldn't be Franny's feelings, but she'd have to consider the feelings of the other mothers she is nursing for, especially those of the gentry.'

'But what'll become of babby, Doctor?'

'I don't know. Like I said, we'll cross that bridge later. I know of a couple of places that take them, but...'

The door between the kitchen and the stairs opened, and Jack and Gertie came through. Jack held himself together, though the effort of doing so was showing in the strain on his face. Gertie would've had a hand in helping him. She was kindly, was Gertie, and always seemed to know the best thing to do. She was already busying herself filling a bowl with hot water from the pan on the stove.

Jack put his hand out to shake the doctor's. The doctor took hold of it and held it in both of his. 'I'm going to miss her, Jack. She were a lovely lass. Everyone loved her. I wish I could've done more. I'm sorry, man.'

'You did all you could, I know that, Doctor.'

'I did, Jack, I did, but it's heartbreaking for me when I fail. I've had to learn a hard lesson over the years: I can't change God's will.' He took out a large hanky and blew his nose loudly. 'Well, I've to finish my rounds – not that I feel like it, but it has to be done. I'll call up at the house and let them know what's happened. I'll tell them not to expect you back to work for a few days. They'll understand, and Father O'Malley said he'll...'

Megan left them talking and went upstairs to help Gertie. She didn't want to find herself alone with Jack.

Gertie had started to wash Cissy's body, and the sight nearly undid her. 'Oh, Ciss! Ciss...'

'Come on, love, get yourself busy. Let's make her look reet bonny, eh, lass? Get her best outfit out. Go on now.'

When they'd finished, Cissy did look bonny, dressed in the pale-blue Sunday-best frock Megan had made for her just last year. It wouldn't fasten up at the back, but as Gertie said, 'They'll not notice that in heaven.'

Jack sat at the table in the kitchen. He hadn't stirred from the same position Megan'd seen him in each time she'd come down the stairs to refill the bowl. The task of laying Cissy out was done, and she had to face talking to him.

'We're all done, Jack. Shall I put the kettle on and make a pot of tea?'

He didn't move or acknowledge that she'd spoken to him.

'He could do with sommat stronger than tea. I'll not be a minute, Megan. Put kettle on and make a pot, and I'll fetch a drop o' whisky to go with it.'

'Right, Gertie.' Her voice sounded normal, but she felt anything but. She bustled around the kitchen, not really aware of what she was doing. Jack's desperation was so agonizing for her to bear. The laying out of Cissy's unresponsive body had made her come to terms with the fact that Cissy had gone, but she could find no words to say, no comforting gestures to make towards Jack.

The bubbling of the boiling kettle broke the silence. The act of making the tea helped her to gain some self-control, and she felt able to speak at last.

'I'll be fetching Sarah after a while, Jack. Do you want me to bring her here or take her home with me, until after doctor's been back?'

'Oh God, Megan, how will I tell Sarah? How am I going to make her understand? She worshipped her mam.'

'I don't know. I don't know how you'll cope with everything. I – I'm sorry, Jack. I just can't think of not having Ciss. She were everything to

282

us, weren't she?'

'Aw, lass.' His arms enclosed her, and his tears dampened her hair. 'How could such a thing happen? Our Ciss ... oh God!'

Her heart drummed a feeling of anguish around her body that threatened to engulf her. Her throat constricted. Her tears fell onto his shirt as her sobs joined Jack's, and their bodies – closely entwined – shook with despair.

Suddenly she felt a new strength enter her. She must keep her sadness locked away; she had to be strong for him. She'd had plenty of practice at dealing with bad times, and she could cope. She would concentrate on Jack's needs.

'Sit yourself down, Jack. I'll help you all I can. I'll fetch Sarah from Jenny's and give her some tea, and I'll bring her over when I've Bert off on his nightshift. I'll be with you when you tell her.'

'Eeh, Megan, it's good to know as I have you by me, lass.'

Jack sat down and wiped his face with his hanky.

Gertie came in at that moment. 'I'm back, Megan. Have you brewed, lass? Oh, good. Pour tea out and I'll get some tumblers down for whisky. We'll all feel better after a nip.'

Jack drank his whisky down in one go, but put his hand up in refusal of a refill. 'I'll just have me brew now, thanks, Gertie.'

After a couple of sips, he picked up his baccy tin from the table next to him. His hands shook as he rolled a cigarette and lit it. After a few deep intakes of smoke, he threw the nub-end into the back of the grate, went over to the cot and peered down at the tiny form.

The babby stirred. One little hand broke free from the shawl and stretched out to him, and her tiny eyes looked towards him. Jack took her hand and rubbed his thumb along her fingers, his other hand brushing the tuft of dark hair from her forehead.

Megan looked over at Gertie. Gertie nodded and smiled. She must have been worrying, too. Things were bad, but they would have been twice as bad if Jack had taken against the babby.

27

A Difficult Choice

The smell of freshly lit tobacco assaulted Megan's nostrils as she opened the door to her cottage. Her stomach knotted with apprehension. The sound of Bert's chair scraping on the stone floor as he rose grated on her frayed nerves.

'Where've you bloody been till now? It's nigh on half-past four, and no bloody tea ready. I'm on shift while six, woman.'

'Aye, I know – tea'll not take me long. I left stew on side, simmering. I've only to pull damper out to have it boiling. You'll not be late.'

As Megan walked past Bert, she held herself ready. The expected blow didn't come, but she hoped her relief wouldn't be short-lived. From one of the shelves of the cupboard next to the grate she took down a clean pinny. The thought of the other one in her bag, red with Cissy's blood, made her pause a moment to compose herself.

'You've been seeing to Cissy, haven't you? Huh? And don't bother lying about it. I got up earlier to use lav, and Mrs Braithwaite said as Ciss were labouring.'

'I had to, Bert. There was no one else as could. I–'

'No one else. No one else! I've bloody told you afore what folks say, haven't I? You can't drop any of your own, but you can see to others. You're a laughing stock, and you're making me one an' all.'

'I'm not, and that's not what's said. That's all in your head. Lassies round here are grateful for me help, and as for me not having me belly up, like rest of them every year, they know as I were damaged when I had our Billy. Aye, and they know whose fault that were an' all. Don't, Bert! I – I didn't mean...'

Bert yanked her round by her hair. He'd pounced so quickly that she'd had no time to stave off the blow. The back of his hand stung the side of her face, and her body reeled backwards. The edge of the table jarred into her. Her breath caught in her lungs.

'You're no proper wife, d'yer hear me? Going all over seeing to others, whilst your own man has no dinner or snap ready. How did I ever saddle meself with you?'

He grabbed the bib of her pinny and pulled her roughly towards him. When she looked into his eyes, the darkness of them seemed to be pulling her into the blackness of his soul.

'Womenfolk might let you think as what you tell them is reet, but does thee know what they bloody well tell their men? Does thee know what talk at pit is? That you turn your back on me and that I've to beat it out of you, and they're not wrong, are they?'

He raised his fist again, but she was ready for him. She placed her hands on his chest and pushed forward with all her might. As he staggered back she told him, 'Cissy died!'

The statement hung in the air between them. He stared at her, his mouth slack and his head shaking in disbelief. 'What? What did you say?'

'Cissy's dead! She lost too much blood. Babby were wrong-ways up, she couldn't shift it, and I couldn't help her. Doctor cut babby free. He cut Cissy with a pair o' scissors. He said as how sommat or other had ruptured.'

The words tumbled from Megan and, once they were released, her throat constricted and her body shook. She could no longer control the sobs that racked her. She wouldn't have cared if Bert had tried to pummel her to death with his bare fists, her grief was such that life didn't seem worth living anyway, but he didn't attempt to hit her again.

'Eeh, lass, I'm sorry. I didn't know as you'd been through that. I thought as you were on with defying me again.'

'It's all right. Sit down and I'll get your dinner.'

She wiped her face on her pinny and looked over at Bert. She wished it was her that had gone. It was getting harder and harder to endure his sudden changes of mood, and now with no Cissy... No, she'd not think about the future just yet. She'd to get on with doing for Bert. She didn't want him to get angry again.

Her actions were automatic as she put the kettle on the grate plate and pulled the damper out. The fire jumped into life, and the stew started to bubble. There was a nice fresh loaf in the pantry. She had made up the dough the night before, left it to prove in the bottom oven and cooked it off before Bert had come in from his shift this morning. She got it out, took it from the muslin cloth that kept it fresh, cut thick doorsteps and spread them with mucky fat. When his snap tin was full, she piled a plate high with the rest and passed him a bowl of stew. He hadn't spoken while she'd carried out these tasks, but after a couple of mouthfuls of stew he surprised her by saying, 'Come on, sit yourself down, lass, and get some of this stew into you. You look done in.'

She did as he bid her. She didn't feel like eating, but it was better to pretend than to protest. They ate in silence for a while, and the knot of fear in her stomach began to release its hold on her.

'She was all right, was Cissy, thou knows, Megan. You're going to miss her.'

'Aye.' She could say no more; she didn't want to break again. She stood up. 'I've to go over to Jenny's to fetch our Billy and young Sarah. She's taken care of them since they left school earlier. You won't say owt to Sarah, will you, Bert? Cos she doesn't know as yet.'

'No, I'll not say nowt. Poor little lass, eh? Eeh, it's sad news, sad news. Don't be long. I'd like some time with you afore I go on shift.'

As she walked, she pondered on how Bert had

taken the news. It was like living with two different people: the one she hated, and the other who touched something in her.

'Megan...'

Helen Bray, a woman who lived three doors down, called her over to her gate.

'I'm sorry to the heart of me to hear of Cissy's passing, Megan. I don't know what to say. Shocked everybody, it has. Anyroad, love, I'll not keep you talking, just to say as Jenny said to tell you she's taken young 'uns round to her mam's. She said with her cottage being next door to Jack's, she'd not be able to stop Sarah from going round.'

'Thanks, Helen. I hope you don't mind if I get on. I've to be back quick.'

Helen just nodded at her. It was a knowing nod, and it ground a humiliation into her.

She hadn't far to go. Jenny's mam's cottage was just two rows away from her own, with only cobbled paths separating the rows. She glanced down the lane opposite as she walked past, her eyes resting on Cissy's cottage. It didn't look any different. Somehow she'd expected it to.

As she rounded the corner, Sarah broke free from Jenny and flung herself at her. 'Oh, Aunty Megan, me mam isn't dead, is she?'

Large innocent blue eyes looked up at her, and the stains of recently shed tears were washed away as fresh ones streamed down the little face. Megan pressed Sarah against her waist and looked over at Jenny.

'Young Graham Pike told her. He said as how he'd heard Gertie tell Manny at corner shop.'

Jenny shrugged, closed her eyes and bit on her top lip. Her head shook from side to side. 'Eeh, Megan.'

A proud claim from Billy interrupted them. 'I hit him, Mam – knocked him off his feet, I did. And I told him as his tongue'd split, with the lies as he tells. It'll not be right, Sarah. Me mam'll tell you.'

Megan didn't answer the appealing looks in their upturned faces, nor did she go for Billy as she would normally have done when he boasted of fighting. Instead, she bent down and lifted Sarah up. 'Come on, love. I'll take you to your dad.'

Sarah clung to her neck, her wretched sobs tearing at Megan's heart. She was right to take her home. Right now she needed her dad – needed to be told by him that her mam had gone – but the decision wasn't without its worry.

'Billy, be a good lad and run and tell your dad as I have to take Sarah straight home. Tell him she's upset. He'll know what's happened. Tell him I'll not be more than a few minutes.'

Billy went to protest, but there was something about the way everyone was acting that stopped him. Was it true then? Was Aunty Cissy really dead? His mam hadn't said different. He thought about what being dead meant, and his mind presented him with a picture of Graham Pike's pet rabbit. He'd made that dead. A smile lit up his face at the memory. He walked a few paces in front of Megan, but put no particular hurry into his steps.

He hated Pikey. He'd especially hated him that day, because he'd been round to Sarah's to play and they'd left him out of the game. He'd made Pikey pay, though. He stole his pet rabbit from its hutch and bashed its head against the wall. By, he could still hear the crunch it'd made. He'd wanted to tell Sarah about it – usually he shared everything with her – but she'd have gone mad. He didn't understand girls sometimes. Ha! Pikey's face was a picture when he found out his rabbit was dead. Billy chuckled to himself at the memory.

28

The Wrath of Not Toeing the Line

Megan stood on the steps of Cissy's cottage and glanced up the lane. A thread of worry wove into her sorrow. It was nearly five-thirty and she should have gone home already. But how could she have left Jack and Sarah whilst the undertakers were putting Cissy in her coffin? She hoped, with all that was in her, that Bert would understand.

An uncanny quiet had settled all around. The womenfolk had gathered at the top end of the lane ready to follow Cissy. They made no sound.

Into the silence came the grating noise of wood sliding along wood, bringing her attention back to the cart and the long, thin wooden box. She held herself together as the undertaker coaxed the horses and the cart departed, taking Cissy away to lie in the church.

It had surprised her when Jack had made that decision, but like he'd said, it was better for

Sarah, and Cissy loved the church. She wouldn't be alone. She and the womenfolk would take turns keeping watch over her when Jack couldn't be there.

The sound of the horses' hooves on the cobbles, and the steel rim of the wheels rolling over the stones, echoed around her. A cry from one of the women broke the spell that held her. It brought into focus the sounds of the lane: the birds singing, the trees rustling and a gate swinging in the wind. Normal sounds that were part of a normal day, but today wasn't normal. Would she ever again have a normal day?

Without warning, Bert's crude, threatening voice cut through the air. 'You bloody can't wait to fill her shoes, can you? After I told you to come home afore I were to leave, an' all! Get yourself home and I'll deal with you in the morning.'

Megan's breath caught deep in her lungs. She held her burning face cupped in her hands. *Oh God. Oh God...*

'Leave it, Armitage.' Jack's voice held a desolate note.

Bert didn't respond. His glare burned through Megan, before he turned and walked away in the direction of the mine.

Nobody moved until he'd rounded the corner, but once he was out of sight, the women's pitying gaze came to rest on her. Her humiliation increased. She wanted to hide away, to disappear and for none of it to have happened. She dropped her head into her hands and ran towards the gate.

Jenny broke away from the group of women following Cissy and caught hold of her. 'Come

291

on, Megan. Don't worry – he'll have forgotten about it by morning. You've had a long day, lass.'

She slumped into Jenny's arms.

'Aye, come on, lass.' A bigger pair of arms took hold of her and she looked up into Gertie's kind eyes. 'Run on ahead, Jenny, and get tea brewed. I'll bring her along.'

As Jenny did as she was bid, Gertie turned and called back to Jack, 'She'll be reet. Me and Jenny'll take care of her.'

Megan looked back at Jack. What would he think? Please, God, don't let him have taken in what Bert'd said. She couldn't bear the thought of him suspecting her feelings for him. It would be a betrayal of Cissy.

The church clock had woken Megan every hour, and this time it struck five times. She didn't want to open her eyes and let in the day, but the memory of Bert's attack came to her and shame filled her body. But then, what did it all matter, compared to losing Cissy? *Oh, Ciss... Ciss!*

If only she could go to Hattie – she'd be able to help. The tears welled up and filled her eyes. She wiped them away with the back of her hand. *Come on, lass, don't start. Get up out of it and get yourself busy. Don't give in.*

Flinging the grey woollen blanket back, Megan swung her legs out of bed. Her feet welcomed the feel of the cool boards. The thought came to her that she must finish the rag rug she was making before winter, as the boards wouldn't be so welcoming then. She shook her head. It was as if her mind wasn't right: thinking of rag rugs when she had so much on her plate, and Bert home in just under an hour! She would be better served making sure everything was just right, so as not to cause him to lose his temper, because if he did, he'd harp back on what had gone on, and that would make him worse. She would try to say she was sorry, but it would depend on his mood as to whether he accepted her apology. She should've thought on and fetched Gertie to stay with Jack and Sarah. Bert had asked her to come home and be with him before he went off on his shift. Cissy's death had been a shock to him, too. He would most likely think she had put Jack's needs before his. Oh God! This thought increased her fear, because Bert had a suspicion in him where Jack was concerned, and he'd had it for as long as she could remember.

After doing all the chores she'd to do before Bert came in, dressing herself didn't take long. Even on a warm morning such as this, washing in cold water was not something to dawdle over. She wouldn't let Bert wash in cold water, though, as that would be a starting point for him.

It didn't take long to rekindle the fire, either. She had banked it up before going to bed, and the hob was still hot. On the back of it was the large iron pot that she kept topped up with water so that Bert always had enough for his wash. She manoeuvred it further towards the middle, to ensure it was piping hot – hot enough so that she could add some cold to it. Bert would have plenty for swilling himself then.

As soon as it started bubbling, she moved it to the back of the hob and swung the grate plate with the full kettle on it over the heart of the fire. Fetching down a heavy iron frying pan from the top shelf, she melted some fat and fried off some sliced potatoes. She had just put them on the side to keep hot when the door was flung open.

'Huh! I s'pose as you thought to soften me up by feeding me as soon as I come in, eh? Well, you bloody well thought wrong! I've had all night to think on how you took no notice of me telling you to keep away from that big-headed sod! Aye, I know he's lost Cissy and, much as I hate him, I feel sorry for him, but you chose to do what others could've done for him, rather than come home to me. Me needs are nowt to you, Megan. Nowt! Well, I'm gonna change that once and for all. When I'm done with you, you'll not go against me wishes again, I can tell you.'

Terror gripped her heart. Bert unbuckled his belt and pulled its length from around his waist. 'No, Bert. No! Not that ... please, Bert. I can't take it. I can't!'

Fear weakened her legs and caused her body to tremble. She groped behind her for the table edge. Finding it, she steadied herself.

'Don't do it. Please, Bert, please don't.' She edged round the table, trying to put something between them.

Her pleas did nothing to stop Bert's snake-like advance. His body curved around the corner of the table, his belt a serpent's tongue snapping in the palm of his hand. With this sound came the knowledge that she would have to accept her fate, and her trembling came to a halt. He was so near to her that she could smell stale smoke, coal dust and the sweat of a night's labour. Bile retched into her throat. She swallowed hard, her voice croaking with the effect of the stinging aftermath of the vile-tasting acid. 'I'll not go against you again, I promise. I – I've thought on and know as me action were wrong. I just wasn't thinking straight when I did it.'

The belt whipped past her face and cracked on the table.

'Aye, you're reet, Megan. You'll not go against me.' His voice lowered until it was no more than a whisper. His tongue slid over his lips, leaving them wet and shiny. 'Come here.' He dropped his belt and took hold of her, pulling her against his body. She could feel his arousal.

Her disgust at how his need heightened when he beat her never lessened, but this time he hadn't actually hit her. Was the thought of doing so enough to arouse him? His groping of her gave her the knowledge that it was.

But the relief this gave her soon left her and a panic set up inside her as she thought, *My protection! I haven't got my protection in place!*

'Bert, I – I've everything ready for your wash, and I've fried off some tatties. Have them first, love.' She kept her voice soft and let her breath fan his ear. 'Then, after I get Billy off to his lessons, I'll come up to you, eh? It'll be good.'

He pulled his head back from her, eyes smouldering with renewed anger. 'Does you want belt first? Is that what you want, eh? Does you have to push me as far as I'll go, eh?'

'No! No, I just thought – well, Billy might come down and...'

Bert pushed himself forward, holding her body as if in a vice between him and the table edge. 'Well, it'll be more of a lesson for the lad than he'll get down that bloody church hall then, won't it?'

She didn't answer.

Bert gave a small laugh and then sunk his mouth into her neck. She felt the wetness and then a deep, bruising sucking, as his hands fumbled with his trouser buttons.

'No. No!' She pushed with all her might, then lifted her legs and kicked him away.

'You bitch. You bloody cock-teasing bitch!'

The back of his hand stung her face and sent her body reeling backwards. She landed on the table, legs bent over the edge. Bert forced them open, pinning her down with his body. He pulled the elasticated leg of her knickers aside, the damp hardness of him brushing the top of her leg. She could do nothing.

The harshness of the shove that pushed him deep into her rasped her back against the wooden tabletop. Her moan of pain joined his moan of pleasure.

'That's reet, lass, thou knows thou likes it. Well, you've got it now, so just relax. Ooh, Megan, lass.'

The coarse material of his work trousers chafed the insides of her thighs and the pain in her back increased with every thrust, as did her anguish.

'Stop, please stop, you're hurting me. No! Bert, don't...'

His dirty droplets of sweat spattered her frock as his thick moans mingled with her cries of pain.

'Good girl. I knows as you likes it rough.'

She sank into despair. Tears flooded from her, some leaving their salty taste in her mouth and others trickling like beads of ice into her ears. A blackness that promised peace loomed in the distance, and she wanted to enter its depth. It was her own wretched cry that penetrated the blackness and drew her back. 'Oh God! Oh God, help me!'

The cry triggered the end. His body became rigid, his face contorted with agonized pleasure. A sound like an injured animal erupted from him and a warm wetness entered her. Her mind screamed, *Please, please don't let me be caught!* When his body slumped, the weight of him was unbearable.

There was a silence before she felt the relief of his weight being released from her as he shifted off her. 'You enjoyed that, didn't you, love? You like to put up a fight, don't you? It seems to make it better for you. Well, I'm pleased an' all. Come here.' He pulled her up, took her into his arms and held her close. There was a small comfort for her body in the warmth of him, but no peace for her mind.

His hand stroked her hair. 'Megan, we could go along together all right, couldn't we? You only have to think on some. You can have it rough when you like, but there's no need to rile me so as I do sommat as I regret, is there?'

She couldn't answer him.

He pulled away from her. 'Don't think, though, Megan, as that's changed owt. It were good – I'll give you that – but I still want you to think on and put me needs first, not everybody else's.'

'I will, Bert. I told you I'd been on with thinking about me actions afore you came in.'

He held her close again. 'Eeh, Megan. You were moaning with pleasure all the while I were doing you. I liked that, love.' He tapped her on the bottom. 'Get yourself cleaned up, lass. I still might have you come up to me, when lad's away.' He winked, picked up his baccy tin and went out of the door.

Megan eased herself across the kitchen, holding onto a chair to steady herself. She was near the sink when the room began to spin and her body fell forward onto it. The edge dug into her ribs, and she could only watch as red streaks of blood from her nose ran down the white surface and disappeared down the plughole. Nausea washed over her. Grabbing the bucket of cold water that stood on the side of the sink, she tilted it so that it splashed over her head. It went some way to clearing her senses, and her only thought now was to get Bert away to his bed so that she could see to herself. Maybe she'd be in time.

His water was all ready for him by the time he came back in. The smug expression hadn't left his face. She managed a smile that belied the hate she felt.

He didn't speak whilst he went about the business of washing, and only grunted something about the tatties being good, while he ate them. She poured him a second mug of tea.

'Will you take it up with you?'

'Aye, I will. I were going to have another smoke, but I feel reet done in. I'll get forty winks whilst you get Billy off, but come up after, eh?' His face

298

took on the same smug expression. 'I've some more in me for you, Megan.'

His smile told her she was forgiven. She wanted to cry out that she'd done nothing that required forgiveness and that he should go on his bended knee to her, but she just smiled back at him.

After Bert'd gone up, she stood a moment and listened for the sounds of him settling. When all was quiet, she dragged a chair to the stairs door and wedged it under the handle. Billy would be stirring soon, and if he tried the door he'd know she was washing herself. He'd wait till she finished.

She lowered the bucket onto the floor, peeled off her coal-black knickers and stood astride the bucket. She douched herself, while praying she was in time to wash out his seed before it planted itself firmly in her.

This done, she went to the bottom cupboard of the dresser and fumbled amongst the clean cotton towels for her cap. Once it was in place, she saw to her other wounds and prepared herself to get Billy up for his lessons.

Billy couldn't look at his mam. He didn't want to see how hurt she was. It was a game he played: if he pretended he knew nothing, then there was nothing to know. But he did know, and he felt confused. The sound of his dad having a go at his mam had woken him earlier, and he'd crept down the stairs and opened the door just enough to peep through. It'd been a shock to see his dad going at his mam like the dogs in the lane did at the bitches. It'd scared him some, as his mam hadn't liked it and was calling out to his dad, begging him to stop. He'd gone back to bed to try to pretend it wasn't happening.

He and Tommy Braithwaite had watched a couple of dogs once. Tommy had told him babbies were made like that, and when he was older he'd be doing it to some lass. The tale had made him feel funny and had made his willy go hard, like it did when he played with it or he needed to pee badly. Not that he was worried over his mam having a babby, as he'd heard his dad say she couldn't drop any more young 'uns.

At times he wasn't sure whether he minded his mam getting a good belting from his dad. It did make him feel a kind of hurt inside, but it was mixed up with his anger. Cos, like his dad said, it was his mam's fault that he got so mad and that must be right, as his mam always said she was sorry. *And another thing: if I'm around when me dad gets mad, then I get a belting as well and that's me mam's fault, an' all!*

'Right, son. Have you got your snap tin, then?'

'Aye. Will I call in and get Sarah, Mam?'

'Well, it won't do any harm, though she might not be up to going. Look after her, if she does go with you, Billy. She's very sad at losing her mam.'

Billy pulled on his boots and grabbed his snap tin. He'd to get out before his mam talked some more about his Aunty Cissy dying.

'Ta-ra, Mam. Eeh, gerroff!'

His mam had tried to kiss him, but Billy still felt cross at her for making his dad mad. He had to get out as fast as he could.

Once outside, he felt sorry. He decided to go

back and give her a kiss, but as he turned to go back in, his mam was just going through the door that led to the stairs. He'd not bother to call out to her.

29

A Decision for Change

'Shift up, Megan, you're taking up all the step.'

'Me? I like that! There's not much room for me, as it is.' Megan dug a finger into Issy's large frame, but squashed herself up some more nonetheless. She didn't mind. Issy's soft body was comforting, and having her close made up some for the loss of Cissy.

'You're cheery the day, Megan. Did Bert pop his clogs in the night?'

Megan laughed out loud.

'No, though I don't mind saying as I've wished many a time as he would. And then at other times I wouldn't wish him any harm. But I'm feeling glad because me bleeding started this morning and I've been at worrying.'

'I s'pose, how you're fixed, you'd have that worry every month.'

'No. If I'm ready for him it's all right, because I have ways of preventing owt happening. Mind, Bert don't know of it. If he did he'd go mad, so say nowt about it in his company.'

'Huh! Can you see me discussing having babbies

301

with *him?* In fact, I'd not talk to him about owt as I could think on. Eeh, Megan lass, you took on sommat there. I always knew as he were a bad 'un, but he seemed that stuck on having you, I thought he'd change when he got you.'

'Me too, but I should've known. The signs were all there. Anyroad, I've to get on with it. Is Bella all right?'

'Aye, she's sleeping. It were a lovely thought of Jack's, to remember Ciss'd wanted to use me name for the babby. I remember telling her once a long time ago that me mam used to call me Bella, and that Issy were sommat as started when I got older. There's only priests and folk such as that as've ever called me Isabella.'

'It's a lovely name.'

'I wonder how things will turn out with little Bella? In the future, I mean, as Doctor were on with saying as Mongol children don't live long lives. Oh, Megan. We've a lot to face.'

'Is there no cure?'

'No. Doctor says not a lot is known of the condition, and that they call it Mongolism because those born with it have features resembling folk as live in Mongolia, wherever that is. He says she's physically all right as far as he can tell, but he could say nothing of her future.'

'Well, I can. She'll be very happy. They are, thou knows. She'll be very much loved and cared for, and she has an adoring sister and dad, not to mention Granny and Aunty Megan. It'll be reet. We'll take it a step at a time, eh?'

'Aye. One day at a time. It's the only way to get through. I can't believe it's on three weeks since the funeral. It were a good turnout, weren't it, Megan?'

She nodded. They sat in silence for a while, but then Megan saw Issy wipe away a tear.

'Are you all right, Issy?'

'No, lass. I'm going to be a long time getting reet, I'm afraid.'

'I know, love.'

'I were thinking what a hard time I had getting caught for a babby. I were on with being in my thirty-second year when Cissy were born, but I lost a few after that. Funny how Ciss suffered in that way an' all. Thou knows, lass, maybe if Ciss had known how to stop getting caught, she'd be here today.'

'Aye.'

They fell silent again. Megan didn't want to tell her that Cissy *had* known. She'd wondered her-self how it was that Cissy had got caught. She'd had a chance to ask her a couple of times, but had never done so. It was always painful to talk of such things with Cissy.

The sound of a motor-car coming towards them from the direction of the big house broke into their silence. The car was the one that had been sent to bring Issy from her home the day after Cissy had died, and belonged to Mrs Harvey's sister.

'Well, would you credit it? Me chauffeur's come to pick me up again.'

They both laughed at this and it lifted their spirits a little, but Megan's laugh was cut short by the look Mrs Harvey gave her as the car passed by. It made her feel uncomfortable, as if she'd no business sitting on the cottage step – or even existing, for that matter.

'Thou knows, I still can't get over them sending the chauffeur to bring Jack to fetch me. Gentry act in funny ways at times. She must think sommat of Jack, though, as he said as she'd told the doctor that she couldn't afford to lose him, so it were important to get me over to look after young 'uns. I wonder what the real reason were. I've never found it in me to trust Lady High-and-Mighty. I mean, it isn't as if Jack's invaluable, with stables going, and he don't know first thing about motors.'

'Well, happen as it were a case of her knowing Jack, and she'd not know who she might get if she put out for somebody else. Besides, she owes him a chance. He's worked for her for a good many years now.'

'Aye, happen. Anyroad, I'm not complaining. I were struggling, thou knows, lass. I'd no job and me reputation were ruined when them as I worked for pinned some stealing on me. I haven't ever stolen owt in me life! Anyroad, I were trying to manage on parish relief, but they give that grudgingly. Last means test as I took, they found out I had a son-in-law in work and told me I'd to put meself in his care.'

'Oh, Issy. If Ciss and Jack'd known that…'

'I know. I were on with being stubborn. I didn't want to be a burden, but if I'd known what were going to happen, I'd have come like a shot.'

'You couldn't have done owt, Issy love.'

'I could've looked after her. Ciss said nowt in her letters about not carrying well, though I did wonder why she kept putting off her trip to see me, which she'd been so keen to arrange. I didn't push it because I knew I'd not be able to help with putting a word in for Jack on the estate, as they'd wanted me to. Anyroad, let's talk of sommat else. Are you still on with your sewing, Megan? Ciss said in her letters as you use the parlour and you've a nice few customers. Only you've never said owt.'

'I didn't like to – not with how things are – but aye, I've garments waiting to be started on. Manny at the shop asked me some two weeks back to see about making frocks for his wife and her friends for a wedding as is coming up.'

'Well, what're you waiting for? Nowt need change along them lines. Whatever Ciss arranged with you still stands, and'll always stand.'

'Ta, Issy. I don't know as I could carry on without me dream.'

'What dream's that then, lass?'

'Didn't Ciss say why I were doing it all?'

Megan told Issy about her dream for the future, but speaking it aloud somehow made it seem silly and impossibly out of her reach.

'Crikey! That sounds a reet good idea, love, and I'd back owt as'd get you away from that Bert Armitage, even though it'd be a scandal to some. But your own shop! That'd take some money. Can you earn that much?'

'No, it's not possible. It'd take at least a hundred pounds, I reckon, and I've been at it for near on eighteen months and I've only got nine pounds sixteen shillings and sixpence so far.'

'That's not much, lass, is it? I mean, you've done well, but you're not going to get far at that rate.'

'I know, but Manny's wife and her friends are me only customers, and they only want frocks now and again, for dos and suchlike.' She paused, wondering whether she should tell of Hattie, then felt cross at herself for feeling embarrassed to talk about her. She ploughed on. 'Mind, I have had another offer, but I'm not sure how I could do it.'

'Why's that, love?'

'It's for Hattie, a friend of mine I grew up with. Well, she's more of a sister, really.'

Megan took some time telling Issy about Hattie, wanting to justify what Hattie did and wanting Issy to see Hattie in a good light.

'Look, I can see you've been at worrying about telling me of this lass, as you've never mentioned her afore. Nor did my Ciss, come to that. But don't worry on account of me thinking badly of Hattie. I've known of her kind afore, a long time ago. It's circumstances, like you say, as gets a lot of them into it. With Hattie, it were gentry as were to blame; and with the lass I knew, it were her own da as took her down and then killed himself in front of her, poor girl. Mind, he'd left her some money, but that were stolen from her. Like Hattie, it was a prostitute that helped her and as a result she landed up on the game. There's a lot as goes on as shouldn't. And this Hattie's involvement in stopping that vile bloody racket and getting them beasts to the gallows – well, that's to be commended. At least, with Hattie, lassies are being looked after, as long as her business isn't enticing others into prostitution.'

'Oh, no! Lassies were in a state when she took them on. Their health is better, they're well looked

306

after, and them as want to get out of the game have every chance, because they can save and better themselves. She does get new ones in, but only when they're seen on the streets prostituting, and then it's only those as has no other way. She won't take lassies as are just after making money and aren't in dire straits. She's funny in how she looks on them as being sinful, and on the others as having no choice and in need of help.'

'Well, there you go. It strikes me as what Hattie does is a good thing, and if she makes money from doing it – well, good luck to her. If I were you, I'd get started as soon as you can on making clothes for her lassies, and get this future of yours sorted.'

'There's more to it, though, Issy. How will I sort everything? I mean, without Bert finding out? I'd have to make trips to Leeds, and on a regular basis an' all. That wouldn't pass his notice, and even if it did, someone would soon make sure he knew.'

'Look, don't put hurdles where there mightn't be any! Get yourself off to Leeds and talk to this Hattie. There might be a way round problems and, if there isn't, well, then at least you tried. What shift's Bert on today?'

'He's on days. Six-while-six for the next two weeks.'

'Couldn't be better then, as it's only just on ten and there's a train at eleven-fifteen, if I remember reet.'

A fearful kind of excitement shot through Megan. Suddenly it wasn't something she couldn't do – it was a possibility! But going off to Hattie's at a moment's notice? That was something she'd never done before. She'd always taken time to make sure everything was in place, so she wouldn't get caught out by Bert, and to be sure Hattie was going to be in.

'What's wrong? You're not having doubts, are you?'

'Aye, some. I'm not used to doing sommat on the spur of the moment, and I'm thinking as to whether I'll catch her. As I told you, Hattie was planning to spend more of her time at the house that she has. What if she isn't in Leeds?'

'Well, leave a message with whoever's there telling her to contact you as soon as she can to let you know when she'll be in. You said she writes to you here, so that won't be a problem for you. Look, lass, if you doesn't go today – right now – you'll never go. You've got money, so use some of it to further yourself. Think of your dream. Go on, lass.'

Issy wriggled her body along the step and stood up clumsily.

'I'll tell you what. I'll come an' all. It'll give me an outing, and I can give this Hattie a once-over. Besides, I'll be an excuse for you to use to Bert. You can say as you went with me to Leeds, as I had some things to do and didn't feel up to going on me own. You could say as I paid train fare an' all, so he'd have no questions.'

'Oh, Issy, would you? Would you come?'

'Aye, I would. Come on, shift yourself. I'll just pop round Gertie's and ask her and Jenny to look after babby and look out for young 'uns when they come in from their lessons.'

Megan rose and went towards her cottage. She

could do this. She could really do this. And she prayed as she walked, *Please, God, help me. Help me to take this step to get meself free.*

30

A Path to the Future

Not two hours had passed since she'd sat on the step talking about it, and here Megan was, standing in front of Hattie's house.

'Well! This *is* sommat. I didn't expect a place like this. I tell you, Megan, they says as we're sitting on a fortune, and by 'eck they're reet an' all. Mind, I've sat on mine so long now that it'll not be worth owt, but it gets you thinking, don't it?'

Megan giggled and tucked her arm into Issy's. 'Aye, it does, but I wouldn't swap with them – not even my life, I wouldn't.'

Issy patted her hand. 'No, lass, you're right, neither would I.'

A young girl, who looked no older than fifteen or so, opened the door. 'What do you want here?'

'Is Hattie in? I'm a friend.'

The girl looked her up and down. 'What's your name, then?'

'Tell Hattie as Megan's here from Breckton. She'll know me.'

The door shut.

'Well! She were no more than a snip of a lass, but she had such a side to her. Surely lassies of

309

that age aren't working on the game, are they?'

'No, I expect as that's Sally. You know, the lass I told you about. Hattie wrote and said she'd found her.'

The door opened again. Hattie stood on the step looking down on them, and for the first time Megan noticed her appearance and how Hattie looked exactly as you'd expect a... She floundered in her thoughts. What was someone who did what Hattie did called? The answer came as a shock and had never entered her head before. Hattie was ... a 'madam', and that's exactly what she looked like, with her dark hair cut short, tightly curled to her face, and her figure squeezed into a red satin dress that showed almost all of her ample bust. Lashings of dark-red lipstick framed her even, white teeth and, as always, she wore long white gloves. For the second time that day Megan felt embarrassed.

'Megan! Oh, Megan love, it's wonderful to see you.' Sweet-smelling perfume filled her nostrils as Hattie's arms engulfed her. It felt good. The uncomfortable feelings she'd had lifted from her, and she hugged Hattie back with just as much enthusiasm, until Hattie held her at arm's length and said, 'Eeh, Megan, I've been worrying over you, and me worry hasn't been without cause, by the look of you. You've took another beating, I see. Come on inside, then you can introduce me to your friend.'

As they followed Hattie into the hall, the door on the left seemed to take on huge proportions, filling Megan with fear. She hoped with all her heart it wouldn't open to let out some man or other and a scantily dressed young woman seeing him off, as had happened on many of her visits here before. How Issy'd cope with that she couldn't imagine, but fortunately it didn't happen and they went through the opposite door on the right. As it closed behind them, some of the tension left her. Hattie motioned them towards the big comfy sofa. As she sat down, Megan told her, 'I'm fine. The last time were a bit back. Things have been all right of late.'

Hattie sighed and shook her head. 'Anyroad, that's not all I were thinking on. How's...'

'Hattie, this is Issy.'

'Issy! Well, what I haven't heard of you wouldn't be worth knowing of. I'm reet glad to meet you.'

A feeling of uncertainty came over Megan as she looked over at Issy. Issy's expression was difficult to read. It wasn't exactly disapproving, but neither was it one that said she was comfortable with where she found herself, as she nodded at Hattie and said, 'Aye, well, I haven't had knowledge of you afore today, so I can't say the same, but lass here told me of you with a lot of love in her heart, so that bodes well. We came with a purpose, and that's to try to sort Megan out.'

Megan held her breath, but she needn't have worried. She supposed Hattie was used to all kinds of reactions from new folk she met, as she didn't seem put out by this and just smiled at Issy. 'Well, it's reet good to see you both. Eeh, Megan, I hope "sort you out" means as you're leaving that bastard and coming to stay with me?'

Megan's giggling response held a nervous sound. She tried to cover it up by coughing whilst

311

she shook her head. The atmosphere hadn't eased at all, and Megan had another worry. She dreaded the moment that Hattie asked after Cissy. She'd not yet written to Hattie to let her know what had happened. The words were not something she ever wanted to write and, though she'd known she should have, she'd put it off. Now she wished with all her heart she had written.

'Is there sommat wrong, Megan? You haven't said yet how...'

'That young 'un as answered door, were that Sally, Hattie?'

Hattie gave her a quizzical look. 'Aye, it were.'

'By, Hattie, you must be so happy to have her back.'

'I am, Megan, I can't say how much. It's like me life's complete. She's on with wanting to stay, now she understands about how I tried to stop what happened, and how the plan I'd made to save her sister and others went wrong. She's finally found some forgiveness within her and we're on with getting on together. But it's going to take time. She's been through a lot, and for years she's been told as it was all my doing by that spiteful Elsie. Thou knows, that sister of Susan's as come and took over and Sally had to go with?'

'Well, I didn't meet her, but I knew she were causing you and Arthur a lot of problems with her interfering and her attitude, and I know as you were heartbroken to lose Sally to her.'

'I were, and I were right about Elsie's motives an' all. She used Sally as a skivvy and didn't feed her reet, and she filled her mind every day with how she were on with thinking as things were.

She never even set Sally to her lessons! The poor lass can barely read and write. Anyroad, we've a long way to travel, but like I say, we're heading in the right direction now.'

'Can she remember...?'

'I think so. We haven't talked about that part yet. It were so horrific for her. What he did to her and what took place after, with me being stabbed. Oh God! I feel so bad about it, Megan.'

'You mustn't, love. You went through hell. Eeh, Hattie, I wished as you could get to a place where you can see that what Sally suffered weren't your fault. It were that police officer. He took a risk with Sally, thou knows that.'

'Maybe I will get there, if Sally does. Like I say, we've some way to go as yet. Now, tell me how Ciss is! Has babby been born? What did she have?'

The ominous silence suggested at what Megan couldn't voice. 'What's wrong? Is Ciss not well? Oh God! No. Oh, I'm sorry. Oh, Issy, Megan...'

The moment she'd most dreaded was now upon them, and Megan didn't know how it should go.

'You knew me lass, I understand, Hattie?'

'Aye, I did, Issy. She were a good friend to me when I most needed one. Tell me what happened. I take it as Ciss – well, is Ciss no longer with us?'

'Oh, Hattie. I miss her. I haven't thought reet since. I should have written.'

'It's all right, Megan love. Come on. Let it all out. Have a good cry. It's the best thing. Oh, Issy, love.'

Megan recounted what had happened, her arm around Issy while she spoke. Issy sobbed throughout her telling, and Hattie sat on the other side of

Issy, stroking her hair.

When she'd finished, Hattie said to Issy, 'Ciss were a lovely lass. When I were thirteen and had just been taken down, I had nothing – not even the means of feeding meself – and Ciss sent over a half-crown for me. And that were without even having met me! That says a lot about someone, don't it? And you have babby, and Sarah and Jack and Megan. You'll be reet, love. You will.'

'I know.' Issy blew her nose, though it sounded more like she was blowing a foghorn. 'It's just that at the moment I can't imagine things feeling any better. One minute I'm fine, and the next I'm like this.'

'That's how it will be, and it's not a bad thing. You can't bottle it up or you'll be ill. I'll go and sort a brew and some sandwiches out, eh? I bet you could do with sommat. You've been here all this while and I haven't offered you even a drop of tea. I'll not be a mo.'

By the time Hattie swept back into the room saying, 'Reet, get your teeth into this lot, girls,' Megan had managed to comfort Issy and get them both to a place where they felt they could cope.

Hattie placed a tray, piled high with sandwiches and cakes, onto the occasional table in the centre of the room. Behind her, and shaking with nerves so much that the large tea pot and cups and saucers on the tray she carried rattled precariously, came the young girl they now knew was Sally. Megan jumped up to help her and sought to put her at her ease. 'Hello, Sally. You'll not know me. I'm Megan, Hattie's mate. Hattie and me grew up together.'

The girl smiled. 'Were you an orphan an' all?'

'Aye, we're all in the same boat. I could tell you some tales of Hattie when she were a young 'un. I will one day. They'd make your hair curl even more than it does already!'

'Oh, no! Don't say that, Megan. She's forever trying to straighten her hair. She wants one of these bobs as they're all wearing.'

'Huh, and there's me tying mine in rags every night to get this fizz to form proper curls. I'd give owt to have your mop, Sally.'

Sally giggled at this.

'I don't like to butt in, but if we don't tell of what we've come for, we'll have to go for our train and miss the opportunity.'

'Oh, aye, Issy, you said as you'd come about Megan getting her life sorted. Well, Meg love, as you've not seemed to come with the intention of leaving Bert, I guess you've thought about making the clothes for the girls. Is that reet?'

'Aye, I am thinking on taking up your offer, but I just wondered if there were a way it could be done with me staying where I am? Issy needs me around. She needs help with the babby and, well, everything.'

'Of course, I can see how it is for you, love. Look, I'll show you the catalogue I told you of and that'll give you an idea of the kind of clothes and undies the lassies like. There's nowt that will be a problem to you. You could make them easily, I know that.'

Whilst Hattie was sorting through a pile of magazines, Sally said, 'Are you a seamstress, Megan? I like sewing, and I'm good at it. I had to

315

do all the mending when I were with me aunt, and she'd accept nothing unless it were perfect. She'd rip it undone and make me start over. And when I got really good, she'd take in mending from her customers and set me at it.'

'She sounds like Madame Marie, the woman who trained me.'

'Here it is. Have a look.' Hattie passed the catalogue to Megan. After a moment Hattie asked, 'Well, what d'yer think, now you've had a flick through?'

'I'd have no problem copying any of this stuff. I could do some designs of me own along the same lines an' all. Trouble is, I just don't know how I'd go about it. I mean, there's a lot of problems, like getting the cloth the lassies choose back to Issy's. And they'll have to have fittings. There'd be such a lot of comings and goings, I'd not be able to keep it all from Bert. It's hopeless. I shouldn't have come.'

'It's not hopeless, Megan. We can come up with sommat. For a start, I'd take care of getting cloth to Issy's. I've a car now and a driver – I had to have one, so as to get back and forth to me house. Daisy and Phyllis are there now. I try to get Sally to stay there an' all, but no, she'll not leave me side, so she comes and goes with me. Isn't that reet, lass?'

Sally looked embarrassed, but smiled at Hattie. The smile lit up her face and held love in it. It would seem that things were a lot better in that quarter than Hattie had realized; if only she could get the guilt to leave her, as it was making her see things that weren't there.

'Now, about the fittings. What if the lass having

sommat made came to your cottage, Issy? I mean, it wouldn't be often, would it, Megan? Once you've got the size of them all, they'd only need to come when they're having a special garment made.'

Issy looked up from the catalogue she'd taken from Megan. 'I don't see why not. After all, nobody knows who me friends and acquaintances are. Lassies could be passed off as them as I worked for, so that'd explain the car. And I don't see how Bert would find out, either, as you'll be doing nowt different to what you've been doing over these last couple of years, and he's not cottoned on yet. I'll tell you sommat, though, Megan: if lassies are willing to pay the prices in this here catalogue, you're soon going to be rich. Nine and eleven! For a pair of knickers! And they'd not cover owt, neither. You'd catch your death in them. They haven't even got elastic in the legs.'

Megan and Hattie burst out laughing.

'You're right about prices, Issy. They are steep for what they are, but there's quite a lot of work in some of them pieces. Though, when I work out what to charge, I'll have to consider the lassies will be buying their own cloth, and Hattie'll have to foot the cost of the delivery, so my costs won't be very high.'

'You come up with a fair price, but don't stint yourself, Megan. You must know the going rate for making up? Well, take that rate and double it, and my lot'll be happy. They'll still be making savings and they've money to spend. And plenty of it an' all.'

'Well! There you go, Megan love. You'll have

317

that shop you want in no time. Eeh, that'll be a grand day, lass!'

Megan felt a smile forming at Issy's words. It was one of relief and hope and excitement and was made even bigger at the thought of all the wonderful colours of the fabrics, the creation of frocks and handling all the different cloths. Ideas buzzed around her head and, best of all, she felt that the future now held better things for her and Billy.

Hattie broke into her reveries. 'Megan love. In a couple of years I'll be ready to invest in another business, and I reckon as it'll take you that long to get near to what you need, so how about I become a partner, eh? Whatever you've got in two years' time, I'll double it.'

'You'd really do that? Oh, Hattie.'

'Aye, I would. It'd give me an income and a means of getting out of this game. Are you sure as you'd have me as a partner? And maybe some of the lassies could work for us? Give those who want it a chance at doing sommat decent for a living, eh?'

'I could help. I've been on with telling Megan about me stitching.'

Megan looked at Sally as she said this, and then at Hattie. In each face she saw a plea. And suddenly it was as if the boot was on the other foot and she held the key that would be the saving of *them*. 'Of course I'd have you. I'll have you both and would be glad to. You say you're good with hand sewing, Sally? Well, how about you do the hemming? That's always a problem if the client isn't present, as getting the right length really needs them there. That'd be ideal for you, as you're based here. I'll come over with the first batch and show you how to pin up and mark the hem so you get the right length, and then we'll see how you go. If you're good, I'll pay you for every hem. We'll work out how much between us, eh?'

'Well! It seems we've got it all sorted. By, you're full of surprises, Sally. And I'm reet glad to hear you putting ideas forward. You can't go wrong, having a trade like Megan has. It always comes back to you and is there for you if you need it.'

'Thou knows, Hattie, it's like me dream's come true already. It all seems really possible now.'

'It is, Megan. And I'll be your first customer. I'll study the catalogue and pick out anything that I like, and you send me a few drawings of winter clothing. We'll start from there. How would that be?'

'That'd be grand, Hattie. I'll send you drawings in the post as soon as I get back. I've been on with designing for you for a good while. I've a whole collection just for you. It includes a lot of the kind of frocks I see in me mind for you to wear when you're with Arthur, as well as what I call your working clothes.'

'Fancy that, Megan. You sitting doing stuff for *me!*'

'I like doing it, Hattie. It keeps you close to me, makes it feel like I'm with you.'

They held each other. Megan knew no more words were needed. She'd not spoil the moment by speaking again of her worries about what might happen if Bert found out.

PART FIVE
'The Affair'
1930

31

Megan's Joy – Hattie's Heartache

Megan drew in a deep breath in a fruitless effort to quell her excitement.

'Look, lass, wait and see. Hattie'll be here any moment,' Issy had said when Megan broached the subject again a few moments ago. Megan didn't blame her for sounding impatient; she hadn't been able to talk of anything else since she'd received the message that Hattie had news and that she herself, not one of the girls, would be coming on the next visit. And that next visit was to be today! Her concentration was nil, and for the umpteenth time she stuck the needle into her finger. She winced and then jumped up. *A motor engine. At last!*

After a flurry of cuddles and kisses with Sally and Hattie, Hattie held her at arm's length. 'Well, lass, I've brought good news, and I hope as you're ready to take on the next stage of our plan.'

'I am, Hattie. Every stitch I've done in these last two years has been for bringing me to this moment.'

'And you've done a few, love. It's a miracle how you've managed to keep it all from Bert.'

'I know, but I've had a few scares – especially with Billy. He's getting to be a handful, but he knows he'll also feel the wrath of his dad if he gets mad, so that's been stopping him saying owt. Mind, he's not been above using blackmail. He worries me at times, Hattie. He seems to have a lot of his dad's traits.'

'He'll be reet. He's just at that age, I reckon – not that either of us has had any dealings with lads afore, but I've heard as they're a handful when they're growing up. Sarah and Sally get on well with him, so he can't be that bad.'

'He's all right, Megan. He's no different to any lads as I've known,' Sally chipped in.

'Happen you're reet. I hope so, and I hope as getting him away from his dad will make a difference.'

'Well, love, if you're ready, I reckon that can happen now.'

Issy interrupted Megan's response as she bustled in with the kettle that she'd been filling out the back. 'Hello, Hattie. Am I glad to see you! Megan's been driving me mad over this visit. I expect as you'll be ready for a drop of tea, eh?'

'It's good to see you an' all, Issy. You look well. I'll not have tea, though. It's too hot for that, thanks, love.'

'Well, get yourselves into the parlour. It's cool in there, and I've some lemonade as I've made. It's in pantry on slab, so'll be nice and cold. I'll bring some of that in to you.'

Megan felt her jaw drop. Had she heard right? Hattie had been keeping all the money she'd made in a bank account for her, and had helped to increase it in such a short space of time by using her contacts to get material direct from the warehouses that supplied the trade. And here she was now, saying she had a total of one hundred and fifty pounds!

'...so with me doubling that, we have a grand total of three hundred pounds, and I reckon that's enough to start looking for a place. What do you say to that, Madame Megan?'

Megan couldn't speak, though a stifled giggle did tickle her insides. *Madame Megan* – Hattie hadn't forgotten what she'd said she was going to call her dream place, then? When she'd first voiced the name she hadn't truly thought it could happen. But now she really felt inside her that it could. She looked down at her hands, on which her own contribution was visibly etched. At times they had been sore and bleeding with the amount of sewing she'd done, and her back had ached until she'd hardly been able to straighten it. Tears welled in her eyes at the thought of all that she'd been through.

'Well, lass? Are you ready?' Issy asked.

Three faces looked at her – three very dear faces that were waiting for her to speak – but she could only nod her head to tell them, yes, she was ready.

Sally clapped her hands. Hattie let out a relieved sigh. Issy stood still, her hands clasped under her bosom, her head shaking. 'Eeh, lass, lass...'

Hattie took charge. 'Reet! That's settled then. I'll get me solicitor onto looking out for a place for us. I thought we'd stay in Leeds, in the suburbs. Somewhere moneyed folk'd find acceptable, though we'd not want to pay a big rent.'

'Leeds? I hadn't thought to stay that close. What about Bert?'

'He'll not find you. For a start, he'll not think for one moment as you've your own business. How could he?'

'No, you're right, but... Oh, I don't know. It all seems frightening, now that it's likely it's going to happen. Me insides are all churned up. I can't think straight.'

'You don't have to, love. I'll do all the thinking. You just have to be ready to leave when I come for you. It's as simple as that. And remember: it's your dream. It's what's kept you going, and it's about to come true!'

The realization finally hit home. 'Oh, Hattie, Issy – it is, isn't it? My dream. I'm about to catch me dream!'

Issy's jaw dropped.

'What's wrong, Issy? Are you all right?'

'Aye. It were just what you said about catching your dream. I've only ever heard that saying once afore. A long time ago.'

'Oh, I know, it's an unusual saying, but ... well, I've only heard it once meself, and it just seemed right for what's happening to me.'

Issy didn't say any more, and Megan was glad. She didn't like lying to Issy and didn't understand her own compulsion to keep the locket a secret. Nor could she understand how it was that Issy often caught on to something she said, or a way that she looked, and went on about folk she'd known in the past. It was unsettling.

Hattie smiled. 'Well, Megan. You're happy, I can see that.' She took hold of Megan's shoulders and looked into her eyes. 'But, love, your happiness is no more than mine, because what you've done,

Megan, has given me hope an' all. I've come to see that in the future I really might be able to change me way of life. The business will grow enough to keep us both in time, I know it will.' She hugged Megan to her and, as she squeezed her, her voice filled with emotion. 'We're going to win through, you and me, Megan. We're going to win through.'

Megan felt uneasy for a moment. Something... But it passed as Hattie continued, 'So, Megan, that's it then. Everything's coming together. Well, we'd better be getting back.'

Sally had already set about the task of emptying the large shopping bag of the paper it had been stuffed with, and filling it with the garments that were ready to be taken back. The shopping-bag ploy had worked well. When there was no material to bring in, the girls always stuffed the bag with paper, so that no suspicion was aroused about them coming empty-handed, but leaving with a full bag.

'By the way, I forgot to tell you about another idea as I've had,' Hattie went on. 'I were thinking of telling the girls they're not to order owt for a while, Megan. And if you've nothing on for your other customers, I thought maybe you could make up a couple of your designs from the material you have in stock. Sommat really special. Say, a day-wear outfit and an evening frock? Then we'd have something to dress the window of the shop, to give folk an idea of what we're about. What do you think?'

'Yes, I've allus thought that's what I'd do, and I've nowt on at the moment for Manny's lot. Thou knows sommat, Hattie? I've an idea to drape the background of the window with swathes of cream satin. Would you get me a few yards ordered? It'd make a really grand background to me designs.' Warming to her theme, she went on, 'Oh, and we'll need–'

'Hold on, love. This is your dream, remember? So I'll find the place, then if rooms above aren't what you can live in straight away, you can stop with me for a bit whilst you get everything you need to make them – and the shop – just as you imagined it all to be, eh?'

Megan laughed. 'Aye, you're right. Ta, Hattie. Me dream wouldn't be mine if I left everything to you. I need to see it all through to the end.'

When they'd waved off Sally and Hattie, Megan clasped her hands together.

'Oh, Issy, I never thought this day would come. But now it has, I'm ready! I didn't think I were at first. I felt scared, like, but I am ready. I can do it. I know I can. Me head's buzzing with lists of things I'll need and...'

'Megan, I'm reet happy for you. But, by 'eck, I'm going to miss you, lass!'

'I know, love, and I'm going to miss you and Jack. I mean – well, all of you. You're me family.'

'I know how it is with you, where Jack's concerned. I know you've never got over your feelings for him, and it's a credit to you that you've never done owt about it. It couldn't have been easy, with Ciss gone these past two years and the way being clear, so to speak. But I knew as you'd think on where the young 'uns were concerned and not cause a scandal as'd outcast them. You've done well, lass. And it'll be easier, now that you're going to be away from him. He'll soon be just a figure from the past.'

'Happen...' She could think of nothing else to say. The way Issy had put it was how it should be, but she knew it wouldn't be. Not ever. Jack was part of her very being and always would be.

Issy had set about clearing away the tumblers they'd had their lemonade in, and Megan gave her a hand. They were by the sink when Issy spoke again. 'You know, Gert'll be at questioning me again, now Hattie's been. She always gets tongues wagging, does Hattie.'

'I know, though she'd not looked so bad today with one of her "Arthur" frocks on.'

'Well, I don't know. There's just sommat about her that gets eyebrows raised.'

'Aye, happen she thinks as she looks reet. Maybe if she could get out of the game, things'd change. Funny, though, how she put so much store on the shop being her means of getting free of it all. I thought she were giving up and selling to Mavis and moving into her house. Thou knows, she never mentioned Arthur. Do you think there's sommat up?'

'I wouldn't think so. They've gone along nicely for years. I'd not think as owt could upset that apple cart.'

Megan didn't say anything else, but she sensed that things weren't right and felt guilty with it. She'd always cottoned on to the fact that Hattie might be in trouble, but she'd been so caught up with the excitement of what was in the offing for her that she'd not taken any notice of the alarm bells when Hattie had hugged her.

'We needed some good news, didn't we, lass?' Issy said. 'It all seems doom and gloom sometimes, especially with Jack as he is. I wonder if he's ever going to come out of his sadness. He's just not the same bloke any more.'

Issy sighed. Megan didn't comment; instead she just nodded. She'd put aside her niggling worry about Hattie and didn't want to give thought to Jack's sadness. Not now, not now that she was going. Her heart had been soothed of late, as Jack'd taken to sitting in the parlour with her as she worked, on the nights when Bert was on lates. He'd talked and talked to her. Oh, aye, it'd been about Cissy and the times they'd had, but his need to be with her for comfort gladdened her. Talking to Issy now – of how upset and wrapped up in Cissy's memory he was – would cast a sadness over her, just when she didn't want to be saddened. She didn't want anything to bring her down from her feelings of excitement and anticipation. In fact she wanted to be alone for a while – alone with her thoughts, her hopes and her dreams. She wanted to hold her locket and talk to her granny and granddad, and try to imagine what her mam was like and wonder who her dad had been. And to quell the feelings of unsettledness that Issy had set up in her with her talk of Jack's sadness and her memories – like the one of hearing the saying 'To catch a dream' before.

Hattie sat in the back of the car. Sally always liked to travel in the front, and today Hattie was glad of that. She was glad, too, that neither Megan nor Issy had mentioned Arthur, and that the excitement of the moment had not allowed them time to speak of him. She tried to relax, but it was hard. Her mind gave her no peace.

Arthur hadn't been in touch this good while. She'd assumed he was still abroad, where she thought he'd been for the last four months. The last letter she'd received from him had been from Italy a month ago, and yet just last week she'd seen his picture in the paper under the heading 'WAR HERO LORD ARTHUR GREYSTONE GRACES SOCIETY ONCE MORE'.

A lord! Arthur had never, in all the years she'd known him, told her that he was a lord. In fact he'd lied to her about his name, calling himself Captain Naraday. Her heart throbbed painfully inside her chest as she remembered the picture. There was Arthur, gazing down lovingly at the beautiful woman in his arms. She knew the piece describing who she was by heart:

Lady Greystone stood lovingly by her husband throughout the dark days when he hid himself away because of the horrific injuries he sustained in the Great War, and throughout his many painful operations. She is now richly rewarded for her sacrifice, as his devotion to her is plain for everyone to see. Society is once more graced with Lord Greystone's charming presence. Lady Greystone wore...

Bloody 'stood lovingly by her husband' – huh! And who bloody cares what she wore. Why? Why all the lies? Why all the hope? Because there had been times when Arthur had given her hope – hope that she would one day be his wife. *You*

331

bloody fool, Hattie Frampton! She wiped away a tear as she silently admonished herself.

A letter had arrived for her while she'd been out. Recognizing Arthur's writing, Hattie went straight up to her room, ignoring Daisy's fussing over her – she and Phyllis had been doing that ever since the day the newspaper picture had shattered her dreams:

My dearest Hattie,
This is a letter I never wanted to write and never thought I would write.
I can do nothing more than be truthful with you, my dear, but our relationship has to end. I know this will come as a blow to you, and I can assure you I am equally saddened.
My life suddenly changed. Nothing was planned. Matilda, my wife, attended a dinner party, not knowing I was to be a guest also. Because of my trips abroad and being with you, it had been over two years since we had been in each other's company. We had conducted our marriage by letter only.
Seeing me as I am now, Matilda is able to cope with my injuries and we have found much happiness.
I will never have the love I had with you ever again, but we could never have had a compatible life, my dear. You would not have been happy in the circles in which I and my friends move, and you know I was not happy with the lifestyle you chose to continue with.
Harry will come to see you in the next few days and inform you of the arrangements I have made for you. I trust you will not ever let the press, or my wife, know of our liaison. My friends in the North never knew of our relationship, other than to know that I did use

your services, but they will not let this be known
publicly. They have many things in their own lives
that they would not want made public. I say all this
not because I looked on our liaison in any other way
than as a loving and wonderful experience, but I
know you will want me to be happy, and I could not
retain that happiness if my wife found out about you.
I will always love and miss you, my dearest Hattie.
Yours, Arthur

The tears dripped onto each beautifully written
word – part of the enjoyment she'd felt at receiving his letters had been to gaze at his writing.
Oh, Arthur... Arthur.
The anger she thought she'd feel didn't visit
her, but a deep sense of loss bruised her heart.
He was right. She knew that. Oh, but the pain of
losing him. How was she to bear it? And describing what they'd had as a liaison! But then he
was top-drawer – she'd always known that, even
if she hadn't known just how top-drawer he was!
To think that she'd been saving the fact that she
was giving up the game as a surprise to tell him
when he came home. Mind, it wouldn't have
made any difference, she was sure of that now.
Thank God she'd insisted on keeping her business, because it was likely this was always going
to happen, and then where would she have been?
At least she was a woman of her own means. Aye,
and it was a good thing she hadn't yet gone ahead
with her plans to sell to Mavis. But best of all, she
had plans for the future. They would help. She'd
throw everything into making her own and
Megan's business succeed, though she'd always

give Megan the lead, as it was her dream. She'd not take that from her, but she'd work hard and give herself no time to dwell.

It was funny how things had turned out. Herself and Megan back together again! They needed one another and always would. That was something. In this new venture she had all the business knowledge, the contacts and the money to back the business, and Megan had all the talent and knowledge of how to succeed in the clothes business. They'd do all right. She'd be all right. *Oh God! Oh, Arthur... Arthur...*

32

Jack's Dilemmas

The sound of himself whistling a tune surprised Jack. And now he thought about it, he realized he'd been doing so for a good while. The realization made him feel better. Something in him had changed. He thought of Cissy, as he had done every minute of the two years he'd been without her, but the memory didn't bring the usual dull ache. Instead his thoughts went to how she used to make him laugh and how she'd always see a way out of things or a different road they could travel. Nothing ever got her down.

'Uncle Jack. Uncle Jack!'

He looked round. He knew it was young Billy, but couldn't see him.

'I'm here.' Billy emerged from behind the big oak tree that stood on the back lawn of the house.

'What're you up to, lad? How many times have I told you not to come that way? You're trespassing. You're to come over field and down through stables. That's if you come at all, which you shouldn't.'

'It's quicker this way, and Mrs Harvey didn't see me. She were at daydreaming. I saw her through the window. Anyroad, I haven't got nowt to do, and I wanted to know if I can be on with helping you some?'

'I thought you were playing with Sarah?'

'I were, but she had that thing ... she had Bella with her. And I threw a stone at a cat and it hit Bella, and Sarah went mad at me.'

'Aye, she would. She'd not have Bella hurt, nor any animals. Thou knows that and should've thought on, and if me little Bella is hurt, I'll be mad at you an' all. And be at giving you a clout.'

'She's not, Uncle Jack, honest. It only skimmed her and she gave me that ug– That smile as she gives.'

Jack felt a familiar worry: young Billy was taking against Bella. He'd nearly used the term Megan said Bert had used when talking of her. He'd have to watch him. 'I'm finished here now, so I haven't owt for you. Look at the car. You can see your face in it, but I'd have been glad of your help to get it like that, lad. I could've used some of your elbow grease instead of all of mine.'

'What's elbow grease?'

'Ha, never mind now. I'll show you some next

335

time. Now get along with you. I'm to take Mrs Harvey out shortly and I don't want you hanging around here.'

'At least you laughed, Uncle Jack. You haven't been doing that this good while.'

'Aye, I know, lad. I'll tell you what, when I go fishing next week on me days off, I'll take you with me. How will that be, eh? Keep you out of your mam's hair for a day.'

Billy ran off, shouting back, 'Ta, Uncle Jack! Ta ever so much.'

Jack shook his head. 'Young 'uns!'

His thoughts turned to Megan – thoughts that Billy had triggered. Megan had been a godsend to him, and she'd been a comfort to Ma. She'd always been there to listen to him. He was going to miss her. He wondered when it was she'd be going. Something in him didn't want her to go. She was a good friend, and lately he'd noticed her beauty. He'd been shocked a few times at the picture Megan made as she'd sat with the light from the window behind her. Funny how he'd never noticed that before. Except well, there was a moment like that on his wedding day. Fancy that coming to his mind after all these years. It wasn't a comfortable memory, happening as it did on that day of all days. He remembered how he'd had a shock when he'd turned and caught her eye. It was as if she'd felt it, too. *Eeh, Megan, lass, it's a shame as you're wasted on that Bert Armitage. By, it'll be a good day when you get away from him, no matter how much I don't want you to go.*

He had a few minutes to spare before he had to take the car around to the front of the house. He leaned back on the car door, and his thoughts turned to Laura Harvey. He realized that this change in him, which he'd thought was sudden, had been creeping up for a while. Because although she'd been up to her tricks again lately, they hadn't been unwelcome. He'd even liked being in her company, though there was a niggling fear at the back of his mind as he remembered how she used to mock him. He wasn't going to forget it was all a game to her, and that she wouldn't really be interested in the likes of him.

'Jack. Jack!'

For the second time he was surprised to hear his name being called, only this time the call held fear and urgency.

'Henry! What's to do, man?'

'Gary's been thrown off Diamond. He's in the lane.'

'Aw, no. Is he hurt bad?'

'He were out cold. Young Billy came screaming into the stables, and I sent him running for the doctor.'

'Reet, get up to the house and tell Hamilton. I'll get to Gary. I'll lift him into the stables, as they're nearest.'

By the time Jack reached him, Gary had regained consciousness.

'All right, lad. I'm here. Can you stand? Doctor's on his way. I'm to get you back to stable.'

'Me leg's badly hurt, Jack, and I'm still at seeing stars. I'll kill that lad, when I get me hands on him. He's turning out to be a right one. Takes after his dad, if you ask me.'

'Who, Billy? Were this his doing?'

337

'Aye. He came, out of bush screaming and yelling, right in me path. He proper spooked Diamond. And just afore I hit the ground, I heard him laughing his head off. I tell you, he isn't right in his head. He'll have done this because I caught him in the orchard scrumping the apples and clipped his ear. He said then as'd he'd get me back, or he'd tell his dad and he'd be for getting me. Sommat needs to be done about him, Jack. He's been at scaring me little lad an' all.'

'I'll see to it. Don't be saying owt to Bert, otherwise Megan'll most likely cop it. And punishment as lad'll get at Bert's hand will be far worse than what his deed deserves.'

'But...'

'I know. You could've been killed. But you've not; you're still here to be at your moaning.'

'You're a cheeky bugger, Jack. Ouch! Be careful, I reckon as I've broke sommat.'

'You will if I drop you, lad. Ha, I've never met such a softy!'

'Eeh, give over, you're on with giving me some stick, and me the injured one. But, thou knows, Jack, I'll say this – it's good to hear you funning again. Are you at feeling better?'

'Aye, I am of a sudden. I feel I'm able to get on with me life some. Funny, that. It were a sudden feeling, like me sorrow were lifted from me and I can think about Ciss now without wanting to break me heart. By, lad, what've you been eating? You're like a ton o' bricks!'

Gary laughed out loud, and Jack joined him. It felt good to be having a joke with Gary again, though Gary was right to be worried over Billy.

338

He'd definitely to do something about the lad. He'd talk to Megan and perhaps find time himself to pay Billy a bit more attention – take him fishing regularly and spend some time talking to him. Provide him with another way of looking at things to what he saw and heard at home.

Laura had been deep in thought. She'd decided recently that it was time Jack came out of his morose mood and had renewed her attempts to seduce him. The signs so far were encouraging.

These last couple of years had been a real trial to her, though she'd had some relief from her frustration. Apart from throwing herself into her work, she'd amused herself with Daniel, Charles's younger brother. He was far too young for her, of course, but it had been fun – the thrill of contrived meetings, teaching him to become a skilful lover, and all without Charles and Daphne having an inkling of what was going on! – and Daniel's mastering of the art of satisfying her had served to help keep her yearnings at bay. But it was over with Daniel now. He'd written her a sweet letter telling her about a girl he'd met and how wonderful she was. She'd written back saying she would never forget their encounter, and that she hoped he would always keep it in his heart as a beautiful shared secret, and not let it become sordid in his mind and a source of embarrassment whenever they met. That had put it to bed nicely, she thought.

She sighed heavily. It had worked well, Jack being her chauffeur. There were ample opportunities for her to have exactly what she wanted, with no chance of anyone on the estate or from the village finding out – or, for that matter, Charles. She didn't mind Daphne knowing, and it'd be quite fun to have someone to talk to. She'd missed that, during her tryst with Daniel.

The trouble was that since his wife's death, Jack had built an even thicker barrier around himself. *Damn it, all I need is an opportunity to present itself. A chance happening ... something! Anything that will pull Jack out of his depression and get him thinking like a man again!*

She impatiently lit a cigarette and inhaled deeply. She'd another few minutes before she needed to leave for the meeting with her works and estate managers. To her annoyance, the hot smoke caused her to erupt into a coughing fit. She stubbed the cigarette out and struggled to catch her breath. The linctus Dr Cragshaw had given her was having no effect. She half-thought about asking him to prescribe her something else, but knew all he'd tell her was that she'd have to give up smoking. He'd already talked about her seeing a specialist, which had worried her. She lay back in the chair, and her breathing calmed. She let the niggling worry over her health drift out of her thoughts and turned her mind back to her quest for Jack.

A knock at the door made her jump. Hamilton, at her bidding, entered the room.

Now what? If he'd come complaining about the kitchen staff again, she'd go mad. Oh God, her life was so boring. She needed something to happen. Anything! Even if it was the completion of the Byron Electric Company deal, though at least the wrangling going on at the moment gave some respite from the boredom. Thank God she was going away with Daphne to her holiday cottage in Scarborough soon.

'I'm sorry to disturb you, Ma'am.'

'What is it, Hamilton?'

'Henry Fairweather's in the kitchen, Ma'am, he's come up from the stables.'

For a moment she couldn't take in what Hamilton had said: Diamond, rearing up and throwing Ardbuckle off his back! It didn't seem possible. Diamond was a gentle creature.

'Where is Ardbuckle now?'

'Fellam has carried him into the stable, Ma'am.'

'Thank you, Hamilton.' She was already standing and reaching for her cardigan. Throwing it around her shoulders, she ran towards the stables, calling out to Jack.

Gary tried to sit up when he heard her voice. 'Oh, no! That's Mrs Harvey, Jack. Now I'm for it. Ouch!'

'It's all right, Gary. Lie still; she'll not blame you. Now just leave this to me, and mind, don't be mentioning owt about young Billy. Just say as horse stumbled, eh?'

'Aye, I will, but lad—'

'Shush now, she's here.'

'What happened, Fellam? Is Diamond all right?'

'I haven't had time to look at him yet, Ma'am. It seems he stumbled on a loose cobble or sommat. Gary's not sure.'

'Well, where is Diamond now? Has someone seen to him?'

'Henry said as how he galloped off down the

lane. He said he were limping slightly, but we were more concerned for lad here.'

Laura Harvey looked uncomfortable and unsure. He could see that she hadn't missed his inference that she was thinking more of the horse than of the lad.

'I'll stay with Ardbuckle. You go after Diamond. Oh, dear, I hope he's all right!'

Diamond hadn't gone far; Jack found him standing near the gate of the bottom field. By the time they were back at the stable, the doctor had arrived and was checking Gary over. 'How is he, Doctor? Is it bad?'

'Well, he'll not be riding horses for a while. It's a bad sprain you have there, Gary. You must have twisted it when you landed. You're lucky you haven't broken it! And I'll tell you something else, lad, you're going to have a headache to boast of in the morning. You've a right bump on top of your head, so you're to rest up and call me if you feel sick or if your headache persists. Is the horse all right, Jack?'

'Aye, he seems to have escaped injury.'

Laura was busy checking Diamond over, and Dr Cragshaw went over to help her. It was well known that he knew as much about animals as he did about humans, his dad being a local farmer. Jack watched him check the horse. 'You're right, Jack, there's not much up with him. He's a little shaken, but nothing serious. Now Gary's a different matter; he's going to have to rest up for a couple of weeks. In fact he shouldn't even walk on that leg for a few days, so if you can arrange to get him home, Laura?'

'I'll take him in handcart, Doc. He'll be reet.' Jack lifted Gary as he spoke, ignoring his protests and placing him in the cart. He laughed loudly at the lad's plea to be put down, but once in the cart Gary stopped moaning and grinned up at him.

'By, like you said, you've certainly changed of a sudden, Jack, but it's good to see, man. It's that good it's taking me pain away.'

Jack caught Laura Harvey's eye at that moment. She had a pleased look on her face, which changed in an instant to a look he'd seen many times before. He didn't shy away from it, and although he was embarrassed to hold her gaze with company around, he managed to let her know he understood, by giving her a quick nod. He hoped the others would just think he was being polite. Something in him told him she'd taken it for what it was, and a tingle of anticipation shivered through him.

Issy stood leaning over the gate, chatting to Gertie as Jack came up the lane. He called out to her as he passed, 'Any old rags, Ma? Cos I've plenty of bones.'

'What's you up to, Jack?'

'I'm running a regular ambulance service, Ma, and Gary here's me first customer.'

'Has he had a drop too much?'

'No, he just thinks he can ride a horse as well as I can, but he found out different, didn't you, lad?'

'Shut up, Jack, and get me home. You're making me a laughing stock.'

'I'm sorry, lad, but you had it coming. By! I've been waiting to get me own back on you for

343

pinching me job from under me nose.'

'Aw, I didn't, man, I didn't.'

'I know as you didn't, I'm only funning. I miss it though, lad – I'm not much for this driving lark. It were good when we had the studs, weren't it?'

'Aye, it were.'

'I'm coming for you next, Ma,' Jack called back to Issy as he manoeuvred Gary into the gate Gertie held open for him. 'I'm going to take you to knacker's yard. Mind, I've to fetch a bigger handcart first, as I'll never fit you in this one.'

Issy's laugh resounded down the lane. Her body heaved, and she dug her fists into her side to ease the ache the laughing caused her. It was good to hear. Gertie laughed too, but not as loudly. She'd taken charge of Gary and was bossing Jenny around as to what it was best to do.

Megan turned into the lane at that moment. 'Hello, Megan,' Issy called out. 'What d'yer think of this pair of daft idiots?'

A sad feeling entered Jack as he saw Megan. She didn't deserve to have to face the fact that Billy had caused Gary to be injured, and he didn't want to be the one to land it on her. He looked down at Gary and spoke quietly to him.

'Don't forget as you're not to say owt.'

'He's not to say owt about what, Jack?' Gertie asked.

'Aw, nothing, Ma. We were messing about and this happened. We don't want Mrs Harvey knowing owt, so we're keeping it quiet from all and sundry,' Gary told her.

'Eeh, Jack Fellam, have you been up to your tricks again?'

344

'Aye, I have, Gertie. I'm sorry, I didn't mean it to end like this...' He made a big thing of helping Gertie to take Gary inside, to cover for the lie, but he soon emerged when Gertie made it clear he wasn't wanted. 'We can manage now, ta very much. But think on, lad, though it's good to see you're feeling better. You should take more care of them around you when you're on with your pranks.' With this, she banged the door shut.

Jack looked over at Megan. She didn't question anything she'd heard and he was glad of that. He noticed she had a lightness about her and thought it was probably down to the hope she'd been given for her future. Something stirred inside him as he saw that hope shining from her. She was close now. Her eyes, beautiful, deep and dark, looked into his and her laughter had a lovely sound as she asked, 'What's silenced pair of you? Was it sight of me? Cos you were making more racket than a playground of young 'uns afore.'

'I've just been told off by Gertie, but I had it coming. Mind, your beauty had sommat to do with quietening me. It took me breath away.'

His tone was light, but he knew inside that he'd meant the words. He heard his ma laugh, but not Megan. As she looked up at him, a warmth flowed between them. It was only for a split second, but he felt as if he'd been punched.

Megan's nervous laugh broke the spell. She moved away and called back at him, her words returning him to normality, 'Go on with you, taking rise out of me. I'll get you back one of these days, Jack Fellam!'

He didn't answer her, but instead covered his

confusion by laughing out loud.

Megan almost ran over to his ma. He could see that her face was red from blushing. He winked at her and she smiled back at him.

'Well, lass, isn't that a sight to gladden you? Our Jack, laughing and carrying on like he was always used to doing! We were only saying about it earlier, weren't we? And I never thought to see day come again, did you, Megan?'

Megan was still looking at him as she answered, 'No, I didn't, Issy.' Then she called over to him, 'Let's hope as it's a turning point for you, Jack, eh?'

He went to answer, but his ma-in-law got in first. 'Aye, and for us all too, lass, because I feel as though me laughing parts have been drying up as quick as me fanny this past while.'

Megan's laughter joined his ma's.

'Now who sounds like a playground of young 'uns? Talk about calling pot black! Your noise is worse than any I were making.'

'It's your mam's fault. I can't repeat what she said, but it feels good to have a laugh.'

'I heard her. By, you're crude at times, Ma. You should be ashamed of yourself!'

'Well, it's good to have a laugh, and I'd like to bet as our Ciss is laughing an' all, lad. She liked a joke, did Ciss.'

'Aye, she did.'

Megan was looking at Jack with a concerned expression on her face. Issy had shocked them both by talking so lightly about Cissy, but he was glad she had. It'd take away the awkwardness he felt when talking of her when Issy was around. He

346

smiled at Megan and felt a gladness that things seemed normal with her, too. He'd been letting his imagination take hold of him, with this new light feeling he had. Megan was like a sister to him.

'Thou knows, Ma, I feel better of a sudden. I can't explain it, but it feels good. I s'pose as I haven't been much fun to be around these last two years, eh? And you've not been able to talk to me about Cissy. Well, that'll change now, love.'

'No, lad, it hasn't been easy for any of us. We suffered a big blow when we lost Cissy, but like I say, she'd be laughing with us now, especially if she knew as I'd wet me knickers!'

This set them off again, and Jack thought it was a healing laughter. For them to mention Cissy's name in merriment was something he'd never thought would happen again. He knew that from now on he was going to find it easier to live with Cissy's memory. It was as if she'd found a place in him that would always be hers, but was letting the rest of him go free to live his life as he wished.

The lightness in his mood stayed with him as he arrived back at the stables, where he found Laura Harvey still tending to Diamond. 'He seems no worse for wear, Jack,' she said as he came up to her. She'd taken to using his first name of late when no one was around. 'All the same, I will ring the vet to check him over, just to make sure. How was Ardbuckle when you left him?'

'In some pain, Ma'am, and he were worried as to how they were to get by without his money coming in. There's four in the household, with his wife and his ma and lad an' all, and they only have what he tips up to manage on.'

'Oh? Well, call by the kitchen before you go home and pick up some provisions for them, and see if they are all right for coal. If not, let me know and I'll have some sent round to them.'

He nodded, unsure of what to say. He'd not thought she would offer help. He'd spoken boldly and had made up Gary's words because he knew they would find it difficult. He'd hoped to nudge her into thinking about what it would mean to Gary to be off work a while, but he'd not expected her to take him up on it. Her words broke into his thoughts.

'Do you think you can cope with the horses while Ardbuckle is off work? I'll need you to drive me into the office first thing each day, as I have important meetings going on this next week, but, we could arrange a time for you to pick me up, so you could return here. What do you think?'

'Aye, I could manage easy, and I'd be glad to.' He patted Diamond's rump. 'I've missed looking after you, lad.'

'So you haven't enjoyed your job as my chauffeur then?'

'I haven't enjoyed much of anything these last two years, Ma'am.'

'No, I can understand that.'

She looked directly into his eyes. He held her gaze. She'd travelled the same road as he had, having lost her husband and son. She understood, he knew that, and this mutual understanding made him feel a kindred connection to her.

She was closer to him now, although he hadn't noticed her move or felt himself lean towards her. When she put her hand on his arm, he could feel its warmth and knew it would be soft to hold.

'I'm glad you're feeling better, Jack...' Her cheeks reddened and he saw the hunger deep in her eyes. 'I'll have this business at the mine sorted out in a few days, then we'll be able to exercise the horses together.'

He held her gaze again. She'd said enough. He understood. He felt acutely aware of her, and the calculating woman he'd known seemed to melt in front of him, until he saw a beautiful, vulnerable one. She removed her hand and held out the reins to him.

'Will you see that Diamond and Prince are bedded down for me?'

Her words, though routine, were spoken in a soft, appealing voice. He felt an urge to touch her and, as he took the reins, he brushed his hand against hers. She flinched. A fear clutched at him. He'd overstepped his mark. He turned and led Diamond away, and the relief to escape the nearness of her quietened his insides.

He had a need in him, and he'd wanted to take her in his arms there and then. But then he wasn't sure if it was just for her or if his need were general, because he'd had a feeling for Megan earlier, too. But that was different. That was... He pulled himself up. By, lad, what're you thinking? He shook his head and raised his eyes heavenwards. He'd not had feelings like he'd felt today since Cissy had died. 'Me little lass, I miss you.' Even as he said the words, the effect they had on him was unlike what he'd felt the other thousand and one times he had said them. His confusion deepened. It had been a funny day.

33

Jack Succumbs

Laura's problems at the mine had been escalating over the last few weeks. Demand was down, and yet the cost of labour was soaring. She had, though, received the boost she'd been hoping for: the contract to stockpile and supply the Byron Electric Company had at last come to a conclusion. She'd made many visits to the new company, negotiating the price per ton, and her chief engineer had worked hard to perfect a screening that would produce the exact quality of coal the company would require. At last it had paid off. The deal was to include them putting an electricity supply into the mine. This would mean she could install one of the new power-driven cutting machines, which would enable her to get rid of a good number of the workforce while at the same time increasing production.

Sitting in the back of the Daimler on her way to sign the last of the contracts, she felt relaxed.

'So, how are you feeling, Jack? A little saddle-sore?'

He looked at her in his driving mirror. He seemed unsure of himself, probably due to what had happened when he'd brushed her hand. She hadn't withdrawn it because she hadn't wanted him to touch her; it'd just been so unexpected.

350

'No, Ma'am. I thought as how I were going to suffer, seeing as it's been a while since I'd last ridden, but I've been all right.'

'Is Diamond doing well?'

'Aye, he's grand, Ma'am.'

'Good, I'm glad to hear it. I've been worried in case he'd suffered any after-effects from that incident with Ardbuckle. I understand from Dr Cragshaw that Ardbuckle is doing well, but won't be back at work for at least another two weeks.'

'Aye, but he's managing to get around, though, Ma'am. He's made himself some crutches.'

She could see Jack was beginning to relax. He glanced at her again in his mirror. She held his gaze, then deliberately put one hand behind her neck and started to turn her head from side to side as if to relieve the tension. She sighed and arched her back, her breasts straining against her tight-fitting blouse. He averted his eyes. He'd noticed!

'Actually, I haven't much to see to at the office, so I'd like you to wait for me. I think today we'll ride out together. I could do with the exercise.'

Jack knew what she meant. She had a way of putting so much into a few words – things that were nothing to do with what she was actually saying. He glanced in his mirror again, once more meeting her penetrating gaze, and he held her eyes for a moment longer before turning his attention back to his driving. They had reached the mine. He manoeuvred through the gates and eased the car to a halt outside her office. He didn't look back at her again, but got out of the car and opened the door for her.

'I'm looking forward to our jaunt out, Jack.'

Her body swayed towards him. 'I won't be long.'

The nerve that had tingled briefly when he'd seen her stretch herself now took a vice-like grip on his stomach muscles. He walked round the car and leaned heavily on the door, with his back to the office. He rolled a cigarette, lit it and drew deeply on it. He paid no heed to the noises of the mine or to the screen boys to the left of him, picking over the coal.

He had no doubt in his mind about what was going to happen, nor did he want to stop it happening, but he had a fear in him. His imagination wouldn't allow him to think about what it would be like to couple with a lady like Laura Harvey. His only experience of love-making had been with Cissy. A picture of Cissy came into his mind. It didn't come with guilt or pain, but with a kind of peace. Not that she'd approve of what he had in his mind, but her memory was no longer intruding on the new sense of freedom he felt.

He jumped when Laura Harvey finally came out of her office and called his name. If she noticed, she didn't comment. Once settled in the car, she leaned forward.

'I think we'll ride out to the south of the estate, Jack, to the paddock we have for family use. You know the place. You took picnic baskets there for us on several occasions a few years ago. It's very secluded. I often ride there when I want solitude.'

Jack wasn't used to talking in subtle riddles, but he'd understood her meaning and hoped she'd know his, too. He turned and looked into her eyes. 'Aye, I know the place, Ma'am. It'll be reet suitable.'

Laura's blushes surprised him and, as he had done in the stables a few weeks ago, he saw how beautiful and vulnerable she could suddenly become.

They had reached Hensal Grange and were turning into the gates before he looked again in the mirror at her. 'Will I saddle the horses then, Ma'am?'

'Yes, Jack, thank you. I'll just need to go to the house to change. I won't be long, I promise.'

This last she'd said with a cheeky grin, and something in him felt at ease. The grin had put them on two footings: one where he was master, and the other where she was. It was going well – better than he thought it would.

As Hamilton came down the steps to help her alight from the car, Jack turned in his seat and smiled at her. He'd never done that before. They'd had laughs together over work matters, but this smile was from a man to his woman. She smiled back in the same way.

They met in the stables half an hour later. He noticed that Laura still had a nervousness about her, and he liked it. Her vulnerability made it easier for him than if she was her usual high-and-mighty self.

'You're all ready then, Jack?'

'Aye, and you'll be glad to know as smell of mothballs that housekeeper had tucked around me riding gear whilst it was in storage has all gone. It was reet strong last week when I first put it on. It made me eyes water.'

Laura laughed.

Making sure his riding habit didn't smell of

mothballs hadn't been the only thing on his mind whilst he'd been getting himself and the horses ready. An odd sensation had come over him at the way things were changing between him and his boss. Had he really spoken to her like he spoke to his ma or Megan?

They went into the stable together to lead the horses out. He helped her to mount. This time she hadn't need of any tricks, and he held her waist and lifted her onto Diamond as if she was a doll. He slid his hand along her thigh as he released her, seeing the pleasure this gave her. But then she frowned. 'I think it best that you ride behind me, in the manner we always used to, Jack, just until we're out of sight.'

She had to bloody do it! She had to put him in his place. He'd not answer her for a moment – that way she'd most likely see as she'd put him out, by not trusting him to know how to go on. Once he'd mounted the horse he said, 'I wouldn't have it no different, Ma'am. I'd not embarrass you, or meself for that matter, in public.'

'I – I didn't mean to upset you. I just wasn't sure. I mean, well, with the new relationship we have, I'm feeling a little unnerved...' She smiled at him in that cheeky way again. 'Anyway, it's about fifteen minutes' hard riding to the paddock, you know. Do you think you're up to it, after your easy driving job?'

The moment had passed. Her smile and her joke made him feel settled again. He'd give as good back. 'Aye, I think I'm up to that. Mind,' he winked at her, 'I'll most likely be in need of a rest when we get there.'

'Yes, I think you will.' She pulled on the reins and set off at a fast pace, her laughter hanging in the air.

He didn't take up the challenge, but followed her as he always would have done until they were about a mile away from any possible prying eyes, when he urged Prince to go faster and came alongside her. She smiled at him but didn't speak, and they rode on in silence until they reached the clearing.

Once there, a deeper silence fell between them. Both were a little out of breath and hot from their ride. An embarrassment hung in the air. Laura broke it by saying, 'I usually unsaddle Diamond when I arrive here and give him some freedom to roam.'

'Aye, I'll see to them.' He looked around him. 'You're right, I have been here afore. I'd forgotten how beautiful it was.'

She didn't answer him, and this increased his embarrassment. He stood a moment and watched the horses gallop away to the other end of the clearing, his stomach clenching with nerves. He glanced at her. Laura looked hot, and he could tell she was feeling as nervous as he was. Her voice shook a little when she spoke.

'I've brought a flask with me. Would you like a drink?'

'Aye, thanks, that'd be reet welcome.' He took off his jacket and laid it out near the tree stump. 'Sit yourself down, lass. I'll get it.'

He found the flask in her saddlebag and undid the cap, the smell of good whisky wafting up at him. He turned to offer it to her, and was stunned for a moment at how different she looked. She'd taken off her jacket and had let her hair loose. It shone in the sun as it cascaded around her shoulders. He sat down beside her and watched as she took a deep swallow of the neat spirit, before handing it to him.

The whisky was the smoothest he'd ever tasted, and as its warmth settled in his stomach, he felt his nerves calming. He touched her hair, running his fingers along its length. 'By, you're lovely, Laura.'

Her name rolled off his tongue as if he'd always used it. She turned to face him. Her body swayed towards him. He kissed her hair, her forehead and the tip of her nose, then cupped her face in his palms and brought her lips to his, in what he meant only to be a gentle caress. A testing. But Laura melted into him and the kiss deepened to a passionate hunger.

The hunger released the last of his tension. She was no longer his boss, but his lover. It felt so natural to caress her body, to feel her soft breasts through her linen blouse. Natural, and yet the urge in him was so strong he was afraid he'd not conduct himself properly. It'd been a long time... He fought for control as, without releasing her mouth from his, soft moans of pleasure came from deep within her throat. Her tongue prised open his mouth, and he tasted the whisky on it as it moved in and out, sending sensations of pleasure shivering through his whole body.

They parted to hastily remove their clothes, and while they did so he couldn't resist touching her and planting small kisses on her breasts. The feelings that were building in him deepened his fear. Could he hold out long enough to give her full satisfaction of her need?

He needn't have worried. The moment he entered her she cried out with joy, her body stiffening beneath him and her thighs clenching him in a vice-like hold. He felt a spasm pulsating deep inside her, gripping and releasing him as she reached instant release. The sensation proved too much. His cries joined hers as he came deeply into her, bringing him an almost agonizing pleasure that he could hardly bear. As the feeling subsided he looked down at her. Her hair was pressed to her face and her eyes were moist and beautiful. He kissed her gently as he eased himself out of her and then, still holding her to him, he lay back.

After a moment Laura stirred and turned towards him.

'That was wonderful. It was beyond all my expectations, and I loved the way you took charge from the moment we kissed. And I like being called *lass*.' She stretched herself, and for a fleeting moment he thought of the yard cat whose movements were the same after she'd had a satisfying meal.

He smiled at Laura and kissed the tip of her nose. 'Nice of you to say so, Ma'am.' She laughed and snuggled back into him.

He felt happy and relaxed. He'd expected a wave of guilt or sadness, but neither came – just a peace. He supposed this was because it hadn't meant anything to him other than a giving and receiving of pleasure and a release of pent-up feelings. He hadn't given his whole self to her and he knew she was content with that. He was under no illusions:

this was just an affair. She was his boss, and they both had a need in them. They'd hurt no one, so he had no need to worry. He hitched himself up on his elbow and looked down at her.

'Are you all right, lass? You've gone very quiet.'

'Yes.' She put her hand up and ran her fingers over his brow and down to his chin. 'Thank you, Jack.'

'Thank you? What's that for?'

'For everything. For the way you handled things. I couldn't have blamed you if you'd taken me out of duty – as just another thing your boss wanted you to do – or if you had treated me like a whore. God knows I behave like one sometimes.'

'No.' He took her hand and kissed the palm. 'I wanted you as much as you wanted me, and have done for longer than you might think. It were just as time weren't right.'

'You knew I wanted you, then? I made it that obvious?'

'Aye, you did, and I'm sorry as you had to wait so long. As I said, it were too soon after I lost me lass. And afore that? Well, I don't know, to be honest. I'd like to think I would've held out against you, cos I wouldn't have wanted to have hurt my Ciss, but you were getting to me even then.'

'I – I'm sorry. I behaved badly. But, well, I was very lonely.'

'No, lass, you've no need to say as you're sorry. It were very flattering, if truth be known.'

'But I know how much you loved your wife, and I could have been the cause of you hurting her or even...'

'Don't fret yourself. It's all right. Nowt hap-

358

pened, did it?'

He lifted her head and kissed her eyes, and then her mouth. Her response surprised him. The kiss became achingly deep and demanding, and before it was over they were coupling again in a frenzy of pleasure.

A fear welled in him. Her giving herself to him in this second coupling was more than he'd expected or wanted, and he felt as though his very being was being sucked from him. And then his fears deepened as she reached orgasm once more, stiffening under him, for her cries throughout told of her love for him.

With his body still shaken with the intensity of his own release, his worry compounded as she clung to him, not letting him leave her. He stayed still for a few moments and then prised himself from her and lay back. Nothing had prepared him for what he'd just experienced. He'd been shocked by the depth of feeling she'd shown. He tried to tell himself all women reacted that way when they reached their special feeling, and he hoped that was all it was. He couldn't cope with anything more. He'd a strong feeling for her, but it wasn't like he'd had for Cissy or Megan. *Megan?* He sat up as this last unbidden thought hit him. *Megan? What made me think of Megan? And in that way an' all!* He shook his head.

'Are you all right?'

'Aye, it's nowt. Just me thoughts haunting me.' He gave his attention back to Laura. Her face looked fearful and he felt sorry he'd caused her distress. 'Aw, lass.' He stroked her damp hair from her face and smoothed her brow. 'You were bonny afore I made love to you, but you're beautiful now.'

Her naked body felt small, clammy and warm in his arms as he held her against him, and he realized once more how vulnerable she'd become in his eyes in such a short time. He'd always been used to looking up to her, being in awe of how rich and powerful she was. And, aye, he'd not always liked her. But then, he'd not understood her.

He'd had a strange day, with strange thoughts and ideas, as well as what had happened here. He'd never have thought it would be like this. His mind brought forth a picture of Megan. *What would it be like to hold her like this?* Sadness made his heart heavy as he remembered that she was going – and soon. Oh God! He couldn't imagine his life without Megan in it, and he knew he didn't want it to happen. He held Laura even closer, but it didn't help. The unsettled feeling inside him didn't go away, but he wouldn't let the reason for it become a truth to him. He couldn't.

'Right, lass, we'd best get dressed.' He released her as he spoke, and eased himself up. He had to busy himself. He gathered up her clothes and passed them to her, and as he stood up he noticed the horses standing together looking towards them. 'Well, I didn't know as we had an audience!' He bowed to the horses. 'That's your lot, lads. There'll be no more curtain calls today.'

Laura burst out laughing. Her laughter released any tension there was between them, and Jack felt glad for it.

When they were dressed, he lit a cigarette. It had been a good decision to bring a packet instead of his baccy tin, as he'd have been embarrassed to have to make a roll-up at this moment. He offered Laura one.

'I'll have one of my own, thank you, Jack. I only smoke one brand.'

Laura found her cigarette case and they sat down together. When she inhaled deeply, a fit of coughing racked her body. Jack felt at a loss as to how to help her, and he could only rub her back until the spasm passed. He'd heard her coughing before and he'd noticed a rattle to her breathing sometimes when she'd come back from riding Diamond, and just now when the excitement of their love-making had made her short of breath, but nothing as bad as this.

'You shouldn't smoke, lass, if it does this to you.'

'I know. I've been trying to cut down, but it's not easy.'

She stubbed out the rest of her cigarette and wiped her streaming eyes. He clipped the end of his half-smoked Capstan and put the nub-end into his pocket. 'Well then, we'll make a pact. When we're together, no smoking!'

'All right, but if we're together as often as I'd like, then I might not be able to keep to it.'

Jack smiled at her and decided to broach the subject that had been niggling at him. He'd intended to talk to her about it while they relaxed and smoked, but her coughing had diverted him. He didn't usually feel embarrassed talking with her about such subjects, but it had been a while since the stud had gone and they'd had any reason to discuss things of this nature. Right now he felt a bit sheepish.

'I were just thinking – well ... we didn't take any care. Against you having a babby.'

Laura smiled. 'Trust a man to think of that after the event! It's all right, Jack. I can't have children, not after–'

He took hold of her and pulled her close to him.

'I'm sorry. We've been through same mill, you and me.'

They held each other and it felt to him as if they were comforting each other's hurts.

A slight breeze that hadn't been there before rustled through the trees above them, and the birds that had provided the background songs to their love-making were becoming quieter and finding somewhere to settle. A dampness entered the air.

'Thou knows sommat? If we stay much longer they'll be sending a search party for us. We'd best get back.' He felt regret as he said this. He'd not wanted to spoil the peace he'd found with her. He stood up and called the horses to him and began saddling them, Laura holding each one steady for him. The silence between them became uncomfortable.

They'd been riding for a while when Laura slowed her pace. Jack dropped back until he was alongside her.

'I've been thinking. I'm going away in two weeks' time with my sis– I mean Lady Crompton. We're going to her holiday cottage in Scarborough. I was wondering... I could arrange for me to go a week earlier. She wouldn't think anything of it. She knows I need a rest, and she herself isn't free until the following week. And, of course, it would mean I would need you to take me and to stay over, to drive me around.'

He smiled. He was getting used to her double meanings. He nodded his head.

As they trotted along she told him more about Lady Crompton's holiday cottage. 'And,' she said as she finished her tale, 'there are no servants to worry about. There is only a housekeeper who comes in daily, so we'll have it all to ourselves at night!'

'It sounds good.' He smiled. 'It'll be sommat an' all, to go to the seaside. I've not been afore, except when I went to France in the war, but that don't count. It were dark when we boarded ship, and we never stayed long on beach when we got t'other side.'

'You'll love it. It's reet grand...'

He laughed out loud at her mimicking of him, and for a moment he felt like a young 'un who had been given a treat to look forward to. An urge to ride as fast as the wind assailed him, as though it would bring the treat to him sooner. 'Come on, slowcoach. It'll be dark soon. I'll race you back.'

'I don't give much for your chances. Diamond can outpace Prince any day.'

'That depends on who's riding him. Are you ready, or does you want a few paces?'

'Ha! Cheek of you, Fellam! Oh, Jack, I'm so happy. I feel happier than I've felt in years.'

'Come on then, gee up.' He tried to sound light-hearted, but her words had dampened his excitement and a heavy feeling settled in him. She was putting a lot more into this relationship than he needed or wanted. She could end up getting hurt, and he didn't want to be the cause of it. But would he be able to stop himself? At this moment he didn't know. There was so much confusion in him.

34

Hattie's Second Chance

Hattie poured the tea. She was on her own territory. Oh, aye, she'd left this patch behind many years ago, but she still came and had tea at Ma Parkin's now and again. It was as if she'd been lifted from here in body, but not spirit, and from time to time she needed the comfort the place had often given her in her dark days.

'How've you been, Hattie?'

Harry didn't look comfortable, and something in her felt that was as it should be. He'd not warned her, and yet he must have known.

'It were a shock, Harry, as I'm sure you knew it were going to be, but I've had some two weeks to get meself to a place where I can cope. I'm not saying as me heart isn't broke – it is. I miss Arthur every day, but not like the way I was used to missing him, because then I knew as he were coming back to me.'

The tears she'd still not shed threatened to stream from her. It was hard. For all her words of getting used to it, she wasn't. Not really. She was still in the midst of the shock of it all. And she'd read the letter over and over to try to get it to sink in.

'I never dreamed as this would happen.'

'I didn't know, Hattie. I promise you. I didn't know. His Lordship–'

'You knew that! You knew he were a lord using a false name?'

'Aye, I did. I was his batman, and me loyalty was to him through and through. I didn't like it, and many a time I wanted to tell you. I did, Hattie. It worried me because, though I could understand it at first, I couldn't understand it being carried on when you got so close. When he didn't tell you, it occurred to me then as he might one day do as he has. I don't think he ever got over his wife's rejection, and I think he didn't lose his love for her or his hope that one day–'

'Don't! It – it's too painful.'

Harry bowed his head.

'Just tell me what it is as he's sent you to tell me, Harry.'

'He says to tell you as you are to keep the house. He's put it into your name. I have the deeds here for you.'

'I don't want it. My God! He's never stopped thinking of me as his whore, and this is the final payment for me services? Well, he can go to hell!'

The tears spilled over and a huge sob escaped her.

'Hattie ... Hattie, don't. Don't, me love. I can't take you crying.'

Harry's reaction to her tears shocked her. He rose and came round to her side of the table. He stood behind her and held her to him. Was that a kiss he'd planted on her hair? Oh, Harry. She couldn't move, such was the unexpectedness of his action. She had always seen him as a dear friend, but he wasn't behaving like a friend now. His soft words were words of love

'Please don't take on. It'll be all right. I'll take care of you, my love. Oh, Hattie, I could never speak of it, but I've loved you from the moment I first set eyes on you. Hattie ... Hattie, forgive my lies. Forgive me.'

She stopped crying with the shock of it all. She didn't want to stop Harry; she didn't want to reject him. It wasn't just that he was a salve to her heart. It was ... oh God! How was it she had never noticed Harry's love for her? How was it she hadn't even known feelings for him like she was feeling now. Or had she? He had been in her thoughts. She had missed him – that was, when she wasn't mad at him for keeping the truth from her, but part of her could understand that. Harry was loyal, and loyalty was a good quality. And his loyalty was so strong that it had come before what was in his own heart. Arthur didn't deserve him.

'It's all right, Harry love.' Hattie covered his hands with hers. 'Come and sit down again. We need to talk some.'

As he sat down, Harry said, 'I'm sorry, Hattie. I didn't ever mean to declare me love for you. I was going to hold it inside me forever. I didn't mean to give you anything more to worry over. Don't think on it. I can go back to how things were.'

'I don't want you to do that, Harry. I – I'm a bit unsure of me feelings as yet, with everything as has happened, but I do feel sommat for you. And it's more than I were used to having. I just don't know if it's ... well, it might be because you are a salve to me.'

'I can wait, Hattie. Patience is a thing as I've been trained to. I'll be at helping you, though, love. I've not just come because of the letter. I've left Lord Greystone's service. I couldn't carry on, knowing what he'd done to you and the part I'd played in it through my loyalty to him.'

'But what are you going to do?'

'I've a mind to start up a business of me own – a cobbler's and barber's shop. Ha! I've even a name for it. I'm going to call it "Harry's End to End".'

Hattie laughed with him at this, and their joined laughter stirred something inside her. She'd always liked Harry.

'Laughing apart, I think as I could make a go of it. I'm skilled in both of them trades and I reckon that if one is slack at one time, then the other will compensate and I'll make a nice little living. Enough! Aye, well, that's for later.'

'Well, we're on with the same idea. Starting a shop, that is.' Hattie told Harry of her own and Megan's plan.

'It sounds grand, love. I've always worried over Megan. She deserved better than she got. I know I didn't see much of her, but I liked her and her mate. Poor Cissy. It don't bear thinking on. Such a pretty lass.' Harry shook his head. 'I've never forgot time as I met her. She sort of got to you.'

'Aye, she were special. And you're right, Megan does deserve better.'

'You do, too, Hattie. What're you going to do about the house and ... and, well, this other

367

business of yours?'

'I'm not for keeping the house, as it has too many memories. It's in me just to tell Arthur what he can do with his gift, but I've to think on. If I sold it, I could get out of game as I'm in. I've wanted to, this good while. I even have someone willing to take it on, but after I lost Arthur, I pulled out of the deal and were at hoping as me venture with Megan would be a way out sometime in the future. But now, though I feel as Arthur is giving me a final payment for me services and it don't sit right, I'd be a fool not to take this chance.'

'In this future you're planning, do you ever think a time will come when you could consider me – well, you know?'

'Are you honestly saying as you'd take me on, knowing of everything? Because I've a past as you'd have to live with, Harry.'

'I know you have, and it's never stopped me loving you. I don't know how it was that you came to be a ... well, you know what I mean, but I can bet it wasn't of your choosing. In my reckoning you've paid the price, lass. You've suffered more than most.'

'Aye, and you're right, this life weren't of me choosing. I will tell you of it one day, but I've a lot to think about at the moment. Let's just say as Arthur's not the first lord to have ruined me life.'

'Don't think on it as ruined, Hattie. What are you: thirty? No more than that, I'm sure. You have most of your life to live yet.'

'You should know it's rude to ask a lass her age, Harry! But you're reet, I am on thirty. And what you say as to me having a lot of me life left to live is true. It's just that at this moment in time I can't see forward without Arthur and all we had together, but I will. I'll take you up on your offer of being patient with me, cos I've a need in me to make sure as what I feel for you isn't clouded by the circumstances I've been brought to. I don't want you to be just someone as fills a gap in me. That wouldn't be fair.'

Harry just nodded, and Hattie thought her life was going to be more bearable for having him with her. She felt hopeful about the future, but for Harry's sake she'd take it steady.

35

The Pity of It All

Megan froze, her hand motionless over the pot of stew she'd been stirring. She held herself stiff and unyielding.

'Oh, aye. It's like that, is it? You can't even bear me to touch you now.'

'No, Bert. I ... you made me jump. You took me unawares. I'm sorry.' She made an effort and turned round to face him. He'd not approached her in this manner for some time. His need was usually satisfied by rolling on her and pounding away until his finish, and then turning over and sleeping. Or after a beating. He still had that sick trait, and beating her always aroused him. But to show a simple affectionate gesture like coming up behind her and stroking her was something he'd not done for an age, and it had shocked her.

'Aye, well, you don't give me any encouragement, thou knows.'

'Maybe I would, if you didn't treat me like you do, Bert. You've never been reet with me. It isn't just a clout on a Friday night with you, is it?'

'Oh, here we go. You have to bring that up, don't you? You have to get me going. By, Megan, you've a lot to answer for. You've made me what I never wanted to be. And yet, knowing what riles me don't stop you, does it?'

'Things could've been different, Bert. We started off all right, and when things began to go badly, there were times as it still could've been sorted. I've not wanted to live like we do. I've not wanted to be beaten from pillar to post, despite your thinking I like it. What you did just now were a nice thing – sommat as should be natural between husband and wife, but instead it were sommat as I never expected. And that's what caused me to stiffen.'

'Well, then, perhaps I should do more of it, eh?'

Bert pulled her roughly to him. His hands cupped her bottom, and she felt the hardness of him dig into her. This didn't worry her, even though coupling with Bert was the last thing she needed, but she'd not deny him. She'd do anything to keep the peace and get through these last weeks.

'Oh, Megan. We'll make a fresh start, eh? Come on, let's go upstairs. Lad's out playing; he'll not bother us.'

The kiss he gave her was a gentle one and, despite everything, it aroused something in her –

something she longed for. A loving. It wouldn't hurt to respond, and that she was able to surprised her. But then, it'd been so long since she'd had anything like this, and she was a normal woman, wasn't she? She wasn't the nothing that Bert had made her feel she was, and even Jack had shown her attention of late. Thinking of Jack made her respond with more passion.

'By, Megan, lass. Come on.'

She giggled at him. 'In broad daylight? Bert Armitage, what's come over you?' She was enjoying herself. 'Go on up, then. I'll just see to stew so it don't burn. I'll not be a mo.'

Bert kissed her again. 'Eeh, lass. Don't be long.'

It only took a minute for Megan to see to the stew, and within no time she had her cap in place. How was it that she could feel like this? Here she was plotting to leave Bert, and yet she was all roused up by him and for the first time in years wanted to take him to her! Well, she'd not dwell on it. Just let it happen. It might be nice to take a happy memory with her.

The shock she'd felt at Bert touching her was nothing to what she experienced when she reached their bedroom. Bert was hopping about on one foot, anger burning on his face.

'I've just caught me bloody toe on that fucking loose floorboard! I've a good mind to rip it up and have done with it. I think I bloody will an' all.'

She held her breath as he bent down. *Oh God! No ... no!*

'Leave it now, Bert. We've sommat better to be getting on with.'

'Aye, and that's a wonder an' all. What's made

you so eager of a sudden? You've wanted nowt to do with me for years. You've bloody needed it beating out of you for me to get owt other than a quick release. I haven't forgot that, thou knows.' He sat down on the edge of the bed and rubbed his toe. 'I've a bloody splinter. Fuck it!'

She held back the retort that came to her. She had to handle this right. Somehow she had to get Bert out of this mood and his attention off the floorboard. It didn't bear thinking about what he'd do if she didn't, and he found what she had hidden there.

'I'll get a bowl of water and you can soak your toe. It'll make it easier to get the splinter out. And, Bert, you're right about the other and I'm sorry. Like you said, let's make a fresh start. You've brought it about, with you being nice to me and touching me, like, so don't let's miss the chance, eh?'

He didn't answer. His expression hadn't softened. She ran from the room and down the stairs. When she came back Bert was having a go at the floorboard.

'Here, Bert. Leave that. Come on, get your foot in here. You don't want it to fester. I'll put rug over the floorboard from my side of the bed. I can make another one.'

'That won't fix it. It'll still stick up.'

In her desperation she emitted a crudeness that wasn't in her nature. 'Aye, but YOU won't, by the time you've sorted it. Are you going to let me down, now you have me going then, Bert Armitage?'

'Ha, Megan Armitage! I never thought to see

the day! Bugger the splinter. Come here.'

She made herself laugh with him and went into his arms. It wasn't unwelcome to her. Her shock at him discovering the loose floorboard had, for a moment, made her forget her feelings of arousal, and Bert's anger had brought her back to reality. But, as he kissed her, the longing rose in her again and she found she did have a need in her for the loving he was offering her.

'Eeh, lass. Let's take it slow, eh? It's always over quick because I've not felt welcome, but with you being willing – well, we can have some fun, eh?'

'Aye, we can.' She could say no more. Bert's kisses were gentle and loving, and his hands were giving her pleasure. Deep inside she felt a response of the kind she'd only ever felt once before. It was a long time ago, when she first learned from Hattie to lie back, let it happen and then to try to take a more active part. Not that she knew what it was her body wanted, only that she'd never reached it and that the wanting of it had always left her feeling unfulfilled.

Bert was in her now, his movements slow and his kisses deep. The feelings in her built and built, demanding to be released. She arched her back, thrusting herself towards him, wanting him deeper and deeper inside her and wanting him to go faster and thrust harder. She knew something was going to happen – something wonderful. She wanted it. She must have it! But then Bert cried out and his body stiffened. *Oh God! Not yet! It hadn't happened. It was so near ... no! No...*

'Aw, Megan ... Megan lass. By, that were grand.'

He rolled off her and surprised her again by

373

holding her to him, when he usually just turned over when he was done.

'Thanks, lass.' He kissed her hair. 'It could always be like that, thou knows. It were as good as what you've given me after I've beaten you. I've never wanted to beat you, Megan. I'd seen so much of it and been the brunt of it, and I used to vow as I'd never treat me own wife like that. It's just as sommat snaps in me. It won't again, I promise.'

His words and his loving hold lulled her, but the throbbing ache she still felt clouded her better judgement. She put her lips to his, and as he responded she deepened the kiss. Her body wanted more. Taking his hand, she placed it between her thighs.

Bert pulled his lips from hers. 'What's up? What're you doing? Wasn't I enough for you? After all we've just done and all as I've said, you have to bloody throw it in me face, don't you? You're a bastard, Megan. A fucking bastard!' He turned away from her.

'No, Bert!' Megan grabbed his arm. 'I ... it were lovely. I didn't want it to end. You've often took me a second time. It were so good I wanted to feel it again.'

'It weren't enough for you, you mean. Get out of it. Go on. I've had me belly full of you.'

Was that a sob she'd heard? Oh God! What had she done? The feeling that had fuelled her action was gone and she couldn't bring it to mind now. And yet it'd been so strong.

'I'm sorry, Bert. I'm so sorry.'

The words were heartfelt. She was apologizing

for bringing him to this – for being the wrong person for him, and for all the beatings she'd taken. It wasn't that she had deserved them or provoked them, but she knew now that she'd not helped him in any way to overcome his anger. Most of all she was apologizing for not having loved him enough and for losing whatever love she did once have for him without even putting up a fight to keep it. She'd known he was the wrong one for her. He hadn't.

She swung her legs out of the bed. They were so heavy they felt like two sacks of coal. Her whole body was heavy. Heavy with her guilt. It was a good thing she was going. Maybe then Bert's troubled soul could find some peace.

If in the future she did well from her business, she'd make sure he was all right. She'd save up to pay for a divorce, so that he was free to find happiness with someone else – someone who didn't rile him. Suddenly she wanted that for him, and wanted it for herself, too. Freedom. Freedom to find happiness. It wasn't much to ask, was it?

As she put her feet to the floor she caught sight of the floorboard, shocked to see it sticking up at an angle. Bert must have got further at prising it up than she'd thought. Her heart thudded against her chest. For all her new way of thinking about Bert, she'd not be able to deal with him finding her money and her locket. Most of all her locket!

What should she do? If she tried to put the board back down and he heard her, he'd start again. As it was, he only needed an excuse – and the floorboard would give him one. Could she get her hand in without making a noise and remove the wrap of money and the envelope containing her locket? She'd have to try.

Every board squeaked as she crept towards it. Why had she never noticed the noise the floorboards made before?

'Where're you going? You said as you're sorry and now you're trying to get away from me.'

This shocked her. There was a change in Bert and he sounded distressed. 'I thought as I'd let you sleep. I've to see to getting dinner done. And I am sorry, Bert. I wouldn't intentionally have spoiled what we did. It were like I said, it were best as we've ever had and I didn't want it to end. I've a lot to learn still. Many a time you've done it again, and I didn't realize as you couldn't always.'

'It were with it being so good, it sapped everything from me.'

'Aye, it were good. Well, I've to get on. You get an hour afore you've to get ready for work. I'll go and put your snap up and have stew ready for you.'

'Just stay until I'm asleep. I'm afraid of losing you, Megan.'

She couldn't speak. He was afraid of losing her? Then why? Why? Why had he done all he could to drive her away? She couldn't cope with this new Bert. What had happened? Had he found out she was leaving? No, it couldn't be that. He'd have knocked two bells out of her if he'd found that out. Whatever it was, his manner made her want to comply, so she got back into bed and pulled the covers over her.

Bert reached out for her and pulled her to snuggle into the back of him. *Oh God! That this change should come now! What should I do? What should I do?*

She lay cuddled up to his warm body. It felt good. This was how it should always have been. Instead she'd spent the whole of her married life lying on the other side of the bed, afraid to move in case she disturbed him. If she did, he could wake up angry and lay into her, or be aroused and pound her with his body, seeking his own release, with no thought for hers. And she *did* have needs, but no, she'd not think on that. She didn't want to wake up the feeling again.

Although she was more comfortable and soothed than she'd ever been, her mind wouldn't rest. The loose floorboard, and the consequences of Bert finding what it hid, roused a fear in her that kept her alert. She willed Bert to fall asleep. He was capable of slipping into a deep sleep in a short time, then waking refreshed after only having an hour or so. Please, God, let that happen now.

His snoring told her he'd dozed off. She took her arm from around him, fear tightening her throat. Should she roll over and lie for a moment, to check if he noticed? It seemed to be the only choice she had. If he woke, she could say she had pins and needles and had had to move.

Nothing happened. She lay with her bottom touching his for what seemed like an age. He'd not noticed her moving. As she edged herself towards the other side of bed, Bert snorted. There was an irritation in the sound. Her body froze.

His breathing became steady again. She inched away from him. Please let her find the boards that didn't squeak!

She'd done it! Her hand was under the board.

She could feel the money, and slowly she pulled it out. She could hardly breathe. As it inched towards her, she kept her head high so that she could see any movement Bert made. Now for the locket.

Just as it came into sight, Bert moved.

'Megan?'

She was lost. She'd nowhere to put the money or the locket.

'I – I'm just dressing. You go back off. I'll give you a call in plenty of time.'

'Aye, all reet, lass.'

He turned back into the position he'd been in. She looked around, hoping an idea would come to her. Her eyes rested on her clothes on the bottom of the bed. She'd have to put the money and the locket on the floor while she dressed.

This done, she bent to retrieve her packages.

'Eeh, I can't get back off. Would you bring me a sup of tea, Megan? Where are you?'

'I'm here.' She stood up, the packages once more on the floor. It seemed an age since she'd taken a proper breath, and her lungs felt fit to burst. 'I were just slipping me shoes on.'

'I think as I'll get up after all.'

He sat up.

One quick movement of her foot and the packages whizzed under the bed. There was a clunking sound. *Oh God! The piddle pot!*

'What was that?' Bert leaned over the side of the bed. Megan collapsed inwardly. It was over. Everything she'd worked for was over. Bert was soon to know it all. 'What's that?'

'What?' Her voice squeaked in response.

'There's sommat under the bed. A package.' He

slid off the bed. Megan wanted to run, but her body wouldn't move.

He had her money in his hands when he rose. If she wasn't so afraid, she would have laughed out loud at his expression. He counted it, licking his fingers to separate the notes.

'Where did this come from?'

She didn't answer. Her body shook. She was going to be sick.

'I'm at warning you, Megan. You tell me where this bloody money came from or I'll swing for you.'

'I – I've been at saving it ever since we got married.'

'Saving it! Then how come we'd to go without, day after day, and live on handouts all the time when I were on strike, eh? I'll tell you, Megan, it don't make sense. There's twenty pounds here – that's more than I earn in a bloody month! Tell me truth of it, or I'll knock it out of you.'

She sank down on the bed. Her mind couldn't come up with a believable excuse to give him, and she wished she hadn't kept so much. A couple of pounds would have been plenty to take her on her trips to Leeds, and wouldn't have needed an explanation. Her only solace was that he hadn't noticed the envelope containing the locket.

'I'm bloody warning you, Megan.'

'Well, why don't you just do it, then? Why don't you just beat me to a pulp? You'll do it anyroad. Your promise not to do it again were a farce, just like all the other times as you've promised me. You know as you'll be at hitting me, whether you find out truth or not!'

379

'Aye, happen as you're reet! Happen as that's best thing. If I beat you to a pulp, I'd be rid of you. And by 'eck, I'd probably be happier in a prison, even if gallows loomed for me. Because I'll never be happy with you, Megan Armitage. Never in a lifetime would you give me any happiness.'

His voice trembled with anger, and yet his words were heartfelt and regretful. Her guilt clothed her. How was it she was always plagued with guilt? Was it her fault that everything had gone how it had for Bert?

'I'll give you one more chance, Megan. Tell me where the fucking money's come from and what you were at, with stashing it away.'

'I – I've earned it.'

'Earned it? Doing what?'

'Sewing. I've been at making frocks for folk this two year or more.'

'What folk? What're you on about? Making clothes? How?'

'I've used Issy's sewing–'

'I might have known as that lot'd be involved somewhere along the line. You bastard! And behind me back an' all.'

The blow held all his wrath. It sliced her face and sent her reeling backwards.

She sat back up; she had to fight him over this. She swallowed the tears down. She had to stand her ground.

'What's the point in that, eh? You can have it all, Bert. It were going to be for your benefit, anyroad. I were saving it to take us on a holiday to Blackpool. It were going to be a surprise for your thirty-fifth birthday.'

Bert stood above her, the second blow he was getting ready to give her held in the air.

'You what?'

Where the lie had come from she did not know, but even to her ears it sounded plausible. 'I've been on with thinking about how hard you work and how you've never had a holiday, and yet what you can tip up hardly covers the basics. So I thought on giving you a treat. I – I never asked you, Bert, because I know what your answer would've been. So I went ahead. I did sommat of me own choosing and without your knowledge. I were going to book a treat for us.'

'Oh, Megan.' Bert sat down on the bed next to her. 'Why? Why does you do it? Didn't I tell you as I'd not have you working? I know as what I tip up isn't much, but it has to be enough. If it isn't, I'll tip up me betting money and give up going to the dog races. Does folk know as you've been doing this? I mean, other than that lot over there?'

'No. Don't you think as I'd have been found out, if they had?'

Bert shook his head. 'How come you could earn this much?'

'I've been at it some two years.'

'But who have you been making for?'

What if I told him? Would he do anything to Manny? She was mystified at how he was taking it. His anger seemed to have disappeared, so she took a chance and told him. He sat in silence a good while.

'So you mean as every time as I went in for me baccy, Manny were laughing behind me back?'

'No, he weren't, Bert. He were in on the secret,

381

and he were pleased for you.'

Again he was quiet. After a moment he said, 'I can't believe it, Megan. I just can't believe it. That you should have a plan such as this. By, it'd be good to take a break, but me birthday isn't till back-end of year. We've plenty here. Shall we sort it now, eh? And I tell you what. How about we take young Sarah an' all? She'd be company for Billy. Keep him out of our hair. What d'yer say, eh?'

What did she say? God! She didn't know what to say. She'd got off lightly with just one blow, and he'd not found her locket. And he wanted to take Sarah along on the holiday that was never really planned. Words failed her, but she knew what she could do. She could jump for joy! That's what she could do, but instead she just smiled at Bert and nodded her head.

36

The Breaking Out of Evil

'What's you got there, Sarah?' Billy laughed. 'He's a tiddler-and-a-half, he is. Let me see.'

'He's the biggest catch of the day, and I've beat you, Billy Armitage. And you're a good fisherman, or so you tell me!'

Billy laughed with Sarah. He'd felt cross at what she'd said, but he was that glad to have her to himself that he took it well. She was only teasing, he told himself.

'Throw it back in then, afore it dies. Anyroad, like I said, he's still a tiddler! Not like fish as me and your dad catch, when he takes me on river. That's what you call fishing!'

'Well then, next time you go, I'll have to come with you and show you how it's done.'

'Aw, give over. Don't start. We're not for fighting, are we? Let's have our butties. I'm reet starved.'

As she passed him a packet of sandwiches from her bag, Sarah said, 'You know, Billy, it's been good being out here on our own. I'm glad as your mam sorted it for us. It's good to have a picnic an' all.'

'Aye, it is.'

'Mind, we won't see much of each other when you go.'

'No. In some ways I'm not looking forward to it. Many a time I feel like telling me dad so as it don't happen. I think I might, because I don't want not to be able to see you every day, Sarah.'

'Don't do that, Billy. Me granny says as if your dad finds out, he'll kill your mam. She says as we have to accept as things change. It happens all through life, she says. Look at me dad – he's away more and more lately.'

'Where's he this time?'

'He's took Mrs Harvey on her holidays today, and he has to stay for the first week as she'd not have a driver. And sommat else has changed an' all. He snapped at me granny! I've never heard me dad do that afore. Me granny were having a go over Mrs Harvey, saying as poor thing must be in need of a rest, and me dad gave her what-for. He said as how no one knows how hard Mrs

383

Harvey works to keep everything going.'

'Well, don't worry. He'll be reet. Happen he don't like going away. One thing I do like changing, though, is us being allowed to come out on our own. Especially as we've not much time left afore I go.'

'I know. It's been good, but Bella weren't for it. She weren't pleased at me coming out without her. She scared me some afore I came. She got hold of me and squeezed until I thought as me life were leaving me. I couldn't breathe! Me granny had to smack her to make her let go.'

'She should be away some place. She takes up too much of your time. She's a nuisance. Me dad says as she should be in loony bin, and I reckon as he's right an' all.'

'Don't talk like that, Billy! Bella's not a loony. She's just a little slow, that's all. I couldn't have her taken from us. I love her, and she loves me.'

'Aw, you're soft, Sarah. You should think on. What if one day she does have a turn and kills you?' He shivered. The thought of Bella made his spine tingle, and now with this latest! He stood up and looked around. Things had changed, given him a feeling of not being safe, and he didn't like it.

'Don't be daft. Bella'd not hurt me. Not intentionally, anyroad.'

He didn't say anything. He just stood looking at her as she gathered up the wrappers.

'Are you stood up because we're going then, Billy?'

'Aye, but I need to pee first. I'll just go into the thicket. I'll not be a mo.'

384

'Hurry up, then. I want to get back to Bella.'

As he climbed the hill, apprehension settled over him. The thicket looked shadowy and menacing. He looked back to where Sarah was. She seemed a long way away. He wondered whether he should wait to pee until he got home, but his nerves had made it more of an urgency. He'd have to go.

When he entered the thicket, the eeriness intensified. He picked the nearest tree and went behind it. As he started to pee, a squirrel scuttled from behind him. He jumped. Fear caused his throat to tighten. The squirrel stood still. He let out a relieved sigh and then, seeing a chance for revenge, aimed his pee at the frozen animal. The drenched squirrel scurried a few paces up the tree, and Billy laughed out loud. He felt better, and his fear lifted some. He aimed again and hit the animal with some more of his pee.

'Sawah! Sawah!'

Fear snapped back into him, threatening to strangle the breath from his lungs. He knew that voice. It was the halfwit. Where was she? He put himself away. Sweat trickled down the back of his neck. He looked around, but couldn't see her. He looked back towards where Sarah was, and couldn't see her, either. He must have gone further into the thicket than he'd thought. Indecision held him still.

'Sawah! Sawah!'

Bella was getting nearer. He needed to see her – that way he could judge what to do. He moved towards the next tree and peeped out. How had she got here on her own? He didn't feel quite so fearful, now that she was in his sight. He'd have some fun – scare her a bit, like she'd scared him. He crept out of his hiding place and bent down to pick up some pine cones. He'd chuck them at her from behind the tree.

Bella was in the clearing, near the old mine-shaft. Perhaps she'd fall down it. The thought felt good. She turned towards him. She'd seen him!

'Biwwy...?'

He'd have to get away; he'd never been on his own with her. The skin on his arms prickled. He stumbled and hit the ground hard. Anger and fear welled up in him. He clawed at the earth to regain his footing, and his hand wrapped around a solid object.

'Biwwy fall? Biwwy hurt?'

The heavy piece of branch burned in his hand as heat filled his body. A redness clouded his head, searing it with pain. It hurt. It hurt bad. He stood up. She was near him, looking at him with those beady eyes. She stank. He hated her!

The sound of the branch crunching down on her head made the pent-up redness burst out of him. He could see her clearly again. She was lying at his feet. The branch was wet, and it seemed like the redness from inside his head was all over it. He threw it with all his might, listening to it swishing through the air. It landed in the mineshaft.

Everywhere was quiet and still. He shivered. Was Bella dead? The shivering became a tremble.

'Billy! Billy?'

Sarah's voice shook him back to reality. He bent down and grasped Bella's ankles, feeling sick to his stomach at the stench of her. Her clothes were wet with her own pee. She was heavy – the big, fat, ugly sod weighed a ton. He was at the mineshaft. One massive effort and she was over. For a split second, nothing. Then a splattering thud. He wiped the sweat from his brow with his sleeve. It felt sticky. He looked at it. Blood! The fat, ugly sod's blood was all over him. He retched.

Suddenly he was hit by the realization of what he'd done. Tears of panic ran down his cheeks. He'd have to clean himself. He grabbed handfuls of leaves and grass and rubbed his face and arms with them.

'Billy, where are you?'

'I'm here. Over here!' He ran towards Sarah's voice. 'Sarah. Sarah ... aargh!'

The earth gave way beneath him, and his body slipped and slid. He couldn't stop it. Earth and stones tumbled with him as his body came to a halt with a thud. His legs twisted beneath him. He couldn't see. The dankness, cold and smelly, cloyed at him. His screams made his throat raw, and he blocked his ears.

'Billy. Billy! What? Oh, Billy, I can't see you down there.'

'Me leg! Ooh, me leg. I can't move.'

'I'll get help. I'll–'

'Don't leave me! Sarah, don't go. Ooh!'

'I've got to, Billy. I'll run. Don't worry, I'll get someone.'

Calling her name was no use; she'd gone and left him. He had best think on and listen out for someone coming. The pain in his leg eased as the cold numbed him. He thought about Bella. She must be dead – she'd seemed dead when he'd dragged her – but he didn't feel sorry. Mostly he felt scared for himself. This was bad. He'd be in more trouble than he'd ever been in. He had to think of a story to cover what had happened. He could say she was near the mineshaft when he saw her and, as he ran to save her, he fell down this hole. Aye, that was it. That's what he'd say had happened.

Drops of rain hit his face. Their pace quickened to a heavy downpour. More earth and rubble slid down around him and puddles of water formed at his feet. He was going to be buried alive, or drowned! His screams echoed back at him through the rain. His voice wasn't strong enough to penetrate it. Blind panic gripped him as he screamed louder and louder.

Issy was distraught. On seeing Sarah running towards her, some hope entered her, but Sarah was screaming and tears were running down her cheeks. What was it that she was screaming? Something about Billy?

'Quieten down, lass. Oh God! Why did it have to start raining? You're soaked through. As if I haven't enough on me plate. Whatever you're shouting about can wait. Bella's gone! Have you seen her? Oh God! Sarah, have you seen her?'

'Bella's gone? Gone where?'

'I fell asleep, and when I woke the door was open and she'd gone. Whole street's out looking for her!'

'Oh, Granny! And Billy's–'

'Never mind about Billy for now. Oh, good, here's Henry.'

'Now then, Issy, what's this I hear about young 'un? I've just come in off fields.'

Sarah spoke first, and Issy stood aghast at what she was saying.

'Mr Fairweather, Billy's hurt! We were fishing at beck and he went to pee in thicket and didn't come back. He's hurt, Mr Fairweather. He's hurt bad. He's down a big hole. The ground just swallowed him. He was running towards me, then he was gone!'

'Billy? I thought as it was Bella as...'

Issy took Sarah in her arms. 'It is Bella an' all, Henry. She got out on her own and I can't find her. She'd nowt on to speak of. She'll catch her death! And now Billy. God, Henry! What's to do? What's to do?'

'It sounds to me like some of the old mine seam has collapsed. I'll raise the alarm, and rescue team'll soon have Billy out. Stay here now, Issy. Look after little lass. Go indoors and get Sarah dry and give her sommat hot and sweet. Aye, and yourself an' all, then if Bella comes back you'll be here for her.' As he turned to go, he added in a softer tone, 'Happen the women who're looking will find her afore long. She'll not have gone far. And if I see Megan round about, I'll tell her of Billy and take her with me.'

37

For the Sins of the Flesh

'Well, Jack, what do you think?' Laura indicated the beach and the sea with her hand, but really she had no need to ask. It was written on his face and in the joy he showed. He was having the time of his life, and was in awe of everything he'd seen since they had arrived in Scarborough just over an hour ago.

'I can't tell you, lass. It's just grand. I feel like a young 'un. Come here, I've a mind to dip you in the sea.'

'No, Jack. No! Put me down!'

'Not until I've wet your feet.'

'No, no, the water will be so cold.'

She wriggled away from him and ran as fast as she could, but he caught up with her. Her screams as he lifted her into the air and swung her round were a pretence. The joy she felt was all-encompassing.

As he lowered her to the ground, he said, 'All right, I'll not dip you, if you promise me I can be at making love to you all night.'

'Jack Fellam! You drive a hard bargain. All night?'

'It's your choice, lass.' He turned towards the sea.

'Yes... You can! You can, I promise. Let me go.'

Their laughter filled the air, and she couldn't remember when she'd felt so happy. She went willingly into his arms and allowed his kiss, brushing away the feeling of embarrassment that she felt at being used so in public. The pleasure of Jack's kiss was worth feeling self-conscious for.

When he released her, he looked out over the sea and on a deep sigh said, 'By, I feel so happy.' He hugged Laura to him, and then his voice changed and took on a wistful note. 'You know, I'd love to bring me family here. They'd love it. I can just see ma-in-law wobbling along on the sand, going for a paddle with her stockings in her hand.'

Laura took this chance to release herself from his arms. She could no longer ignore her embarrassment, and that of onlookers. To prevent Jack from noticing, she asked quickly, 'How is Mrs Grantham keeping? Is she well? I've never forgotten her husband. He was a good horseman.'

'Oh, aye, nothing ails Ma, but she still misses her old man. She gets on with things, though I think she's finding it hard to take care of little Bella. She's on two years old now, is Bella. She can be a handful at times. Mind, me little Sarah helps. She adores Bella, and she's a sensible head on her, has Sarah. Sometimes it's hard to remember she's only just on ten years herself.'

Jack had taken Laura's hand and they were walking back towards the car.

'And then there's Megan. Ma'll miss Megan. She's a grand lass, and for all as she goes through and all the hard work she does, she always finds time to help Ma with Bella. And, well, she's a big

391

help to me an' all.'

A small twinge of worry shot through Laura. Jack talked of this Megan woman with great affection. Even ... no! She hadn't let herself think there could be another woman in his life.

'Megan? I haven't heard of a Megan before. Is she a relative?'

Listening to Jack telling of Megan and her life, and of the beatings she took from her husband, deepened the worry she'd felt. His passion when he spoke made it obvious that he had deep feelings for this woman, even if he didn't realize it.

'If I could do owt about how Bert beats her, I would. In fact I'd gladly swing for the crime of killing him. And if I ever did interfere, that's what I'd have to do: kill him. Because just giving him a hiding would only make things worse for Megan.'

'You said that your mother-in-law is going to miss this Megan. Does that mean she's planning to leave?'

'Aye, she is.'

Hearing how Megan had worked hard to earn enough money to better her life made Laura feel desolate. Jack loved this woman – it was clear from the way he spoke of her – and the know-ledge of it was breaking her heart. Jack was hers! She'd longed to have him for so many years. Well, one thing she did know: now that she had him, no one was going to take him from her. No one!

'So she is actually going to leave her husband? Surely she realizes that such an action will make her an outcast? I mean, even amongst the lower classes there is a certain code of honour and a sense of right and wrong. I can't imagine that breaking marriage vows and taking a child away from its father is looked upon in a very good light. She will have to resign herself to being on her own for the rest of her life, unless this – whatever his name is – gives her a divorce. But really, I can't see it. These things are expensive, and very hard to come by.'

'His name's Bert Armitage. He works for you down your mine and has done for some fifteen years or more. And you're right: us lower classes do have a code of honour and a sense of right and wrong.'

'I didn't mean... Oh, Jack, I'm sorry. I was just thinking of – well, you wouldn't want a friend, especially a close friend, to suffer the stigma that Megan is certainly going to suffer. Not to mention her son.'

'No, and she's thought on that. She's going to pass herself off as a widow. Lad'll go along with it. He suffers a hit at his dad's hand, so is looking forward to getting out of it. That's why he's kept quiet over what his mam's up to.'

'Well, I hope it goes well for her. Anyway, that's enough talk of Breckton and the goings-on there. Shall we have our picnic? I'm suddenly feeling really hungry.'

'Aye, here's as good a place as any. I'll nip over to the car and bring the baskets and the blankets over.'

There was a note of discord between them, and Laura was cross with herself for highlighting the fact that they were from different classes. She was troubled, too, because it occurred to her that when the woman had left, Jack might – in the

393

missing of her – realize his true feelings for her. And, worst of all, the way would be clear for him! Oh God, she couldn't bear it! She wasn't going to let that happen.

Laura woke first and lay looking at Jack. Images from the night before flashed into her mind, and her body tingled with thrills at the memory. They had made love three times during the night. He'd completely sated her.

Scrunching up into a satisfied ball of pleasure, she pondered how different things would be, if only Jack was of her own class. They could be more open with their relationship, go out socially together and there would be opportunities to stay in hotels without causing a stir. Or even marry!

But all that was impossible. Just one night away with him, trying to live as equals, had shown her that the social gulf between them was unbridgeable. Knowing this didn't lessen her need of him or ... or her love for him – because she knew beyond any doubt that she did love Jack, and always would.

The thought brought with it a fear: what of that woman?

She had to do something. Jack had said Megan's husband worked down the mine and that he beat her, sometimes near to death. A feeling of jealous rage snaked around inside her as she thought that if the husband didn't 'near kill her', as Jack had put it, then she would! Well, that wouldn't be possible, but she'd have to think of a plan that would get rid of this Megan woman and at the same time scupper her idea of setting up on her own, because, to ensure that Jack would never stand a chance with Megan, Laura needed her to stay with her husband.

There was only one way. She'd have to sack Armitage and evict them from the cottage – that way the woman would find it almost impossible to get away from her husband. And to make sure, she'd see to it that Armitage knew of his wife's plans and the fact that she had money. Yes, that was what she must do, and the timing was perfect. With plans already in hand to cut the workforce, Armitage would just be one of many she'd be getting rid of. It would have to be soon, as didn't Jack say there was someone helping Megan – a partner of sorts – who was already looking for a place for her? One had to admire someone of the lower classes, especially a female, putting into action such an elaborate plan, and about to actually pull it off! Well, almost pull it off. A part of her felt sorry for her rival, with the plans that she'd been dreaming of for so many years so nearly in her grasp. Ha, she didn't think so!

The thought of the battle ahead gave Laura pleasure. She turned over to face Jack. Brushing her naked body against his had the desired effect. He opened his eyes.

For a moment Jack felt disorientated, but, as memory flooded in, a little smile curled his lips. Laura raised herself onto one elbow and looked down at him. Her hair tumbled over his face, and as she put her hand up to sweep it back, her nipple brushed his lips. He kissed it gently. 'By, that's a nice way to be woken up.' He put his arms around her, eased her down by his side and rolled over, so that he was looking down on her. His throat felt dry. His body reacted to the feel of her. He'd thought he'd not be ready to take a woman to him again for days, so it surprised him to find that he was in fact ready. He pushed his hardness against her soft skin. 'I've a feeling on me again, lass. I...'

'Kiss me, Jack, kiss me.'

The kiss didn't end before he'd entered her, and her pleasure filled his being. She was receptive and yet surprisingly demanding. He hadn't expected this, after he'd sated her beyond anything he'd known the night before, but he wasn't for arguing. He allowed her to roll him over and take all she wanted from him. He lay back, soaking up the intense thrills she gave him, until her moans turned to hollers, her body stiffened on his and the pulsating deep inside her told him she was done. He knew then the ecstasy of taking from a willing and satisfied woman. He'd no need to think of her needs, or how to pleasure her. His mind could wander. She could be who he wanted her to be. *Megan... Oh, Megan.* His pleasure intensified with the thought, and the fantasy engulfed his senses as he thrust into Laura, gently at first and then harder and harder. *Oh God! Oh God!*

The release brought feelings that racked his body and took all control from him. It took all his effort to keep from calling out to Megan. When it was over, he slumped down on Laura, exhausted.

They lay facing each other. An unease crept into Jack and guilt plagued him. He wasn't sure if it was because he'd used Laura or because he'd thought of Megan in that way, but it wasn't a comfortable feeling. Suddenly he felt at odds with himself, with what he was doing and with his surroundings.

This grand bedroom was larger than all the rooms in his cottage put together. Even the softness of the sheets, which had added to his excitement when he'd first got between them last night, now felt strange.

He wondered how it could all have seemed right to him yesterday. He had excused himself with the thought that he was hurting no one, but now he wasn't sure. Laura talked as if they had a future together, and it frightened him. He wished she would see it all like he did. How could it be any different? They were two people who had a need in them and an attraction for each other. Nothing more. There could be nothing more. Their lives were worlds apart.

'What's wrong, Jack? You look worried. I hate that look you sometimes have on your face. I can't make up my mind if it's regret, or if I'm just the wrong woman.'

'There's no look, lass. I'm still trying to get used to the situation, that's all. Me having an affair with me boss don't always sit easy. But we're not hurting anyone, are we? We're free to do as we like, and any one of us can stop it when we want to, can't we?'

Laura looked dismayed, and he felt a sorrow creep over him. He had to lighten the moment, bring in some fun and make an excuse to get away from her for a while, so he could gather himself together. 'Anyroad,' he sat up and playfully grabbed her pillow from under her and put it over

397

her face, 'I've another need on me just now. And it's not the same as the one as I've just had on me. It's for a nice pot of tea!' Laura pushed the pillow away in an agitated manner, a look of fear clouding her face. His fun-making hadn't seemed to work. He tried a cheeky grin before getting off the bed. Her expression changed, but not so that she was showing less worry. Her eyes travelled over his body. They'd been naked with each other all of the times they'd been together, but she hadn't actually looked at him – not the way she was doing now. He twirled around. 'Like what you see, eh?'

The smile crept back over her face at last. 'Jack Fellam, you take my womanly pleasures from me, and then all you can say is that you need a pot of tea! But I can forgive you, as you are so beautiful to look at.'

He laughed at her. 'So you didn't have any of me manly pleasures, then? By, you're a hard woman to please!'

Laura didn't answer him, but as he left the room he saw her lean over and take a cigarette from her packet on the side of the bed – the 'no smoking' rule hadn't lasted, then. He was glad of that, as there was nothing more he wanted at this moment than a smoke. Maybe it would ease the unsettled feeling inside him.

The sound of her coughing followed him along the corridor to the bathroom. Hesitating, he nearly turned back, but the hacking stopped. Why she didn't have the tests that Dr Cragshaw wanted her to have was beyond him. That cough was more than an infection.

As if he'd been doing it all his life, he ran a hot

bath for himself. This so-called 'cottage' was like a palace to him. No tin bath to haul in and fill with buckets. *By, this is the life!*

Refreshed as never before, he made his way to the kitchen. He knew where everything was, as he'd made Laura supper the night before. Having heard her go into the bathroom and start running a bath for herself, he knew he had a few minutes now, so he poured himself a mug of tea and sat on the wooden armchair next to the grate. His mind was still troubled over what had visited him whilst he was making love to Laura. He had to pull himself up; thinking of Megan in that way wasn't any good. God knows what she'd think, if she knew. By, if he knew anything, she'd laugh at him and tell him not to be so daft.

When he returned to the bedroom, he found Laura sitting up in bed, her complexion rosy from the hot water. He avoided her eyes. 'I just missed the daily help. She was opening back door as I scurried out of the kitchen.'

'I wondered what you were laughing at. Oh! Have you poured my tea?'

'Aye, is owt wrong?'

'No, no. Well, I'm not used to having it poured for me, and I'm used to having a tray. Oh, never mind.'

He ignored this. A lot of her ways were different from his, and it wouldn't hurt for her to keep being reminded of them. He hoped it would bring their situation into perspective for her. Aye, he knew she was used to a tray with a silver pot of tea and a jug of hot water and another of milk, as well as slices of lemon and cubed sugar. He'd seen it all prepared in the kitchen back at the big house, but he was used to a mug of tea and he wasn't about to change his ways. 'Well, I'd better hop on up to the attic-room, where I'm supposed to be sleeping, and make the bed look as if I did,' he told her, then left her to the irritation she showed at his service.

A short time later he was sitting in the kitchen with Janet, as the daily had told him to call her, enjoying the hot breakfast she had cooked for him. She had already served Laura in the dining room and was having a cuppa before cleaning upstairs.

Making small talk, Jack asked her, 'Do you have far to come?'

'No. I just live t'other side of park. If yer get some time to yerself, yer want to walk round Peasholm Park. It's grand—' The sound of the front doorbell interrupted her and she got stiffly to her feet. 'There must be some rain in the air. Me rheumatics are giving me gyp the day.'

She was back in no time.

'It were a telegram for Mrs Harvey. I wonder what's up?'

The muscles in Jack's stomach clenched. A telegram meant urgency. He waited, his nerves on edge. A sixth sense told him the telegram concerned him.

The sound of the bell summoning Janet had her getting to her feet, but he stayed her. 'I'll go. Whatever it is, she'll more than likely need you to fetch me anyway.'

'Jack, I ... I'm sorry.' Laura's hand shook as she held the telegram out to him.

The edgy nerves gripped him harder. His eyes

400

read the words. His body trembled, disbelief forcing him to read the telegram again. The brutal truth of it sank in. Bella, his little Bella. 'Aw, no. No! No...' He sank down into the nearest chair.

Laura knelt down in front of him and clasped his hands in hers. 'Oh, Jack. Jack.'

He wouldn't take hold of her hands and clamped his own together inside hers. The deep anger and hurt in his eyes caused her to look away from him. He couldn't blink. She flinched under his gaze as she tried to comfort him again, then she rose and went round behind him. Her arms enveloped him and she tried to cradle him to her, but he didn't want this. He heard a moan – a moan that came from deep within him. Pain trembled through him. He felt her kiss the top of his head and smooth his brow with her hand.

'No!' His body swayed away from her, bringing him to his feet. 'How could it happen? A mine-shaft! I thought as they were all covered.'

'It must be one of the old ventilation shafts. A closed seam. Probably from before I took over, but what would she be doing near one? Did she play that far from home? Oh, I wish to God that Charles had put a telephone in this place, so we could find out more!'

'She must've gone with Sarah and Billy to the beck. It says a boy tried to get to her, but a seam collapsed and he was hurt. It doesn't give his name, but if it is Billy, then Megan... Poor Megan.' He looked at the telegram again, thinking he might have missed something about Sarah, but no – she must be safe. But how was she to cope with this? There was only one thing he needed to do: he

401

must get back to her. Guilt flooded into him. He'd left his family unprotected, for the needs of his own body.

'Jack?'

Hate welled up in him. It was the same burning feeling he'd felt a few moments ago. He watched Laura recoil again, and it seemed right that she should, because the hatred he held in him came from blame. It was Laura's mineshaft that Bella had fallen down, and it was Laura who was responsible for the safety of the closed seams. And it was the pleasures of her body that had kept him from his family. Aye, and he hadn't had to ask for them, either! She'd given them to him on a plate.

Turning away, he went out into the hall, took the stairs two at a time and made his way to the attic. It only took a minute for him to gather his things together, but in that time he saw the unjustness of his thoughts and sank down onto the bed.

Laura entered. 'Jack. Please. I...'

'It's all right, lass. I'm sorry. I shouldn't have looked at you like that. It's not your doing.'

When she came to him, he opened his arms and took comfort from her. She was just a lonely lass and he'd taken advantage of the fact that she was attracted to him. He knew now the blame was solely his own. The warmth of her embrace helped to ward off the cold that had clutched at his heart. 'I'll have to go home, and I need to go this minute.'

'Yes, of course, darling.'

The endearment brought him renewed guilt,

reminding him that she was getting in too deep. He couldn't cope. It wasn't her he needed it was Megan. He let go of Laura and sat down heavily on the side of the bed. All of a sudden he felt as if someone had turned a light on inside him. In his mind it had been Megan he'd made love to last night. He could admit it now and feel no guilt. The love that had flowed through his veins had been for Megan, and his need at this moment told him the truth of it. He loved Megan. He loved her so much it hurt. He wished to God it was her by his side.

Laura sat down beside him. He saw a desperation in her, but she didn't question him. Instead she went into all the practicalities that he couldn't yet allow his mind to think of. 'You get yourself home right away. I'll be fine, and if things haven't settled down for you by the time you are to fetch me home in a fortnight, just get Hamilton to telephone Lord Crompton and inform him.' Her voice droned on in his ears, an intrusion on his feelings. It confused him. He wanted to be away from her. He wanted to be with his little Sarah and his ma-in-law, and he had a desperate need to be with Megan. He wanted to hold them all, say how sorry he was, and tell them of his love and how he'd never leave them alone again. An urgency in Laura's voice penetrated his confusion. 'Listen, Jack, I know you don't want to think of these things now, but when your head clears and you are faced with them, you'll need to know what I want you to do.'

He made an effort to listen to her. Laura was different from him. She was of the stiff-upper-lip class. He'd listen to her orders, and then he could go.

'If you are not feeling up to taking the car into York next week for its service – you remember, I arranged for it to be done whilst I am still here, and have the use of Lady Crompton's car? Well, if you are unable to, don't worry. You can get Hamilton to telephone through to the garage and rearrange a date. But we do need to concern ourselves with the horses...'

Some of what she was saying was going in. And it helped. It helped him to put up a curtain in his mind, to block out what he really had to deal with.

This feeling lasted until after he'd said goodbye to her, promising that he would take care and that he would contact her if he needed any help from her. It didn't lift during the drive home, but the moment he entered his home and saw Issy, it fell away and the pain hit him afresh.

PART SIX
The Consequences
1930

38

A Future Hope Cut Deep with Sorrow

'I can't believe it, Harry! That we should find two shops in the same road! And both are fit for purpose. But, best of all, I haven't told you yet, but there's a house for sale just two streets away that I'm going to bid for. It'll be perfect. I can have it turned into two flats: one for Daisy and Phyllis, and the other for me and Sally.'

'You've not thought any more about my proposal then?'

'Aye, I have. But I'm still not sure. I need time to get over Arthur. I'm flattered as you want me, Harry, but it's only been a short while since it all happened. I want to take it slow. It's for your sake as much as mine.'

'But I want you so badly, Hattie. I – I need you in all ways. I mean, whilst I was just keeping you hidden in here,' Harry tapped his chest, 'I could cope. But now as I've declared meself and think as I have a chance, it isn't so easy to ignore the nearness of you and–'

'Harry – Harry, stop this. You're not being fair to me or to yourself. You promised me...'

'But can't I just hold you, and maybe a kiss?'

'Oh, Harry.'

'All right, lass. I'll not mention it again.'

Harry turned his attention back to his paper,

and Hattie poured the tea Ma Parkin had brought to their table. Her mind was troubled over Harry. She knew she had feelings for him. He even occupied more of her thoughts than Arthur did of late. *But what if that wore off? How can I be sure?*

Her thoughts were cut off by Harry's sudden exclamation. 'Oh, no!'

'What is it, Harry?'

'Didn't you say Cissy'd called her babby "Bella"? And wasn't she a Mongol?'

'Aye, I did. Why?' She almost didn't want to know the answer.

'I'm afraid as she's been killed. Poor little lass. It appears she was playing near a mineshaft and fell down it.'

'No! Let me see. It must be her. Oh God, poor Jack. Oh dear, how will Issy and little Sarah cope? They doted on that young 'un.'

As Hattie read the story, some gladness returned to her. It appeared that Billy had shown his better side. He'd tried to save little Bella and had sustained a broken leg in the process – not that that bit of the story gave her any uplifting, as she didn't want him hurt; but it was Megan she was thinking of, and how it would be good for her that her lad had showed he did have a good streak in him.

'Oh, Harry, I don't know what to do. That this should happen just as everything is almost ready for Megan! I daren't go to them. There'll be so many folk milling around. How would I answer their questions? I mean, Issy's always passed me and the girls off as lassies as she worked with, on an estate out York way. It'd be difficult for me to keep that up, as I don't know what she's said about me role and suchlike.'

'I should write them a letter, if I was you, love. They'll understand. And put in it as you've found a place. Give Megan some hope, at least.'

'No, I don't think that's the right thing to do. Me finding a place is the last thing as Megan needs to be thinking of. She'll have her hands full helping Issy and Sarah and Jack. I will write, though, and offer me condolences. And then I think as I'll concentrate on getting all the paperwork for the shop completed, and get the upstairs ready for her, so as when I do go to tell her she can come straight away.'

'Aye, all right. You know best. But I'll not be of much help to you, I'm afraid, as I've only to sign on the dotted line to finalize the papers on my shop. So I'm going to be busy with buying equipment and setting it all up. Will you be all right?'

'I'll be fine. I'm experienced at this side of things.'

She couldn't tell him so, but she was in fact glad that Harry was going to be out from under her feet for a while. She needed to sort out how she felt about him, and if she was to take him on. Some part of her wanted to, but it wasn't easy to give herself fully again. Not so soon; she'd no trust in her. That was the worst thing Arthur had done to her: destroyed the trust she'd had for folk she'd thought of as good, and it'd left her feeling alone. Afraid and very alone.

Hamilton's voice droned on. Jack looked around the kitchen at all the familiar faces. He was still

409

closed off from the outside world. They'd all tried to help, but he wasn't for being helped. He needed to work his own way through the grief that held him, and he was doing that. He knew he had to; knew he couldn't let it take hold of him, as it had done after Cissy had died. His family needed him. He was to be there for them.

'...so Lady Crompton informs me that Mrs Harvey will not be home for at least another two weeks, though she is making excellent progress and is getting back to full health again,' Hamilton said.

Hearing of how Laura had suffered a bout of pneumonia after he'd left had not touched Jack deeply. He was sorry to hear it, but that was all. He tried not to think of her, or of what they'd done. He'd had a letter from her and had been shocked by the wording of it. It spoke of her love for him, and of how she wanted to be with him to comfort him. He'd burned it and hadn't replied, even though she'd asked him to.

At this moment he didn't know which way his life was going. The only good thing was that Megan had been delayed from leaving. Hattie had had personal problems, and the finding of a shop was not something she could put her mind to at the moment. He was selfish in feeling glad – he knew it, but he couldn't have got through this without Megan around. She didn't know how he felt about her. He'd kept himself closed when he was around her. It wouldn't do for her to find out. He couldn't imagine what she'd think of him, as she'd more than likely be put out and it would spoil the friendship they had.

'I will speak with you after, Jack. There are some special instructions for you from Mrs Harvey. If you will be good enough to come to my room, I will convey them to you.'

Jack nodded at Hamilton.

His thoughts turned to Billy. The poor lad had suffered for his heroics, with his leg broken in two places. But he was getting around some now, as Gary had given him the crutches he'd made. He'd cut the length down to size, but you had to smile at the sight Billy made, with the top bits being too big for him. He looked like a scarecrow with his arms propped up. He was showing a better side of late, was Billy. He'd have to find some way to thank the boy – give him a reward, so that he knew that when he was good it was appreciated. If only he could take them all to the seaside. By, that would be something. Give them all something to look forward to.

Hamilton had finished talking and was motioning for Jack to follow him.

'Come in, Jack. Now, Mrs Harvey is worrying over the service of the car. She says it is getting well overdue. She understands the position you are in, but wonders if you feel up to taking it in yet?'

'Aye, get it sorted, and I'll see to it.'

'She has also instructed that you go over to Lady Crompton's cottage in Scarborough and take some clothes for her. Her maid has packed them. Mrs Harvey is leaving hospital tomorrow and will be convalescing at the cottage.'

'Well, if you could fix up the service for this week – let's say, Friday – and arrange for me to take clothes and stuff next week. Tuesday'd be a good day, then any new parts will get a good run-in.'

'Very well, I'll let you know if that is suitable. Thank goodness Lord Crompton has had a telephone installed in the cottage at Scarborough, as it means I can contact Mrs Harvey direct. Well, thank you, Jack – that will be all. I'll confirm all the arrangements with you as and when they are settled.'

As soon as he left the office Jack's thoughts returned to Megan. It was dinnertime and he'd taken to going home to have his snap. He'd found it a comfort to be with his ma-in-law, and it put his mind at rest to see she was all right; and, with any luck, Megan would be there and he could talk of his idea to go on a day out.

On his way home he stopped off at the graveyard. The mound of fresh earth on Cissy's grave tugged at his sore heart. 'Bella, me little Bella.' He knelt down. 'Ciss love, I'm glad as she's with you, lass. You had no time with her when she was born, and doctor said as she'd a lot of suffering to face in the future. Be happy together, lass, and remember: whatever I do in the future or whichever path me life takes, you and little Bella will always be in me heart.'

When he approached his cottage Jack was surprised to hear laughter coming from the kitchen.

'Eeh, Jack. You should have been here five minutes ago. Your ma was in full swing. She's had me in stitches.'

'Well, I'm glad of it, though you needn't be

412

telling me what she's been saying. I can guess as it was on the crude side.'

'Aye, you know Issy. Anyroad, how're you feeling, Jack?'

'I'm all right, Megan. I've been at graveyard. Thou knows, despite everything, it feels good that Bella is with Ciss. I like to think of them together at last.'

'Aye, you're reet there, I'm sure of it. And, like you say, it's good to think on. Well, I've to make tracks. I'll...'

'Wait on a mo, Megan. There's sommat as I wanted to talk to you and Ma about. Ma, what d'yer think on us all having a day out. A trip to seaside?'

'A trip to seaside! Where did that come from?'

'Well, I thought on it when I was in Scarborough with Mrs Harvey. But...' The memory of holding Laura to him shuddered through his body. Never, never again! But then, would he have any choice?

'That'd be grand, Jack. But how're we going to manage it? I mean, we could go on train, I s'pose, but I've looked into that in the past and, with all changes as you have to make, it takes hours. It isn't worth it for a day. And what of Megan? She'd not be able to get out.'

'Oh, Jack didn't mean me.'

'I did, Megan. I were thinking on giving Billy a treat, to sort of thank him for how he tried to save Bella and for being a good lad this last couple of weeks. And I've a lot to thank you for an' all. D'yer think as you could sort sommat, so as you could come? We'd go in car, so you'd be back in time for Bert coming in.'

413

Megan's cheeks reddened.

'Well, I ... I s'pose as I could. It'd have to be when Bert is on six-while-six day shift. He's on that next week. I've managed many a time to get to Leeds on them days and he's known nothing of it. How far is seaside?'

'It's some sixty to seventy mile. I'm to take some stuff to Mrs Harvey on Tuesday of next week, and I were thinking on taking you all to the next resort. It's called Bridlington. I don't know what it's like, but if it's owt like Scarborough, it'll be grand. I could then go on and take Mrs Harvey's stuff and be back with you about an hour later.'

'I couldn't get into the car with you, Jack. Somebody'd say sommat to Bert.'

'No, I know, and nor can Ma, for that matter. I've not got permission to take me family anywhere. Look, I've thought all of this through. You and Ma and Sarah and Billy could catch the train to Church Fenton, and I'll pick you up there. The Leeds-to-York train runs on the hour from six a.m. till last one at ten p.m. If Bert's off to his shift by five-forty, say, you could be on the seven o'clock train. How does that sound?'

'I reckon as we could do it, Megan. Eeh, lad, you don't know what this is doing for me. Planning sommat as exciting as a day out! It's bucked me up no end.'

'I'm glad to hear it, Ma. But Megan's still looking unsure. Come on, Megan love, it's only one day.'

'Aye, it is. And if owt goes wrong and Bert gets to know, then so be it. Yes, I'll go. I'll sort everything so as I can.'

414

'That's settled then. I can't wait. Seaside! I've never been, have you, Megan?'

'No, I haven't, Issy. We were going once. On a charabanc outing with miners' welfare, but Bert put a stop to it at the last minute–'

There was a knock at the door. Opening it and seeing Hattie stood there stopped Megan in her tracks.

'Hattie! Oh, Hattie. It's good to see you. I never heard your car.'

'Well, it's outside. And you three look like you were up to sommat. You jumped out of your skins when you opened the door.'

Issy took hold of Hattie. 'Oh, it's good to see you. Come on in and sit yourself down. And thanks for your letter, lass. It meant a lot to receive it. It were a comfort, and we all understood how it were as you couldn't come. Anyroad, you've been through the mill yourself an' all. How're you coping, love?'

'I'm doing all right. It isn't easy, but I have Harry and he's a comfort.'

'Oh, Hattie, I couldn't believe it.'

'I know, Megan. It's still not sunk in with me.'

'But I'm glad as you have Harry. He's a good bloke, is Harry, and it were always obvious as to how he felt about you.'

'Was it?'

'Aye. He were a proper gentleman to us all. Our station being a lot lower than he was used to dealing with didn't matter to him. He treated us all as if we were young ladies, but with you there were a tenderness in how he was. I hope it works out for you, love. I mean, it's what you always

415

wanted – a proper relationship. A man as wanted you for yourself. A man as you could go to as his wife.'

'I did, didn't I, Megan? And I remember even saying once as I wished that could be Harry.'

'There you go then.'

'Aye, Issy, there I go.'

'Well, that's poor Hattie sorted out, between the pair of you. Now, when's a man to get his snap? I've to go back to work soon, thou knows.'

'Trust a man to think of his belly! Your sandwiches are in the pantry under that linen cloth. Now, I'll put kettle on.'

'I'll see to the kettle, Ma. Take Hattie through to the parlour.'

'Ta, Jack, you're a good 'un. Sometimes!'

'Come on, Hattie, before they start up with their banter.'

As soon as they were in the parlour Hattie asked, 'Well, what were you all on with, when I came in? You all looked guilty.'

Issy told her about their planned outing.

'That's sounds just the thing. It'll cheer you all. I only wish as I were coming, but some of us have work to do! No, I'm only fooling. I've done it all now, and all it needs is your presence, Madame Megan.'

'You mean...'

'Aye, I've found a place and it's all ours, and you know what? Harry's place, you remember? I wrote you about Harry starting up? Well, he has a place in the same street!'

Jack came in before she had time to reply. He put the tray of tea down on the occasional table.

'Well, I'll leave you ladies to it. I've to get back to work. I'll see you later, Ma.'

As he went out, his heart was heavy. The joy he'd felt at the prospect of having one day with Megan had dissipated. Hattie's arrival had taken it from him. He'd heard all that had been said. Hattie had news that would take Megan away from him for good. And he didn't want that. He couldn't even begin to imagine a future without her.

39

The Beginning of a Plan Is Put into Action

'You look ... worse ... than I do ... Daphne.'

'Well, darling, I have lain awake for most of the night. I'm worried about your health. I've contacted Charles and asked him to make some enquiries in York as to who is the best specialist for you to see.'

'Oh, don't fuss, Daphne. I'm feeling a lot better now. Is there any tea left in that pot? I'm–'

A fit of coughing prevented Laura from finishing what she was going to say, and she held her napkin over her mouth. Daphne came to her side, and her arm on her sister's shoulder gave comfort. The coughing subsided. Laura lifted her head. The glaring red stain on the napkin filled her with terror.

'Oh God! Daphne, what is wrong with me? That's never happened before.' Tears trickled down her cheeks.

'I don't know, darling. We'll have to get to York right away. I'll telephone Charles.' Daphne's arms tightened around her. 'Don't be afraid, darling, it may be that you've an infection in your throat and the coughing has made it bleed.'

Laura looked up into Daphne's face. She read her sister's fear, and knew she knew more than she was letting on. She allowed her head to droop and rest on Daphne's shoulder. She didn't ask any questions – didn't want to know what Daphne knew. Not yet. She needed to gather herself a little.

When her limbs stopped shaking, she lifted her head. 'I'll need to get a little stronger ... before I travel such a distance and ... face what's wrong with me, Daphne. I feel like a caged animal. I need some air. Couldn't we just go for a drive out? Get my sea-legs, as it were?'

'I don't think ... no. On second thoughts, I do think that's an excellent idea. Look, it's only eight o'clock. Let's get you back to bed for an hour and we'll see if you still feel up to going out then.'

As Daphne helped Laura to rise she heard her intake of breath.

'You've lost so much weight. No wonder you feel weak. We'll get some fish and chips and sit and eat them out of the newspaper! You always liked that. I think it must appeal to the bad girl inside you. Anyway, we've to fatten you up.'

'I am a bad girl, aren't I? I haven't told you all about my conquest of Jack yet. We'll have a good gossip as soon as I'm feeling ... better. Is it today that he is coming with ... my things?'

'Don't try to talk so much, Laura. Save your

breath. Come on, I'll help you back to bed. I'll ask Janet to bring you a tray at about ten-ish.'

'But if Jack comes – you will wake me?'

'I most certainly will not! For heaven's sake, Laura! Besides, you don't want him to see you in this state. I'll tell Janet we're expecting him, and she can deal with him. Now, that's right. Snuggle down. I'll see you later. And if you are up to going out, Johnson can drive us along the coast. We might even get as far as Bridlington. You remember? We visited it the last time we were here.'

Laura felt so drained and weak, and the fear hadn't left her. If only Daphne understood. She so wanted to see Jack. He would settle her mind. But she hadn't the strength to fight her sister over it. Oh, she couldn't bear this illness much longer. Please God, that the specialist would be able to help her. There was so much that needed her attention. She would do some of it when she got up. Things at the mine must start to move. That Megan woman had to be got out of the way. Oh God! Her head hurt so when she worried over it all.

The thought of the drive out cheered her and yet wearied her at the same time. She closed her eyes. Her thoughts drifted to Jack. If only ... if only...

'Here we are, Mrs Harvey. I've brought yer a nice pot of tea and a toasted crumpet. I'm to see to it that a hot bath is ready for yer, when yer done.'

Laura was surprised to be woken. She hadn't thought she would sleep.

'Thank you, Janet. Put it on the table in the window. Would you get my writing case for me,

419

please? It's in the top drawer of the chest over there.'

While Janet pottered about, Laura managed to get herself up. It took a massive effort to reach her chair. She flopped into it, feeling utterly exhausted. The nap hadn't benefited her at all, although her breathing seemed better.

The letter to her manager was hard to compose. She needed to tell him to get rid of twenty men, as of the end of the month. He was to notify them at the end of next week, and tell them she would be looking into vacancies in other areas for them. She would meet them in about three to four weeks, hopefully to inform them of where they could transfer to. Her estate manager was already instructed to make enquiries.

That part was easy enough, but to specify one of the men was more difficult. Eventually she realized the only thing to do was to be blunt:

I want you to make sure that a Bert Armitage is one of the twenty. I have heard stories of him beating his wife and drinking heavily, and I do not want to employ such a man.

This would surprise her manager, but he wouldn't question it. She sealed the envelope before she changed her mind. Sure that she had covered everything, her mind felt at ease now. Though how she was going to let Bert Armitage know what his wife was up to was another matter. She'd have to think about it in more detail, but not now. Oh, how she needed to escape the confines of the cottage and the fears in her heart!

40

The Clarity of Jack's Love Brings Heartbreak

'Issy, I've got butterflies, and I feel as though all of this isn't happening. I can't take it in that we're going to the seaside! And as for me not coming back here – it just don't seem real.'

'Aye, I feel that excited meself. I've mixed feelings on you going, though. Part of me's glad, but I can't get the sad feeling out of me, try as I might.'

'I know. It's a big step. And I'm going to miss you all. And, strangely, I feel bad about Bert in a way. He's been trying to be a better husband lately, and he were that looking forward to trip to Blackpool. I've left him all the money, though. And I don't wish bad on him. We should never have got together in the first place, and I blame meself for that. I hope everything works out well for him.'

'You need to stop feeling sorry for him and carrying guilt of it. No one has the right to beat anyone, like he beat you. You tried – in fact, you did your best – so put it behind you. And, lass, think on: you and Billy start your new life today, and I reckon as it's all fitted in nicely with us spending our last day together at seaside. I'm reet glad you decided to stay long enough so we could.'

'It couldn't be a better send-off and I wouldn't miss it for the world. But I've not said owt to Billy yet about us not coming back. I thought to let him enjoy today, then tell him at the last minute. Jack says as he'll help me. We'll tell him in the car as we get back to Church Fenton tonight. He'll not have time to think on it all then. What did you and Jack decide on telling Bert when you get back?'

'We decided Jack would take me all the way home, instead of me doing the last leg on the train. I can say then that I left you earlier, as I wanted to meet up with the lassies as I used to work with, and you went to catch the train home – and that were last as I saw of you. Did Bert swallow excuse as you gave him?'

'He were over the moon. Mind, telling him as I were going into York with you to fix up the Blackpool trip for him has made me feel bad.'

'As long as he believed you, that's all that matters. After all, there'd be nothing else he'd let you go for. Let him stew. He's had it coming this good while. I reckon as we can relax and enjoy ourselves. Except ... well, I know as I've said it a dozen times, but I am going to miss you, lass. And I doubt if I'll get to see you for a while, as I'm to be careful not to alert Bert as to where you are.'

'It'll be reet, love, we will see each other. Just let things settle down. I'll write to you. I'll tell you everything about the shop, and me flat above. Mind, I'm that nervous, I'm shaking. I wish train'd hurry up. I feel as though Bert'll come round the corner at any moment with some reason as to why I can't go.'

Jack made good time. They were at the seaside and he was back with them, having delivered Mrs

422

Harvey's clothes, by noon.

Megan saw him arrive. She'd not been able to stop herself looking for him every few minutes. He called over to them as he got out of the car.

'Hey, haven't you been on the sand yet or dipped your toe in the sea? I didn't expect to find you sitting just where I'd left you.'

'No, we wanted to wait for you, Jack. We didn't want to do owt until you came back. We've been for a pot of tea at the cafe over the way, though. Mind, it's been hard keeping Billy from going off – he and Sarah are that excited.'

'Oh, and you and Ma aren't, then? Ha, I bet as you're dying to wet your feet! Come on, you young 'uns!'

Jack grabbed Sarah's hand and picked Billy up and ran with them onto the beach. Their laughter carried on the breeze.

Megan stayed with Issy. Issy was in awe of it all.

'By, lass, it looks big, don't it? It's most water as I've ever seen in me life. Shall we take our shoes off and go and have a paddle?'

Megan laughed. She couldn't speak. The sight of it all had overwhelmed her, too, and if truth be known, she'd felt nervous to go onto the sand until Jack had come back. She did as Issy said and took off her shoes and stockings and, clasping Issy's hand, together they picked their way towards the sea.

Jack and Sarah came up to them. They were flushed with excitement, their smiles lit their faces and their eyes were full of joy.

'Come on, pair of you, come on. Sea's just grand,' Jack said.

'I'll tell you, Jack lad, it's like nothing I've ever imagined.'

'I know, Ma. Come and dip your feet.' He took hold of Issy's hand and led her down to the water's edge, then turned and ran back to Megan. 'Come on, me love, come on.'

The endearment came so naturally from him that Megan wondered if he'd realized what he'd said – but *she* had, and her heart sang.

'Come on, Aunty Megan!' She felt Sarah grab her hand and looked down into her lovely little face, so like Cissy's, and felt a warmth and a sadness fill her. It was going to be so hard to part from this little one; Sarah was like her own daughter. The sadness left as quickly as it had arrived – Jack saw to that. She felt her other hand being squeezed, and she looked up at him and smiled. He held her eyes for just a moment and then turned and ran back to the wall to get Billy's crutches.

When he came up to them again Jack said, 'I'll take these down for lad, then he can have some independence to wander away with Sarah. She's going on about collecting shells or sommat, aren't you, me little lass?'

With that he took hold of Sarah's other hand, and together they all ran towards the sea. They lifted Sarah into the air as they ran. Their joy sang out in the raised tone of their laughter and made them immune to the cold waves that splashed over their feet as they came to the water's edge.

'Are you all right, Issy?' Megan had let go of Sarah and gone over to her. The water lapped around their ankles.

'Aye, lass. I'm grand, just grand.'

They watched as Jack lifted Sarah and Billy, so that he had one child under each arm. He waded further into the water, all the while saying, 'I'm gonna drop you. I am. I am...'

Their squeals were deafening.

'Give over, Jack. You're worse than the nippers.'

'I am? Am I, Ma? Well, you wants to thank your lucky stars as you're too heavy, else I'd have dunked you in sea by now!'

'Ha, I always knew this padding would come in handy for sommat. At least I'm safe from your games, you big daft sod.'

'Ah, but Megan's not.'

He brought the children back to safety, and then surprised them all by bending low and gathering Megan up high over his shoulder and running with her into the water. Megan cried out in mock-anger, asking to be put down at once, and at last he lowered her down. The water lapped around their knees. A tangible silence fell between them. Jack looked into her eyes. She couldn't look away, even though she knew she was baring her soul.

'Megan, Megan...'

Her name was a whisper on his lips.

'I – I ... oh, Megan, I love you.'

Her heart swelled within her, causing her breathing to constrict. Tears sprang to her eyes. He loved her. Jack had said he loved her!

'I love you too, Jack, and I have done since I first met you.'

Their bodies swayed towards each other. Megan's skirt swirled around them. They were oblivious to everything and everyone as their lips met and a deep and unbreakable bond connected them forever.

'I'm so glad you felt up to coming out, darling. It's a lovely day. Oh, look – there's the beach. What do you think? Are you feeling well enough to get out for a while?'

Laura looked wearily out of the window. Her eyes fell on the young couple in the water, who were just parting from a sensuous kiss. She gasped in horror. 'My God! Oh God!'

'What is it, darling? What's the matter?'

'It's Jack. He–' She was stopped from going any further as a spasm of coughing gripped her.

'Where? Oh, dear!'

'How ... how could he?' Tears streamed down Laura's face. Through the mist of them she saw Jack release the woman and put his head back. He was obviously laughing with joy. Then he bent down and lifted the woman up and carried her back to the sand, kissing her face as he did so.

Daphne turned Laura's head away from the scene. 'There, there, darling, come on now. Don't get upset. It will make things worse.'

'How could he d – do that to me?'

Daphne didn't answer her, but leaned forward and spoke to her driver. 'Mrs Harvey is delirious, Johnson. She is very ill. How long will it take to get to York from here?'

'Well, if we get a clear run, m'Lady, it'll take us two hours.'

'Right, head for York, Johnson. Just get us there as quickly as you can.'

No ... no. I – I must speak to him.'

'Drive on, Johnson.' Daphne leaned forward and pulled the curtain across. 'Oh God, Laura. How did you get into such a state over him?' Her voice was little more than a whisper.

Laura couldn't answer. The spasm of coughing started up again. Fresh blood tinted her hand-kerchief. 'I – I need air.'

Daphne slid the window down. Gradually the coughing subsided and Laura caught her breath. 'Why? Oh, Daphne, why?'

'Oh, darling. I've never seen you so miserable. What can I do to help? How did it get to be like this?'

Daphne slipped off the seat and helped Laura to lie down. She didn't resist. Once she was lying down, Daphne wiped her sister's mouth with her hanky and snuggled her up in the car rug. 'Try to sleep, darling,' she whispered. 'We're going home to York. Charles will know what to do.'

Laura made no protest. Her heart was break-ing. Her mind was screaming for release from all the pain. Sleep was a blessed sanctuary.

41

Where Are We Going, Hattie and Megan?

'Look at them, Megan. They're tired out, and Sarah was that insistent on coming onto the station to see you off, and now she's dead to the world.'

'Aye. Mind, train'll not be more than about ten minutes now. It was a grand day, wasn't it, Issy?'

'It was that, Megan.'

'Issy? Well, about what happened. I...'

'You don't have to say owt, love. I've known how you've felt this good while, as thou knows, and I've seen it in Jack an' all, lately.' She sighed heavily. 'Whether it can lead to owt is another matter, but then that's up to the pair of you to sort. I will say one thing, though: it's only heartache as you'll be getting, because you'll not be able to be together, not proper like. It wouldn't be fair on young 'uns. The shame it would bring down on them would cast them out. I'm not saying as I'm not for you, because I am. I'd not give a damn for what folk'd say, but I'd not be for owt as'd hurt these young 'uns.'

'I know, Issy. It means a lot to me that you're not against us. And don't be worrying. I'd not bring shame on you all. I don't know what the future holds for us, but just knowing as Jack loves me helps some. Were young 'uns upset? Did they say owt? They've not mentioned it to us.'

'I took their attention away, and just told them as Jack'd hurt you by lifting you like that, so he were kissing you better. They just took it as it was. Mind, I'm sorry for you both. I am. I tell you what: put Billy's head on me lap. There's room, if I shift Sarah a bit. You go back down to Jack and spend last five minutes with him. You'll hear train coming. Go on.'

'Thanks, I'll not be long. I just...'

She didn't finish her sentence. She didn't have to, she knew that. How was she to live without them all? The next five minutes that she'd spend with Jack might be the last for a long, long time. But at least she would have had time with him – time during which she would know that he loved her. That would have to do for now. She'd to get on with things, as she always did. Her new life was starting, and for that she'd paid a price. She only hoped she'd no more to pay.

They were on the train. Megan had watched until Jack, Issy and Sarah were lost to her in a cloud of smoke, all the while waving. Her face was wet with tears when she turned and went in search of Billy.

She found him in an empty carriage, lying along the bench. Once Billy had said his good-byes, Jack had helped him onto the train and he'd disappeared out of sight. He sat up on his elbow when she entered, and she'd hardly sat down opposite him when he spoke.

'Mam, I feel reet funny inside. I don't know if I want to go to a new life or if I want to go back to me dad. I do know one thing, though: I want to go back to Sarah.'

'Aye, I know. I feel the same. But it's going to be better for us, Billy, I'm sure of that.'

'Does Uncle Jack love you, Mam? Thou knows – like I love Sarah?'

The question, and the comparison he'd made, threw her for a moment. She sat back and looked at him, uncertain how to answer.

'I'll be truthful with you, Billy. Your Uncle Jack and me, we do love each other, and aye, it is like you love Sarah. But we'd not do owt as would bring shame on you all. We want to be together as

429

a family. But it's not going to be easy, and we don't know how or when, but we will. One day we will, I'm–'

'What about me dad? He'd not have it, thou knows.'

'No, he'd not have it. You're right there. And, Billy, he'd not have us living in a shop away from him, either. He'll near kill me if he finds us. So we've to be secretive, tell no one where we come from, and be on the lookout when we go into Leeds for anyone as knows us, and make sure they don't see us.'

Billy's body shuddered, and Megan felt sorry she'd put him through all she had.

'Don't be worrying. I'll take care of you. He'll not find us.'

Billy just smiled and closed his eyes again and she saw his body relax. Her own body couldn't relax; she felt the tension in every sinew.

The rhythm of the wheels on the track took her back in time. She was ten years old. She and Hattie were part of a group on a trip out for the day, which had been paid for by a charity. Sister Bernadette was there, too.

Something about the way she felt today was like the way she'd felt when she'd finally parted from Sister Bernadette and had gone to make her way in the world. She put her hand in her bag and found the locket, tucked in one of the pockets. She pulled it out and put it around her neck. She suddenly felt safer, more able to face the future. Her granny and granddad would look after her.

A little ditty started to go round in her head. She and Hattie had chanted it in time to the noise the train had made that day of the outing:

Where are we going, Hattie and Megan?
Where are we going, Hattie and Megan?

And, as the train had gone faster, it had changed to:

You two wait and see.
Wait and see ... wait and see...

Where were she and Hattie going? Were they on the up and up? She had to believe they were. She had to conquer the fear and uncertainty that lay within her.

Issy took the steaming mug of cocoa Jack offered her, and he watched as she relaxed back in her chair. They'd been home almost an hour, but had hardly spoken. The air needed clearing between them, he knew that. But getting Sarah settled, and rekindling the fire, as well as a few other chores they'd been doing in readiness for the next day, had helped him to avoid the issue. He could do so no longer.

'Now then, Ma, I s'pose as you've sommat to say to me?'

'Aye, but it's not what you're thinking. I'm not disapproving. In fact, I'm glad. As I told Megan, I've known a good while how she felt, and I've come to see it in you of late an' all. But I'm reet worried, Jack. How's it all to work out? You need to think on. Don't do owt as'd bring shame down on them young 'uns. Billy's out of it in a sense, as

431

no one knows him where he's gone, but Sarah...'

'I hear what you're saying, Ma, and I agree with you. But, thou knows, love and need sometimes make morals take a back seat. And you've said many a time as God has given Megan a rough deal up to now, so surely she deserves some happiness.'

'You're reet there. I've ranted and raved at Him above on Megan's behalf, and I'd have nowt to say about the pair of you finding happiness together, no matter how you found it. Circumstances weren't of yours or Megan's making, but folk don't take breaking marriage vows lightly. Even if the law does sanction divorce, it isn't sanctioned by us Catholics, nor Methodists, and most folk around here are one or t'other.'

'Aye, I know.' He sipped his cocoa. The steam blurred his vision for a moment. He sat back in his chair. Neither his body nor his mind would relax, and his needs conflicted with reality. His affair with Laura had ended inside him the moment he'd held Megan in his arms, but, in truth, would Laura let it end? Would she understand if he told her he'd found love? Somehow he knew she wouldn't. And he knew that having an adulterous affair with him wouldn't sit easily with Megan, either. She was made of different stuff from Laura. That wouldn't stop it happening, he knew that, as he'd felt Megan's need in her kiss, but as time went on, the conflict inside her would make her unhappy. He heaved a deep sigh of frustration.

'Don't worry, Jack, these things have a way of working themselves out. I've told Megan and I'll tell you: I'm for you both, and I'll help all I can.

Love's a powerful thing and they say as it conquers all, so just hold on to that.'

'Thanks, Ma. It'd be a lot harder for us if you were against us. I don't know how–' He jumped up as the sound of a heavy banging on the door filled the room.

'Fellam – Fellam, you bastard! Open this door, I'm gonna kill you! Open this fucking door.'

'Ma, go upstairs, I'll deal with Bert. Go on now. Thou knows what he can be like, and I'll not have you getting hurt.'

'No, Jack, I'm staying. I'm not afraid of the likes of Bert Armitage!'

Issy's anger gave fresh life to her body. She shot off her chair and was through the door that led to the outhouse before Jack had crossed the room. And just as Jack opened the front door, she was back again, armed with her thick wooden copper stick, which – though worn down at one end from poking and lifting laundry – presented itself as a mean weapon as she swished it back and forth through the air. 'Bugger off out of here, Bert Armitage. We don't want the likes of you in our house, shouting your bloody mouth off.'

Bert stopped in his tracks. 'Get out of the way, you demented fat bitch! Come near me with that thing and you'll be on your fat arse afore you know it. Where's Megan? And don't say as you don't fucking know.'

Bert turned. His fist sank into Jack's stomach. Jack's knees buckled and the air left his lungs. He'd no time to recover before Bert's fist crashed into his left ear and sent him reeling to the floor.

'I'll fucking kill you, you bastard. Where is she?'

The kick he'd been about to give to Jack's head never landed, as Issy got to him first. The copper stick smashed across his back.

'Stop that, you bloody bugger. If anyone's a bastard, it's you! What are you talking of? We know nothing about Megan's whereabouts. Get out of here.'

Bert turned and raised his fist. Issy was ready. The copper stick cracked down on his raised arm, and then another blow caught his shoulder. 'You just bloody try it, you bastard! Get out, you filthy scum, you slimy bastard. Only one as is going to get killed round here is you! Get out, I tell you!'

Jack was on his feet again. He grabbed Bert and locked his arms behind his back. 'All right, Ma, that's enough. Open door and let's get him out.'

Issy did as she was bid. Jack could see her body was shaking, but she stood tall, her head high as she held the door.

Bert didn't struggle. When Jack got him to the door, he pushed him so hard he fell like a rag doll down the steps leading to the gate.

'What's to do, Jack? Issy? Are you all right?' Henry was at the gate with Gertie.

Bert got himself up and pushed past them. 'I'll get you, Fellam – and that fucking bitch of a mother-in-law of yours. You'll not pull one over me. Just watch your backs, because I'll get you!'

'What's going on? Issy, oh, Issy, you're shaking! Come on, sit yourself down.' Gertie had almost leapt up the steps. She held the trembling Issy by the arm.

Henry had followed behind her. 'What's got him going, Jack?' he asked.

434

Jack closed the door. He'd have to be careful what he said. No one must suspect that he and Issy knew where Megan was.

'It seems Megan's left, from what he was saying, but Ma...'

The story they'd concocted rolled easily off his tongue. It sounded that convincing, he almost believed it to be a truth himself, and Issy played her part like she was going for an acting award as she said, 'We knew as Megan were planning to go, but that's all she told us – not when, nor how, nor where to. In fact I didn't really believe as she'd do it. God! I hope she finds some way of letting me know as she's all right. She's like a daughter to me.'

Jack almost clapped her performance. 'Don't upset yourself, Ma. Be happy for her. She deserves some happiness in her life, and she'll not get it with Bert Armitage. She'd not have done this lightly – not leave you, she wouldn't.'

'But where would she go? She'd no money or owt. She wouldn't go to workhouse, would she? Oh God, surely not? Even living with Bert would be better than that,' Gertie said.

'Happen she's gone into one of them big houses,' Issy said. 'I were always telling her they'd snatch her up as soon as they looked at her. They can't get servants these days and are taking on without references.'

Jack walked over to the sink and turned on the tap. He dipped his head under the cold running water. Their speculation was only the beginning, as talk would be rife tomorrow and for weeks ahead. His actions distracted them. Henry was beside him, asking if he needed him to fetch the doctor, and Gertie resorted to her cure for all ills.

'Put kettle back on the hob, Henry,' she instructed. 'I'll fetch bottle over. It's not the doctor as is needed, but a hot sweet drink and a good stiff tipple!'

When she'd gone, Issy asked, 'Is your head all right, Jack? Are you sure you'll not need doctor?'

'I'm fine, Ma. Anyroad, I bet mine's not as sore as Bert's. Ha, I'm glad as I never made you mad like that! I thought as you'd kill him with that copper stick. And swearing! I've never heard likes of it, nor I bet has Bert, not even down pit.'

Issy laughed with him.

Jack winked at her. It's funny, he thought, but despite the Bert episode, they could laugh. They'd had a grand day, and Megan was away and safe. He never knew he was such a good liar. Well, before his affair with Laura, that was. Carrying on like he was with her always called for untruths to be told, or implied.

Still, all that mattered was that Gertie and Henry were taken in by the story. And if he knew anything of Gertie, it'd be gossiped around and would be the truth of what happened, by the time the cock crowed in the morning. He sank back in his chair. *I'm going to miss you, lass. But I wouldn't bring you back to that man for all the coal down pit. Things will turn out well for us. I know they will.*

42

A Fragile Canopy of Lace

It was two weeks to the day before Megan saw Jack, Issy and Sarah again, and she couldn't believe they were with her so soon. She'd thought it would be months before she saw them again. After hugs, kisses and squeals of excitement, Jack explained that he'd told Hamilton he had to give the car a good run out, to stop it seizing up, because with Mrs Harvey still away, the car was hardly moving.

Issy chipped in with her part of the story. She and Sarah had had to catch the train to Leeds, and Jack had picked them up at the station.

'I tell you, Megan, fooling that lot back in Breckton is as easy as taking a titty from a babby's mouth. And Sarah was that excited when I told her on train where we were coming.'

'How's she been, Issy?'

'Not good. She's missing Bella and Billy, and you. Mind, young Annie Bradshaw helps, but...'

'Well, that's good. She needs someone.' Megan took Issy's hand. 'There's only time as'll heal her – well, all of us really. Bella's loss is still like a big knot inside me. So God knows how you all feel.'

Issy nodded. Megan knew she was struggling with her emotions, and changed the subject.

'Anyroad, let's not waste any of your visit. It's

just on eleven, so I'll shut early. It's half-day closing in this area, so I've all afternoon for you. Come on, I'm dying to show you all around. Eeh, Hattie's going to be mad at missing you! Her and Harry have gone off for the afternoon. Things are moving along nicely in that direction. Sally's here, though. She's at stitching some hems. I'll call her. We were both going to be working at our stitching this afternoon, but we'll not now.'

'You mean you're trading already? By, lass, it didn't take you long!'

'Well, not trading exactly, Issy. As soon as the flat were ready and me stock of material and stuff arrived, I dressed the window with the garments as I'd made, and within two days I had me first customer call. And what a customer! It was a lady's maid. She'd come to see if I'd go to her mistress's house and discuss making her a new wardrobe. Come upstairs and I'll tell you all about it.'

The tour of the shop and flat complete, Megan asked Sally to take everyone through to the front room. 'I'll make a brew. Go on, there's a good lass.'

Sally had started to protest, and Megan knew she was about to offer to make the tea, but she needed a little time to herself. She felt suddenly very shy of Jack. She couldn't have said why, but by the time she'd poured the tea out for them all she felt better able to cope.

'So how've you been in yourself, Megan?'

'I've been grand, Issy – better than I thought. Every day's been a new adventure. I've so much to tell you.'

'You're looking lovely, Megan. Your new life suits you.'

438

'It does, Jack, it does, but thou knows it's not complete. Not without you. I – I mean...' A hot colour flushed her face. 'I mean, all of you.'

'We know what you mean, lass. Look, your news can wait. Jack, take Megan for a walk in that park as we passed up the road. I'll stay here with Sally, and Billy and Sarah can play together. Go on – get yourselves off. Have an hour on your own.'

'Are you sure, Issy?' Megan's heart leapt at the chance to have Jack to herself, but the feeling of shyness and uncertainty she'd felt earlier gripped her afresh. Jack seemed a little distant to her. He'd never been far from her thoughts, and her body had longed for him at night. But now that he was here, she felt unsure.

'Go on, pair of you. You're acting like you've just met or sommat.'

Once out on the street, she felt her shyness increase. It was as if she'd imagined what had passed between them before, and she was back to the days when she loved him and he didn't know it. Some of this dissipated when he took her hand.

'It's good to see you, Megan, and you're looking more beautiful than ever.' He lifted her hand to his lips.

'Oh, Jack, I've missed you.' Jack did love her. She hadn't imagined it.

'I've missed you an' all, me little lass. Come on, let's get to that park and find a big tree to hide behind, so as I can hold you. I'm so near bursting to do so. I'll do it right here in the street, if I've to wait much longer.'

The barriers were lifted. The awkwardness had gone. Laughter bubbled up in her and burst out as

439

they ran towards the park. Never before had she been so glad of a bad-weather day as she was now. The slow drizzle meant the park was deserted.

They found their tree – a sprawling old oak. It was majestic, surrounded by poplars and elms. Its wizened roots had pushed through the surface and accepted them like huge arms. Its dense foliage sheltered them from the drizzle.

They didn't speak, just clung together in a kiss so deep that Megan felt her very heart being tugged from her and pressed into Jack.

Jacks actions weren't those of a normal taking of a woman. It was more like a giving. A giving of body and soul to each other. Jack whispered his love between every kiss and with every touch. 'This is meant to be, my darling Megan. Tell me you feel it too.'

'I do, I do. Oh, Jack.'

Her heart burst with her love for him. She wanted him to stay inside her forever. When the sensation rose, she did not deny it, and rode the wave of love with him. It was so right it should be Jack who took her to those heights, the first time she experienced them. 'Oh, Jack ... Jack, oh...'

She clung to him as she tried to cope with the spasms of pleasure. She knew she was holding him in a vice-like grip, but she didn't want him to move. She'd not be able to bear it. As the waves subsided, she felt her inner being let go. Her limbs shook, her body heaved and huge sobs racked her. It was a kind of crying she'd never known in her life – a crying of great joy.

Through it all she felt Jack covering her face in kisses and licking her tears, while calling her his love, his own sweet Megan, and thrusting himself ever deeper into her, until she felt she would die with the pleasure and the love she had inside her.

The feeling started to build again. She heard Jack's name coming in a moan of pleasure from her lips. Heard her own name being spoken in love. Felt his movements become stronger and ... she was lost. Lost in a world of pleasure so deep it fragmented her very being. Jack was making her his own. Their souls were fusing together.

There was a quiet moment – a moment broken by the sound of gentle sobs. Her Jack was crying. She moved herself, just a little, not wanting him to take himself from her, but needing to hold him.

'Jack?'

His arms encircled her. His weight pressed down on her. 'Megan, Megan, Megan.' He kissed her nose. His tears rolled onto her cheek. She put a hand up and wiped them away. She didn't have to ask. She knew they were tears of joy, just as hers had been, but knew, too, that there was an anguish mixed with the joy. Once he'd found control, he smiled down at her, then rolled to her side, taking himself from her.

'Megan, I love you beyond all I know. Thou knows that, don't you?'

'Aye, I does.'

The small worry she'd felt over the anguish she'd detected dissolved, and she lifted herself onto her elbow and looked down on him. 'And I accept your love with all me heart and body. I love you, Jack. And, like I said afore, I have done since I first set eyes on you.'

'Oh, Megan.' He pulled her down and rested

441

her head on his chest and stroked her hair.

Stillness surrounded them and she knew she'd remember the feeling she had inside her forever, and knew the love that encased her body would be with her till the end of her days.

The drizzle had stopped, but she couldn't have said when. The sun dappled down through the leaves, and as she looked up the pattern it made was like that of a lace canopy. *Please, God, let this canopy cover us forever, shrouding our love with protection.*

Without warning, her peace was shattered. An ugly image of Bert shot into her mind and fear rippled through her. Jack stirred.

'Are you cold, love?' He took her hand and sat up. 'I s'pose as we'd be best to get back.'

He helped her to her feet, and held her near-naked body to his. It felt so right. The fear left her. Bert could never hurt her again, not now – not now that she belonged to Jack.

Her frock was one that buttoned at the front from the hem to the scooped-out neckline. Jack helped her to button it up, and their giggles at his clumsy attempts lightened the moment until he stopped and pulled her to him. 'Are you alreet, lass?' His hand came up to her chin and he lifted her head until she was looking at him. 'I mean, no regrets?'

'I've no regrets, love, and I've never been better than at this moment in me whole life.' Some of her shyness was creeping back, but she found the courage she needed and told him, 'I've never had feelings like you gave me, Jack.'

His kiss felt sweet, and yet at the same time she

442

felt a great sadness. She wanted to be with Jack forever, but she knew that couldn't be.

When they returned, Issy busied around without looking directly at them. Or was it Megan's imagination? Whatever it was, she felt a blush redden her cheeks. Jack laughed and winked at her.

'There you are! We thought as you'd never come back. Me and Sally have made some sandwiches and kettle's boiling for some tea, and I'm starving to skin and bone.'

'Right then, Ma, we're ready and waiting. Do the business and serve up.'

Issy huffed and puffed, but didn't pursue it. Jack didn't help matters, as he looked like a cat that had just caught a mouse.

'Sally's been telling me more about your first client, Megan. It sounds as though you're off to a good start.'

'Oh, you mean Lady Gladwyn?'

Jack drew in a loud, deep breath as she said this. She turned to look at him and caught the look of shock that passed over his face. But then he smiled – a little too quickly, but she didn't have time to quiz him before Issy spoke.

'Sally says you're on with making her a whole new winter outfit.'

'I am, Issy. I feel reet lucky, getting Lady Gladwyn as me first customer. It seems she drove past me shop and were taken with garments as I had on display. And best of all is, if she's pleased with what I make for her, she's said as she'll recommend me to her friends. In fact, I were surprised as she didn't recognize me. She were a regular at Madame Marie's. I told her as I were trained there, and I nearly told her as all clothes she bought from there were my designs, but I didn't. Somehow it would've been like a betrayal to Madame, and she didn't deserve that.'

'Well, that's good. Once you get a foot in door with that lot, you'll not look back. I'm reet glad for you, lass.'

'Thanks, Issy. Like you say, it's a start. I need to build up a few more clients, though, and fairly quick, if I'm to keep going. There's not much of me start-up capital left, so it's a bit of a worry at the moment. But it's worth it. Me life's that different in just two weeks, it's like a miracle!' She squeezed Jack's hand. She couldn't help herself, and she looked at him and whispered, 'A real miracle.'

He smiled at her, but once again she felt there was something wrong. A worry entered her. Was he regretting what had happened?

To cover her fear she chatted on, telling them about Lady Gladwyn's house and how she and Sally were going to have to work from early morning until late at night to get the work done. It was to prove they could deliver on time, just as much as the fact that the gentry were slow in paying, that would drive her, she told them.

'It'll work – I know it will. I'll make it work,' she said as she finished her tale. 'Anyroad, that's enough about me goings-on here. What's been happening back at Breckton? I s'pose as Bert's created some trouble. Has he had a go at you both?'

They skipped over the incident that had happened just after she left, as if it was nothing, but Megan knew what it must have been like, and loved them both all the more for trying to ease her mind.

The next piece of news they told of shattered that ease and sent a quiver of fear through her. Bert had been sacked. Oh God, he'd be looking for her as it was, but his time would have been limited. Now he'd not rest until he'd found her, she was sure of that.

'That news has upset you, hasn't it, love? We knew as it would, but we decided we had no choice but to tell you. You're going to need to take care. I'm only sorry as you've already had contact with customers, before me and Ma could get over to you. We thought p'raps you could change your name or...'

'Change me name? Oh, on shop you mean? Well, I have, Jack. I mean, I haven't put a sign up or owt as yet. But I have registered the business in Hattie's name. Bert knew nowt of Hattie. We've called shop "Frampton's Exclusive Frocks and Gowns". I know as I'd always said as it'd be "Madame Megan's", but thinking about it, that'd be daft, as if Bert found out I were on with carrying me dream through, that'd be the first shop name he'd look for.'

'And you've not thought on changing your own name? What does Lady Gladwyn know you as?' Jack asked.

'I don't know as she knows me as owt. Her maid introduced me to her as "Megan from Frampton's", but she'd not think on it. She never used it. Well, you know how top-drawer are. They can talk to you without really talking to you. Why? Do you think it's important as no one knows me real name?'

'Yes, I think it'd be best. I think as you should change your name completely, for business purposes.'

'But why?'

He didn't answer her for a moment. She looked from Jack to Issy. Both seemed tense. Afraid even. They glanced at each other and then looked away quickly. 'What's wrong? What should I know? Issy? Jack?'

'It's Mrs Harvey. She's not back yet from her sister's, but I've heard tell she's coming back soon. She knows folk. Folk as you're dealing with – like this Lady Gladwyn. In fact she's one of Mrs Harvey's closest friends. She's bound to tell her about you.'

'But why are you worrying over her, Jack? I can't see her running to Bert to tell him. She probably don't even know as he exists. I think you're worrying over nothing, love.'

The look passed between them again, and this time Issy's face held a warning. The fear that clutched at Megan's heart held a more sinister coldness than did the fear of Bert. This was fear of the unknown. Whatever it was they were holding back held terror for her. *No, I'm being silly. There is no chance in heaven or hell that these two would do that to me.*

'Look, lass, our worry is if Mrs Harvey becomes a customer, right? Well then, her household's going to know – at least them as deals with her clothes. And thou knows as none of them can keep owt to themselves. They thrive on the fact that it's news about goings-on up at the big house as keeps us all entertained, and as most of them live in the Miners' Row...'

'Oh God! You're right. I never thought about it like that. It were always a possibility, I s'pose. Mind, it's not too late as, like I say, Lady Gladwyn'll not remember what I'm called.'

There was a silence for a moment, and during it a thought occurred to her.

'Happen as I could stop all home visits – make it a rule as clients come to me shop, like they had to at Madame Marie's. Then, if Mrs Harvey does become a customer, she won't expect me to go out to hers.'

'Well, that might work, but it still has its worries,' Issy said.

'It needn't. I mean, they never bring their maids shopping, so that's not a worry. And thinking on it, it might turn out in our favour, as you might have to pick up stuff when it's ready for her, Jack. Or at least you could warn me if someone was to come with you.'

'It sounds good, I know, but...'

'I shouldn't worry, Jack. Mrs Harvey wouldn't recognize me if she saw me. I can only recall one occasion in me whole life that she looked at me. It were a funny look and it made me feel a bit ill at ease. It were as if she had a loathing of me. It happened just after we lost Ciss, and me and you were sitting on step together, Issy. I couldn't understand it at the time, and still can't. Though I'd not thought about it till now.'

Jack once again drew in a deep breath. His

discomfort seemed to have increased. *Why?*

'Anyroad, Bert losing his job might turn out for us an' all. He'll probably just disappear down to Sheffield, or somewhere he could get set on at a pit again.'

'Happen as you're reet, lass. We're probably meeting trouble halfway, when it's not even travelling our road. But we wanted you to be aware of the dangers.'

'Ta, Issy. I know, and I'm glad as you've made me think on, but now stop worrying, pair of you. Come on, time's passing and you've to go in a bit. I don't want to spoil the last half-hour thinking about Bert. He's in me past, and that's where he's staying.' She wished she felt on the inside as convincing as she sounded on the outside.

Jack's hand curled round hers, and a warmth entered her. All the talk of Bert had overshadowed what had happened between them. She squeezed his hand. It was going to be hard to say goodbye. Would she ever get used to it? And, worse, how would she cope not knowing when she would see him again? And, her body asked, how would she keep her yearnings for Jack's love-making stilled?

All too soon the time for them to go arrived. Jack stood on the steps with Megan. Issy and Sarah were already in the car, and Sally and Billy leaned through the car windows, talking to them.

'I need a few minutes with you, Megan. I need to say me goodbyes in private.'

They drew back into the shop. Jack pulled her to him and held her. His face buried into her neck. 'Megan. Megan...' An anguished love

448

croaked audibly in his voice. 'I'd never mean to hurt you ever, Megan. Not ever.'

He felt her stiffen. 'What is it, Jack? I feel as sommat isn't right. I know, without you telling me, that you'd never hurt me. Oh, me love, when can you come to me again? How soon? I can't bear to be apart from you.'

He skipped over her first question as if she hadn't asked it. How could he do any other?

'I don't know, love. It's not going to be easy. I've to be careful, as I'd not be able to live with meself if I led Bert to you.' His heart, heavy with guilt, made his chest squeeze tightly. He knew that her greatest danger of being found was through his affair with Laura, but how could he tell her?

Johnson had been over to Hensal Grange to collect some things for Laura. It had surprised Jack that he'd not been instructed to take them to her, but after listening to Johnson, he'd known why. Johnson told him all that had happened: how ill Laura had been at the cottage, and how she'd become consumed with grief when she'd seen him kissing a woman in the sea at Bridlington.

All kinds of fears had attacked Jack since that day: fear for Megan; fear of losing his job and home; fear for Sarah and his ma-in-law. And fear of Megan ever finding out. Oh God! He held her even tighter as his shame burned through him. It'd been bad enough telling his ma-in-law, but he'd had to. He'd had to discuss with somebody what Johnson had said. Issy had been shocked, but as ever she'd understood. Like him, her main worry had been for Megan and the danger this all posed her.

Megan stirred in his arms. 'Hey, you're crushing me bones and ... well, you're getting me feelings going inside me.' She drew away from him.

'Oh, Megan ... Megan.' He drew her near again. 'I'll work sommat out, lass. I promise. I'll be back soon. Somehow, I'll be back.'

Again she drew back from him. 'Come on, me love – they'll be shouting for us. You need to calm yourself.' She took his hand, then leaned forward and kissed his cheek. 'Just hold on to my love. Hold it safe inside you. Touch it whenever you touch your heart, and we'll always be together.'

They walked back through the shop. They stood together for a moment, not talking or touching, and yet they were joined, as he knew they always would be.

The parting was happy, full of hugs and kisses and promises to see each other soon, but it didn't lessen the weight of Jack's guilt. *What will Laura do? What will she do? Was the sacking of Bert part of her plan to get revenge? Or am I just being silly? Somehow, I don't think so...*

43

Adding the Final Link

'Darling Laura, you look much better. How are you feeling?' Daphne held her sister at arm's length and then hugged her to her.

'I'm loads better, darling. Two weeks in this

clinic has done wonders for me. My breathing is fine now and I'm eating well. I'm nearly finished packing, so we needn't hang around for too long.'

'Charles is just having a word with the doctor. He wants to know how long before all your results are in. The shadow they found on your lung is very worrying, but hopefully now that your infection has cleared, your last X-rays will show that it has gone.'

'Oh, I'm sure it has. I've hardly coughed for a few days now. I'm eager to get home and deal with some important matters. One thing I've done while I've been in isolation this last two weeks is to think, and it's been good for me. I have a plan formulated in my head, and I now need to get home and put it into action.'

'You don't mean you're going home straight away, dear? You can't – you're not strong enough. Come home with us. Stay a week or so. Charles is talking about taking some time off and arranging a cruise for us, somewhere really hot. Now that would be lovely, wouldn't it?'

'It would, and I certainly won't rule that out. But as for staying with you, it's not possible. There is so much that needs my attention, both on a business and on a personal level.'

'Hello, old thing.'

'Charles, come in. Don't stand there with your head poked around the door like that. You look silly! Oh, it's good to see you. I'm going to need someone sensible to help me with this sister of mine.'

'Come here first and give me a hug. You look – well ... better. A lot better, my dear, but you've a long way still to go, and I expect Daphne has been trying to persuade you to take it easy? Thought so. I told you, my darling, that you would do no good. Now, now, I'm not going to start a fight with you. I know you mean well and you're right in everything you say, but if I know Laura – and don't forget I've been in the ring with her, when it comes to arguments about what she should or shouldn't do – she's having none of it. Am I right?'

'Yes, you're right. But I'm not for saying no to everything. That cruise sounds good and you could do with a rest yourself, Charles, so don't let me stop your plans on that one. But I have so much to see to. You understand, don't you? You know I have such a lot going on. The Byron contract's going to be the saving of me, and I've a lot to put in place for it to happen on time. There's recruiting of experienced men for a start, then accommodation for them. I need some good men in place to oversee the installation of the cutting machines, so that has to take priority, and–'

'Hey, hold on, old thing. You're making me feel exhausted, just listening to you. Look, I can take some time off. How about Daphne and I come with you? That way I can help you with it all.'

'It's not that simple, Charles. I – I have some personal things to see to. I need to straighten out my life. I've been silly. Well, Daphne knows what I mean. So it's better that I go home alone and sort it all, whilst I'm feeling so well. You are only at the end of a telephone line if I need some advice. Besides, if the worst comes to the worst and I need prolonged treatment, I can have it knowing that everything is ticking over well, both

452

in my business and in my private life.'

'You know, she has a point, Daphne. What do you say, darling?'

'Oh, all right. But you will contact us if you need the slightest help, won't you?'

'Yes, of course, darling.'

Matters settled, Charles left them to go in search of Johnson.

'Darling, how are you really? I mean – well, you know, about ... well, that chauffeur of yours, and that awful business of seeing him with another woman?'

'I'm all right about it. At least I think I can handle it. How did I let such a thing happen, Daphne? I feel such an idiot. But I fell in love with him. I know: I can't believe it myself, but it's true. There's no future in it, I know that, and it looks like he's fallen for someone else anyway.'

'He's a cad! No, that's not right. A man of his class cannot be called a cad, but – oh, I don't know. What do the lower classes call men like him?'

'That's not fair, really. Jack didn't ever commit himself to me. Oh, he said nice things and we were good together, but he always cautioned me about taking it all too seriously, and he was right. It's a pity we can't make our feelings behave to order.'

'I'm so relieved, darling. You seem to be well in control. You'll be fine. Look, just do one thing for me. Stay a couple of nights. I've got something organized for tomorrow night. Nothing big – only Charlotte Gladwyn rang. She and Derek are going to be in York and I've asked them to dinner.

She can't wait to see you. Now you're set on going home, we could arrange for them to drop you off. At least then you won't have to see Fellam too soon, and you will have company on the drive. What do you say?'

'All right, if it will make you happy. It will be nice to see Charlotte. I haven't seen her for ages. And no, I'm not yet ready to see Jack.'

Laura thought she'd pulled that off well. Daphne seemed quite content, and now the coast was going to be clear when she got home. It shouldn't take much to pull Jack back into line. It was only a hitch, she was sure of it. That woman would be out of the way in less than two weeks once the sacking of her husband and eviction of them both from the tied cottage was completed. *Surely then, if I threaten Jack with losing his job and home, he'd want to carry on with things as they were. After all, he has enjoyed it as much as I have.*

Finding something to wear the next evening proved a problem, but Laura eventually settled on one of the frocks that belonged to her niece.

Daphne's daughter Theresa had had her coming-out ball the year before and was now enjoying a year in Europe with her twin brother Terence, before deciding which of the many beaux who had offered for her hand she would marry. Theresa was the same height as herself, but tinier in build, so the frock fitted perfectly. Examining herself in the mirror had been a painful experience. She needed to put back on the weight she'd lost. And she needed to feel stronger. Her mind was strong, but she tired so quickly.

'Are you ready, darling? Can I come in? Oh, you look lovely. No, don't look like that, you do. I think Charlotte and Derek are going to be pleasantly surprised. They've been very worried about you.'

'Is that the truth as to why they've come all this way? Oh, don't bother denying it, Daphne. You've been scheming, I can see that. You and Charlotte are as bad as each other. I don't know why I love you both so much – well, her anyway. I suppose I've got to love you.'

'Come on, we're not up to anything, I promise.'

'No? I'll believe that when I see it. If this isn't a dummy run for something bigger, then I don't know you two as well as I think I do.'

The evening had gone well and they'd retired and left the men to their port when the 'not up to anything' surfaced.

'You know, darling, you look really lovely. I think it suits you – being thinner, I mean. It shows your lovely bone structure to its best advantage.'

'Come off it, Charlotte, you know I look awful.'

'You don't, darling, really! You should socialize more. We all miss you, and there are one or two interesting men on the scene at the moment.'

'Uh-oh, here it comes!'

'No, really, darling – it's nothing we've planned. But it won't hurt to enjoy yourself and have a look at what's around. It must be lonely on your own.'

'Yes, it is, but I've no time, and I'm not up to doing the rounds at the moment. Anyway, I shouldn't think there's anything interesting going on until the winter season, and I couldn't stand the intimacy of a dinner party. Not with strangers

455

there. All that polite conversation! No. Count me out.'

'Ah, but that's where you're wrong. You remember Lord Fennington died – oh, about two years ago now? Well, his eldest, John, didn't outlive him by many months, and so the younger one, David, has come back from France. He married a French aristocrat. Anyway, it appears he is a widower with one son and is now the new lord. He's about your age, handsome and well set up, and they say he has started to accept invitations. Jocelyn Withers has taken it on herself to introduce him to everyone. She's giving a late-summer ball in about three weeks' time.'

'No. No. And it's no use you two ganging up on me, either, as I'm not fit enough yet to think of attending a ball. And you're not going to match-make me with this Lord David Fennington, or anyone else for that matter! I knew you had something up your sleeve. You're incorrigible, both of you.'

'Oh, I see, so you're fit enough for business, but not for pleasure?'

'Daphne, that's below the belt, and you know it. Besides, I've nothing to wear; nothing fits me, and I'm not going in one of Theresa's coming-out gowns. Everyone will recognize it. And you can pretend all you want to. I know that nothing will look good on me. I'm too thin.'

'Ah, but I have an answer to that. You'll never believe it, but I've found myself a new dress-maker! No, not an expensive London one – it's a new place just opened in Leeds. And wait for this: the woman who is designing for me used to work for Madame Marie! Anyway, her designs are exquisite, and her materials are out of this world. And the best bit is: they are not expensive. In fact I've ordered a whole new winter outfit...'

'What's the matter, darling? Are you all right? Laura?'

'I – I'm all right. I'm just tired. I'll go up now, Daphne, if you don't mind. It's early days for me yet. But I will go to Jocelyn's ball, Charlotte, and I will treat myself to a new outfit from... What did you say this woman's name was?'

'Oh, I can't remember. Wait a minute: I wrote it down. Megan – Megan of Frampton's. That's it. I don't know if she's the only designer they have, but as she is so good, I made a note of her name. Yes, here it is. I'll tell you what: I'll telephone you in a couple of days and arrange to pick you up and bring you over to mine. I'll arrange for her to come over as well and bring some swatches and designs and things. We'll have a lovely day picking and choosing something for you. How's that, darling?'

'That would be wonderful, thanks, Charlotte. Megan, you say? May I see? Hm, Coppery Street, Bramley? Well, I never! Frampton's of Bramley. Quite a posh name for – I mean, well...'

'I know, and this Megan is part-owner of it. Though it's hard to imagine where she got her money from, as she's very low-class. It would be interesting to find out. In fact Madame Marie must have had her work cut out, getting the woman to such a high standard. Why she took her on is a mystery. I thought she only took on middle-class girls who at least had an education.'

'No, I recommended a girl from my estate. She

457

took her on and did very well, by all accounts. Now you'll have to excuse me, darling. Say goodnight to Derek and Charles for me.'

'I'll see you up, darling. Oh dear, you're trembling. Here, take my arm.'

'Thanks, Daphne. I do feel shaky.'

It took a while to convince Daphne that she would be all right, but eventually Laura found herself on her own. To her amazement, tears began to stream down her face as soon as the door was closed. So she'd done it – it must be her! It was too much of a coincidence, the name Megan. And having worked at Madame Marie's! Oh God, that woman was all set up now and away from Bert Armitage – just what Jack had wanted to happen. She'd surely lose him now. How could she keep him? If she sacked him, he'd have somewhere to go, and he'd soon find work in Leeds. All her planning had been to no avail. But wait a minute. What about Armitage? Surely he wouldn't take all this lying down? Not from what she'd heard of him, he wouldn't. What if she was to make sure he found out where his wife was?

The tears dried, and Laura rubbed a weary hand over her face. Her head ached and her chest felt tight. No, she mustn't be ill again. There was so much to do. So much...

Once home, Laura found that most of what had seemed like a huge burden during her illness turned out to be simple to achieve. Her manager had already done most of it. He'd found there were a large number of very skilled men on the market, so the hiring had been easy. Dealing with the union, though, had proved to be a hard task, and costly, as she'd had to agree to meet the cost of relocating the men she'd sacked. And then there was Jack.

She'd decided she would ignore his presence while she sorted herself out. She needed a scheme. She needed him to need her – to rely on her totally, as he was used to doing – as that way he'd do as she bid. But whilst he had that slut waiting to give him a home, what chance did she stand?

It had been planned that her manager was to pay off the men who were to leave, but she decided she'd have to be there. It was the perfect opportunity, and the only one she was going to get. She'd give out the payments herself and speak to each one. She'd have to get the proceedings to take place in her own office at Hensal Grange, as not only did she not feel well enough to venture out to the office, but that would have meant Jack driving her, and she definitely wasn't ready for that.

The day of the payments had arrived and Laura didn't feel so confident. Her stomach twisted with nerves. Could she pull it off, without anyone knowing she was doing it deliberately? But then it wasn't just Armitage – it was the whole thing. These men had been working loyally for many years for the company. Many had started in her father-in-law's day. Suddenly it seemed like a betrayal, and she wished she was anywhere but in this room waiting to face them.

Thank goodness she had been able to put Charlotte off for a couple of weeks. Seeing Megan

459

Armitage would have made her task a little too personal. By the time the appointed day came round again, everything would hopefully be sorted, one way or the other. If not... No, there was no *if*. Her plan would succeed.

Five men had been in front of her when she heard Bert Armitage's name. It was turning out to be more of an ordeal than she'd anticipated, and one she could have saved herself from, if it wasn't for this bloody business of getting rid of that woman.

Bert Armitage was in front of her, and he looked nothing like she expected. He was a strong-looking individual and had a power about him, an evil power. She shuddered and took a deep breath.

'Well, now, I'm here for two purposes, Armitage. One is to express my regret at how progress at Hensal Grange Colliery has unfortunately meant some of you lost your jobs. And the other is to give you a resettlement payment, which I think you will find very generous and should tide you over for a while. Have you found another position?' She knew he hadn't.

'No, Ma'am.'

'You have somewhere to go, I take it?'

His look darkened. Her nerves enhanced to fear.

'Only on the road, and I'll not stand here talking to you so that you can pretend as you bloody care! I'll take me pittance and be off.'

Out of the corner of her eye she saw her manager move. She put her hand up to stay him.

'But surely you will be going to your wife? I hear she has a nice little place in Coppery Street, in Leeds. I was quite surprised and pleased to hear that one of my tenants had done so well, and that it had come at such a time, when you most needed it. I imagined that it was all planned that way. I–'

The sound of a sharp intake of breath from behind interrupted her and she turned and looked at her manager. She feigned a worried expression. 'Have I said something wrong?'

Armitage's raised voice brought her attention back to him.

'What does you mean – a place? What bloody place? And how come as you knows of it?'

She let her voice falter. 'I – I'm ... well, I didn't realize. Perhaps I shouldn't have spoken of it. I...'

He leaned forward, his hands on the desk in front of her. He stared straight at her, his blackened, evil soul exposed in the depth of his eyes. Her body trembled with the knowledge of her own devious self – the self, deep in her own soul, that had prompted her to do what she'd just done. Oh God, what if he killed Megan? She hadn't thought about the consequences. She'd thought he'd perhaps knock her back into line, but now she wasn't sure. Her legs would hold her no longer. She sank back into her seat.

'I asked you a question, Miss High-and-Bloody-Mighty. What place?'

'That's enough, Armitage. Get out of here. You've got your money.' The manager stepped forward and faced him squarely.

'I'm not going until she tells me what she knows of me wife and her doings.'

Once more Laura found herself looking into those evil black eyes. But she'd composed herself. She might as well tell him, if only to get rid of him.

She stood up. 'It's a ladies' fashion shop on Coppery Street. It's called Frampton's, or something like that. Now leave this office at once or we'll call the police.'

Bert glared at her for a few seconds. His body trembled. His mouth opened and then closed again, and then he turned and slammed out of the office.

Her manager looked at her with concern. She sat down, happy in the knowledge that her distress looked as real as it had seemed a few minutes ago.

'Well, what was all that about? How come he didn't know his wife had set up a shop in Leeds?'

'She'd left him, Ma'am. No one knew where she was. Mind, I'm surprised to hear as she's set herself up like you say. How's she managed that, I wonder? Well, well! Anyroad, I'm glad for her, but God knows as to what'll happen now Armitage knows of her whereabouts. As thou knows, Ma'am, he gave her a pitiful life afore, but now as she's dared to leave him...'

Laura looked at him, feigning ignorance.

'You asked specifically for him to be one of the men to go, as you'd heard of his cruelty to his wife.'

'Ah, yes, I remember. So that was him? And now I've told him where his wife is. Oh, dear! I never dreamed he didn't know. After all, she told a friend of mine that she'd achieved her success by making clothes here, and saving the money. How could she have managed that, without her husband knowing?' *Jack will rue the day he gave me this knowledge. Well, at least he's learned a valuable lesson, and he'll never, ever cross me again.*

'She must have managed it without anyone knowing, because it's first as I've heard of it, and there's not much as goes on that I don't get to hear of. Well, I never!'

'Oh, well, what's done is done. She'll probably take him back – they always do. Shall we continue? Who's next?'

A banging on the door startled Issy out of her nap. 'What? Who is it?' Before she could rise from her chair the door opened.

'It's me, Issy. Oh, love, I've bad news for you!' Gertie could hardly catch her breath.

'What is it? What's happened? Sarah? Jack?'

'No, love – it isn't none of them. It's Megan. He knows. Bert Armitage. He knows where Megan's at. Mrs Harvey told him, when she gave resettlement money out. Oh, I'll have to sit down.' She pulled one of the chairs out from under the table. 'It all beggars belief! Megan's in Leeds, and it's said as she has a shop! How did she manage that?'

'Never mind that now. Oh, Megan! Poor Megan. Has Bert gone? Does Jack know?'

'Yes, talk is as Bert went straight to station. When I were told, I went over to see Henry and asked him what he knew. He told me as he were stood talking to Jack in the garage, when the manager of the mine came out of the house and told them what'd happened. Henry said Jack took off in Mrs Harvey's car like the world were on fire.'

'Oh, dear God! What am I to do, Gert?'

'Happen as you're best leaving it to Jack. He'll get there about same time as Bert, and hopefully

463

sooner. He'll not let Bert hurt her, I'm sure of that.'

'No, I've got to do sommat. Look, Gert, I'm going to Dr Cragshaw, and I'm going to ask him to take me over there. I'll beg him, if I have to. Emotions are running too high for Jack. He's in love with Megan.'

'What? Jack? And Megan? No!'

'I know, I know. It isn't right, but it is how it is. Neither of them planned it, and they'd not do owt as'd bring me and young 'uns into shame. But now Bert will know, and it was bad enough thinking on what he'd do to her, just on her leaving him. But when he realizes there's someone else for her, and who that someone else is, it don't bear thinking on.'

'Well, I never dreamed! And you know where Megan's at?'

'Never mind that now. Will you help me, Gert? Will you see to Sarah when she comes in?' Gert was nodding. 'Mind, don't tell her owt – nor no one else, for that matter.'

'I wouldn't. I...'

'Now then, Gert. No offence, but like me, you likes a snippet. "An exclusive", as papers call it. But I also knows as you don't use owt you know in malice. So think on. Thou knows what this'll do to Sarah. I want no shame bringing down on her. Right?'

'I'll not say nowt, I promise, Issy. Now go on, and go as fast as you can! Oh God, I hope as doctor'll take you and you get there in time. I dread to think what'll happen if Bert realizes what you've just told me.'

44

Fatal Revenge

'Mam! Mam ... Mam! Maaaam!'

'What? What is it, Billy? Have you hurt your-self? Have you been stung? Calm down, love. Tell me what's wrong.'

'I – I've just seen me dad. He's coming, Mam. He's coming up street!'

Terror gripped Megan. It tightened her throat and threatened to strangle the life from her. Her legs gave way. She sank back on the chair she'd just risen from.

'Mam? Mam! I – I'm scared.'

Billy's fear wrenched her from the depths of her own.

'Sally, close the door. Quick, lass! Lock it and put all bolts in place. Billy... Billy.' She stood up and took him by the shoulders. 'Run upstairs, get some money out of me purse and get yourself out of the back door. Take the key and lock it from outside and get yourself over to Hattie's. Go on, lad. Hurry! Hu–'

'Get out of me fucking way! I'm here to see me so-called wife.'

Megan turned and saw Sally being shoved to the floor by Bert. But before she could react, a piercing scream of terror filled the room. She froze. It was as though she was in a cold cocoon,

465

wherein the only knowledge she had was the fear of her own imminent death.

'Stop that fucking racket, you bloody little wimp!'

The vicious push that Bert had given Billy sent him reeling backwards. His arm was raised above the cowering boy, his belt coiled around his fist. The glint of the buckle caused Megan to slip out of the fear that had held her.

'No!' She sprang forward, placing herself between Bert and Billy. A tearing pain ripped through her, and her cry of agony was joined by Bert's cry of pain. Sally had sunk her teeth into his leg.

'You fucking bitch!' His movement was swift. His body twisted and the buckle whipped through the air. Sally moved, but she wasn't quick enough. The buckle caught her, and a raw, gaping gash appeared on her head. Her body crumpled to the floor.

Releasing the breath that the stinging pain had caused her to hold within her, Megan lunged forward. Bert's boot lifted and was aimed at Sally's head. He didn't find his mark. Instead his body fell heavily, unbalanced by the force of the hold Megan managed to get on his raised leg.

In a flash she was sitting on him, beating his vile, hated face with her fists. 'You bastard! You bloody bastard!' The spittle ran down her chin. Years of pain oozed from her. She grabbed his hair and banged his head on the floor. 'No more. Do you hear me? No more!'

In one swift movement he twisted his body and unseated her. Before she could right herself, he was up and standing over her. The arm she put up to protect herself was ripped open as it caught the full thrust of the lashing. 'No... Nooooo!'

'I'll give you fucking NO! You scum! You fucking whore!'

She tried to crawl away. The buckle stung her buttocks. The stinging, unbearable pain took the breath from her. The smarting of her back as another blow caught her drew that breath back, only to be released with an agonized cry as more crushing blows bore down on her. 'Oh God! Oh God, help me! HELP MEEEEEE!'

'You're rotten, Megan Armitage! Fucking rotten through and through. You'll do no more to me, you cow!'

She kicked out and caught Bert's shin, causing him to step back. Using everything she could muster, she scrambled away and managed to stand and face him. Her own broken spirit mocked her, reducing her to a whimpering, begging animal. 'Please, no more. I – I'm sorry I left you. I'll come back. I'll do anything – anything as you want of me – but...'

'Back? Back to what? I've got nowt. Nowt! Does you hear me? I'm on streets – me family gone. You fucking left! And I thought when I came home, me trip to Blackpool would be all sorted. You cruel bitch!'

He sprang forward. She had no escape. His arm was around her neck. She couldn't breathe.

'I'm going to kill you!'

Her body hit the floor. She was nothing ... nothing...

Blood squirted into Megan's eyes and mouth,

mixing with her tears and her snot. Her agony drummed in her ears and filled her mind, blocking out all that was going on around her. No begging, no praying – nothing. She was the vilest of creatures...

Jack slammed on his brake. The barrel boomed down the cobbled road towards him. It had happened just a few yards in front of him. The car that had hit the dray had seemed to come from nowhere. The horses hadn't stood a chance. The dray had overturned, spilling its load of barrelled beer.

Just as it seemed the barrel would hit him head-on, it veered and the passenger side of the car caved in. The noise deafened Jack. His shock held him suspended.

'Are you all right, man? Can you get out?'

Jack looked at the policeman, unable to take in what he was saying.

'Are you hurt, man?'

All he could do was shake his head at such a thing happening, but he'd not let it delay him. He couldn't. He got out of the car.

'Hey, where do you think as you're off to?'

'I'm all right. I'm not hurt. Look, Constable, I can't stay. I've got to get to Coppery Street.'

'You're going nowhere, Mister. You're the only witness. I need a statement from—'

'No! I must go. I must – me lass is in great danger. Her life depends on me, please. I'll come to the station to give evidence ... please!'

'What're you talking of, man? Happen shock's playing tricks with you. You can't leave the scene of an accident. Now, what's your name?'

'Jack – Jack Fellam. I'll be in touch.'

'Hey! Come back here. Well, I...'

Jack's body took on the challenge. His legs gained a speed he'd not thought possible. He was so near. So near...

As he turned the corner he could see the shop door. It was closed. He sent up a prayer: *Please, God, let me be in time.*

'What the–? Jack Fellam! You bastard, you knew all along where she were! Well, I'll do the two of you in one go. Come on then, big fella. Let's see how big you are, with no ma to defend you.'

'Jack? Jack?' Megan could only mouth the words. Some comfort came to her.

Jack and Bert both leapt at once. Their bodies landed near her. Her bench crashed to the floor and a loud echoing boom filled her head. The paraffin stove was on its side. Flames flared, snaking round the workbench. Within seconds her rolls of material became flaming torches. Horror engulfed her. Her throat stretched to yell out, but no sound came.

Through the swirl of smoke she could see Bert on top of Jack, his fist raining blows down onto Jack's face. He couldn't defend himself. His arms were trapped – one under his own body, the other pinned down by Bert's knee.

'Please, God, help him!'

The unbearable heat and smoke was closing in on her and clouding her view of what was happening. She felt a desperate sense of fear for Billy, but then she saw that he wasn't in the path the flames were taking. But what of Sally ... oh God! The flames were all around her.

The swirling smoke choked Megan as she crawled towards Sally. Stinging tears streamed from her. But somehow she managed to reach Sally and drag her to the door, with every ounce of her being. Once Sally's head was outside, Megan's strength drained from her, but she *had* to find enough to go back for Billy.

Through the haze of her tears, Megan saw Billy standing behind his dad. He held what looked like a huge, menacing hammer. 'No, lad ... no!' But the words didn't come out.

She had no voice to use. The smoke smarted and stung her nostrils. A blessed blackness took her into its peace.

'You leaning forward isn't going to get us there any quicker, Issy. Rest back, woman.'

'Aye. I know, but I'm scared with every bone in me body.'

'And with good reason to be.' Dr Cragshaw shook his head. 'I've not taken in all you've told me yet. It was bad enough Megan upping sticks and leaving. Talk was rife then, though it was tempered by the fact as folk were glad for her. But her and Jack! That's not going to be accepted. Folk are going to be on Bert's side, even those as despise him. If he murders the pair of them, it'll be said as he was justified.'

'I know, Philip lad, I know. But what can I do? I know what you're saying. It isn't right, but ... well, they both deserve some happiness.'

'I'm Dr Cragshaw now, Issy, not Philip. I know

that sounds pompous, but it took me a long time to get the older generation to accept me as their doctor – me being a local lad. But that aside, Megan and Jack do deserve some happiness; and in other circumstances, yes, I can see them together and would be the first to wish them luck. But I can't as things are, much as I'd like to. I'd be hounded out of my job. Medical Council would–'

'Take it as understood, Doctor. And I'm sorry me use of your first name offended you, but try as I might, I can't get the cheeky lad as you used to be out of me head, but that don't mean as I don't respect you. I respect you more than anyone I know – you getting your scholarship and doing so well. Anyroad, what you've done today in bringing me here will be seen as you going to help your patients. After all, that's what they all are, and I've fetched you to them because they're all in danger. Right?'

'Well, put like that, yes. I'm only doing my duty. Now then, which way do I go from here? We're in Bramley now.'

'Turn here. Yes, I'm sure it's–'

As they turned into Coppery Street, Dr Cragshaw slammed on his brakes. 'Oh no! Is that Megan's place?' He didn't wait for her to answer. 'Stay here, Issy!'

Issy stared in horror at the flames and smoke belching out of every window of the building. Fear made her body surge forward. She was out of the car and by the doctor's side in a flash. 'I'm coming with you. Oh God!' She looked around her. 'There's no car. Jack can't have got here, he...'

The clanging bells drowned out her words. A

fire engine screeched to a halt in front of them. Two ambulances followed behind.

'Stand back now. Come on, everyone, out of the way.'

'I'm a doctor – Dr Cragshaw. I'm from Breckton and I know the owner of the shop. Is everyone out of the building, do you know?'

'I've had no time to check that, Doc, having only just arrived,' the policeman answered. 'I was seeing to another accident, and fella as witnessed it ran off. Said his lass was in danger in Coppery Street. I come as quick as I could and–'

'Oh God, Doctor, there's Jack coming out. He's on fire. Oh, my God! Jack! Jack...'

One of the fire officers leapt from the engine and sprinted across the road, taking off his jacket as he did so. In seconds he had Jack on the floor and had smothered him with the jacket.

'I couldn't reach...'

'It's all right, man. It's all in hand. Don't worry yourself. Doctor, quick. Over here!'

The doctor was just behind the policeman, as was Issy. Jack's body was trembling from head to toe. It was impossible to see how badly injured he was, as black soot covered all that was visible of him.

'Oh, Jack. Jack love...'

'All right, Issy, leave him to me.'

Issy stood as if in a trance. She looked from the blackened body of Jack to where an ambulance man was working on Megan, and it seemed as if her world was crashing down around her.

'There's another bloke still inside!'

The shout from the fire officer brought her back

to reality. Her decision was made in seconds. She could trust Philip with Jack, but she needed to see that the ambulance men were taking proper care of Megan, then see to the young 'uns. She looked over at Billy and Sally. They were sat huddled together on the pavement. Sally, her face covered in blood, sat with her head resting on Billy's, her arm around his shoulder. Billy was in a daze. His eyes stared out into nowhere and his body trembled all over.

It was two days later that Jack woke. At first he thought he'd had a nightmare, but his pain soon brought him back to reality. 'Megan, Megan – where...?'

'It's all right, Jack. Stay calm. You're in hospital.'

'Doctor, Megan's hurt.'

'I know. Now I'm here to examine you, Jack. I've just–'

'Is Megan...?'

Dr Cragshaw shook his head. 'I'm sorry, Jack, so sorry, but things look bad for Megan. I can't honestly say she'll survive. It's suspected there may be internal injuries and there's a very real risk that she'll develop pneumonia. She's very weak from loss of blood. Her injuries are – well, I've never seen the like. To think as a man could do such a thing to a woman. To anybody, come to that.'

Jack sank into himself. His eyes closed. He swallowed hard to try and stop the stinging tears, but they seeped through and ran freely down his face.

Dr Cragshaw took hold of his hand. 'You've been through a lot, Jack.' He hesitated and then took a deep breath. 'I'm afraid there's more, though. I'm here at the request of the police.' He turned and for the first time Jack saw two men standing behind him. 'These men here are detectives. I'm to check you over to see if you are well enough to answer some questions.'

'Questions? Can't they wait? I know I'll have to sort things out. I left an accident just afore I got to Megan, but I had to. I were only just in time, as it was. Are Billy and Sally all right? And Ma? I saw Ma with you.'

'Billy and Sally are going to be fine. Sally has a nasty gash on her head and they're both in shock, especially Billy. He seems unable to speak at the moment, but that's a natural reaction to the horror he witnessed. And Issy? Well, you know Issy. She has some friends supporting her. Hattie and Harry, I think she said their names were.'

'Oh, thank God. Hattie'll take care of them all.'

'Yes, she's an odd-looking character, but she has a kindness and a level head on her. Now, roll over, Jack, I need to check your dressings. You were lucky. Your burns are only superficial and you seem to have suffered very little from the smoke. Although how you managed that, I don't know, seeing as you made several trips back into the building and managed to catch your clothes on fire!'

'I only went back in once. Sally was already by the door. And Billy could hop along whilst holding onto me, and I carried Megan at the same time. When I went back for Bert, flames had blocked me return. I held me breath and tried to get through, but...'

'That's why you're to be questioned. You see, Bert – well, he didn't come through it, and it wasn't fire or smoke as killed him.'

'We'll take over now, thank you, Doctor. Now then, Mr Fellam. It was a bad day's work, what with fire and cruel beating as lass took. But more seriously than that, a man is dead, and he didn't die from natural causes, neither. So what light can you throw on that matter, sir?'

'I – I don't know. I mean ... what killed him? I tried to get him out. I couldn't reach him: the smoke, the fire... How did he die?'

'Couldn't reach him? Or didn't want to, because you knew he was already dead, eh? Knew blows as you landed him had done for him? Isn't that how it was? Nice and convenient if his body was burned up and no evidence to trace. Isn't that what really happened, eh?'

'No! No.'

The larger of the two men, who hadn't spoken until now, moved forward and sat on the end of the bed.

'It must have been a terrible scene – lass being beaten, young 'uns crying and scared, and the man causing it all half-crazed and capable of anything. No one would blame you. What did you use? And what happened to the weapon?'

Jack didn't answer. Billy's face, and the evil intention he'd seen in it, flashed into his mind. *Oh God! Billy had killed his dad! Aye, and meant to an' all... Oh God!*

'You and lass were having an affair, was you? Nice and convenient to have her husband out of the way, eh? And if body can burn an' all – well, the perfect crime.'

'No!'

'What then? Young lass wasn't one as you went to save, was she? Oh, we know you went there intentionally to save someone, as you told policeman at the accident scene. In a state, you were. Desperate.'

'I ... no, not Sally. Megan. She'd left Bert – he found out where she was. He was going to kill her. I had to stop him.'

'It wasn't enough just to restrain him, though, was it? Most would say as he was in his rights. His missus got what was coming to her – that is, except you, Fellam. You had other motives. Saw an opportunity, didn't you? Kill him. Get him out of the road and set the fire to cover up your crime. And all under the guise of wanting to save this Megan, your mistress! Folk'd see you as a hero and the path would be clear.'

'We – we fought. Paraffin heater got toppled. It were an accident.'

'Oh no! Bloke wasn't killed by accident or as a result of fighting, nor fire. It was blows you landed. Remember? Vicious blows to the back of his head. Blows that were meant to kill him.'

'I didn't mean to kill him – just stop him. He were raging. I didn't mean...'

'Jack Fellam, I am arresting you for the murder of Albert Armitage. You do not have to say anything...'

Jack didn't register what the detective said to him, after the first statement. Fear and shock held him rigid, his terror intensified by the thought that he could be hanged for this. *Megan... Megan, oh God!* He looked over to where the doctor was registering the look of horror on his face. 'I didn't mean to, Doctor, I–'

Dr Cragshaw shook his head. 'Oh, Jack, no. No!'

PART SEVEN
The Coping
1930

45

Taking the Blame

The clanging of the prison gates grated on Jack's nerves. Each set he went through underlined his dread. He was being taken to the visitors' room, where Dr Cragshaw was waiting to see him. *Please, God, don't let him be coming with bad news.*

But then why else would they allow him to visit? They'd not let him have any visitors since he'd been formally charged with Bert's murder. They'd said it was on account of all the folk who could visit him being witnesses; or, in the case of Hattie, they refused her because she had the witnesses staying with her.

'Jack. How are you, man?'

'I don't know, to tell the truth, Doctor. I'm in a kind of trance most of the time. I can't feel anything or think on things.'

'That'll be the shock. It's a funny thing, is shock. It can in some ways protect us from what we have to face.'

'What do I have to face, Doctor? Have you come with news? Is Megan...?'

'Megan's doing well. She's out of hospital and is at her friend Hattie's house, and as you can imagine, she is being looked after well by Issy and Hattie. There are two women living in a flat at the back who seem to know Megan and Issy

481

well, and they are helping. And, of course, Megan is helping her own recovery. She's a very strong and determined young woman and wants to get better, so that she can support you. In fact she's shocked us all with how quickly she is getting better. Not to say she hasn't still a long way to go, but she will win through.'

'Oh, thank God! Thank God.' Jack sank into the chair and put his head into his hands. He'd not cried since he'd been in this awful place, but now it was as if he was a babby again. Sobs racked his body.

'Let it all out, Jack. It'll do you good. Help you to break free of the shock, and help you to make decisions about your future.'

'How can I do that? Me future isn't in me own hands.'

'Yes, it is. Look, I haven't got long – I am meant to assess you medically, but I came chiefly to give you news and, in my opinion, you knowing what is going on will help your health, especially your mental health.'

'Thank you, Doctor. Tell me how everyone is.'

'I'll not go into detail.' The doctor told him how everyone was coping as best they could, and that the young 'uns had been told he was away at work, so as not to worry them. 'Billy is worrying us all. He hasn't spoken a word since it happened. It's the shock. As I said, it can affect us in different ways. But Sarah is paying him a lot of attention and looking after him like he was a babby. I'm just leaving him alone at the moment. His physical health is fine. These things often resolve them-selves, with time.'

This news gave Jack mixed feelings. Part of him was glad the lad wasn't having to face the truth of what he'd done. *But what that means for me doesn't bear thinking on.*

'I have other news,' the doctor continued. 'And I need you to give me your agreement to it. Mrs Harvey–'

'I want nothing to do with *her!* She caused all this. She is the real murderer! Only it was Megan as she wanted to see dead.'

'Listen, Jack. She is what she is. Aye, I know the whole story. And you're right, this was her doing, though I'm going to speak straight. You know that's my nature. You, Jack, must shoulder some of the responsibility. Lady Crompton tells me Laura fell in love with you, and you knew and didn't take her feelings into account. In the eyes of her family, you dropped her without as much as a by-your-leave and went on to your next conquest.'

'What!'

'I'm not here to judge one way or the other, but from what I have heard, you were very insensitive to Laura's feelings. If you knew as she'd fallen for you, you should've been more of a gentleman in how you let her down. And you weren't being fair on Megan, either. Well, I needn't say any more. The price has been paid, as I see it, and now we've to deal with the mess that has been caused.'

Jack couldn't speak. The guilt hit him like a punch in the stomach. The doctor was right. He did know Laura was getting in deep. He should have talked to her, written to her – warned her where his true feelings lay. God, he was guilty! He was as guilty of Bert's murder as he would have been if he'd rained the blows on Bert's head himself.

'Well, as I see it, Jack, you're getting a bit of luck. Lord and Lady Crompton are anxious that Laura isn't caused any more harm. She is quite ill. The shock of what her actions led to – and especially what has happened to you – has caused her to collapse. It is confirmed that she has TB of the lung. She is going to Switzerland, where she will have the best chance of getting better, though in my opinion her chances are very slim. Lord Crompton has asked me to speak to you. He wants to keep Laura's name out of all this. He has asked if you will allow them to pay for a very good lawyer to act on your behalf.'

Jack stiffened. Laura had done what she'd done because she was a woman crossed. Aye, he'd played his part, but the part he'd played hadn't deserved all this. Not for Megan, it hadn't.

'Jack, if you're thinking of refusing, think on. You need help.'

'But how can anybody defend me? All the evidence is against me.'

'Are you saying as you did it?'

'No! No, I'm not. But who's going to believe me? I've had it, Doctor. I'm going to hang...'

'You mustn't think like that. Listen, Jack, a good lawyer will help. He might even be able to get the murder charge dropped and one of manslaughter put in its place. You'd only be facing around five years in prison then. Be sensible, man, and take the Cromptons' offer. All they're asking is that Laura's name, and her affair with you, is kept out of it all.'

'And you think that's right!'

'No, I don't, as it happens, but if it can keep you from being hanged, then I'd go for it. I'd see it as right in them circumstances. Look, dragging it all out can only make things worse for you. Think about it. Think how it makes you look. Having an affair with your boss, then with another man's wife – it don't look good, especially as the husband of the woman you had an affair with has been murdered and you're implicated! If I didn't know you, and know that you are not capable of such a despicable thing, I'd be the first to put the noose around your neck. So think on. Them as are dealing with you don't know you. If they get to hear the full story, you *will* hang, and make no bones about it!'

'Alreet, I accept that I have no choice. But it don't sit easy with me.'

'Good. Never mind how it sits. It's your only hope. Now then, the lawyer is already engaged. He's the best. My solicitor knows of him...'

As the doctor told him about the lawyer, Jack's emotions alternated between anger and despair. If only he could lie in Megan's arms and have it all not have happened. *Oh, Megan, me lass, will I ever see you again?*

'Anyway, he will be in to see you tomorrow. Tell him the whole truth, Jack. Don't leave anything out. Then he will know what he is dealing with and how to act. Thank God you had the foresight to plead not guilty at your initial hearing. Your trial date isn't set as yet, though, as the police have asked for more time. So, you'll meet this lawyer, then?'

'Aye, I'll meet him.'

'Good. Now that's done, I can concentrate on contacting Bert's sister.'

'Bert's sister?'

'Yes. It's a funny tale. I don't mean funny in an amusing way. But it turns out as Issy and I know Bert's sister. Her name's Bridget Hadler, or was. She was brought up in Breckton. There was a lot of to-do around the time her dad died. All sorts went on. You should get Issy to tell of it. I was only a young 'un when it happened. Anyway, it seems as Bridget's mam, Bridie Hadler, married again and had Bert. I tried to contact Bridget as soon as all of this happened, but she and her husband were abroad on holiday. They will be back now. And nothing is lost, as Bert's body hasn't been released as yet. Megan had their address.'

'Megan knew?'

'Yes, but she'd been sworn to secrecy, at least where Issy was concerned. Bert didn't want any interference. Megan had told Hattie, though, and we found the address amongst Megan's things.'

Jack had no time to ask any further questions. The prison officer stepped up to announce that their time had come to an end.

'Well, Jack. Think on now, man. And do as I say: tell the truth.'

Jack didn't answer this. He quickly gave the doctor messages for everyone, especially Megan.

As he was led back to his cell he thought: *The truth? How can I ever tell the truth? The truth would kill Megan. Or at least kill all the life that is in her.*

Jack looked across the table at James Pellin. The

man wasn't much older than himself! It beggared belief that he was a top lawyer, of whom it was said that he could get the devil off a charge of arson, if he'd a mind to. Or so Dr Cragshaw had told him.

Pellin sat in silence, his piercing eyes lowered now. Jack felt a relief in him at that. It was like he could see your soul when he looked at you.

'You're lying, Jack.'

'I'm not. It's the truth, I'm telling you. I couldn't get the better of him. The fire were taking hold. I had to do sommat. I hit him. I picked up Billy's crutch and I hit him as hard as I could. I did it so as I could save the rest of them. We'd have all burned to death if I hadn't done it.'

'The only thing I believe about your story is the weapon. A crutch could have been used to kill Armitage. And if you're not for telling me who it was that wielded it, then I have two options. One: I can go for self-defence, but given the circumstances I can't see that holding up. Two: I can dig and dig until I find out the truth...' As he paused, Jack felt again that the lawyer's eyes were piercing his very soul. 'And that truth is not going to be that you killed Bert Armitage.'

Jack's body shook. He closed his eyes. In his mind flashed the scene of the blunt, heavy end of the crutch smashing down over and over. His ears heard the sound, the terrible crunching sound, and the moan as air was forced out of Bert's lungs, never to be drawn in again. But he wouldn't let in the evil – not the evil he'd seen in Billy. He shook his head and looked up at Pellin.

'Why? Why don't you believe it was me?'

'Why? Because I have this thing called intuition. And that intuition is not letting me believe you. Now, which one was it?'

'It was me. I keep telling you.'

'You can tell me till you're blue in the face. My intuition tells me you probably will, because you are protecting someone you love, and you are the kind of man who would go to the gallows rather than betray them. But I won't give up on you, Jack. I'll find out the truth. Unfortunately the only other two who know can't remember the incident. But they will. I'll have to get the Cromptons to cough up some more of their hush-hush money, to pay for psychiatric help for them.'

'Will you be able to keep Lau– Mrs Harvey's name out of all this?'

'I doubt it. I'll let them think so for a time, but it doesn't matter one jot to me that they are paying. My loyalty is to you, Jack, as I believe you are innocent. I will use every bit of information I deem necessary in your defence, regardless of who may be hurt in the process! Besides, I may not have any choice. If it becomes apparent that the involvement of Mrs Harvey is crucial evidence, I will have to share it with the prosecution. I'm duty bound to do so.' Pellin let out a heavy sigh. 'Jack, you are admitting to having killed a man! You had a motive for that killing. A motive that will be judged as premeditated. There can be only one sentence. *You will hang!*'

Jack watched as Pellin wiped the sweat from his brow and around his neck. The handkerchief he used looked as if it had never been used before. Funny, that.

'Don't turn away from me, Jack. Listen! Let it sink in that you are going to be hanged by the neck until you die. It isn't quick, Jack. You kick and kick. Your body swings. Your head swells. Please, Jack. Look, if it was Megan, I'd be able to get her off with self-defence. She'd serve a minimum time, or more than likely no time at all, when what she has suffered is taken into account. If it was Billy – well, he's a minor. His mental state would be looked at. They'd take into consideration whether or not he knew that his action would kill. Umpteen things will be taken into consideration, and the worst that could happen is that he would be committed to an institution and helped to get better, then possibly in years to come he would be rehabilitated. But neither of them would die! Do you see what I am saying, Jack? Death is final.'

Jack made no reply. He couldn't. It all seemed so simple to Pellin. And yet he knew that any of those outcomes would be too much for Megan to bear.

'Look, I've done my best. But this isn't the end. I am going with my gut feeling. I am going to do my utmost to prove I am right. In the meantime there is a plea hearing tomorrow. We are going to stick with a not-guilty plea. I'll see you tomorrow.'

'I don't want you to represent me.'

'Oh, don't try that one, because I'm telling you it won't stop me digging and digging until I find the truth.'

As Pellin left and the guard took him back to his cell, Jack felt out of control of everything. He couldn't contact anyone. He could do nothing. All he could do was hope – hope that the Cromptons refused to pay for medical treatment for Billy and Megan, so that they would remain in a world where they had no recollection of the horror of what had happened. And he wished to God he didn't, either.

The phone call was the best news they'd had. Dr Cragshaw was with Hattie and Issy when the telephone rang. James Pellin had asked for him, and now here the doctor was, telling them that Megan and Billy were to receive help.

'Look, on the face of it, it does sound good. But this kind of therapy can take a long time to work. It isn't always the best idea to bring back the memory. It may cause worse problems, particularly in Billy's case, so we must all be prepared for that.'

'Shall we see what Megan says? She should be the one to decide.'

'Yes, Hattie, you're right.'

Whether the doctor thought she was right or not, Hattie wasn't in favour of anything happening that Megan didn't know of.

Megan was propped up by a number of pillows. She looked pale and gaunt and yet managed a smile. The bruising around her eyes was receding and the blue-black colour was fading, though her eyes were still very bloodshot.

'How are you feeling today, Megan?'

'A little better, thanks, Doctor, but I'm reet troubled. I need to know what is happening. Is there any news as yet from that lawyer? Does you think as he's seen Jack?'

'Yes, he has.' Dr Cragshaw told Megan what

490

Pellin was proposing.

'But why? I mean, why is Mrs Harvey's sister doing so much? I mean, it's kind of her, but...'

Hattie held her breath for a moment. She looked at Issy and then at the doctor, and each indicated with a look that Megan shouldn't be told.

'What? What is it? Hattie, don't keep it from me. You know we never keep owt from each other.'

Hattie took a deep breath. *What should I do? Is it my place to tell?* Megan was right that they'd never kept anything from each other – especially something as big as this. Rightly or wrongly, she decided she had to hold fast to what had formed the very basis of her own and Megan's life to-gether: the truth.

'Look, love, what I tell you...'

'No.'

'Issy, let Hattie tell me. I have to know. I already know as it's sommat as will affect me by how you're all acting. Go on, Hattie.'

At the end of her telling about Jack's affair, Hattie was no longer sure that she'd done the right thing. Megan looked devastated. Hattie sat on the bed.

'It doesn't affect how Jack thinks of you, Megan love. Megan...'

The laughter started deep within Megan and erupted out of her mouth, causing her immense pain. And yet there was release – release from the agony of knowing the truth. A truth that left her feeling cheated: cheated out of a time she could have been with Jack. Cheated that he'd lain with another woman. Cheated in the trust she'd placed in him. Because she hadn't ever envisaged him doing something like this. Not just taking to sate his need. Not Jack!

'Eeh, lass, lass, don't take on.' Issy's stroking of her hair gave her comfort.

Hattie held her hand. Megan gripped onto it, trying to make it the saving of her.

'Megan, Megan, do you want me to give you something to help?' The caring voice of the doctor offered her blessed oblivion.

'No. No, I've to face it. I – I can. I have to. Oh, Jack ... this'll do him, won't it? I mean, if it comes out, how will it look? Oh, Jack – why?' No one spoke. She looked around at them. None of them could help in a situation such as this. 'And to think as he must have talked about me when he was with her!'

'Megan love. Let me tell you, lass, as that woman were after Jack for years. Even when Ciss were alive! And he managed to avoid being seduced by her until Ciss were two years in her grave, but then – well, his need... You know how it is with men.'

Aye, she knew how it was. Only she'd thought Jack was different. She could understand Issy trying to justify it all, but it was hard to accept.

'Anyroad, he was afraid of sommat like this happening. That's why he wanted you to change your name.'

'Why didn't he tell me, Issy? Why?'

'He was scared to tell you. He didn't want you thinking badly of him. I agreed with him that he shouldn't. Not yet. You'd been through so much, and you were just starting a new life. He were going to tell you sometime in the future. He'd not live a lie with you.'

'But he did! He should've told me.'

'Let me give you something to rest you, Megan.'

'No, I – I want to see Bridget. She ... she will need me. I need to make her understand. She'll be here this afternoon, you say?'

'Yes, she will. But she does understand. I have told her most of it. She says she knows first-hand what it's like to go through such violence. She doesn't hold you or Jack responsible. Look, a mild sedative wouldn't put you out for long. It would just help you to rest a while.'

'All right, thanks, Doctor. Is Billy all right? And Sarah? And Sally? I haven't seen them today.'

'Aye, they're fine. Billy's happy as long as Sarah's paying attention to him. He shows no sign of re-membering. Maybe it would be the best thing for him to have some help. What do you think?'

'But isn't he better not knowing, Doctor? What I can remember haunts me, whether I'm asleep or awake. Shouldn't we let Billy live without the memory?'

'We can't. We need you both to remember. We need the truth to come out, for Jack's sake. Pellin thinks Jack is innocent. But he is confessing to it all.'

'Is he? Why? No ... no! Doctor, he mustn't! Why is he?'

Megan sat up with the shock of these words, despite the pain it caused her to do so. 'He didn't do it!' Images shot into her mind. Flashes... 'Oh God! NO. NO!'

'What is it? Megan, love.'

'It – it were Billy... Oh, Hattie, it were Billy!'

The horror of it all played through her mind as if she was there again. She retched and retched. Someone put a bowl under her mouth and she heaved until she felt her very heart would come out of her.

'Megan, Megan ... oh, love.'

Issy's sobs filled the room. How did we get to this, Megan asked herself. Oh aye, me and Jack sinned, but did we deserve so much punishment for doing so?

The pinprick of a needle going into her arm calmed the retching. 'Doctor, I didn't want to be put to sleep, I told you.'

'I know, but as your doctor, I overrode your decision, as it will rest you for a couple of hours. You need that, Megan. I don't want you going into shock again. If you get pneumonia, we will be lost.'

'Hattie, what should I do?'

'Sleep for a while, love. Then, if you feel up to it, tell us all about it and we'll take it from there, eh?'

'I'm sorry, Issy. That I should bring this down upon you. I've never told you, but I love you. You are like a mam to me.'

Issy patted her hand. 'Oh, Megan love, I love you an' all. We'll get through this, we will.'

'Doctor, get that help for Billy. The truth has to come out.'

As her body relaxed, Megan felt someone wipe her lips and put water to her mouth. She sipped the cool liquid. She'd let her body rest. But what of her mind? Would she ever have peace of mind again?

494

46

Coming to Terms

As she emerged from sleep, Megan knew she hadn't rested. Not properly. She'd dreamed, seeing horrific images of Jack and Billy hanging by their necks. She'd tried desperately to take their weight, but every time she'd reached them, they'd moved. Her body was racked with pain, but her mind was racked with agony. She opened her eyes. Hattie sat by the side of her bed.

'I don't suppose as you're much rested, love. You've been very agitated. I've done wrong. I shouldn't have told you. Issy's out of sorts with me, and so is Harry.'

'No, Hattie. They don't understand the trust as we have. Most people have broken our trust – even those as we love the most and should've loved us – but we've not broke each other's. That means a lot to me. Folk have a false sense that they're protecting you by keeping the truth from you. And, aye, they do it for the best of reasons. I just wish as Jack'd told me or, if he hadn't the courage, at least Issy should've said.'

'Aye, Issy should've advised him better, but you can't blame Jack. You can't put a woman's head on a man, love. They're not the same. They can justify anything to themselves, though I reckon as no one regrets his actions more than Jack. You've put him on too high a pedestal, love. He were bound to fall off. My Arthur did. He crashed right through the floor. I thought as he were different. You'd have thought as I'd have learned about men enough to see the fall coming, but I didn't.'

Megan felt she'd nothing in her to give Hattie, so she just patted her gloved hand. It was an action they both used at such times.

'Is it going to be all right for you and Harry? I mean, can you learn to trust again?'

'Oh, aye, I think as you can. I'll not bring me pain from Arthur and crucify Harry with it. He don't deserve that. But I'll be more careful, as I know *you* will. I'll not look on Harry as some kind of God just because he loves me. I'll keep in mind that he's a person and can make mistakes. But I know what he's offering me is a truth. He don't want to just take me – he wants to marry me. That's first time that has happened to me, and thou knows sommat? I'm not for going to his bed until he does make me his wife! But I'm not letting him know, so poor thing keeps trying.'

'Oh, Hattie ... oh, don't make me laugh. It hurts. And stop messing with him. He doesn't deserve that. You know you love him, so put him out of his misery. Your games might come back to haunt you.'

They were interrupted by the opening of the door, and Issy put her head around it. 'Megan lass, Bridget and her husband Edward are downstairs. I thought I'd come up first and see as you're ready.'

Megan gave her a smile. She wanted to put Issy's mind at rest about her having known all and not told her.

Issy came into the room, talking as she walked.

'There's sommat that's reet funny, lass. Bridget looks just like you! They say as men often pick women as look like their mam or their sister. Well, you wouldn't credit it. And, you know, she takes after her da. He comes right back to me mind, when I look at her. Though I've often said, haven't I, as you remind me of someone? And I still can't get over the coincidence. Fancy her being Bert's sister! And fancy him landing up here, where she were brought up.'

'That wasn't chance, Issy.' Megan's hand went to her neck. She wanted to hold her locket, to feel the comfort it always provided her. But it wasn't there! She looked around her as she told them how Bert had come to these parts because he'd wanted to be near where his mam and sister had lived.

'What is it, love? Have you lost something?' Issy asked.

'Me locket.'

'It's here. They had to take it off you in the hospital.' Issy opened a drawer of the chest opposite the bed. As she brought it over, it twirled in her hand, glinting as the light caught it.

'Oh, look. There's an inscription on it.' Issy squinted at the locket. *To Catch a ... a Dream...* Good God! No, it can't be the same one.'

'What do you mean: the same one?' Hattie asked. 'The same one as what?'

'I – I've seen this afore. A long time ago. Where did you get it, lass?'

Megan felt her stomach muscles tighten. She

told Issy and Hattie the story of the locket and of her mam dying at her birth.

'Well, well! I'll have to sit down a mo.' Issy shook her head from side to side. 'Megan love, I feel as though all me coincidences are coming together, but I'm afraid of the outcome. If this locket holds the pictures of Will and Bridie, then ... my God! If they are your grandparents, then ... then Bridget – no! No, it couldn't be. You said as your mam died. And yet, how like Will and Bridget you are. The same dark eyes, the lovely olive-coloured skin and the high cheekbones.'

'What ... what're you saying, Issy?'

'I don't know, lass. I need to look inside. Will that be all right, love?'

Megan's 'Yes' was little more than a whisper.

Issy's hands shook and her mouth dropped open. 'Tell me, Issy. Please tell me.'

Issy stood up and came over to her side. 'Megan love, I have no alternative but to tell you, but I wish I had. I'm afraid me news isn't all good.' She held the open locket up. 'This here is Will and Bridie Hadler, and they were Bridget's mam and dad. They had no other surviving children, so if they were your granny and granddad...'

The silence that followed was fraught with tension as each absorbed the information.

Megan slumped back on her pillows. She could hardly breathe. Bert's half-sister was her mam. She was about to meet her mam! Her mam was alive! Her world had gone mad. Bert and her mam, related!

Nobody spoke. Megan knew they'd already come to realize what had just dawned on her.

498

'Billy and me ... share the same grandmother. Billy's an inbred! Oh, Hattie, Issy...'

They both looked distraught. Both seemed dumbstruck. 'What do I do? How do I face Bridget? Will she know me?' The emotions that were churning about inside her provoked so many questions, the answers to which all held fear in her. And yet didn't some of the answers hold what she'd always longed to know? Who her family were? Who she was?

'One thing you can do nothing about, love, is Billy's inbreeding. It weren't your fault.'

'It were in a way, Issy. I could've shown me locket to Bert afore we were wed. I nearly did. But I always wanted to keep it to meself. It were the first thing as ever belonged to me, proper like. I kept it from everybody. If only I'd have shown it.'

'*If only* begets *if only*. But it don't alter nowt. We've to deal with things as they are. Now, how Bridget and you deal with finding each other – and what the tale is behind her giving you up – will soon be upon you, and that's me worry at the moment. Are you feeling up to it, Megan love? Or does you want us to put Bridget off for a while? After all, you've so much to come to terms with.'

'No! I mean ... no, Issy love. I want to see her. I need to.' A tear trickled down her cheek, and as she turned to talk to Issy another ran over the bridge of her nose. 'It should be a joyful time – me finding me mam – but it's not. I have so much inside me. So much to tell. I...' A sob caught in her throat. How much more could she possibly take? How much?

'Oh, Megan love.'

499

'Shift over, Issy.' Hattie put a stop to Issy's sympathetic flow by pushing her way nearer to Megan, then kneeling in front of her. 'Megan lass, I know it's come at a bad time, but isn't it what we always dreamed of: finding our mams? Well, no matter what else has happened or is happening, surely that's the one bright spark amongst it all? Think on it, love. You've found your mam!'

Megan looked at Hattie. She was right. How often had they lain awake together into the early hours, two lost little souls, longing to know who they were and where their mams were? And, in the years since, how often had she felt pain when she'd been told her mam was dead? But she wasn't dead. She was here. Here, in this very house. And she had no idea what she was walking into.

'Hattie, you're right. I just can't take it all in. I – I mean, how will it be when I see her? On top of that, I have some things in me as I've not spoken of, and I'm scared.'

'Don't be scared, love. Like we said, we're all here for you. We'll help you. Is it about what happened?'

'Yes. Billy did kill Bert. He hit him with his crutch. And … and he meant to. Oh, Hattie. He hit him over and over – me little lad. Me little lad. He – he had an evil in him. And – and it were all my fault.'

'It weren't your fault, lass; it were Bert's. And, aye, Jack has some guilt an' all, as does that Mrs Harvey. But not you, Megan love. You were just the victim of it all. Look, love, we had an idea that's how it all happened, from what you said earlier. Jack has a good lawyer, and we'll tell him

500

all about it.'

'But what will happen to Billy?'

Hattie told her what the lawyer had said would most likely happen.

Megan's heart, though already splintered, seemed to shatter in her breast on hearing this. Aye, Billy had killed his dad, but the sin wasn't his. It was hers. Hadn't she put a terror in him about what might happen if his dad caught up with them? And it did happen. In front of his very eyes! He must have felt that he had no choice. Poor Billy, how would he bear being locked up in an institution? No! No, she'd not be able to bear it, either. There would be no help for him. Those places were... No, she couldn't think about it.

She lay back and closed her eyes. She wanted to be alone. She wanted to try to sort everything out in her head. She didn't feel that she could face Bridget, or face having her confirm that she was her mam.

After a few moments she heard the door close. She opened her eyes. Hattie was standing by the window, looking out. Megan closed her eyes again. Her head throbbed. The turmoil inside was too much to cope with. She longed to be lying in Jack's arms, looking up at that protective canopy. She wanted to feel the happiness and peace she'd felt then. *Oh, Jack, Jack...*

Her thoughts turned to Bert. He was gone – gone forever. The thought should have made her feel relieved, but it didn't. Not that she'd wish him back, but in his death he'd won. He'd destroyed Billy and Jack, aye, and her as well, because she'd never be the same again. None of them would.

501

The tears she'd stemmed earlier came back to sting her eyes. The pain in her heart twisted and turned to agony, as she tried to imagine what it was like for Jack.

She became aware of a hand holding hers and opened her eyes. She looked into Hattie's. Her eyes, too, were misted with tears. 'Don't give up, Megan love. Don't give up. Jack's going to need you, and so is Billy. And, aye, Issy and me an' all – all of us need you.' The mist dissolved into a wetness, and a tear flowed down Hattie's cheek.

Megan leaned forward and wiped it. 'I'll try not to, Hattie.'

Suddenly it was as if they were children again, with all the pain of their childhood now piled high with the turmoil of the present. Hattie rested her head in Megan's lap and they allowed the tears to flow silently down their cheeks.

'I'm scared, thou knows, Hattie. After all we dreamed it would be like, and it's not. I feel that scared, I feel like changing me mind and not seeing me mam. I don't know how it should all happen, or even if we should tell her what we know. And s'pose as Sister Bernadette were lying to me, and the folk in me locket are not me grandparents.'

'No, she weren't – I know that. Anyroad, Issy said as you looked like Bridget's dad, and you do – the features on his face are yours. And, Megan, Bridget herself is like an older version of you. Not that much older. I reckon as she had you very young. Look, love, how about I get Issy to tell Bridget, afore she comes up? Wouldn't that be better than dropping it on her in front of you?'

'Aye, it would. It'd be better for her an' all. Give her a chance to get used to the idea afore she meets me. It's going to be a shock to her. Her own half-brother's wife ... oh, Hattie.'

'All right, love. Shall I take the locket with me? I think it would help in Issy's telling.'

Megan handed over the locket. Hattie's hand shook as she reached out to take it and in a hurried movement she bent forward and kissed Megan on the cheek, then left. Megan knew that Hattie was anxious because she would have to face seeing her united with her mam, whilst still not knowing of her own mam, or knowing of a time she ever would. *But then that's how it'd always been with us – me getting the best end of the stick. Though it changed some when I got Bert.* But even then Megan sensed that Hattie would have liked her status as a married woman. Dear God – status! Oh, aye, she'd had status, but for the most part it had been a living hell.

To think that Bert was the half-brother of her own mam! Was it bloodline that had drawn her to him? Because she'd always sensed something about him, although she'd known it wasn't love; and, despite all Bert did, she never lost that feeling for him. In a way she even felt some pity for him now. She could see the tragedy of their ever getting together with one another. Maybe, if he'd met up with someone else who really loved him, as a woman should love her man, he'd have been different. And what of Billy? Was he unstable? Aye, she had to face it. Deep down inside her, she'd known a lot of his actions were not just a lad's way, as they were put down to. Billy was unstable. Billy

503

needed help, and it wasn't to be wondered at; after all, he was an inbred and it was known that inbreds often had sommat wrong with them. She couldn't take it in; she'd sinned by laying with a close relative, and hadn't even known it.

The painful laughter threatened to erupt again, but Megan wouldn't let it. No. If she did, she'd not be able to stop, and she'd fall into a deep pit of madness. She was needed. Despite the horror of everything, she had to stay strong – strong for Billy and Jack, and strong enough to meet the woman who might be her mam. In some ways it would be better if she wasn't. It would be better if a mistake had been made by Sister Bernadette. At least then one part of the nightmare that she was currently living wouldn't actually be real.

47

A Reunion Marred by Revelation

'Megan. Megan, love...'

Megan hadn't realized she'd had her eyes closed so tightly. The voice brought them open, and as the concerned and loving face of the voice came into focus, she knew it was all real. 'Mam?'

There was a silence. Megan waited, holding her breath, then sighed with a relief that she hadn't expected to feel as Bridget said, 'Yes, dear.'

'Oh, Mam.'

A gentle hand stroked hers. Glistening tears of

joy fell down the smiling, beautiful face. 'I can't believe it – it's like a miracle. My own baby...'

They stayed like that for a moment, neither knowing what to say. Megan felt a surge of love for Bridget. It was a love that forgave all. Nothing mattered – not why, not all the loneliness – nothing. All that mattered was that her mam was here. Her very own mam.

It was Bridget who asked the first question. 'Has all of your life been awful, Megan dear? I mean, have you had some happy times?'

She thought for a moment. Recent events stopped her mind from giving forth any happy memories to speak of, but then a laughing Cissy came to her, and with the image came many happy moments of their time together. And then she thought of Hattie and all they had been to each other. And of the moment little Billy was born. And how lucky she was to have Issy and Sarah and Jack; above all, Jack... Yes, she'd known happiness. She'd known the greatest happiness of all – the love given to her by Jack. She nodded. 'Aye, Mam, I've had a lot of happiness mixed in with the bad.'

'I'm glad, dear. Oh, Megan, I'm so sorry, I–'

'No, don't be sorry. It's all right. You're here now, and that's all that matters.' But it wasn't, and suddenly she did want to know why she had been left, who her dad was and what had happened to him. What had her mam's life been like? What...? Oh God, she wanted to know the answer to so many things that had troubled her all her life. But then she remembered that her mam had just lost her half-brother without ever being reunited with him. 'Bert – I mean, he was your half-brother and he... Well, I didn't know he were...'

'I know, dear. The fact that we're all blood relatives is marring our coming together. How could anybody ever prepare for such a thing happening? I did ask Sister Bernadette to tell you everything. I told her to tell you about Bert, and where he lived, and ... and about me. And I contacted her just as soon as I was in a position to take care of you. She told me you had been adopted and that I should keep you in my prayers, but that I would never be allowed to have the details of your adoption. Why? Why did she do such a thing? I trusted her.'

'She told me you were dead, and that I had no family alive. That you'd never revealed who me dad were. Only thing she said were that it wasn't your fault – you had been attacked by someone you trusted.'

Bridget bowed her head.

'Yes, that is true.' She paused and took a deep breath. 'The man who raped me was someone I trusted. I worked for him and his wife at the corner shop on the street where we lived. I'd loved him and his wife, and they were very good to me and Bert. They seemed so happy together, but then I found out the truth – or realized it as I grew up. He wasn't a nice man. I'm sorry, I know I am talking about your father, dear, but he was a malicious individual and his wife suffered. The shock of what he did was beyond anything I'd known – not just the rape, but Bert's dad, my step-dad's involvement in it and his future plans for me.' Tears ran down her cheeks and her face filled with distress.

'It doesn't matter, Mam, I understand. Don't upset yourself further. It's in the past. All that matters is that you are here now. Have you any other children?'

'Yes, two boys, Richard and Mark. They don't know where we are, or anything about their Uncle Bert dying. We will tell them when they are older. They think we are on holiday – they are with their grandparents. They'll be having a good time getting spoilt. Richard is eleven and Mark is ten.'

'That's grand. Not only a mam, but two brothers as well! Only you don't have to tell them about me, either, Mam. They are too young to hear our tale. Best we give them time to grow up without any complications. We can say I am a long-lost cousin or sommat.'

'No, darling, they have always known about you, though they think I was married before. And every night, when we say our prayers, they pray for Mummy's lost little girl and my lost half-brother, and – funny, this – but after your letter, they pray for Bert's wife and his son, whom they thought was their cousin, which of course Billy is, and yet... Oh dear, it is all so complicated.'

'We'll have to find a way round it all for them, but not yet, not yet, Mam.'

'I know. As it is, they are going to be surprised at how grown-up you are, as we always spoke of you as a little girl. And now I find I am a granny, too! That is a shock.'

'Aye, you are. And it's lovely to think that all these years you and me brothers have been pray-ing for me – ta, Mam. Mind, it makes you wonder if Him up there ever listens. But thou knows sommat, Mam, Bert did...'

She went on to tell Bridget how Bert had kept her letter and how he'd wanted to be in the place where she was brought up, and had searched for the burial place of the babby her mammy lost. 'And like I told you in me letter, he named Billy after your dad.'

'That's a comfort, Megan. Thank you for telling me. If only he'd answered my letter...'

'He told me that he did. But then, he could have lied just to stop me going on about it. Bert were a stubborn man. Billy can be like him. I – I'm worried over Billy, Mam. I've heard tell as inbred children can suffer – well, mentally.'

'Yes, it is possible. I know what you are worrying over. Issy told me everything. Billy may need help. I'll bring Edward up to meet you soon: he has friends in the profession. He can see that Billy gets the best possible treatment. Everything will turn out, you'll see. Now, my dear, you're tired. We've covered a lot of ground, and we've both been hit by something akin to lightning, finding each other like this. It's the happiest and yet the saddest day of my life.'

'I know what you mean. We've lost so much, and so much has happened to us, and all because of Sister Bernadette thinking she was doing right by us. We've a lot to tackle. But we won't lose each other again, will we? No matter what happens and no matter how all this concludes, we won't lose each other.'

'No. You'll never be able to get rid of me, even if you find you don't like me! I'll not go away.'

'Mam, I'll never come to not like you. I know as I love you even now, and I know as I will for the rest of me days. I'm so happy to find you. It's what me and Hattie... Oh, poor Hattie. We used to dream of this moment, but I can't ever see a day when she'll find her own mam.'

'Megan, I think I know who Hattie's mother was. In fact, given her name and that Hattie looks so like the girl I think was her mother, and you two being brought up together in the same convent and being the same age, I'm certain I do. The person I'm thinking of was in St Michael's with me. We became very close, like you and Hattie. She was a lovely girl. Her name was Lucy. Sadly, she died during childbirth.

'Her story was heartbreaking, in that it was a calculated rape by a member of her own family, specifically to get a child. The rape was instigated by Lucy's aunt, her mother's younger sister, who was childless, and whose husband was on the verge of leaving her. My friend Lucy didn't know it was a plot. Her shocked parents, who had thought she was in France with her aunt, dis-covered the truth, partly through what Lucy had told me about her young man, and partly by Sister Bernadette knowing of a sum of money being paid to the Reverend Mother.

'Lucy had been taken to France by her aunt as a companion and had been introduced to a relative of the aunt's husband. The young man's attention to Lucy made her think that he had fallen in love with her and they would be married. One night he forced himself on her, but was sorry afterwards and she forgave him. They continued their intimate relationship, but once she was with child he disappeared. Her aunt put all the blame onto Lucy, and then told her she had a plan to keep everything secret from Lucy's parents and society. The plan was to send her to St Michael's to have the child.

'During the pregnancy, the aunt stayed in France. Her husband believed her to be pregnant and was happy again and visited her occasionally. Once the baby was born there was a plan that her aunt's maid would collect the child and take it to France and the aunt could announce that she'd given birth. But, with Lucy's death, her parents had to be informed, and the whole story came out.

'Lucy's surname was Grampton, which is similar to Hattie's, as your maiden name is to my maiden name. Sister Bernadette must have changed your surnames. Why, we will never know!

'The Gramptons were a well-to-do family, but there aren't any close relatives alive now. The shock of what happened to their only child and the deceit they suffered proved too much for Lucy's parents. They were an elderly couple and had had Lucy very late in life. They both died within two years of Lucy's death.

'So you see, Hattie really is an orphan, with no one who would care to be found. And though she is probably entitled to a legacy, she could never prove it, as it was all hushed up and all traces of her were banished. She was even named by Sister Bernadette. But one thing: despite her deceit in not telling you and me the truth, for whatever reason, Sister Bernadette did her best for you both. She used her knowledge of what happened to Lucy to blackmail the Reverend Mother of St Michael's to arrange things so that she was always going to be with you both.'

Megan had lain still throughout the story, her heart heavy for Hattie. 'It's strange about Sister Bernadette. It will take me a long time to forgive her. You and I could have been together. She stopped that, and yet she protected Hattie – well, both of us – because she did take care of us and she intervened on our behalf, if things got really bad. Thou knows, things have gone better for me throughout than for Hattie, and I've always carried a guilt about it.'

'That's not your fault, my dear. Anyway, if Hattie is like a sister to you, she can be like a daughter to me. I know it's not the real thing for her, but I'll try to make it the next best thing, and it will be my way of paying back her mother. She was very good to me.'

'But, Mam, I need you to understand about Hattie...' As she had done with Issy so long ago, Megan carefully told her mother Hattie's story. True to form, she didn't want anyone to ever think badly of Hattie.

'Don't worry, Megan. I'd guessed some of it when I met her. It won't affect me. As I've said before, there's stuff in my past I can't tell of yet – oh, not about me, but ... well, others, so I know how it is. Anyway, from what I understand, Hattie is trying to put it behind her.'

'She is. She has a good stash now. She was left a house – well, sort of. Anyroad, it's been sold, so she's been able to get rid of her old business. Her

511

and Harry – he's the fella as loves her – well, I think... I'm hoping they might marry soon and... Oh, I'm not making much sense, but well, thou knows, Mam? Afore all this happened, everything was going good for me and Hattie.'

'It will again. I know it's hard to believe that it will, but we are together now, and I think everything will turn out right for Billy and Jack, and you could start up your business again. You hadn't been going long, so you can't have lost it all. I mean, orders will be delayed, but, like you told me, your customer was very taken with your designs and is likely to recommend you. Give me her address and I will contact her. I imagine that, as she is a friend of that despicable Laura Harvey, she'll already know what has happened and probably feels some guilt and doesn't know what to do about the situation. Did you take a deposit and leave carbon copies of the designs that she wanted with her?'

'Yes, Lady Gladwyn did give me a deposit; but no, I didn't leave copies of what she wanted making. I had them all in a book. Me idea was to have a book for each customer, and then they could point out things they really liked on one outfit and might want on another. Now I think on it, though, I should make copies.'

'Yes, you should in future, but it won't matter. I'll try to persuade Lady Gladwyn to see you again, and together you should come up with what it was she wanted. What do you think?'

'I don't know. You can't be sure how top-drawer folk'll act over owt, but I'd not be against you trying. It would be grand if she would give me another chance. I've probably got enough of me start-up capital to buy the materials, and Hattie will help me out. I could use Issy's sewing machine. It's slower than them as I bought for shop, but I managed for over two years on it. And even if Lady Gladwyn won't have me back, I've still got hope. I can start up again. I can.'

'Well, I'm glad you think so, dear. We all need something we can hang on to. Just a thought: would you consider a restart in another area, rather than staying around here where there are so many memories? It would be lovely if you could move nearer to us. We can build a proper family. Edward and I can help you. I'd certainly become a customer, and I know I could get you some business amongst my friends. Some of them are on the fringe of being *top-drawer*, as you call it, and they have some good connections.'

Megan felt her mouth drop open at this information.

'I know. Look, it's all too much for you to take in at the moment. I'll tell you all about it when you are better and when I'm more able to disclose more about my life. Anyway, I'd better go and bring Edward up to meet you. He'll be worrying about us. We've left them all for such a long time, they'll be wondering how we are doing.'

As she got to the door, Bridget turned back and said, 'I'm very proud of you, Megan love. You know, I think you get your talent for drawing from my dad, your granddad. He loved to make sketches. Oh, and I chose the name of my Granny O'Hara for you. She was my mother's mother – oh, I've such a lot to tell you.'

Megan smiled. She lay back and allowed the wonderful feeling of really belonging, and of being part of a family, to wash over her. She knew there was still a lot to face, but she had her mam to face it with her. That was something to be thankful for, she told herself. But then a thought came to her. 'Mam, will you ask Hattie to come up first, and will you come, too? I can't keep the information about Hattie's mam from her. She has to be told.'

'All right, dear, if you are sure?'

'I am, Mam, I am.'

48

The Truth Will Out

The sweat ran freely down Jack's cold body. His legs shook as he stood looking at the judge, whose voice droned in his ears.

'Jack Frederick Fellam, you are charged that on the fifteenth day of October 1930 you did murder, by beating, a Mr Albert Armitage. How do you plead?'

His 'Not guilty' didn't sound convincing. But then it wasn't what he'd wanted to say. He'd not wanted to drag it all out. Why had he let Pellin convince him to?

The wrangling didn't take long. Pellin had warned Jack that he'd not have much of an argument for getting him bail.

'Mr Fellam, bail is refused. You will be remanded

in custody until the eighteenth of March 1931. At which time you will appear here, at Leeds Crown Court, to stand trial. Do you understand?'

'Yes, Your Honour.'

He understood, all right. Five bloody months cooped up in that cell! Oh, Megan. Megan! he thought with despair. He held on to the message she'd sent him. It added to his shame that she knew of his affair with Laura, but to know that she had come to an understanding of it and had forgiven his part in it was a help. If only he could talk to her.

He was glad to hear that Megan had found her ma, though her being who she was beggared belief! Still, no matter what the circumstances, it was something that would be a help to her. He wished as it was him helping Megan. Holding her – would he ever do so again? And what of Billy? He was glad it was a friend of Megan's step-dad who was going to help him, and it wasn't to be paid for by any more of Laura Harvey's stinking blood-money. But how would the lad cope with having to face what he'd done? What if it tipped him over the edge, as Dr Cragshaw had warned? *What then? Oh God! It all seems so hopeless.*

'Oh, dear, Doctor, will Billy be all right?' Issy asked the consultant psychiatrist. 'Should I go after him?'

'No, we'll leave him for now. But you must all be prepared for a long-drawn-out healing process. It is going to take a long time to get through to him. I will have to gain his trust, which I have already damaged. You saw his reaction when I mentioned

515

his dad. He took flight. That's a typical reaction to this kind of trauma. Billy is a very frightened young boy. I'm going to have to go slowly – very slowly indeed.'

'But we don't have time.'

'Don't get upset, Issy. Surely, John, there are other, quicker ways. What about the new regression techniques? I was reading something only the other day that servicemen, suffering from similar mental traumas due to their experiences in the war, have been helped by taking them back to their pre-war life and then bringing them forward.'

'Yes, it is an option, Edward.'

'Is it safe, John?' Dr Cragshaw asked. 'Only I am afraid your field is something I know very little about.'

'Yes, the trials have been good, but all of those who were on the trial programme were much older than Billy, and they could be told what would happen and talked through all the implications.'

Issy felt all this medical talk was above her, as were the three doctors discussing it. But she knew that Phi– No, she wasn't to think of Dr Cragshaw as that; it wasn't her place to call him Philip, even in her mind. But, whatever his status, she knew he'd watch out for Megan and Billy. He knew how far all this should go.

A sudden scream cut into her thoughts. The scream held a terror. It was Megan – what was she screaming? Issy stood as if she'd never move again, but Edward grabbed her as he went by and pulled her along.

Hattie and Bridget emerged from the kitchen,

just as they entered the hall. Sarah was right behind them, but thankfully Issy saw that Daisy was there too, and that she took Sarah by the hand, led her back into the kitchen and closed the door.

Edward held Issy back as they reached Megan's room. When he opened the door, the sight caused Issy to freeze. Billy held aloft a wooden rolling pin as if he would bring it down on Megan's head. His eyes stared out of their sockets, and froth foamed from his gaping mouth. Issy knew she was looking at living evil. Her blood ran cold in her veins.

Megan had quietened as the door opened. She turned towards them. She looked desolate, and Issy wanted so much to go to her, but knew she had to allow Edward to get things under control.

'Put that down! Do you hear me, Billy? Put it down! Billy, Billy, can you hear me? Don't be afraid, put...'

Edward had a commanding tone to his voice, but Billy took no notice.

'She's got to die – it was her fault.'

'No, Billy, it wasn't your mother's fault. Don't–'

'I – I have to. I have to kill her. It's telling me I'm to do it.'

'What's telling you, Billy?'

'The redness, the red...' Billy's body broke out in sweat and his skin paled. 'The redness says she's to blame. She left me dad! She made him mad – he hit Jack. He ... he was going to kill him!' Billy swung his arm even further back.

Issy felt her body sway. 'No! Oh God! No.'

'I've to get the red out. I–'

'No!' Edward leapt forward.

517

Billy swung round to face Edward. He felt his arms drop. They were heavy. Everything was heavy. That fella that claimed he was his step-granddad was near him. He'd to stop him.

'Get away, else I'll do you an' all!' The redness inside his head burned. It swelled – his head would burst! It had to come out. He thought of the first time it had come to him and given him such pain. The thought carried with it an image of Bella at his feet, and he laughed.

'The stinking halfwit. Ha!' His body shook and the laughter took hold of him. The pain in his head increased. The redness was eating him! He needed to stop laughing.

It was making him weak – he'd to beat it. Look at them all – he'd have to do them all in.

The redness would help. It was helping him; it was coming back, giving him strength.

He swished the rolling pin backwards and forwards. He could still see Bella, and she was looking back at him, the ugly sod. He lashed out at her. Heard once more the crunching sound of her head.

'She's dead – I've done her! Ha! She's heavy, she stinks ... the ugly sod stinks. I've got to get her to the mineshaft.'

'Billy, what are you saying, lad?' Issy's voice penetrated the redness. Billy liked Issy.

'It was the redness. It told me to – it come out; it was on the branch. Then on me – it come out of me head. I didn't know what to do. I hid her. I dragged her to the mineshaft...'

He was losing his power again. He'd only to do his mam in and it'd be over. His eyes hurt. They felt like they were leaving his head! The agony of the redness crushed him. He swished the rolling pin again.

'You killed–'

'Shuddup! I have to listen.'

'Who are you listening to?'

That was the new bloke they'd brought in. Why didn't he listen to what he told him?

'The REDNESS! I told you: he's in me head!'

A pain seared through Billy. He had to get it out. Had to do his mam in – it was all her fault. He raised his arms. A strength came into him. He felt huge, bigger than everyone in the room. He looked round at them. They were all staring. He laughed out loud.

Someone was shouting. It was his Aunty Hattie.

'Tell the redness to go away, Billy. Go on. Tell it. It isn't your boss. It'll do as you say, lad. Tell it as you don't want to kill your mam.'

'No! It won't. It made me ... it made me kill Bella and me dad. It made me.'

'Well, you bloody well tell it it isn't going to make you kill your mam, or it'll have me to answer to, and that'll frighten it. I'm helping you, lad. We can beat it together, eh?'

'Billy, I'm your mam, I love you. I'll join with Hattie. I'll help you fight the redness.'

'We all will, lad. We'll not leave you on your own with it.'

Everybody was nodding. The fella who had been talking to him earlier started to move. Billy didn't want him talking at him again. He wanted his mam. The redness was going – he'd beaten it. His Aunty Hattie had made them all help him to beat it. He didn't ever want it to come back. 'Mam... Mam...'

He was in her arms. He was safe. 'Ouch!' Someone had jabbed a needle into his bottom. It hurt. His mam held him tighter. His eyes felt heavy, he couldn't keep them open...

Megan felt the mattress sink as it took another weight. Hattie had come to lie beside her. Her arm came round her and Billy. There were no words Hattie could say. She knew that.

Issy stepped forward, her body bent over. Megan wanted to take Issy's pain away, but knew she couldn't. For a moment Issy just looked at her. Her head shook from side to side. Her body sank down in the chair next to the bed.

Was it all over? Could Issy forgive? Issy's shaking hand reached out for hers, and Megan took it gladly.

Bridget came further into the room. She motioned with her head to Edward and he steered the rest of the doctors out and closed the door. Bridget came over and knelt in front of Issy.

'Issy. Issy dear.' She brushed a stray strand of hair back from Issy's desolate face. 'Everything will be all right, Issy.' Issy looked up into Bridget's face. Bridget paused a moment, then said, 'Issy, I've never stopped thinking of you as a second mother. I just wished I'd conquered my shame and contacted you. When ... when I realized I was carrying a baby, I wrote a letter, but I couldn't post it. I so wished I had. I'll look out for you now, Issy love. Just like you looked out for me when I was a girl, remember? You were all I had whilst

Mother was in that workhouse.'

Issy patted Bridget's hand, then turned to Megan. 'Oh, lass...'

Megan understood. It was enough to have Issy's warm, chubby hand in hers. It told her she still had Issy's love. Despite everything she had brought down on her, Issy was still there for her.

So many questions were swimming about in her mind. Her granny in a workhouse? And Issy caring for her mam? But she didn't voice them. The tears running down her mam's face stopped her.

Megan looked at each of the women – women she loved, and who loved her. She could see that the pain pitted into her own heart was etched into each of them. It was a pain cut deep by others' brutal acts.

She held Billy to her. She had no more tears left in her. No more. Surely Jack would come home now? And Billy would get the help he needed.

Megan relaxed back and let her head fall, so that she was looking at Hattie. Hattie smiled. It was a smile that held courage – enough courage for Megan to hold on to. She smiled back.

EPILOGUE
Finding Peace
1933

49

Reopened Wounds Bring Healing

'Megan love...'

Megan did not turn round to look at him. The distance between them was a void too gaping and cold for Jack to cross.

'What are you thinking, lass?'

'I'm for feeling all the pain again. Not that it ever goes from me, but the letter has reopened the wounds and made them sore.'

'I know, lass.'

'Why can't she leave it alone? I – I know she's dying. And, well, I understand she wants forgiveness, but why do you have to go to her? That woman broke me, Jack. She brought me so low that I've never properly recovered. She gnaws away at me thoughts. It's like a war in me. I fight a daily battle with my hate for her.'

'We'll never be reet until it's settled, lass. Going to her, and giving her the chance of getting our forgiveness, might settle it all.'

'She wants you, Jack, not me. You! It says so in the letter.'

'Well, that's not going to be how it is. In the past I had to do Mrs Harvey's bidding, but not now. If I go, you come, too.'

'Wouldn't a letter do? Did you ask Lord Crompton if we could write a letter saying as we

525

forgive her?'

'Aye, I did. He begged me to consider going.'

'How can she do this? We're just getting sorted. The year you spent in that prison... Oh God, Jack. And Billy – he's settling, and doing well on the treatment. The shop's beginning to make a profit. You have your job.'

'It is as you say, lass, but there's sommat between us. Sommat that's not letting us be happy.'

'You're not happy with me?'

'I didn't say that, Megan. What I'm trying to say is there are loose ends. Stuff we need to face. Just living with it isn't working. Once it's done we can–'

'And going to Laura Harvey on her deathbed and giving her our blessing will end it? I don't know as I can do it, Jack. I don't know as I want to. The hate in me wants her to rot in hell!'

'That's it, Megan. That's just it. The hate in you – the bitterness – it is eating you away. You're letting her win.'

'Win! Don't you see, Jack, she *has* won. She has the power to open all the vileness, and lay it raw between us.'

Megan turned to face him, and what Jack saw in her face made his heart ache.

Two years had passed, and one of those they had spent apart. He could still hear the judge: 'Jack Frederick Fellam, you have been found guilty of perverting the course of justice, in that you withheld information that would have assisted the police in their enquiries. Taking into account all the circumstances, and the time you have already spent in prison, you are sentenced to be detained for twelve months...' And so it had droned on.

In some ways he and Megan had been stronger during that year – determined not to let their lives be ruined. It had been hell, but it was a hell they had got through. Megan kept busy rebuilding her business. Billy was sectioned for an indefinite period, but – with the help of Bridget and Edward – he was in one of the best mental hospitals available and had started to make progress from the very beginning. His newfound affection for his mam was a salve to Megan.

On Jack's release from prison they had married, making it a double wedding with Hattie and Harry. It had been a good day, a happy day. And, to top it all, not long afterwards and right out of the blue, Smythe's had offered him a job. He could never understand why, but it was welcome and he was plodding along there. The other blokes knew all about him and what had gone on, and didn't seem to bother about it all. They respected his knowledge and his skills with the horses, and all in all it was working out for him there.

On the face of it, everything should be grand. Oh, he'd known there would be a lot of healing to do. He had thought his love could do that. But the letter from Lord and Lady Crompton had shown that it couldn't:

We feel we have no right to contact you. Please forgive us for doing so. Mrs Harvey is very ill. Her life is coming to an end. She has a dying wish to see you and to ask you to forgive her. She is deeply troubled and holding onto life for this one thing. As her sister and brother-in-law, we appeal to you on her behalf to

consider making the trip to Switzerland and ex-
tending your forgiveness to her. We fully understand if
you are unable to oblige.
Please contact Lord Crompton...

Lord Crompton had been very humble when Jack had contacted him. 'I beg of you, Jack, to allow my sister-in-law to die in peace, and my wife to be able to know she did do so.'

'I need to think, Jack.' Megan's words cut into his thoughts now. He lifted his head. The void was still there. Megan walked towards him. She didn't stop by him or speak again. Her feelings were echoed in the slam of the door. After a few moments the front-door latch clicked, and then that too banged shut. Jack raised his eyes. Was he asking too much? Well, if he knew anything, Megan would have gone to Hattie, and that was a good thing. Hattie would help her.

'Is everything all right, Jack?' Issy came into the room. Jack looked at her and saw the worry etched into her face. It was a worry that he wasn't able to relieve her from – he didn't know how to. If anything, she was the one who helped the situation. Oh, and Sarah, of course. Sarah was growing up with a sensible head on her shoulders. Together, she and Issy kept them all going. Kept some balance in the fraught atmosphere.

'Make us a cuppa, Ma, and I'll tell you all about it. I could do with your advice.'

'If it's advice you need, Jack, then you most likely know what you need to do, and you just want me to help you decide. Eeh, lad. Will it ever end?'

'Megan, I'm going to talk straight. It's not likely as you're going to like what I say, but it has to be said.'

Hattie had that look on her face that Megan knew well. Frustration frayed her temper. 'I know you're going to side with Jack...'

'Look, lass, if you've a mind not to listen, why did you come? I'm not letting you off the hook with this one, Megan. Jack is right. The bitterness in you is destroying the person we love. Every one of us can see it and feel it. Your mam's worried over you – oh, yes, we've spoken. And we both agree: you have to reach a conclusion to all of this. Some of it you have to live with, but Mrs Harvey's involvement you don't have to!'

'But, Hattie...'

'I won't listen to your side, because I know it. Where d'you think as me and Harry would be, if he harboured feelings in him about me past, eh? None of us can alter our past. Jack had an affair; it meant nothing to him. I've told you afore, men are different to us, but Jack is different to most. He had his chances when Ciss were alive – God rest her – but his love for her stopped him. That marks him as a good 'un, in my books. He has told you that when he spoke of you to Mrs Harvey it was with pride, aye, and with love. He had no idea it would lead to what it did.'

'I don't blame Jack, Hattie.'

'You say you don't, but he feels blamed, and that on top of everything is wearing him down. He cannot say sorry all his life, Megan.'

'I – I...'

'Oh, love.'

Megan went into the fold of Hattie's arms. Her tears, locked away so long ago, tore from her body in a torrent that she felt she'd never be able to stop.

'Forgive, Megan. Forgive.'

A feeling as if a door had opened in Megan's heart drained her tears to nothing. Her sobs became sniffles. Hattie was right. Jack was right. Her mam, Issy – all of them were right!

'Why d'yer think you and Billy are at peace, love? It's because Billy has been helped to forgive you. Oh, I know what the little chap thought was your fault wasn't, but to him it was. Once those working with him managed to get him to forgive – to understand – he was able to return your love. They are working on getting him to forgive his dad, now. And then...'

'How d'yer know all this, Hattie?'

'Yer mam – my pretend mam, bless her. She telephones me and we have long chats.'

'About me?'

'Yes, mostly. As I said, we are all worried sick for you, love.'

'It'll be all reet. I can see that now. Ta, Hattie. Oh, ta ever so much. I understand. I'll do it. I'll forgive Mrs Harvey. I will. And, thou knows, I need to work through all the folk involved, just like Billy is. Mam said not long back she could get that psychiatrist bloke to help me. I snapped her head off, said I didn't need help, but I do, don't I, Hattie?'

'You do, love. We have all tried, but we are too close, and we only make you cross. Oh, Megan,

I'm so glad. I'm so glad.'

Jack and Megan's journey by rail and sea to Switzerland gave them time to talk and, free from everyday cares, they had time to listen to each other, too. Jack told Megan he'd long since come to an understanding in himself and had found forgiveness for Laura's actions, and he hoped she had forgiven him.

Megan couldn't help feeling a small pang of hurt as he spoke. Part of her wanted to say that he had no right to forgive the woman, not until she had.

As if he had read her thoughts, Jack held her close. 'Megan, I'm not saying I forgive her for what she did to you. I can't do that until you do. It is what she did to *me* that I can forgive, as I shoulder half of the blame. I should have held out against her, but in a funny way I came to understand her. Her loneliness, her grief – all of it mirrored my own, and it drew us together.'

'I can only say that I want to forgive her. I want to understand. And I will try, though I am hoping sommat happens that will make it all come naturally,' Megan told him.

They met up with Lord and Lady Crompton on their arrival and found that they had booked them into a small guesthouse. Arrangements were made to take them to the clinic later that day.

Jack felt he was entering a gulf of silence as they went inside the clinic. The squeak of their every step on the polished floor of the long corridors only deepened the dread in him. He held onto

Megan. Lord Crompton walked ahead of them, showing them the way. Lady Crompton had stayed in the car. Neither of them had commented on Jack having brought Megan to the clinic with him. They were allowing him to handle the situation in his own way.

When they reached the room, Lord Crompton stopped outside. The doors stood open. A set of doors on the other side of the room opened onto a balcony with a spectacular view across a shimmering lake, mirroring a backdrop of snow-covered mountains. And yet it wasn't cold. The late-September sun beamed warming rays into the room. Jack could see that the staff had wheeled Laura's bed out onto the balcony.

The moment they stepped into the room, a weak but unmistakable voice called out, 'Jack?'

Megan clutched his sleeve. He looked down at her. 'Go to her, love. Go on your own, first. I'll wait in the corridor. Fetch me when you are ready.'

'But...'

'It's all right, Jack. Go on. Do what you have to do. Say what you have to say. I am never going to ask you about it. This has to be the end. I will come in. I will, but not yet.'

Jack didn't answer her. He knew she meant it. If it was possible, Megan's newfound understanding had only helped to deepen his love for her. He held her close, then waited for her to leave. Lord Crompton went with her. It was Megan who closed the door behind them. At that moment Jack knew her trust in him had been re-forged. He took a deep breath. Whatever was to come, he was ready.

But nothing prepared him for the sight of Laura. Her features had sunk into her face. He could see nothing of the beauty he remembered, as the small amount of flesh left on her made her appear skeletal. And yet something of the old Laura remained in her eyes. He hoped she hadn't noticed the shock that the sight of her had caused him, or the overwhelming pity that swamped him – a pity that mingled with other emotions churning inside him. This dying woman had lain in his arms, had made love to him, had loved him and wanted him. He crossed over to her side and sat on the chair provided. He could think of nothing to say other than, 'Hello, Laura. How're you feeling, lass?'

It was a stupid question. He wanted to tell her he would make everything right for her. He'd change things – she wouldn't die. But that, too, would be stupid.

Her thin, trembling hand stretched out to him and he took it. 'Oh, Laura lass. I–'

'Shush. You're here now. It's all I wanted – just to see you again before ... and to tell you something...' She was overcome by a fit of coughing.

He leaned forward and held her. He waited while she calmed.

When she did, she said, 'I've had a lot of time to think. I'm sorry. So sorry – tell Megan...'

'Megan's here. She's outside, and she wants to see you when you are ready. For my part, everything is all right. Don't think on it. It's done with. And, listen, I'm not without guilt, as I didn't treat you right. I should never have–'

'No. No, don't take on any of the guilt, Jack. It was my doing – all of it – and I want to make amends.'

'There are no amends that have to be made.'

'Tell me, Jack. Did you ... ever love me?'

This is what he had been dreading. But he'd made up his mind that if he got the chance and was on his own with her, he would lie. If that was what he could do for Laura, to help her die happy, he would do it.

'Aye, I did, Laura. I did love you. It died in me when everything took place, but now I know you are sorry, I can feel it again.'

'You ... have made me very happy – very happy, Jack. I have always loved you, though my love was selfish and made me do things ... to hurt you. It isn't now. It–' She could not continue, and her body was again racked with coughing and her breath so laboured that Jack got up and called out for help.

The room filled with nurses and doctors. Megan rushed in, along with Lord Crompton. Once the nurses had dragged the bed back into the room, Megan stood next to Jack on the balcony, looking out at the beautiful view. Jack felt his eyes mist over. The action going on in the room behind him filled him with a sense of helplessness.

The doctor eventually came to them and, in heavily accented English, told them that Laura did not have long. 'Lord Crompton has gone to fetch her sister. It is hoped they will be in time.' His head shook from side to side as he said this. 'We will wheel Laura out here again. She has many times expressed a wish that she be allowed to die looking at the beautiful mountains.'

Megan held Jack even tighter than she had done before. The sense of helplessness deepened. He could only stand transfixed as the nurses manoeuvred the bed back out onto the balcony. Once this task was completed, Jack looked down at Laura. He would have said that she had shrunk even more, had it been possible for her to do so. He knelt beside her and held her hand. 'Megan is here, Laura.'

Her eyes flickered open. Her hand clawed weakly at the sheet.

'For – forgive me, Meg...'

Megan knelt down. 'I do. I do. Jack has made me understand how lonely you were and how you had no real idea of what might happen. You weren't used to folk like Bert. You didn't understand what the consequences of your actions would be. You lived in a different world. I don't think you would have done it, if you'd been like us and knew the way of us. You were fighting to keep your man. I can understand that.'

Laura's half-closed, glazed eyes showed a flicker of light. Her lips moved, but no words came out, then they closed in a small but lovely smile.

Jack kissed her hand and assured her again that all was forgiven.

This brought a peace to Laura. She relaxed and closed her eyes. Her hand tightened in his and then went slack as a heavy sigh released her last breath.

They stayed still for a moment and gazed at her. To Jack, some of her beauty returned in her death. Her passing had been peaceful, and he was glad they had been able to help it to be so. A deep sigh escaped him as he gently placed Laura's hand back on her breast and joined her other one to it. Leaning forward, he kissed her still cheek and whispered goodbye. Megan kissed her too as she said her goodbyes. They got up to leave, holding each other as close as they could. As they reached the door, Lady Crompton entered the room.

'Am I too late, Jack?'

He nodded. He didn't trust himself to speak.

'Oh, Charles!' She collapsed into her husband's arms.

'Come on, my dear, she's at peace now.' Lord Crompton steered Daphne towards the balcony. 'Jack, will you wait outside for us? I'll need to talk to you.' Over his shoulder he said, 'We'll only be a few minutes.'

'Take all the time you need, m'Lord. Me and Megan'll be walking by the lake.'

The full beauty of the lake and the mountains engulfed Jack. 'This must be the most beautiful place on earth, Megan. Thou knows, if I could choose where I wanted to die, I would choose somewhere like this, with you by my side. I love you, Megan, more than I can say. In fact, I'm going to say it as loud as I can. I'm going to listen to it being echoed all around the mountains.'

He put his head back, but it wasn't a shout that came. It was a strangled sound and then a sob, and he sank down onto his knees and wept. Megan sat down beside him as his sobs brought forth all the grief that was knotted tightly within him.

'Oh, Megan, I'm crying for Cissy, our sweet

Cissy. And for me little Bella ... me mam and me dad, and me brothers – all gone. But they are all still so very dear to me. And Laura, poor, sad and lonely Laura. But mostly, Megan, me heart breaks for all you have been through because of me affair with Laura. The deep scars on your back: they're a daily reminder of your pain, and of the fact that I so nearly lost you an' all. Every night I have nightmares. That prison – oh God! – and the hell of only seeing you once a month, and then not being able to touch or hold you. How could I have opened those wounds again? How could I have thought Laura's forgiveness of me, or us forgiving her, was worth that?'

'Don't – oh, my love, don't. Don't torture yourself any more. It is over. It is truly over, Jack.'

After a while a calm feeling came over him and he felt cleansed. He knew he and Megan had both been cleansed. There was no bitterness left in Megan to gnaw away at her. He knew that; he could feel it. He took his hanky and blew his nose and then went to wipe Megan's tears.

'Eeh, Jack Fellam, I'm not having that all round me face!' Her giggle was the best sound he'd ever heard in his life.

Megan wiped her own tears on her own hanky, then snuggled into him.

The peace of the mountains settled them and they sat in silence, allowing the cool air to bathe them. The lowering sun dappled on the lake.

'Ah, Jack ... Megan, here you are. Well, it's a sad day. Poor Laura. She was only thirty-eight, you know. Well, well, poor Laura. She had a sad life, really, what with everything.' Lord Crompton stood for a moment looking at the ground.

Megan and Jack rose.

'I want to thank you both for coming. All the arrangements will be made for your return.' He paused.

Neither Jack nor Megan said anything.

'Bad business. Sad. Very sad.' He paused again. They could see he was fighting for control.

'We're very sorry, m'Lord,' Megan said. She felt Jack squeeze her hand.

'Yes, thank you, very decent. Well, must be off. I'll send everything you need to your guesthouse, and I'll contact you when I get back. Did Laura say how she left things?'

'What things, m'Lord?' Jack asked.

'Her last will and testament, Jack. She's – well, I'm not speaking out of place, I'm her executor. I am charged with arranging everything. The will is to be officially read, of course … after… Anyway, she meant to tell you today. She has left the bulk of her estate to be shared equally between you and Megan. By way of an apology. Quite right, too.'

Megan looked at Jack. He had an incredulous look on his face.

'I can see it's been a shock to you, on top of everything. Laura wanted to tell you herself.'

'But – no, she shouldn't have. We can't accept. It wouldn't be right. We all played our part in it. Me, Bert, Jack … we were all as much to blame. I told her. What she did, she did because she didn't understand. We forgave each other, and it's over. That money is yours and your family's.'

'I have never heard such generosity of spirit, Megan. But no. It is what Laura wanted. She has thought of us all, and you are not to worry about that. Look, I must get back to Lady Crompton. You have everything you need at the guesthouse?'

'Aye, we're being well looked after. They told us dinner is laid on for us tonight, and breakfast in the morning,' Jack told him.

'Good, now don't worry. My man will bring over your return tickets and sort everything out for your journey home. And about the will – I'll help you. Laura made a couple of requests as to how she would like you to use some of the money, but she stipulated that they are only requests. You're not to be beholden to them. I'll be in touch as soon as I have everything sorted. But, Jack and Megan, your life is going to change quite significantly, as the sum you will inherit is around ten thousand pounds. Take care and, like I say, I'll be in touch, probably in about two to three weeks. Goodbye, and thank you once again for coming. I know your doing so will have helped my sister-in-law to die peacefully. She looked ... beautiful. Yes, beautiful.'

As he turned to go, he shook hands with both of them. They could only nod. Megan stood stock still in shock, and Jack looked as though he'd been all but turned to stone.

'Meg...'

'I know, Jack. I can't take it in.' A nervous giggle escaped her. 'Oh. My. God!'

'Eeh, Meg. Meg...'

Her feet left the ground. She was being held aloft by Jack. The mountains swirled around her.

When he lowered her, Megan looked down at the lake. In its depths she saw the reflection of the swishing pines. She was reminded of the pattern made by the sun dappling through the leaves of the tree when she had first lain with Jack. She had likened it then to a protective lace canopy. That canopy had slipped from over her, but it was back in place. She could feel its protection once more. Everything in her world was coming right. She thought of Hattie. *Oh, Hattie. We came through, lass. Me and you. The unbreakable bond we formed as young 'uns brought us through. And aye, the one between me and Jack has proved true an' all. For now forgiveness has removed the shackles that held me bitter towards him and nothing will ever come between us again.*

Author's Note

The use of the word 'Mongol'

'Mongolism' was the medical term for Down's syndrome during the historical period in which this book is set. At that time people born with this condition were known to the profession as 'Mongoloids' – or 'Mongols' for short. This term is now considered an insult, but for authenticity I use the expression in this book. I do not intend to use the term in a derogatory way.

Just as they are today, Down's-syndrome children were very much loved and cared for by their family and immediate neighbours, but all of these people would use the word 'Mongol' then, as they knew no other. Like today, there were ignorant and hurtful people who would call names and cause problems. There are two characters of this ilk in this book. Their ways, and their use of language, are not mine, and they depict the worst of our society, then and today. I do hope no one is offended by my use of the term 'Mongol' – as soon as medical science discovered the real cause of the condition, it became obsolete, and rightly so.

Yorkshire dialect

An Unbreakable Bond is set in a fictional West Yorkshire town in the North of England. The following words are used in the dialogue and are common to this area:

Ginnel – an alleyway

Beck – a brook or stream

Owt – anything

Nowt – nothing

Reet – right

Neet – night

Eeh – an expression often used before a sentence

By – another expressive word to begin a sentence

Sommat – something. For example, 'It will be sommat and nowt' means 'It will be something and nothing'.

Acknowledgements

A book begins with an idea, it is nurtured and sweated over, and yes, has tears shed over it by the author, but no one person can bring it into being. I am lucky that when I self-published the first edition of this book, I had the expert help and guidance of freelance editor Rebecca Keys, proofreaders Julie Hitchin and Stanley Livingstone and talented cover artist Patrick Fox. And I am very grateful to them. I was also encouraged along the way by many, many people – too many to mention – but you know who you are and how grateful I am to you all.

And now *An Unbreakable Bond* is going out into the world thanks to all at Pan Macmillan whose faith in me, and whose guidance and help and belief in me have fulfilled my dream.

This new edition, the follow-up to *To Catch a Dream*, has been expertly and sensitively edited by Laura Carr and her team, especially Mandy Greenfield, whose input has enhanced the novel in a special way. Thank you all.

And how can I thank my wonderful editor at Pan Macmillan, Louise Buckley, who spotted my ebook self-published works and had faith enough in my ability to help me to make the step into traditional publishing, and has since taken care of me, encouraged me, and brought me through the stages of the traditional publication route? Thank you isn't enough, Louise.

No acknowledgement would be complete without giving my thanks to my brilliant agent, Judith Murdoch. Always in my corner, always guiding me and encouraging me, I'm very lucky to have you. Thank you.

And lastly, but most importantly, I am blessed to have such a wonderful family, who all support me in every way they can; my husband Roy and children Christine, Julie, Rachel and James, and my grandchildren and great-grandchildren, who are all a source of great joy to me. Not forgetting sisters and brothers and nieces and nephews of both my Olley and Wood families. Thank you, I love you all dearly. With your help I am able to reach the top of my mountain.

The publishers hope that this book has given you enjoyable reading. Large Print Books are especially designed to be as easy to see and hold as possible. If you wish a complete list of our books please ask at your local library or write directly to:

Magna Large Print Books
Magna House, Long Preston,
Skipton, North Yorkshire.
BD23 4ND

This Large Print Book for the partially sighted, who cannot read normal print, is published under the auspices of

THE ULVERSCROFT FOUNDATION

THE ULVERSCROFT FOUNDATION

... we hope that you have enjoyed this Large Print Book. Please think for a moment about those people who have worse eyesight problems than you ... and are unable to even read or enjoy Large Print, without great difficulty.

You can help them by sending a donation, large or small to:

**The Ulverscroft Foundation,
1, The Green, Bradgate Road,
Anstey, Leicestershire, LE7 7FU,
England.**
or request a copy of our brochure for more details.

The Foundation will use all your help to assist those people who are handicapped by various sight problems and need special attention.

Thank you very much for your help.